MAN OF
STEEL AND VELVET

Aubrey Andelin

Updated Edition

Pacific Press Santa Barbara

Pierce City, Missouri

Man of Steel and Velvet

Printing History

Pacific Press Santa Barbara edition, 1972
Bantam edition, 1983
Revised Pacific Press Santa Barbara edition, 1990
Updated Pacific Press Santa Barbara edition, 1994

ISBN: 0-911094-23-7

Published by Pacific Press Santa Barbara

P.O. Box 219

Pierce City, Missouri 65723

The Steel and Velvet

What qualities within shapes a man's destiny, impels him to success as a husband, father, and builder of society. In this work I have described these qualities as *Steel and Velvet?* This is a term I have taken from Carl Sandberg who used it to describe Abraham Lincoln. Sandberg did, in fact, consider the steel and velvet in Lincoln the secret of his greatness. I know of no other expression which so adequately portrays the perfection of manhood.

Carl Sandberg, on Lincoln:

Not often in the story of mankind does a man arrive on earth who is hard as a rock and as soft as drifting fog, who holds in his heart and mind the paradox of terrible storm and peace unspeakable and perfect.

During the four years he was President he took to himself the powers of a dictator, commanded the most powerful armies till then assembled in modern warfare. He directed politically and spiritually the wild, massive, turbulent forces let loose in the civil war. As chief executive he issued the paper by which he declared the slaves to be free. Nearly four billion dollars worth of property was taken from those who were legal owners. Such actions are a clear demonstration of the steel qualities in Lincoln.

And of his gentle traits Sandberg says:

In the mixed shame and blame of the immense wrongs of two crashing civilizations, often with nothing to say, he said nothing, slept not at all, and on occasions was seen to weep in a way that made weeping appropriate, decent, majestic.

Mark Van Dorren:

To me Lincoln seems, in some ways, the most interesting man who ever lived. He was gentle, but this gentleness was combined with a terrific toughness, an iron strength.

Every man can develop the steel and velvet within him, and by so doing develop his manhood. In this work I point out clear guidelines to this goal, how you can reach your potential by developing both gentle and firm qualities.

When A Man's A Man

There is a land where a man, to live, must be a man. It is a land of granite and marble and porphyry and gold, and a man's strength must be as the strength of the primeval hills. It is a land of oaks and cedars and pines, and a man's mental grace must be as the grace of the untamed trees. It is a land of far-arched and unstained skies, where the wind sweeps free and untainted, and the atmosphere is the atmosphere of those places that remain as God made them, and a man's soul must be as the unstained skies, the unburdened wind and the untainted atmosphere. It is a land of wide mesas, of wild rolling pastures and broad, untilled valley meadows, and a man's freedom must be that freedom which is not bounded by the fences of a too weak and timid conventionalism.

In this land every man is, by divine right, his own king; he is his own jury, his own counsel, his own judge, and, if it must be, his own executioner . . . in this land a man, to live, must be a man.

Harold Bell Wright

The above is quoted from the book *When A Man's A Man,* in which is described the vigorous breed of men necessary to endure life in the early western United States. Although this tough breed of men is no longer necessary in order to exist, we do still need real men if we are to achieve a world worth living in.

Our present times are more complex and demanding than in the past. *Wild pastures and untilled valley meadows* are not our challenge today, but some of the greatest challenges of history are before us. Our time demands excellent men more than ever before.

Contents

Introduction

This is a book which teaches men to be men. It helps the young, single man visualize the man he ought to be in full maturity. It provides the mature, married man with a pattern to consider for more effectiveness in his role as a husband and father. The teachings presented here are greatly needed, for in spite of the millions of men who make up our society, there are few role models from which men can pattern.

It may seem presumptuous that I should declare *there is a need for men to be men*, for what man is there who doesn't think he is already a man. He was born male and has grown into manhood. Being a man is self-evident. In childhood he was proud to be a boy, and no one dared call him a *sissy*. Everything in his nature demands respect for the masculine in him. So fundamental is this that to suggest a loss of manliness is the greatest affront that can be made. Yet, the sad truth is that men, speaking generally, are no longer men. This becomes obvious when the average man is measured against the undeniable criteria I present in this book.

American men received a stinging insult from British psychiatrist, Dr. Joshua Bierer, who described them as a *bunch of weak-kneed, lily livered sissies*. He originally thought women were at fault, declaring American women to be domineering. *Before I thought the women wanted to rule the country. I changed that opinion. Women are compelled to take over, not fighting to take over,* he continued, *I thought the men who attended some seminars I spoke at with their wives would shoot me for my remarks, but instead they all agreed with me. It's still the fatherless society. The husbands are not husbands. All the women are crying out for a strong man, and he's just not there.*

Throughout our society we find men who are weak, spoiled, pampered, spineless, and lacking in moral, physical or mental strength. There are men who fail to take their position as head of the household, allowing women and children to push them around, not wishing to accept the responsibility which is rightfully their own. Some blatantly encourage their wives to assume this burden. Many of our so-called jokes center around the wife *wearing the pants*. Her husband is portrayed as a bungler, inept and incompetent to understand or control his family.

To a great extent men have failed to assume the primary responsibility of providing *bread for their tables*. Women must come to the rescue. Every day millions of them leave their households to assist in earning the living. The *working mother* is more the rule than the exception. The deterioration and loss of effectiveness in so many homes is in great part a consequence of the neglect resulting from the mother deserting her post, a situation she often laments but can do nothing about.

Lack of chivalry is apparent on every hand. Of necessity, women must take care of themselves. They change their own tires, wash the automobiles, mow the lawn, repair the furnace, paint the house and lift heavy objects. Where are the men waiting to offer masculine assistance?

In addition to failing at home, men are failing to measure up in society. We are in a period of crisis where it is likely the great inheritances we enjoy from the labors and sacrifices of generations past may be lost. Freedom is in jeopardy. It is a time of turmoil, strife and numerous problems. Our only hope is for men to rise to their feet as real men. But where are the heroes of today? Where is the man who will proclaim, *Give me liberty or give me death!*? Where are men willing to sacrifice time and energy to rescue a dwindling society?

Social Problems Caused by Lack of Manliness

The general lack of manliness is producing far-reaching social problems. The man who fails to stand up as the head of

8

the family creates trouble in his home. There is a lack of order. The weak-kneed father also creates the *dominant mother*, for someone must add substance to the family, someone must determine policy and make decisions. Often urgent demands make it necessary for the wife to step into the leadership role when her husband fails to do so.

Such default in leadership causes great unhappiness and frustration to women. If she must be the *man of the family*, she isn't free to function as a woman, to devote her time and thought to making a success of her equally demanding duties as a wife and mother. Her lack of a strong man to preside over her, *something she has every right to expect*, may cause severe emotional reactions. She becomes insecure and sometimes desperate.

Children of a recessive father also suffer as innocent victims. They feel insecure due to lack of firmness and decisiveness. Growing up in a home where the father doesn't demand obedience, they learn disobedience. They learn they don't have to yield to authority. When turned out into the world, they are likely to be rebellious and are often troublemakers and delinquents.

The man who allows and encourages his wife to work outside her home creates further social problems. She must divide her interests between her work and family. Since her work is usually more demanding, the children and home life suffer. She can't serve two masters. Her neglect at home results in lack of love, attention, and development of the children and her failure to serve as the understanding wife.

Homosexuality is another social problem caused by lack of manliness. When a father fails to portray a strong male image, there is a blurring of roles between mother and father. The distinction between male and female becomes obscure. Boys and girls don't see a clear sex image they can identify with. Because of this, girls don't grow strongly feminine, and boys don't grow strongly masculine. A ridiculous term, *unisex* comes into usage, which in itself describes something that can't be. When men are *truly men* and women are *truly women*, this contrast keeps the sexes attracted to one another.

Homosexuality is a perversion encouraged when normal heterosexual drives are interfered with.

Still another social ill, party caused by the weakness of men, is the feminist movement. Had men been strongly masculine, sensitive to the needs of women, holding them in high regard with appreciation for their contributions in their feminine role, it's unlikely so many of them would have deserted their posts. As it is, many of them feel like *second class citizens*, the victims of an oppressive male population who have taken to themselves the jobs that are exciting and fulfilling. Feeling unappreciated and consigned to a position of minimal value, women have wanted to be *liberated* from female duties. When functioning successfully at home, they feel the importance of their work and gain fulfillment doing it. Seeing men fulfill their masculine duties causes women to esteem them as well as themselves.

And last, when a man is weak or in any way fails to measure up as a man, women and children lose respect for him. This weakens these important relationships, leading to marriage problems and a gap between parent and child.

These serious social problems illustrate the urgent need for action. Truly, there has never been a time of greater urgency when men and women must understand how best they can contribute to the well-being of themselves and society. It appears that if we do not produce a generation of real men immediately, our entire civilization, as we know it, may be lost. In peril are our most sacred and cherished institutions - marriage, family life, freedom of country - the very foundations of organized society and religion.

The Need

Our crucial times require men of strong minds, kind hearts, and willing hands, men who find joy in labor, men of courage, honor and strong opinions, clear minds and high goals, men who are not afraid of responsibility, men who are dedicated to a task and will surrender their selfish desires and pursuits to a life of service. These are men whose word can be depended upon.

But along with this fiber of steel there must be a gentle nature. We need men who can appreciate the beauties of nature, men who love their families with passion and honor, men who adore womanhood, yet dislike weakness or coyness. We need men with compassion, sensitive to the needs of the less fortunate, men who are tender with their wives and children, men who have developed an ability to love.

This book outlines the way to become such a man. *It is the way to a man's greatest fulfillment.* Fulfillment does not come, as many suppose, by recognition, honors, money, security, material goods or sex. Although these contribute greatly to his well-being, his greatest fulfillment comes in being a man.

This goal is attainable, regardless of one's station in life. No one is shut out if he obeys definite and unfailing principles. One is not limited by restrictions which usually accompany so-called success.

This book will teach you how to understand women, their feminine nature and peculiarities, and how to build a beautiful relationship and an enduring marriage. It will teach you how to stand at the head of your household, gaining the utmost respect from wife and children. It will teach you how to succeed as a man in your work, in your community, and in your duties as an integral part of society.

Among Other Things You Will Learn:

1. What it means to be a man.
2. How to understand women.
3. What women appreciate in men.
4. What brings security to women and children.
5. How to handle a woman when she *tries to take over*.
6. How to handle children in a way to win their hearts.
7. The role of a man as a divine calling.
8. How to handle difficult marriage situations.
9. The fulfillment every man is seeking.
10. Why some successes cannot be sustained.

1

The Ideal Man

The ideal man as I see him, is a man of *Steel and Velvet*. This term I have taken from Carl Sandburg who used it to describe Abraham Lincoln. I know of no other expression which so adequately portrays the perfection of manhood.

The Steel

The ideal man has the strength, endurance, and temperance of fine steel. He is a composite of many sterling qualities. Foremost among them is his willingness to assume masculine burdens, to *earn his bread by the sweat of his face*. He provides for himself and family with pride as he fulfills this masculine duty. He delights in this opportunity to serve, and does so enthusiastically. He doesn't face his responsibility sullenly, as though there were no escape. He is not looking to others to do what he should be doing. When his problems become difficult, he takes pride in trying to solve them. Only in emergencies does he look to others for solutions.

He shoulders this obligation, not only for the moral responsibility to do so, but because of the positive masculine feeling he has in doing it. If placed in a position where he cannot function in this important capacity, he is most uncomfortable. His acceptance of this responsibility adds substance to the faith his wife places in him when she leaves the security of her parents' home to make her way with him. She must rely on his sense of duty to provide for her, to shield her from the harshness of the world, and to strengthen her in her new experience.

Not only does he assume responsibility for himself and

family, but he is also a *builder of society*, a contributor to the welfare of others. He recognizes the world's urgent needs and, with a sense of social responsibility, contributes his measure to making the world a better place. He is not afraid of responsibility, even when it requires time, toil, and personal sacrifice. All this he does because he feels a moral obligation to others. He helps without complaint.

A man of steel is a masculine man. He is aggressive, determined, decisive, and independent. He is efficient in a man's world, demanding quotas of himself in reaching his objectives. He is competent in a task, fearless and courageous in the face of difficulty, and master of a situation. He has convictions and steadfastly holds to these convictions. He sets high goals, goals which require dedication and patience. He is not afraid of strain and diligence. He rejects softness and timidity. When he has made a decision based on his best judgment, he is unbendable as a piece of steel. These qualities set him apart from women and weaker members of his own sex.

A man of steel has a sterling character. He remains steadfast to his convictions even under pressure. He is a man of honor and integrity. He is fair, just and honest in his dealings, possessing moral courage and self-dignity and those diamond traits which make a strong character. He is master of himself because he has learned to discipline himself. When subjected to pressures, he stands firm.

In addition to all of this, he has achieved a feeling of confidence and peace *because of his victory over himself*. And physically, the man of steel has a body of strength and skill.

The Velvet

The velvet qualities include a man's gentleness, his tenderness, kindness, generosity, and patience. He is devoted to the care and protection of women and children. He understands and respects their gentle nature and recognizes it as a complement to his masculinity. He is chivalrous, attentive and respectful to women and has an ability to love with

13

tenderness. He has an enthusiastic and youthful attitude of optimism which he maintains in spite of increasing years. Humility is also a part of the velvet, subduing the masculine ego as his rough nature is refined.

In considering the function of the steel and velvet traits combined, they may be compared to a large, tall building. The steel qualities relate to the sturdy framework of steel and concrete which tie the structure steadfastly together and anchors it to its foundation. Without this strong inner framework, the building would not hold nor function under the pressures of its use and outside forces. The velvet relates to the building's decor, its art forms, its landscape and interior finishing which add softness and beauty to the otherwise stark and stern mass of steel and stone.

When properly blended, these traits of steel and velvet comprise the ideal man, a masterpiece of creation and the greatest contribution to the well-being of society. The attributes characterized as steel are the framework of his being, demonstrating a steadfastness in purpose born of the self-respect he feels when he is true to himself . . . when the quality of his life is such that he can live comfortably with himself as his own best friend.

This produces confidence analogous to the strength of a bar of steel which is thoroughly refined and tested. When the velvet qualities are added, a masterpiece results. That firmness which otherwise might appear harsh is softened. It is not unlike the large, heavy hands which are trained to play the violin. Such hands have the raw strength to crush the instrument in a moment, but there is no danger of such a thing, as the gentle strokes bring forth beautiful music with a softness and appreciation for the artistic. Both the steel and velvet are necessary to produce a great character. There has never been a truly great man who was not a possessor of both.

Men Who Are Steel Only

Throughout history men who have had certain strong steel traits have left their mark on the world, but lacking character, refinement, tenderness and other velvet qualities, they have not been great men. Such are some of the military geniuses and political leaders as Napoleon, Caesar, Stalin, Hitler and Mussolini. The eminence these men achieved was not done without some merit.

It must be recognized that each possessed qualities which inspired confidence and trust, at least initially. By providing forceful leadership, an assurance of protection of the rights and interests of their people, and by doing it in a strong and confident manner, they won support. The virtues of an upright character were largely missing. Also missing were most of the velvet qualities. Yet they won support because of strong steel qualities.

Although strong steel qualities were sufficient to establish them in power, yet they were insufficient to sustain them for an extended time. The lack of character and the crudeness and coarseness of their lives was self-defeating. Instead of being numbered among the great, they are classified as enemies to mankind.

Men Who Are Velvet Only

There are scores of men throughout history who have been *velvet* men. Although they do not stand out as enemies to society, they do not stand out for anything else. They are nonentities, being remembered for nothing of note. Not being real men, they did not build a better world, nor were they adequate as family leaders.

Jesus Christ

Only such men as achieve a balance of the steel and velvet stand securely on an unshakable pedestal. At the apex of this relatively small group of individuals stands Jesus Christ, who was the epitome of all that was good and strong. In no area was He lacking.

A study of His life reveals an intriguing demonstration of the steel and velvet. He never lost sight of His responsibility

15

to complete *the work he was sent to do*. He maintained His devotion to it until the end when He said, *It is finished*. He was a leader of men, women, and children - true to His convictions until death. He had the moral courage to introduce ideals and standards which were in conflict with popular teachings of His day.

He dedicated His life to the service and salvation of others, lifting people to higher planes of thought and living. He was a builder of society. And He was masculine, possessing courage, determination, fearlessness, decisive judgment, and aggressiveness. He was skilled and masterful in a difficult situation, never afraid to face the hardness of his enemies.

Some artists have pictured Him as thin, effeminate and physically weak and shy. He was just the opposite, having a strong body, sufficient to drive the money changers from the temple and adequate to perform strenuous masculine tasks.

His character was spotless, built on the highest of moral principles and standards of perfection. He was eager and enthusiastic about life, promising, *I am come that ye may have life and that ye may have it more abundantly*.

Yet with all of His strength and courage, there was about Him a gentleness that drew to Him women and children. Women wept at His feet and children surrounded Him. With all this He had humility. Though He was worshiped as perfect, He denied His goodness, saying, *There is none good but the Father*. Yet with this humility there was a self-dignity which commanded respect. As He stood before the judgment of the high courts, He bore His false accusations valiantly and faced the scoffing multitudes with superb dignity.

Abraham Lincoln

Christ stands alone. None can be compared to Him. However, in a modest way some ordinary men have left a mark that will not be forgotten. Such is Abraham Lincoln, who was described by Carl Sandburg as possessing qualities of steel and velvet. Note the following quoted from his writings:

Not often in the story of mankind does a man arrive on

earth who is both steel and velvet, who is as hard as a rock and as soft as drifting fog, who holds in his heart and mind the paradox of terrible storm and peace unspeakable and perfect.

During the four years he was President, he at times, especially in the first three months, took to himself the powers of a dictator; he commanded the most powerful armies till then assembled in modern warfare; he enforced conscription of soldiers for the first time in American history; under imperative necessity he abolished the right of habeas corpus; he directed politically and spiritually the wild, massive, turbulent forces let loose in civil war. He argued and pleaded for compensated emancipation of the slaves . . . failing to get action, as chief executive having war powers, he issued the paper by which he declared the slaves to be free under "military necessity." In the end nearly four billion dollars worth of property was taken away from those who were legal owners of it, property confiscated, wiped out as by fire and turned to ashes. Such actions as these are a clear demonstration of the steel qualities of Lincoln. Of his gentle traits, Sandburg says:

In the mixed shame and blame of the immense wrongs of two crashing civilizations, often with nothing to say, he said nothing, slept not at all and on occasions was seen to weep in a way that made weeping appropriate, decent, majestic. An Indiana man at the White House heard him say, "Voorhees, don't it seem strange to you that I, who could never so much as cut off the head of a chicken, should be elected or selected, into the midst of all this blood?"

Mark Van Doren tells us, *To me, Lincoln seems, in some ways, the most interesting man who ever lived. He was gentle, but this gentleness was combined with a terrific toughness, an iron strength.*

The greatness of his character is revealed by the way people revered him at his death. As Carl Sandburg describes it: *In the time of the April lilacs, in the year 1865, on his death, the casket with his body was carried north and west a thousand miles; and the American people wept as never before; bells sobbed; cities wore crepe; people stood in tears with hats off as the railroad burial car paused in the leading cities of seven states.*

17

Such is the greatness of a man who has the strength of steel and the gentleness of velvet.

That this combination of the steel and velvet in men has always been admirable is evident throughout history. Some have won public acclaim by steel virtues alone, but the true heroes, those men who have won the hearts of people and stood out as great among their fellowmen, have always been the combination of steel and velvet. And it has always taken both to win the hearts of women.

In no way does a man need steel and velvet more than in the manner in which he handles women and children. It is the combination of both strength and gentleness that makes women surrender their lives to a man, giving him unconditional love and devotion.

Petruchio

For a perfect example of the use of steel and velvet in dealing with women, let me refer you to the character of Petruchio in William Shakespeare's *The Taming of the Shrew*. Although fiction, the character of Petruchio is accurate as it relates to real life.

Petruchio was a strong, rough, and unyielding man who was looking for a wife, in haste. He approached Katherina, the daughter of a wealthy man. Katherina was beautiful and young, but a shrew. She was sharp-tongued, unruly and defiant. No one, not even her father, could subdue her. But Petruchio, intrigued by the challenge of her unruly nature, as well as being tempted by her wealth and wishing to find a wife in haste, approached her with gentleness:

Bonny Kate, and sometimes Kate the curst:
but, Kate, the prettiest Kate in Christendom;
Kate of Kate-Hall, my super-dainty Kate,
For dainties are all Kates; and therefore, Kate,
Take this of me, Kate of my consolation;
Hearing thy mildness prais'd in every town,
Thy virtues spoke of and thy beauty sounded, -

18

> *Yet not so deeply as to thee belongs, -*
> *Myself am mov'd to woo thee for myself.*

Each time she snapped back at him he ignored it and called her, *sweet Kate, gentle Kate.* And finally he won her and wed her. And then his firmness, his steel, came to light on their wedding day: The father had prepared a wedding feast, but Petruchio announced he and Katherina would take their leave. To which Katherina said:

> *Do what thou cans't, I will not go today,*
> *No, nor tomorrow, nor till I please myself.*
> *The door is open sir, there lies your way;*
> *You may be jogging whiles your boots are green.*
> *For me I'll not be gone till I please myself.*

And then, as she marched forward to the bridal dinner, he pulled her back:

> *They shall go forward, Kate at thy command.*
> *But for my bonny Kate she must with me.*
> *Nay, look not big, nor stamp, nor stare, nor fret;*
> *I will be master of what is mine own.*

And to the others, he said:

> *She is my goods, my chattels; she is my house,*
> *My household stuff, my field, my barn,*
> *My horse, my ox, my ass, my any thing;*
> *And here she stands, touch her whoever dare;*
> *I'll bring my action on the proudest he*
> *That stops my way in Padua, Gumio,*
> *Draw forth thy weapon, we're beset with thieves;*
> *Rescue thy mistress, if thou be a man.*
> *Fear not, sweet wench; they shall not touch thee, Kate;*
> *I'll buckler thee against a million.*

Most people in our day vehemently oppose such possession of womanhood, terms such as chattels or goods. But the story, true to life nevertheless, brought out the best, not the worst, in Kate. His firm masculine leadership combined with gentleness, won her heart devotedly. In the final scene she valiantly defends the man's position as master of the woman:

> Thy husband is thy lord, thy life, thy keeper,
> Thy head, thy sovereign; one that cares for thee,
> And for thy maintenance commits his body
> To painful labor both by sea and land,
> To watch the night in storms, the day in cold,
> Whilst thou liest warm at home, secure and safe;
> And craves no other tribute at thy hands
> But love, fair looks and true obedience;
> Too little payment for so great a debt.
> Such duty as the subject owes the prince
> Even such a woman oweth to her husband;
> And when she is forward, peevish, sullen, sour,
> And not obedient to his honest will,
> What is she but a foul contending rebel,
> And graceless traitor to her loving lord?
> I am ashamed that women are so simple
> To offer war where they should kneel for peace;
> Or seek for rule, supremacy or sway,
> When they are bound to serve, love, and obey.
> Why are our bodies soft and weak and smooth,
> Unapt to toil and trouble in the world,
> But that our soft conditions and our hearts
> Should well agree with our external parts?
> In token of which duty, if he pleases,
> My hand is ready, may it do him ease.

Lancelot

Another example of steel and velvet is in the character of Lancelot in the legend of King Arthur. It is important to first make clear that the movie version of the story is not correct. Lancelot and Guinevere did not have an illicit affair. They did love each other, but it was from afar, withholding any affection or demonstration of their love.

Lancelot was unanimously regarded as the strongest, bravest, most admired knight in the kingdom. With almost superhuman strength he won against all his opponents in the tournaments of the knights. But it was not until he revealed his velvet side, his tenderness and concern for his fellow knight, that he won the heart of Queen Guinevere and the undivided respect of his countrymen. After defeating his fellow knight in battle, his heavy masculine body bent over the dying knight and he prayed with fervor and kindness of spirit for the suffering man to return to life. This concern for his fellowman, this gentleness of velvet, combined with his proven strength and manliness, made him, in the eyes of the Queen, the *perfect man*.

It must be remembered that not all great men are recorded in the pages of history. There are many, perhaps thousands, who have been both *steel and velvet* who are unknown. They are men who have valiantly served their families, standing strong and firm as the leader of women and children. They have faithfully earned their bread *by the sweat of their face*, and have been men in every sense of the word. Although they have not won acclaim in the eyes of the world, they have nevertheless been real men. Their existence only proves that every man has within himself the possibility of being a man of steel and velvet.

The blending of the steel and velvet, then, becomes the objective of this study. First, to learn the essential ingredients of each. Second, to learn how they may be achieved on a personal basis. These are not opposing forces, as good and evil, but are complementary qualities which should be developed to the utmost. Only when the steel and velvet are adequately developed *together* does a man become truly great. A deficiency in either category will result in inevitable difficulty.

In teaching fundamentals of truth which serve as precepts for men to live by, one may wonder if I'm trying to make men alike, as carbon copies of one another. This is not so. The fact is only too obvious that the human personality is created with distinct individuality which makes it unique, separating each person from all others. The identity of personality will always be preserved.

But it's well to recognize that certain fundamentals serve as guides. The qualities I describe as steel and velvet serve as an aspiration to all men. They are deep running fundamentals which know no distinction, are not altered by age, personality or background. They do not destroy the uniqueness of the individual. They enhance the man, helping him to become his better self.

On the opposite page is a chart of *The Ideal Man*, divided into the qualities of *steel and velvet*. Listed are the qualities which will be taught in this book. If understood and applied, they will guide men to a more perfect manhood.

THE IDEAL MAN

Steel	*Velvet*
1. Guide, protector, provider	1. Understands women
2. Builder of society	2. Gentleness
3. Masculinity	3. Attentiveness
4. Character	4. Youthfulness
5. Confidence	5. Humility
6. Health	6. Refinement

Makes women and children feel secure. Arouses admiration of all. Makes women feel womanly.

Promotes good human relations among all people. Awakens love in women and children.

When a man has both *Steel* and *Velvet* qualities,
it brings him peace, happiness and fulfillment

Part I
The Steel

The steel qualities, which we will now discuss, are the foundation upon which a man must build his masculinity and make the most of his life. These are true principles which will endure throughout all periods of time. In our fast moving world which is characterized by change, *these principles will not change*. They are immovable, and because of this, provide a sure anchor.

While this study is serious business and not to be taken lightly, it is not a litany of onerous obligations from which one would shrink. To learn a new truth is exciting and invigorating. To walk from darkness into light changes one's whole perspective. To apply principles of truth solves endless problems and brings satisfaction to the soul.

Important as these principles are, knowledge on this subject is extremely limited. It is ironic that in a world where knowledge abounds, and where information of all kinds can be called up instantaneously, some of the most important information of all is not available.

It is hoped the reader will study this text with an open mind and heart. The truth of what you are learning will become increasingly clear as you make these principles a part of your life. The benefits to you will be extended to others.

2

Man's Basic Role

A man's most important responsibility is to be the guide, ✓ protector and provider for his wife and children. This role is not merely a result of custom or tradition, but is of divine origin.

The Holy Scriptures designate man as head of the family. The duties of both Adam and Eve were defined by God in explicit instruction. Eve was told, *Thy desire shall be to they husband, and he shall rule over thee.* Gen. 3:l0

Many years later the apostle Paul reaffirmed this principle when he said, *The husband is the head of the wife, even as Christ is the head of the church . . . therefore, as the church is subject unto Christ, so let the wives to their own husbands in everything.* Eph. 5:23. He also told women to *reverence* their husbands. Eph. 5:33.

Peter, the apostle, also supported this principle by saying, *ye wives, be in subjection to your own husbands.* 1 Peter 3:1.

That man is born to *protect* women and children is apparent when considering his body build which is larger, stronger, and has greater endurance. The woman is different. She has a body build that is delicate and sometimes fragile, uniquely adapted for bearing children. Both men and women have a temperament adapted to the complementary relationship they bear to one another.

Proof that man was commissioned to provide the living is supported by God's instructions when He said, *In the sweat of thy face shall they eat bread.* (Gen. 3:19) This command was not given to the woman, but to the man. Although she was to be a *helpmeet* and sometimes worked in the fields with him, it was not her direct responsibility to provide the living.

27

Man's role as the guide, protector and provider is his first and foremost responsibility. No other duty can compare to it; no other duty replace it. Urgent, of course, is his additional responsibility to contribute as a builder of society in assisting to solve problems and meet needs in his community. But these things are secondary to his obligation at home. *His usefulness in the community is realized principally as he builds a happy home and marriage and produces well-adjusted, useful children.*

Man's God Given Role is Challenged

While God's instructions are as valid today as when first given, many people discount them. They say we are living in a new age under different circumstances. They feel the complicated problems of our day require a new approach allowing for accommodation to the many crises which have arisen in our complex civilization.

These crises include adjustments which confront families having both parents working as breadwinners. Single parent families have special needs. Women have been taught that their traditional role in the home is demeaning and unfulfilling, so many of them want modifications so they might compete with men. Many children grow up without an adequate male and female image and are therefore confused. They are often without moral guidelines. Our value system is assaulted. We are asked to accept perversions as an alternate way of living.

Because of such difficult circumstances as these, many people feel that a replacement or alteration of God's plan for the family must be made. In a broken home solutions less than ideal may be all that is available. But artificial legs will never come into vogue as a preference. There has not yet been found a suitable substitute for the family structure God has ordained for us. Nor will there be. His plan is flawed.

When a Man Fails In His role

A failure in the home is a man's greatest failure. If he fails in marriage, if he fails with his children, if his home is troubled or divided or if his children are unruly, wayward and irresponsible, he has failed in his most fundamental duty as a man. No success in life can compensate for this failure. He may accomplish great things in the world of men. He may be a man of science, industry or government with notable achievements, but what can atone for a failure in the home? He is principally responsible for its success or failure.

The home is the most basic unit of society. The strength of a country lies in the home and the security and happiness of the families which comprise that nation. It is difficult, if not impossible, for anyone - man, woman or child, to contribute much of value if his home is troubled. The troubled home affects a man in his work, a woman in her homemaking, and children in their personal development. The man stands as the head of the household, the shepherd of the flock; only when he functions successfully in this calling is his house in order. And only when his house is in order can the community and thus the nation function as it should.

When He Succeeds

On the positive side, when a man functions effectively as the guide, protector, and provider, when his home is ruled with firmness and kindness, love and good leadership provided, with the security and comforts needed, and when his children develop into happy, well-adjusted citizens, *then he has made his most notable contribution to the world*. Other contributions may be added, and they are important, but they are secondary to the success of his family.

It has been said that a sign of a man's success is when he walks up the path leading to his home and his children run with eagerness to greet him; his wife, smiling, lovingly greets him at the door. This is achievement not often seen.

The Woman's Role

The woman's role is to be the wife, mother and homemaker. Her role as the wife is indicated by the following:

When God made man he said, *It is not good for man to be alone. I will make a helpmeet for him.* And thus she was given as a wife, a supporting companion, his encouragement, and sometimes his strength. Her position as mother was established when God blessed her with the function of bearing children.

A woman's household duties are clearly defined in the description of a virtuous woman in Proverbs 31: *She seeketh wool and flax and worketh willingly with her hands . . . she bringeth her food from afar . . . she giveth meat to her household. she planteth a vineyard . . . she is not afraid of the snow for her household are clothed with scarlet . . . she looketh well to the ways of her household and eateth not the bread of idleness.*

Besides her domestic role, a woman needs to give benevolent service outside the home. She has a debt to society to make the world a better place, as does man. But in her case, it is a feminine service, such as helping the poor, serving in the church or community, assisting in youth problems, etc. Giving such a service enriches her life and makes her a better wife and mother. *At no time should this role supersede her duties in the home.* Her first and sacred obligation is to her family, to serve them as the wife, mother and homemaker.

The Complimentary Partnership

In the ideal home the man's and woman's duties are distinctly divided. There is little overlapping except in emergencies. Not only does this follow divine command, but also logic and reason. Every group must be organized to avoid chaos. This consists of delegating duties to each member, making each accountable for his assignments. A family is a small organization and thus must also follow this pattern.

The joining of these roles forms a complementary partnership. Neither the man nor the woman is superior. *Both are indispensable and of equal importance.* But as we see so plainly, there is a difference of responsibility. Longfellow compares the partnership in the following way:

30

> As unto the bow the cord is,
> So unto man is woman;
> Tho' she bends him, she obeys him,
> Tho' she draws him, Yet she follows;
> Useless each without the other.
>
> From *Hiawatha* by Henry W. Longfellow

This partnership has also been compared to a lock and key that joined together form a perfectly functioning unit. Each has a different function, yet each is necessary. Neither is superior. One is useless without the other.

Capabilities to Function in Roles

When God blessed man with the responsibility to guide, protect and provide for his family, he also blessed him with the temperament and capability to function in this role. He was given the capacity to shoulder heavy responsibility, to endure the stresses and strains of the marketplace, to struggle with difficulties and make weighty decisions. Although his burdens may be heavy, and discouragement enter in, *he has the capacity to do his work.* God has promised it, and will bless him when he seeks divine guidance.

The man was not created, however, with the capacity to function as a woman. He does not have the temperament to assume the monotonous and trivial tasks of the household, to tend the children, do the wash and cook the meals. He may do well with woman's work in an emergency and may have a deep appreciation for the service she renders, but he does not thrive on her responsibility.

The woman, on the other hand, was created with the temperament to cope with the problems and responsibilities of the feminine world. Although delicate in body build, she has great endurance in her own sphere. She can spend sleepless nights with a crying baby or caring for a sick child. She can struggle with demanding tasks, all of which seem to need doing at the same time. She is patient with trivia and endless meals which come three times a day throughout the year. A *feminine* woman not only copes with such problems, she thrives on them.

As a man is not so adaptable to feminine tasks, a woman is not adaptable to masculine tasks, to be a carpenter, bricklayer or auto mechanic. Her feminine make-up does not suit her to build her own shelter, fix the roof, repair the furnace or worry about finances or make weighty decisions. Her temperament is not that of an executive, a leader of industry, a scientist or a politician. She was made to be a wife and mother. Here is where she functions best.

Many women do, of course, take on masculine responsibility, especially when their husbands fail in this respect. But when they do *they lose some of their femininity*. When a woman rises to a position of leadership in the business world, she must develop *masculine* capacity. Masculine capacity is contrary to femininity. It works against it. She must, in fact, reject her femininity if she is to do a man's work.

It is a fact that men and women differ temperamentally, psychologically, physically, socially and in capacity to do a specific job. Although they are equal in intelligence, their intelligence is not on identical subjects. They do not think alike, have the same perspectives, nor do they react the same way to a given circumstance. They worry about different things, and they worry differently. Men and women do not have the same capacity in a specific job.

These unique differences are undeniable to even the casual observer. Frustrating as these differences frequently are, as men and women try to understand one another, they are nevertheless an important part of the divine plan and add much to the attraction and excitement the sexes feel for one another. Each was given the capacity to function best in the specific male and female role.

Marriage

The security of the partnership of a man and woman lies in binding them together in marriage. Only then will each have the incentive to do his best and build an enduring life together.

32

Any other arrangement, whether it be an assumption, oral agreement or whatever, is not sufficient to endure for any period of time. It does not provide sufficient incentive to make a whole-hearted effort towards a high goal and overcome the obstacles and trials which are sure to come. The underlying reason for rejecting marriage is rooted in *lack of faith*, which is in itself an admission of doubt of one's own self-worth, or the value of the person he is considering as a partner. The deep feelings of romantic love which should exist could not endure such an insult. Defeat is therefore built in.

The most important reason for matrimony, however, is that *marriage is ordained of God*. It is a sacred covenant. *What God hath joined together, let no man put asunder* implies that it is part of the heavenly plan. This seems reason enough to respect the institution of marriage.

In spite of the sanctity of marriage, there is a threatening trend to do away with it. Many people are afraid of marriage, hesitating to step into its binding obligations. This fear is undoubtedly due to the many marriage failures and the trouble observed even in those marriages which remain together. Although we can sympathize with these fears, it must be recognized that the solution does not lie in abandoning the institution of marriage. We must learn the principles which will allow us to be successful and happy in marriage.

At the time David V. Haws was chairman of the department of psychiatry at the Country General Hospital, Phoenix, Arizona, he said, *Marriage, imperfect as it is, is still the best solution we have to keep the family intact and make a man responsible for the children he has procreated.*

The most important way a man can contribute to the security and happiness of his marriage is to successfully live his masculine role. This means, in review, that he rules his household with firmness, kindness, and love - that he provide an adequate living, that he protect his wife and children and in every way serve as a man.

As we progress in this study we will see that a man is much more than a *pay check*. He will learn to understand women and children, and how to meet their needs. He will learn how to achieve a happy marriage.

Trends Opposing Male and Female Roles

There is a world wide trend to do away with the traditional male and female roles and achieve equality between the sexes. The goal is to eliminate any differences in responsibility so that all duties are shared equally. This includes decision-making, earning the living, housekeeping and child care. This rejection of traditional male and female roles asserts that such roles are no longer useful to society.

Known as *Feminism*, this movement, initiated by a group of women who were dissatisfied with the woman's traditional role, attempted to reshape the thinking of both sexes. They considered homemaking a second-rate job and advocated that women move into the man's world on an equal basis.

They view their work in the feminine world as confining and isolating and limiting to personal development. They say *While our husbands have the freedom and opportunity to be out in the working world, experiencing new people, new ideas, and perhaps the creative joy of seeing the world change for the better, we are at home in the isolated household with no one to talk to but little children.* They view themselves as a shadow to their husbands and a servant to their children. They want to be freed from *the shackles of male supremacy*. In total, they want liberation from their mundane existence and a share in the world's *more interesting work.*

These women have ignored some fundamental principles. They have failed to realize that happiness and fulfillment come only as people give of themselves in service and duty to that work which is important to be done. No work anywhere is more important than caring for children and doing other domestic duties. No work is more essential to the national interest, economy and well-being. And no work requires more love, patience, resourcefulness, raw intelligence and managerial ability than being an efficient mother and homemaker. This work naturally falls to women and can best be done by them.

It is a sacred responsibility, and failure to perform is a

serious dereliction of duty with dire consequences. Each passing year since this vicious and fallacious concept was announced there has been an acceleration of trouble. In large measure the parents of our present generation are at fault. Their daughters are now mothers who are unprepared and perplexed. Many of their sons are irresponsible unwed fathers.

It makes just as much sense for a man to say, *I'm tired of earning the living. I want to find something more exciting and less demanding*, as it is for a woman to feel she should desert her place in the home.

In the woman's sphere there is a record of failure. Our generation is one of divorce, troubled homes and rebellious children. Drugs are a consequence as is violence in the street. This is not the problem of government and will not be solved by government. Women must return to their homes and serve there. They are thinking too much of what they *want to do* ✓ rather than what they *ought to do*. But even before I blame the women, I accuse the men who are the leaders in the homes. My displeasure focuses on them. They cannot cowardly shrink back and blame the women.

Only when men and women willingly assume responsibilities they were born to do, devoting themselves to making a success of them and losing themselves in the challenges incident to it, will they find happiness and will we have a better world. It is primarily the duty of the man to fulfill his responsibility first and encourage his wife and daughters to be competent and happy in female duties.

Advocates of the *share alike* philosophy demonstrate an unusual lack of insight as they ignore the serious social problems arising from this blurring of male and female roles. Countless children grow up in an environment where the distinction of the sexes is so obscure that no clear-cut example exists for them to follow. Many homes lack definitive leadership, and the very differences which should be emphasized are purposely minimized as men act like women and woman act like men. This often leads to under-development of the child to his own sex and in some cases to homosexuality.

Children cannot come into existence without a male and a female. To deny the specific duties of each is absurd.

Harm In Women's Lib

In review we can say that equality of the sexes leads to a blurring of roles, giving no distinct male or female image. Women are encouraged to desert their posts. The greatest harm comes to children as they are deprived of a mother's undivided interest. A mother who works outside the home by choice casts doubts in the minds of her children as to her love and interest in their welfare.

Besides the harm that comes to children, there is a distinct harm to both the man and woman. With the emphasis on equality, the man does not fulfill his masculine role. He is robbed of this opportunity for personal development - those experiences that develop his masculinity. The woman is harmed in a different way. As she divides her life between two worlds, she takes on masculine attitudes and abilities and loses some of her femininity. Neither the man nor the woman develop to their full potential, nor does either experience real fulfillment.

The advocates of *Feminism* are seeing the failure of their concepts. Based on false principles, this was inevitable. Young women who accepted these ideas find themselves short changed and drifting without guidance. Believable role models are a rarity. A few of the early advocates of the feminism philosophy have been courageous enough to admit the failure, but most of these are not willing to accept the reality that there is no adequate remedy other than a whole-hearted acceptance of the principles advocated in this book. For an enlightening and comprehensive study of the woman's role there is no better resource than *Fascinating Womanhood* by Helen Andelin.

How Young Men Face the Masculine Role

Many young men are fearful of stepping into the responsibilities of marriage. Being untaught and then misled by the prevailing philosophies, it is no wonder they are apprehensive. For this reason, it may be that only the emotion of intense love will cause him to overcome his fears and take the step.

Even after marriage many men have severe adjustments to the load they have assumed. They are suddenly faced with an additional dependent, a household to run, furnishings, the prospect of children. Before, they were relatively free. This adjustment is natural and deserves understanding. But always there is the assurance that the step of marriage and family life is a desirable one - one that will lead to personal development, happiness and peace within if one is successful. Those who reject this responsibility without just cause, demonstrate a weakness of character and sacrifice the opportunity to grow. Growth comes through adversity and difficulties - not through the pursuit of the easy life.

The Second Mile

The secret of gaining satisfaction and fulfillment in this important role is in going the *second mile*. This instruction was given by the Savior when He said, *If any man compel thee to go one mile, go with him twain.* There is in this simple statement a key to mastery over a situation. Let us refer to Jewish history at that time to understand its meaning.

When this instruction was given, Israel was ruled by the Roman government. Common among the Roman soldiers was the practice of oppressing the Jews with such tasks as forcing them to carry a burden or a pack for some distance. In this instance, Jesus instructed them to be willing to carry it twice as far as they were compelled. He recognized a fundamental principle - the only way to take the burden out of work is an abundant willingness to do more than is required.

Going the second mile is the way a man lightens his burdens and learns to enjoy his responsibility. A half-hearted effort nets nothing in satisfaction. As one devotes himself to his family, going beyond the call of duty to be as completely responsible as possible, he experiences satisfying fulfillment.

Another great principle of truth was given when Jesus said, *He who loseth his life for my sake shall surely find it.* As one loses himself in the responsibilities that are his, forgetting about his personal or selfish desires, devoting himself to making a success of the calling God has given him, he finds himself.

Pride In Responsibility

Equally important is that a man have pride in his many manly responsibilities. These duties, he realizes, are his alone. He does not lean on his wife or children or others in his family; nor does he expect society to support him. The job is his. A masculine man takes pride in his God-given responsibility.

If his burdens become heavy, he does not run away from them or turn to others for assistance. He looks to himself for solutions. He may have to reorganize his life, reevaluate his situation and possibly eliminate unnecessary obligations. He may have to move to a less expensive residence, or cut down the family budget, or make other sacrifices. But he independently solves his problems as best he can and then carries on. This is having masculine pride. This does not mean there will not be emergencies when assistance from others must be had, but this is accepted as a last resort.

Fulfillment In Masculine Role

Inborn within man is a desire for personal fulfillment. This is a feeling of satisfaction towards himself derived mainly in the following ways.

1. Proving one's worth, i.e. reaching objectives, overcoming obstacles and exercising unique talents and abilities.
2. Making a worthy contribution to society.
3. Character development. Becoming a more worthy person.

Fulfillment may come from many sources - any avenue which requires talents and abilities and produces worthwhile achievements. The successful artist, writer, scientist, politician or any worker in a legitimate occupation receives a measure of fulfillment for worthy contributions made. It is important that his work should be beneficial to mankind. Whether the work is ordinary or not is not the point. It must be something that must be done. If it means cleaning the public street, that would certainly qualify as a worthy contribution.

His greatest fulfillment, however, lies within his role as the guide, protector and provider. As he works patiently and diligently to provide comforts for his family, he becomes unselfish. Overcoming obstacles and solving problems develop character and refine the spirit. His leadership over his flock develops this masculine trait more fully, and as he stands at the head of the family he must be a shining example for them. He must overcome his weaknesses and take on strengths. He has incentives which were unknown before marriage. Marriage is his greatest field for personal development.

As a man reaches high objectives in this way, he attains the greatest rewards life can offer. His children are his kingdom - his wife his queen. As his children become young adults, he enters the best period of all. He begins to enjoy the *fruits of his labors* as he delights in the company of his mature children. The beautiful relationship he has built with his wife is the center of his joy.

Proof that his home is the center of a man's fulfillment is evident in viewing a man who has failed to make a success of family life. His children will be a heartache and his marriage may have left scars of defeat. The most fundamental area for his fulfillment has not been fruitful. He may have achieved his goals outside his home and may be honored among his associates, but this success does not compensate for his failure at home. His happiness is as an empty shell and his fulfillment robbed of its full measure.

When Men Fail in their Work

During middle age many men who have not reached the measure of success they anticipated realize their sad situation.

The work they devoted themselves to these many years has not amounted to much. They may say, *I missed the boat. What I have been doing hasn't paid off. I'm getting older, and if I don't do something exciting and different now, it will be too late.* They are concerned over advancing age and loss of physical strength. Many such men turn to the world of pleasure, seeking before it is too late, some measure of life's enjoyment. Others make a last desperate attempt to achieve the status they felt would justify their years of toil. Regrettably, some turn to other women and a life of degradation.

But if a man has reared a successful family, he has before him a monument that speaks for itself. His family is his achievement, his children the richest fruits of a successful life, and his joy the love, respect and devotion of a wonderful wife. God did not command that he be on the pinnacle of success in his work. He commanded only that he earn his bread by the sweat of his face. This he will have done. He will now find satisfaction in seeing the greater success he has made at home.

Married children continue to need counsel, strength and encouragement. A man is a father as long as he has children. All home ties are strengthened through these conscientious efforts, and one enjoys a deepening feeling of joy.

But regardless of a man's need for fulfillment, let us keep in mind that there are certain areas in which we must serve. A man has a God-given responsibility to his family to be their guide, protector and provider, and as he loses himself in this important responsibility, not thinking of reward, fulfillment will naturally follow.

To Others

All family members are greatly benefitted by the effort of a man who succeeds in his leadership of the family. His strength in doing what he knows is right gives security to all of them. The home is their base, the center where values are established and is their shelter and refuge. A woman's security does not lie in money her husband earns. She finds it in him as a person of character and dependability. The same is true for the children.

As a man does his duties well, a woman is free to concentrate on making her career in the home successful. She has a man to lean on, and is not responsible for earning the living or doing his work. She can devote herself to the feminine arts and building a happy family life. Because her husband is a man, she is more of a woman.

Together they build a happy home and make their most worthy contribution, not only to themselves but to the nation in which they live. The gift of wonderful children and a happy home is priceless!

3

The Guide

Again I emphasize that man is the divinely appointed head of the family. This is not a self-assumed position acquired because he is stronger than his wife and able to force his way. Society did not assign him this position because, after years of research, it was found to be the most workable plan. It is God who placed him at the head.

The leadership position is one of trust for which man is *accountable to God*. It is not a position he may decide he does not want - nor can he pass it to another whom he considers better qualified. To allow others to forcefully steal his position indicates a weakness of character and lack of obedience to principle. The least that could be said is that he does not understand. There is no way a man can neglect this calling with clear conscience. To turn aside from this sacred responsibility is a serious dereliction of duty in the eyes of God.

Some people dislike the God-given plan for family leadership, feeling it places too great a burden on the man or is unfair to the woman. There is an effort to do away with the patriarchy, substituting instead equality of leadership between the sexes. Such advocates do not realize that God's plan is not a flawed plan. It did not come to us in need of revision. It is not one which burdens, frustrates, nor deprives the individual. It is rather one with blessings attached - the most ideal plan for the family to live by in attaining order, unity and peace. It also provides the greatest opportunity for both men and women to develop as individuals. In the eternal scheme of things, this earth life is a period of learning with a view to having the experiences for maximum happiness. A man grows as he learns to function as the leader. A woman becomes more feminine when relieved of this position. She is free to concentrate fully on the responsibilities in her sphere.

Logic of the Man Being the Head

Not only is leadership of the family of divine origin, it follows logic and reason. No organization can function without a responsible head. We observe this in government, business, social groups, military, every place where people work together. There must be someone to direct activities, to initiate action. There must be someone ultimately upon whom responsibility rests. Without a head, disorder and chaos result.

A family is a small social group of intelligent beings and therefore must be organized with a leader. Policy and rules must be established. Decisions must be made daily, and sometimes at the moment. These are not necessarily momentous decisions, but may be as simple as *May Larry take the car tonight?* Suppose husband and wife disagree? When the wife yields, order results. Some will ask, *Why must the man lead? Why not the woman?* The reply to this is also very logical.

The man is the bread-winner and protector. If he is to succeed in this role, he must have the power of decision. Should he, for example, be having difficulty making his income cover expenses, he may feel a change of jobs, perhaps a move to another city, is necessary in the solution of the problem. He must be free to make such a choice and move his family to a new location. If his wife is the leader, she may choose to remain in their present location. This would be unjust to the man and disruptive to the family. It is logical that the role of the provider and leader belong inseparably together.

Leader Not a Superior Person

A leader may be in a superior position or more highly favored, but this does not mean he is a superior person, or even a more valuable person. He is merely functioning in an office or calling. The wife honors her husband's position of authority and gives it the obedience and respect it deserves. She is as supportive as she possibly can be in an effort to see that the venture in which she also has a part is successful.

To illustrate, a commander of a naval fleet has a position superior to his fellow officers. Those who honor him or yield to his authority are giving obedience due a superior officer, not a superior man. This is a matter of law and order through which every person involved in the operation is benefitted.

In the home the father and mother, husband and wife are equally important! The leader soon learns he cannot succeed without the support of his wife. She finds she cannot succeed without the leadership of her husband. His duty is to lead; hers to follow.

Duties of the Guide

The duties of the guide are: To guide the family in establishing policies, rules and laws for them to follow. He is also responsible for the final decisions. He is expected to make plans and motivate the family towards worthy goals.

The father has the right to establish rules of conduct, expenditure of money, laws of the household, religious affiliation of the children, educational planning, etc. His right and obligation to make these decisions are the consequence of his assignment to be the guide, protector and provider. He will need to delegate some of his authority to his wife, especially in affairs of the household and matters concerning the children. She is closer to them in their day to day activities. The fact is, there is no way a household could operate without such division of labor. But he maintains the right to step in when necessary.

The father should seek his wife's viewpoint in matters of family planning or decisions. She is a counselor with valuable wisdom and advice. Her perspective is an all-important one. But the power to determine is his, even if in opposition to hers.

The father may also wish to consult with the children, by calling them together in a family council. He should listen to

44

even the smallest child, regard his feelings and consider his viewpoint. But the responsibility of decision is ultimately his.

Contrary to what some may think, the family organization √ is *not a democracy*. This was brought to my attention by a family who tried to establish a democracy in their home. Each member was given one equal vote, including the parents. The first issue to be reviewed was how the daily dishwashing was to be accomplished. The children voted that each person in the family was to do his own dinner dishes. The parents were out-voted by their children. A democracy in a family is not a workable arrangement.

The father stands as the shepherd of his flock. His √ decision should be honored and respected by all members of the family, even when they disagree. They are honoring him in an office. They are also learning obedience, which is one of the greatest needs we have in our nation.

Every Man a Leader

Every man must he a leader. He may not be a leader in industry, government, or even a local men's organization, but if he is married he will be a leader of a family. The importance of this position cannot be over-stated. The home is the most basic unit in society. How it functions to meet human needs directly affects all other institutions to which we belong. In any given family, the consequences of the leaders success or failure inevitably goes beyond the threshold of his own home. The man's conduct as head of the family will, for better or worse, affect all society. This crucial organization needs prime leadership. Leadership is required on every hand, but where is it more urgent than in the home? Where are the opportunities greater?

The Ideal Leader

The ideal leader assumes his position as a sacred trust. √ He takes pride in his masculine role, does not set it aside or turn it over to others. He has a keen feeling of responsibility for his place as leader, realizing that it is the most important function he has. He serves patiently with dedication, devotion and pride.

He is a leader of steel and velvet. He has those steel qualities which accompany great leadership - firmness, decisive judgment, courage, steadfastness, and a keen sense of justice.

He rules over his flock with firmness, not allowing others to dictate or steal his leadership. He does not yield to pressure on matters contrary to his better judgment. Nor does he make concessions which would dilute the effectiveness of a decision he feels is in the best interest of his family. In all this he is *fair*. In making decisions, he is always careful. If he lacks knowledge sufficient to make a sound decision, he will search for that knowledge. He will seek the counsel of his family when necessary. But once he has made a decision based upon the best of his judgment, he will have the courage to carry through with steadfastness. He will make mistakes occasionally, but allows for those mistakes. He has the confidence that his judgment is usually sound. Because he has confidence, others believe in him and follow readily.

The ideal leader has velvet qualities also. He is kind and tender-hearted. He is willing to sacrifice his own pleasures for members of his family. This quality of unselfishness is a most important one. No leader can be great unless he is unselfish.

But along with his velvet tenderness, a great leader must be a little hard-hearted at times. He must have the toughness of steel in following through on what he considers a *right decision*, even if it means bitter disappointment to those he is leading. This unalterable courage of his convictions is the supreme quality of leadership that brings order to a household.

A great leader has humility. He is not too proud to listen to the counsel of his family and, in fact, seeks their opinions. If one of them is right or has a better idea, he is humble enough to admit it. He realizes his limitations. Others have much to offer. He will be alert to pick up worthwhile suggestions.

With this combination of qualities - firmness, courage, decisive judgment, and justice, and the velvet traits of tenderness, consideration, and humility - a man is equipped to offer excellent leadership to his family. Order and peace thrive. He has established an ideal situation to rear well-adjusted, happy children.

Every Man Has Capabilities to Lead

Since men were born with the sacred responsibility to create a family and appointed to be their leader, they were also born with capabilities to lead. It is a religious truth, that God gives no commandment to His people without also giving them the means to carry it out. Therefore, since God blessed the man with the leadership of the family, He also blessed him with the capacity to lead. I am not saying that because a man has the capacity, that he is prepared immediately. He must learn the principles as you are in reading this book.

But he has the physical, emotional, and temperamental make-up to lead. Consider his physical structure. Is he not superior in strength and capacity to those he leads? Although it is not likely he will have to force a family member, yet he has the capacity to do so and can overpower them when necessary. His physique is a reminder or visual aid that he is the leader.

Emotionally he is equipped for the burden of leadership. He has the fortitude to make weighty decisions. Sometimes he must, within a few hours, make a decision that may affect his family for a lifetime. Based upon a few facts and the best of judgment, he hurriedly draws conclusions and comes to a decision. Such risk is frightening to most women. They would find it impossible to reach a decision in such a short time. But men have the ability to make such a determination. They have the emotional stamina to take the strain.

Men also have the temperament needed. Being more decisive by nature, he is able to size up a situation rather quickly. A woman, on the other hand, is inclined to waver, and wants to postpone as long as possible. This often produces stress, and disturbs her tranquility which means so much in a household. A man is not so apt to be frustrated with the continual demand of decision-making, as he has an inborn

47

ability to cope with such matters.

If a man is lacking in any of these qualities, it may be due to his childhood background. Growing up with a weak father or a dominating mother would have deprived him of the example and teaching he needed. Furthermore, who is there to explain these principles? It is not likely he would have been taught correctly. But worse than that, we can be sure he has been subjected to much false information. If for any reason a man feels he does not measure up in his role as leader, he can rest assured that he does possess the innate qualities to lead. The capacity is there, and with a desire on his part and the help of God, he will succeed.

It is important to remember that *this work in family leadership is God's work as well as our own.* We must keep in mind that we are commanded *to ask* that we might receive. This is not on idle promise on Deity's part, but is given to assure us that we not only have the right to ask, but in asking are obedient to a commandment which is, in itself, worthy of a blessing. But we must ask *in faith*. The truth is, He is more anxious for your success than you are. Our materialistic world would have us believe we must do it ourselves or it can't be done. Call on Him and expect answers.

Failures of Man

The American male, more than any man in the world, is a failure in regard to leadership of his family. Referring again to the statement of Dr. Joshua Bierer, *It's the fatherless society. All the women are crying out for a strong man and he's just not there.* Let's review some of the failures of American men:

First is the man who fails to assume his position as leader: He does not lead. He does not determine family policy, make plans, set down rules or issue commands or make decisions. The family is like a ship without a rudder, tossed in a tumultuous sea. If the family is to be led, the wife must do so. Occasionally children must. The husband sits back without concern. He has defected, and his responsibility goes to another. His attention is on other things. He is irresponsible.

48

Second is the man who allows his wife and children to ✓
push him around: He may wish to lead, but because of
weakness or fear he allows his family to dictate. He is a
pushover, a jellyfish. He follows the course of least resistance.
Instead of claiming his position, he cowers to the demands of
others. Some men are actually afraid of their wives, even with
fear of bodily harm. The pushover is a miserable failure in his
masculine position. He feels he should lead, but does not have
enough backbone to make a fair attempt.

Third is the man who succumbs to pressure of women and ✓
children: This man is no jellyfish. He exerts himself to lead, but
due to insufficient strength and firmness he gives in to pressure
against his own convictions. Pressuring may take the form of
harping, needling, bugging, convincing, moral pressure,
weeping, whining, wailing, and other means to get their way.
Or they may go so far as to make demands, issuing ultimatums
with a threat of consequences.

Some men succumb to pressure because they are busy or
preoccupied with other important matters. They feel they
don't have time to wrestle with the problem. It seems easier
to give in and keep peace than hold firm to the position of
leader. They do not give their responsibility the priority it
deserves.

Other men grow weary from pressures. They are like the
judge in the scriptural parable of the importuning widow who
became weary of the widow's requests night and day and so
gave in to her wishes. The man may believe he should stand
firm, but due to constant harping he relinquishes rights and
prerogatives which should be sacred to him.

I was once in the company of a man who had two
teen-age daughters who were guilty of this practice of harping.
The father had bought a horse for the girls which was to be
delivered to their ranch several days later. But the girls urged
the father to borrow the farmer's truck and take the horse
immediately. They pleaded and begged, as they had done in
the past for other things.

The man, embarrassed and torn in his feelings, turned to
me for advice. *Tell them "No," in no uncertain terms,* I said, *and*

stick to it. Supported by my advice, he faced the girls with a firm *no.* They were in tears and coaxed continually until we were in the car and well on the way home. They sat in total silence for awhile, then began mumbling to themselves and looking harshly at their father. Such a denial was new to them and a severe adjustment. They were used to having their way. They had thought before that it pays to plead, but for the first time, they felt the weight of their father's words. If he kept up this firm sort of leadership, his girls would soon learn that pressure is of no avail, and they would be smart enough to stop.

The fourth failure of men is to compromise: In this case the man does not give in completely. He stands his ground to a degree, but makes concessions, or appeases in one way or another. This weakness is a mark of a poor leader and one which will lead to future trouble. Appeasement weakens one's position. So many decisions in the home have a moral tone or inference that one must be exceedingly careful not to do anything that would allow rationalizing from a strong position to a weak one. Standards must be maintained.

Men must be aware that, although it is wise to listen to family members, to consider their ideas, to accept good suggestions, it is never good leadership to give in against one's better judgment. A mark of great leadership is to stand firm to one's convictions, regardless of the feelings of others. This is not only a leader's right; it is his obligation.

Fifth is the man who allows his wife to steal his leadership: In this case she doesn't pressure her husband. She usurps his authority. She is a dominating woman and therefore tries to take over. She believes it is her right and duty to be the leader in the family, for whatever reasons she may have. Her husband's wishes are of no matter. He may wish to lead, but she overpowers him. She makes the decisions, determines family policy, makes plans without his sanction. The children turn to her for consent.

If she is more subtle, she offers endless suggestions, gives advice and counsel, always telling him what to do and when to do it. In either case she is out of place. The man who allows his wife to hold the reins is also to blame and has failed in his leadership. He must, if he is a man, overpower her and regain his position as head of the household.

Sixth is the man who fails to "make his leadership stick" or to command obedience from his family members. In this case the man may give instructions to his wife (or children), but she does not obey. She feels her opinion prevails; she does not have to follow his word but can do as she pleases. The children also follow this pattern of disobedience, for they have learned it from their mother. For children to learn disobedience at home, especially from their mothers, is most serious and often has far-reaching consequences. The man who allows this conduct becomes an *accessory to the fact* and bears a burden of accountability he is going to regret.

In some cases the wife (or child) would not argue against obeying, but would justify disobedience because to obey is difficult in the face of a selfish desire. She would minimize the consequence of her disobedience by trying to rationalize her way out of it. A husband who can teach obedience without rancor and with patience is a remarkable man indeed.

The seventh failure of men in leadership is lack of velvet: This is an opposite problem. This man leads with strength and firmness of steel, but lacks consideration for those he leads. Simple requests are brushed aside; heartfelt desires are denied. When a family member pleads for consideration, the man is without compassion. Filled with selfishness, he is not willing to be inconvenienced or make sacrifices for the benefit of others.

When a family member has been disobedient, he is severe in judgment, harsh in punishment. Such men rule as tyrants and fail in one of the most important qualities of great leadership. A man must rule with kindness, consideration, justice, mercy, love, and unselfishness. The prime quality that gives velvet to leadership is unselfishness. A man must have both the firmness of steel and the softness of velvet to rule properly.

The eighth failure of man is due to a weak ego: This problem is so subtle that men may not understand the fault they have. A man will say *no* when he would prefer to say *yes*.

He does this just to show his authority. He will resist a well-thought-out idea or suggestion because he does not want his family to forget that he is the leader. He has a weak ego and has a need to prove himself.

He does not realize that he doesn't have to say *no*, just to show his authority. There are numerous legitimate situations when he should say *no*. As he learns to be firm, decisive, and have the courage of his convictions, he will deserve and have the respect he seeks.

A man with a wholesome ego will respond as follows: If a family member makes a suggestion which is reasonable he will say, *That sounds like a good idea. Let's try it.* He doesn't need his position as leader as a proving ground for his self-worth.

The ninth failure is due to an oversized ego: In this case a man feels superior to those he leads. This is not a superiority of position, but a superiority of total worth. He may feel more intelligent, more gifted, capable and otherwise qualified than his family members. Therefore, he resists their advice, ideas and suggestions. He lacks the humility to listen, does not seek their counsel, and therefore separates himself from them. Strange as it may seem, and probably confusing to him, his superior image does not command the respect expected. Instead, it arouses contempt. Only a man who recognizes his fallibility can become an effective leader.

The Value of Humility in Leadership

A humble person is a teachable person. Without this attribute little progress can be made. For one who desires to be successful as a husband and father or in any field of endeavor, this fact must be recognized. As we consider the awesome responsibility a family leader has, it is apparent we need all the help we can get. There is much to learn from the experience of others. Children are not to be discounted, for their wisdom is sometimes astonishing. Women are noted for insight and intuition. A wise man is open to learn from all possible sources. If I have learned anything in life it is that one

52

should be slow to judge and ready to listen. Bits of truth come from the least expected sources.

Causes of Men's Failures

It is helpful to discover the major causes of men's failures to lead. They can be listed as follows:

1. Lack of Knowledge: This is the greatest problem of all. Although the disposition of a man is to lead, it being an √ integral part of his nature, *he has not known how to lead.* Consequently he has failed, and because he has, the idea that he should lead has been thrown out and alternative suggestions such as dual leadership or experimental leadership has been recommended. Let both husband and wife make the decisions together, or negotiate and see if something can be worked out. It is a case of *the blind leading the blind.*

2. Lack of Conviction: When a knowledge of this principle has been taught, it may be that it was not understood in a way to comprehend its tremendous importance. The knowledge may not have been supported by the Holy Scriptures, which lead to a conviction of truth. Whatever the failure, there are many men who, although they understand at least in part, lack conviction to apply these principles.

3. Lack of Self-Discipline: Even with knowledge and conviction it takes energy to use discipline. Using discipline is √ like thinking - it's easier not to. And perhaps not seeing an immediate reward, a man will lazily set it aside. It is not easy to be unselfish and kind, to control one's temper, to be forgiving and understanding, and persist in well-doing when the rewards are not evident. Doing what one knows he should do is the problem of life. Obstacles always arise, and no one likes obstacles. If a quick, short term alternative is available, that is usually the one we want to take.

The incentive to muster the self-control needed is to keep in mind the advantages if we do, and the consequences if we don't. We will save much time and frustration when we realize there is not an acceptable short cut. This is not a circumstance where we dare to face the consequences of not doing a job upon which so many people can be adversely affected.

The temptation is always there to blame someone else. In this case it would be the wife or children. After all, it is they who are making it difficult. Teaching and leading would work well were it not for those we are trying to teach and lead. We can't blame others for our failures. The responsibility is clearly ours and we must face up to it. The trend to weak leadership has been going on for several generations with disastrous consequences.

Social Problems Caused by Poor Leadership of Men

The general lack of manliness has led to many social problems. These I want to emphasize again.

1. The Dominating Woman: The dominating woman has become one of our major social problems, leading to a multitude of related problems. To sum it up, *When you have a society of dominating women, you have a society of unhappy, insecure women. You also have an equal number of frustrated, unfulfilled men. This affects their relationship and brings trouble into marriage and the home.*

The reason for the unhappiness of men and women, as the woman dominates, can be explained. In taking over leadership, she acquires masculine characteristics which accompany leadership. She learns to be aggressive, decisive, efficient, and competent in the leadership position. This may go on for a number of years without her realizing that she is less of a woman than she once was. Although her husband may not understand what is happening, he would surely have noted a change in feeling for her.

One day she comes to the rude awakening that she has lost much of her feminine charm. This is as important to her as masculinity is to a man. The hurt is compounded when she realizes her husband's default has brought it on her. It is like contracting a contagious disease from him. As she loses femininity, his feelings for her are adversely affected. He may appreciate her and love her, but he regards her as less of a woman than he once did. The tender, protective feelings he once had are gone. Such a loss is tragic indeed.

As the husband defects in leadership, he suffers a loss of masculinity. He is less aggressive, less dominant, less decisive. *He is less of a man.* This frustrates him and causes him to feel unfulfilled. His wife loses respect as she detects this loss of manliness. This diminishes love. The entire home scene is affected in a tragic way.

It would be unfair to place all responsibility for the dominating woman on the man. Women themselves have taken initiative beyond justification to dominate the household. Some have usurped authority, trampled on men's rights, pressured and demanded their way. But in spite of women's aggressiveness to lead, men are principally to blame. With a strong man, the dominating woman doesn't exist. Women take over as men allow them to. The responsibility to retain his position is his. This he must do at all costs.

2. Trouble in the Home: The home where the father's word is not obeyed is a home of trouble and discord, chaos and confusion, affecting all members. These troubles are subsequently poured out on society where everyone pays a penalty for the neglect of the father who fails to be the shepherd of his flock.

3. Youth Rebellion: Children who grow up in the home of a weak father who has not commanded respect for his word or obedience to his instructions grow up unprepared for life. Their own desires predominate, and they often find themselves at odds with the law and acceptable social behavior. A pattern of rebellion in the home leads to rebellion against authority, established customs, and accepted principles and standards when they go into adult life. These are the young lawbreakers, guilty of crime and delinquency. These are the young rebels who will not comply with the rules. These are the youth who are seeking to experiment with free sex and other forbidden practices. They are rejecting refinement, culture, and the disciplined life. These young rebels are usually the products of undisciplined homes.

Young rebels are sometimes produced by an overly strict father, who lacks the velvet of leadership. Such men do not respect the rights of children and unjustly demand or deny too much of them. Because of such unfair treatment, children may rebel against the teachings of their father. He has failed to win them to his way of life.

4. *Homosexuality:* It has been discovered that homosexuality is often the result of the home where a strong father image does not exist. There is a blurring of roles between the father and mother. The father does not stand out as strongly masculine nor the mother as strongly feminine. Children in such an environment lack a sex image with which to identify. Therefore they do not develop as strongly masculine or feminine. The maladjustments of homosexuality and lesbianism are a major problem and national concern.

This aberration in behavior has long been an affliction of mankind. But it *is an aberration*, whatever may be said to the contrary. We were born male and female and designed to function accordingly. Whether man or woman, each functions to the optimum with the association of the other in a relationship that is holy. Through this association come children as a blessing from God, a stewardship of his most precious gift to us. Our whole social order is dependent upon a continuance of this process.

All homosexuality could not be the consequence of failure of men's leadership in his role. Nothing is ever that simple. But this failure is one of the causes. And I would not suppose it is mere coincidence that the overwhelming rise of this affliction comes at the same time the structure of our homes has deteriorated so badly. Certainly when children don't understand the proper relationship of the sexes, the duties of each with a clear picture of true masculinity and femininity, it is no wonder they wander off into forbidden paths.

5. *Feminism:* Underlying the complaints of this movement is a dislike if not an open hostility and hatred towards men. At least a portion of this discontent is aimed directly at man's failure in leadership. Women are crying to be liberated from the shackles of male supremacy and eventually desire to eliminate the patriarchy which honors the man as the decision-making head of the family.

In thinking of men's guilt as it relates to the feminine rebellion, one observes that the lack of velvet in dealing with women is probably the main cause. Had men been more considerate, more unselfish and fair in their dealings with them, there would have been no need for women to seek freedom from such leadership. They would have enjoyed the security of strong leadership because it was tempered with gentleness and thoughtfulness.

It has been my opportunity to be interviewed on many talk shows and to face advocates of the feminist philosophy. Most of them are persons of deep feeling, usually hurt and disillusioned. The idealism I speak of is usually met with contempt, but some have been open minded. I have warned them their plan will never work for it is rooted in error. Contrary to their beliefs, their goals will best be met through the philosophy I teach, for it is the truth.

Probably their worst enemies are men who advocate feminism. Masquerading as defenders of women's rights, they prey upon them and take feminine favors with no responsibility or commitment. They are happy to see women solve their problems independently of men, leaving men free to selfishly follow their own pursuits.

* * *

We have viewed the weakness of men's leadership and have observed a lack of both steel and velvet. We have also observed the many social problems which occur when the father is not a proper head of his house. Let us now turn attention to the principles involved in good leadership and how they may be applied in daily living.

57

4

How to Lead Women and Children

There are fundamental principles which, if understood and followed, will aid immeasurably in leading women and children. Such leadership is frequently difficult and exasperating in the extreme. In this field of leadership a man is tested as in no other, for the relationships are far more intimate and often fraught with emotion. But if a man will study and apply the seventeen principles outlined below, he will find his task much easier, and will grow in a way that will greatly surprise himself and those he leads.

1. Take hold of the reins and keep them: A man must first assume the mantle of leadership, taking responsibility for making the major decisions, for directing family members, for delegating authority and dividing responsibility. In this way the household is put in order.

Many women do not realize the obligation they have to follow their husbands. His responsibility as leader is not self-assumed, but is divinely appointed. A divinely appointed assignment is not to be taken lightly. Women must be taught this principle and understand the sacred responsibility the husband has and the magnitude of his calling. For many women this concept is new. For nearly two generations there has been a barrage of contrary teaching. But the failures of the feminist philosophy are now apparent. She may be more open now.

Her obligation to respect her husband's position, honor his word and obey his instructions is difficult, particularly so when he makes mistakes. But the principle is a true one, and will work to the benefit of all when practiced.

It would be ideal if parents would teach their sons and

daughters this order of God at an early age that they might understand these principles as a guide to establishing their own homes later on. First, the sons would learn that they must prepare themselves for leadership, and the daughters would learn to yield to this leadership and to encourage it in the man. If these principles are clearly understood before marriage, it is likely more thought would be given to mate selection than seems to exist in most cases. The father must seek to clearly and unwaveringly establish himself as the undisputed leader and not deviate from this position.

2. *Teach the way of life:* If a man is to be the guide for ✓ his family, it is essential that he teach them principles to live by, standards and ideals which will serve as guides throughout their lives. He can sit at the bedside of his little children and teach them concerning the origin of man, how he was created in the image of God, the purpose of life and man's destiny after death. They can be taught their responsibilities as children of God and principles to follow in becoming better persons. If a man is unsure of himself in these basic beliefs, he can seek God through prayer and search the scriptures seeking a revelation of truth as a guide.

An effective way of instructing family members is the holding of a family home evening once each week. During this evening the father instructs his family, teaching them principles as a guide for their lives. The children are encouraged to ask questions and make comments. Mother is an active teacher also. This brings a family together. Recreation and fun are essential. Children will be reminding you, so you won't forget this important event.

A man must not only teach the way of life, he must be aware of the teachings they are receiving by way of TV, school, friends and employment. This is not a job to be passed to the clergy, social workers or day care centers. Nor is it an option to expect children to develop their own value system. They must have positive input from someone of conviction whom they trust.

3. *Provide a sense of direction:* There are always ✓ numerous uncertainties facing us. Indecision and unrest exist,

plans fluctuate, change, or hang in a state of flux. Problems are often unresolved. These situations are not too difficult if the father provides a sense of direction. This means presenting a positive picture - giving them something to hold on to.

During times of unrest or uncertainty, a man must reassure his family that he is giving careful thought to the future, plans are being considered and *problems will be resolved*. People need something to hang their hopes on, whether the dream is vague or specific. A man's thought for the future, his effort to conceive some type of plan, provides security for his family even if the plan is vague. He is their captain. When they are tossed about, as at sea, he is the one who charts the course.

Some men hesitate to make plans fearing they may not materialize. This would cause disappointment. Perhaps he fears that if he felt it unwise to proceed, he would have a moral obligation to go ahead anyway. Perhaps he fears that confidence in him will be shaken. This may be true if the plan is outlined in specifics and great enthusiasm built up. But if he will keep to generalities, emphasizing desire and hope and avoiding binding commitments, he will bring a feeling of security to his household and provide a sense of direction.

4. Act confidence: A good leader acts confident. He speaks with a self-assured voice, walks uprightly, trusts his own judgment, and is not plagued with doubts and fears. Because he appears confident, it is easy for others to follow. People naturally trust a self-assured leader, whereas it is difficult to support a person who lacks this quality.

Now, most men are not as confident as they need to be or would like to be. They suffer doubt, fears and complexes of all kinds. But even so, it is important to *act confident*. You must hide your fears for the sake of those who follow.

The future may look bleak and unsure to a man who has suffered financial reverses. He has doubts and fears. But as much as possible he should protect his wife and children from his anxieties. His wife needs to be aware of the general circumstances so she can offer comfort and confidence, but he should not allow himself to lose heart and place the burden on her. There *will be* solutions to the problem. After all, *it is God who has charged him with the duty of supporting his family and His assistance can be drawn upon.*

5. *Seek knowledge:* A good leader may be confident, but he is also humble. He realizes his limitations and therefore seeks knowledge from reliable sources before making plans or decisions. If he is considering a move to a new community, he does not rely on his own limited knowledge. Instead, he checks out the facts. He investigates the schools, housing, business opportunities, weather, the people, and special problems. He opens his eyes and takes a good look and disregards emotion or whims.

A young man planning a future occupation will have his special concerns and will not rely too much on the opinions of others. If he is considering a change of jobs, he finds out what his daily responsibilities will be, his potential, his problems or limitations, the pay and benefits. What he does not already know, he finds out and does so thoroughly. He does not trust to luck, an impression, or the opinion of others. He gets an accurate picture.

The advice of others is often very useful. In the business world men frequently pay a high fee for the advice of consultants, advisors, and counselors and feel that the money is well spent. But in seeking the advice of others, it is essential to choose a person who is knowledgeable and unbiased. It is especially important that you not seek advice from just anyone. The temptation to seek out someone who will give you the advice you want is hard to resist. Such advice may be worse than none. In general, it is better to avoid opinions of others as you would a plague. Seek only the advice of those you can trust, people with knowledge and wisdom on the subject. Avoid the opinion of someone who has a vested interest in the outcome. If in doubt about a person's qualifications, it is best to rely on your own judgment, for your perspective is usually better.

After you have gained knowledge and competent advice, weigh out the facts considering your own deep feelings. Make a determination based on your own judgment. Do not trust completely the knowledge or advice of others. Remember you may still have better judgment than they. Also, God may be guiding you in a direction that seems illogical in the face of the facts. It is best to heed strong feelings and follow your own convictions.

If you find you lack important knowledge upon which to base a decision or plan and do not know where to turn for the necessary information, remember you can always turn to God for answers. He will give to you in full measure whatever you need to know. The Savior taught, *If any man ask for bread, will his father give him a stone?* And in the book of James, *If any man lack wisdom, let him ask of God who giveth to all men liberally and upbraideth not. But let him ask in faith, nothing wavering.*

6. *Consult family members:* In matters which concern the family, it is usually wise to consult them. There may be some exceptions to this rule. For example, if the father is considering a change in his business, a change which will affect their future, and if the reasons for this change are too complex or too difficult to comprehend, it may be better not to talk with them. But in most cases the family will comprehend. They deserve to be consulted and can serve as valuable aids in making a wise decision.

The wife especially should be consulted, for she is usually a man's most loyal friend. She has a perspective that no one else in his life has. She is closer to his objectives and problems than others, yet not so close as he is. The consequences of the decision will likely affect her more than anyone. Her perspective is more accurate where his may be distorted and exaggerated. She stands back a little from the situation, making her viewpoint valuable. Women may be limited in knowledge, but they are inclined to have valuable insight. Voltaire has said, *All the reasoning of men is not worth one sentiment of women.* And Christine Rossetti commented, *Men work and think, but women feel.* Women can be fountains of wisdom. But it is to be remembered that hers is not the dominant voice. A man need only consider her viewpoint and then follow his own convictions.

Children also should be consulted, for they have interesting and valuable viewpoints and should never be underestimated. Many times they are intimately affected by the consequences. They will appreciate being a part of family planning and will be more cooperative and willing to sacrifice for objectives. It will, in fact, bring father and children closer together if he invites their ideas.

The best arrangement for the father in consulting with his family is a private meeting with his wife first in which they discuss all aspects of the matter and come to a unity of feeling. This would be followed by a family counsel to which everyone is invited. After laying out the proposal, each child would be invited to express himself. No one would be excluded just because he did not volunteer. The opinion of each would be known. Each person is asked for his ideas. At the end of the meeting the father assures the family he appreciates their ideas and will weigh them carefully, but will have to hold the right of final decision based on his own judgment.

The husband-wife meeting and the family counsel may be held when the need arises, or as a routine once a week. It can be held in connection with the family home evening, mentioned previously, or at a separate time. If it is held as routine, it has many benefits. If the father does not have matters to discuss, the wife and children will, and it will assist the father in bringing greater harmony into his family.

7. *Be decisive:* The dictionary defines the word decisive as *having the power or quality of deciding*. A decisive man is able to gather facts and draw conclusions quickly and come to a firm decision. Indecisiveness is to fluctuate or vacillate. There is usually hesitancy to come to a firm decision even after all the facts are known and considered. The tendency to postpone creates anxiety. For a decision never to be definitely made leaves unfinished business and the annoyance and pain of always having it *on the table*.

A leader who has this fault is handicapped, and his job becomes an onerous one. Decisiveness, on the other hand, helps a family immeasurably. It is like adding grease to the wheels. There are many decisions to be made on a daily basis.

Some are of momentous importance, some are small; but all must be faced in one way or another. For a leader to be decisive is a wonderful asset.

This trait can be cultivated. One must force himself to draw conclusions quickly and firmly. But before doing so, he should make a careful study of the facts. Risk in some measure is usually involved, and one will have to realize that this is an integral part of the matter. Most indecisiveness is caused by fear - the fear of making mistakes. This problem will be discussed in the following point.

8. *Allow for mistakes:* Fear of humiliation is a strong deterrent in decision making. This fear can be minimized by facing life realistically and allowing for human error.

Every man will make his share of errors in judgment. Not all decisions will be wise, not all plans fruitful. Success is never assured nor can results of a given decision and course ever be accurately measured beforehand. Therefore, a man must be willing to face this fact and allow for mistakes, not worrying about the consequences. If he has followed the principles of good leadership, being careful to gain adequate knowledge, and consider the viewpoints of his family, he will avoid an unnecessary number of mistakes.

As far as the wife is concerned, she is usually less concerned as to the outcome of a decision than she is to the confident attitude of her leader. Women tend to be very understanding, and in the face of defeat will extend great understanding and sympathy. They do, in fact, enjoy being the *understanding angel* in a man's moment of need. Women do not criticize a man for his failures and mistakes so much as they admire him for his courage to venture out, take risks, and do the things he believes in.

But it is important to say something about mistakes. We view them as totally destructive and probably without redeeming value. It is doubtful anyone would deliberately make a mistake. Yet experience teaches that many mistakes are important learning steps. There is usually a compensation somewhere. (I am speaking of errors in judgment or calculation - not sins.) Somewhere down the line we will likely see that, although the calculations we made did not turn out as expected, the overall results are good.

9. Win their support: Even though it is not always necessary, it is wise for a leader to win the support of his family. If they don't agree, try to explain your point of view with patience. Tell your wife you need her support, you value her opinion, but you are sure she will understand that if you are to lead you cannot do so unless you follow your convictions. Emphasize that her support is invaluable to you. Try to sell her on your ideas so she will be in harmony.

If this is not possible, at least try to win her support to your right to lead. Remind her that you alone are responsible for the leadership of the family, the decisions and their outcome. Do not try to win her support by pressure or ridicule. If you do, she may feel an obligation to support you, but this is not the kind of support that will strengthen your position. If a man does not make an effort to win his family's support and willfully goes against their wishes, they may have the impression he does not consider their feelings of any worth. They will then feel more opposed than before. This makes for trouble, for the man stands alone.

But if support is gained, it may prove invaluable later on. Should disappointments arise and plans fail to materialize, your wife, although she may not have agreed fully, did give approval and support to your decision. You will not be alone. You will not need to apologize for failure, and she will have no reason to point out your mistakes.

10. Keep reasons confidential: When announcing plans and decisions, it is not always necessary to explain your reasons. Sometimes it is an advantage if you keep them confidential, especially if the reasons are difficult to explain or may arouse questions. *Your decision may be sound but your reasons may seem wrong or illogical.* This may cause others to question your judgment or present opposition.

Often, a man is impelled to lead, not by logic or sound judgment, but by inspiration, perception, or even hunches. In these cases he may not know the reasons for his actions. The reasons may appear illogical, even to him. Any attempt to explain may seem futile. He can say, however, that he *feels* his decision is one he should follow. He can win family support even if he cannot sell them on his reasons. This is all that is necessary. People like to follow a self-assured leader.

God does not always reveal His reasons to us. We must learn to trust Him. We are instructed in the Book of Proverbs: *Trust in the Lord with all thine heart, and lean not to thine own understanding. In all thy ways acknowledge Him and He shall direct thy paths.* God's path is always right, but His purposes may seem illogical to us. We are not able to comprehend the full meaning of His divine plan. So He conceals his reasons and teaches us again and again to trust in Him. And such it is with any leader. His followers must learn to trust him in many situations.

11. Consistency and follow-through: When a man has conceived an idea or plan. given it careful thought, laid definite plans based on his best judgment and set an objective, the time comes to move ahead. A good leader does not turn back unless an unforeseen emergency arises.

Let's take an example: Suppose a man desires to take his family on an extended trip which will not only be a wonderful adventure but will have great educational value. He gives the idea careful thought. He convinces himself that the idea is not only feasible but is sound. He announces his plans to his family, and they excitedly start making preparations. They build up to a high peak of enthusiasm and set a definite objective.

As the date of departure nears, deterrents arise. He *loses heart.* If the object is high, it begins to look more difficult than expected. A man may wonder why he ever conceived such a wild idea. There are so many problems he didn't think about, and perhaps the advantages he thought about are not worth the trouble. This new view of an objective is much like the view one takes of a majestic mountain. Seen from a distance, it does not seem like such a great task to climb it. As one approaches, however, and finally reaches the base, the mountain seems much higher. It now looks insurmountable. From a distance your project seemed easy to accomplish; now it's hard.

Self-doubt is another hazard. Because the goal is unusual and someone may have expressed doubt or surprise, you wonder if the idea was a good one. You begin remembering past mistakes and fear a repetition. You question your judgment and wonder if it is really worth the sacrifice.

The tendency to become sidetracked is also a hazard. You start out with every intention to follow through, but find yourself involved with other things which take precedence. You are now too busy to go. Important as the plans seemed when you laid them, now they seem unimportant when placed beside your present involvements. These are *not* unforeseen emergencies, but self-assumed obligations. Justified as you may feel to cancel plans, you reveal a weakness in not placing a high enough value and priority on your project. These three tendencies are weaknesses and should be overcome.

The lack of follow-through on the part of the father can have a disheartening effect on the family. Not only is there a loss of enriching experiences that could just as well have been had, but the family suffers a certain lack of security, especially if it happens often. They will come to distrust their father's word. When new plans are presented, there will be doubt concerning the outcome. The family will lack faith that the plans will materialize, and disillusionment will set in.

Considering these doubts, it appears it would be better to follow through even if it may not be quite so prudent as originally thought.

Unforeseen circumstances do arise which make plans unwise. But the amazing fact is that women and children adjust to emergencies. They understand these situations. But they do not understand or make adjustments easily when there is no justifiable reason for turning back. They suffer disillusionment in the face of this retreat. It shows honor, justice, and fair play for a leader to follow through, not only for the benefit of those he leads, but for what it does for him. He feels true to himself.

12. Listen to their ideas and suggestions: A part of the √

67

velvet is listening to the family when they come with ideas and suggestions. Especially is it important to listen to your wife, as she is in a secondary position and feels the consequences as you do. I am not referring to those times when you seek their viewpoints. I am referring to *unsolicited voices.*

A man may resist listening to his family's suggestions, considering it an affront to his authority. He may expect women and children to remain silent unless asked. He may be humiliated to listen when he thinks he has the answers. It can even cause him to feel a little unmanly to listen, especially to women. If he does listen, he may do so impatiently, giving the impression he is in a hurry or imposed on.

A wise leader will listen and carefully consider other viewpoints. Valuable ideas come from many sources. It is not only wise to listen, but a leader has an obligation to listen. Although he is the leader, they who are led have a right to be heard. They are entitled to a voice in matters which concern them. A leader has an obligation to consider other viewpoints, even if they are in opposition to his own. When a family member comes to the father with a suggestion, the father can deal wisely with him as follows:

a) Stop all activities and give full attention. If this is not possible, make an appointment for a time free of interruptions. Then give undivided attention.

b) Listen carefully. If you are not in agreement, withhold your opposition. Do not present negative thoughts at this time. To do so shows great inconsideration for his right to speak and your responsibility to consider his thinking.

c) Be understanding. Express sympathy for his ideas. More than anything else a person wants to be heard and considered. This is more important than to have his ideas materialize.

d) Tell him you will think about it and will give it careful consideration. Do this although the answer may be so evident to you that you have no doubt about it. This shows courtesy and consideration. He will feel he has a voice and that his ideas are important. There is always the possibility that that which seemed so clear will be altered as you consider more facts. On the other hand, if you give a fast answer or quickly toss the suggestions aside, it shows thoughtlessness, perhaps arrogance. If the matter is of vital importance, tell him you will seek the Lord in prayer for guidance.

e) After you have carefully weighed the suggestion, if the idea is sound, admit it and express appreciation. If the idea is unsound, point out why in a manner that is kind and firm. In doing this, be sympathetic with the opposing viewpoint. Do not belittle ideas or regard them as unimportant. Show respect for others' thinking, but explain that you must follow your own convictions even if they are in opposition. Sometimes your reasons may be difficult to analyze or for others to understand. In such cases, explain that you do not have a good feeling about it and feel responsible to follow your convictions.

13. *Listening to requests and special desires:* Much the same procedure is followed as when listening to differing suggestions. After you have listened and had time to consider it carefully, if the requests seem reasonable, give consent. Don't be afraid of spoiling them, especially your wife. It develops her femininity and gentle side. She will feel more loved and therefore more loving. And with children, although it is not wise to provide them with an overabundance of material things, they can be granted many little concessions which are absolutely harmless.

For example, one of our little girls once asked her mother if she could wear her new dress to bed. Sensing how much it would mean, her mother said *yes.* This child is an adult now and has never forgotten this unusual concession. The more ridiculous the request, the more children seem to appreciate it.

If the request is not justified, if it is selfish or unwise, make your refusal gently. Show sympathy for feelings. If the desire is right, but you cannot possibly grant it at present, express regret. Express your desire to give it if you could.

Let them know there is nothing you would rather do than give things to those you love. Your attitude in giving, your willingness to give, is more important than the gift itself and just as much proof of your love.

Whatever you do, never ignore or disregard a request, however insignificant. Very often a little boy will request a sailboat or some other item which seems of no consequence to his father, but to him it means everything. His heartfelt desire needs to be recognized. A man might think he would like something else just as much and, because it may be easier to obtain, might supply a substitute. If it is not wise or possible to have what he wants immediately, he must somehow be taught patience to wait. Sacrifices often must be made. This sympathy and understanding may mean more than the toy itself. Whatever our children ask, they should have our listening ear and sympathy and consideration. The Savior taught, *If your children ask for bread, do you give them a stone?* A cold denial of a heartfelt desire can make a woman or child feel you have given them a *stone*.

14. *Listening to problems:* As their leader, your family will confront you with many problems, great and small. Some are of major importance and must have careful consideration. Solutions should be sought or pointed out wherever possible. But all problems, great or small, should be listened to and considered. The wife especially needs her husband's help, for she is dependent on him.

With small problems and especially with children, it may be only sympathy they need. They must know that someone understands. They do not always need or want solutions. For example, if Johnny is shunned at school, it may be difficult to find solutions. Nor is this necessarily what he needs or wants. He wants your sympathy. He needs to know you are with him, that he is not alone. Often children will resist solutions, since what they really want is understanding. You can be assured that if either wife or children resist your solutions, you are failing to give what they really want - sympathy.

This is not to suggest, as in the case of Johnny, that you should not point out methods of dealing with the situation. Perhaps he must make improvements in himself. Although these may not be the full solution, they teach a person how to cope with problems. Even this should be preceded with sympathy for the problem itself.

Never use negative means of minimizing a problem. For example, never say, *I had it far worse,* or *Others have a harder time than you,* or *You should be thankful for what you have.* These remarks make a person feel foolish or ashamed. They will regard you as critical and lacking in sympathy. A positive means of minimizing a problem, however, is this: *You have lived through more difficult things than this.* This makes a person feel heroic and is a recognition of your faith in him.

15. Listening to objections, complaints, and dissenting voices: This is a difficult time in leadership. No one likes this unpleasant task, so it is easy to minimize or turn aside. Sometimes the complaint is in opposition to your plans and decisions. This is a time when a man is most apt to become irritated and resist listening, feeling that his judgment is being questioned. It is upsetting to have an opposing view when one's mind is settled in another direction.

A man who will not listen to a dissenting voice is not equipped to lead. He does not have to yield - he only needs to listen and consider. To do so is a valuable aid in promoting good relations. Right or wrong, they have a right to speak.

In ancient India, kings held what was called a *dunbar court.* These sessions were held almost daily at which time opportunity was given the subjects to appear before the king to voice suggestions, criticism, or complaints. These courts were highly successful and promoted good relations. It will do the same for a father who is willing to listen.

It is important to stress that a leader need not heed all complaints. Without the knowledge he obtains from listening, how is he equipped to judge? It is difficult to be sympathetic with someone who is bringing a criticism, but such is one of the tests a leader must face. He will not immediately take a defensive attitude or point out others' mistakes nor make them feel foolish or ashamed. He will be patient and sympathetic and attempt to view the problem from their point of view. This is respect for human rights and dignity.

16. Hold to your convictions: The supreme quality of leadership is for one to hold to his convictions. With all the velvet suggested - kindness, patience, consideration for ideas

71

and feelings of the dissenting voices, a good leader will hold fast to his convictions. He will have the courage to follow his judgment and conscience even in the face of opposition from those he loves. He will not be moved by pleas or tender feelings. If necessary, he is willing to bring bitter disappointment in his obligation to do what is right and wise. This quality is compared to the strength of fine steel that may bend slightly but will not yield to pressure. It is a trait of greatness. It makes for peace, order, and harmony. It brings security to women and children.

It is interesting to know what this quality in a man does for a woman. Although she loves the velvet in him, she needs his steel. This is her security. She may seek to rule, she may try to dominate, but always *she loves only her master.* What I'm saying is *she wants a leader!* This explains why a woman will sometimes stay with a tyrant when one would think she would leave. He may be hard and sometimes even cruel, but she sticks to him like glue because his firmness brings security.

Weak men, on the other hand, often lose their women. The man who can be dominated and pushed around does not have the respect of his wife and robs her of the security she needs. In spite of a million kindnesses, years of sacrifice and devotion, she can not tolerate her life with him.

A man I have known for many years married a girl of ambition and drive for worldly possessions. She had dreams of special accomplishments for her husband and in her mind had him fitting a different role from that which he had for himself. Although this was probably the greatest difficulty, it was compounded immeasurably by the fact that he would continually give in to her pressures - whims as well as deeper feelings.

Going against his better judgment, he would go into debt for things she just had to have. Always there was the thought that she would be satisfied if she could have these things that meant so much. It became a matter of continual appeasement.

This man was a good worker, a reasonable provider, and true to his wife. His moral standards were above reproach. He was the epitome of kindness, long-suffering and temperance. He dedicated his life to looking after his family, always sublimating his interests to theirs.

The consequences were that the more he gave in, the greater was her disrespect for him. Although the couple were *religious,* her feelings for him degenerated into a near contempt. The natural kindness and tenderness which was so typical of his character and which was actually so admired by many of his friends was, ironically, the quality which destroyed his marriage. Always compromising to avoid a showdown, being willing to give in rather than face her demands or unpleasantness, was finally the thing which brought on the ultimate failure. After twenty-five years of marriage, they went their separate ways.

Children also benefit from their father's firmness. They do not respect a father they can push around. He does not provide security. They may as well be put out in the world by themselves. He is not a guide they can rely on. They only feel security when they have a father who will not yield to pressure. In divorce courts children usually choose the parent who has been the most firm.

Women and children are *entitled* to firm leadership. They do not understand this need themselves. This explains why they so often try to dominate and pressure to get their way. In reality they are testing to see if the firmness they need is really there. They will love you more, respect you more and feel far more secure if you will not yield against your better judgment.

17. Seek God through prayer in your leadership position: When we realize the responsibility we have as leaders - a role that extends for a lifetime - and when we contemplate the necessity of discerning wisdom from foolishness, dealing justly with the rights of others, and the consequence of our decisions, it is apparent we need the daily help of God. Without His help the risks are too great - with His help success is assured. If you will seek the Lord in daily prayer, naming specific needs and problems, placing your trust in Him, He will aid and sustain you.

This point was brought into focus for me several years ago when being interviewed on a call-in radio program. A lady called to tell about her wonderful father who was an example of all I was saying. He had reared a family of thirteen children and they had all turned out well. He was an excellent father and respected by his family. And yet, he was an uneducated man. He could not even read or write. But, he was a *very prayerful* man and his life had turned out surprisingly well.

He was now ninety three years old. She had recently visited him and, at the time, had asked him: *Dad, how come ninety five percent of your decisions were always right?* He answered thoughtfully, *Ninety five percent of those decisions were not mine*

Understanding The Woman's Subordinate Role

A woman is in a *very subordinate position* to her husband. The man leads; the woman follows. He holds the right of decision, the final say in everything. She is dependent on him for all she has, for every freedom, every consideration, for everything she does and every place she goes. He holds the reins in the family.

And yet she shares equally the responsibility of the family. She shares the same sacred responsibility for its success, is a partner in its problems and burdens. She has a desire, probably even greater than his for a happy home and successful children. Yet, to accomplish her goals, she is dependent upon him - upon his decisions, his wisdom and judgment. She is at his mercy for justice, fair play, and understanding of her needs and desires. Hers is a case of responsibility without final authority. She does not have control over her life. In a way it is similar to the problem of our early American forefathers who had *taxation without representation*.

To see the position she is in, and then to see the abuses to which she is vulnerable, is it any wonder many of them chaff under the leadership of men? It is vital that a man understand and appreciate this subordinate position.

Suppose that you are partially responsible for the success of a large industry. You have a desire for its success, feel keenly its problems, and are personally affected by its success or failure. Your hands are tied if you have a president whose ideas you feel work against your interests. If he is more interested in showing a short-term profit so he can sell the business for his advantage, rather than the long-term investment that would make the business more profitable later, you might find your interests disregarded. Everything you hope to accomplish, every goal or objective, is directly dependent on him. You are at his mercy. You can quit, but that is not what you want to do in marriage.

A woman has goals. She wants a happy home and children. There are numerous things she believes are necessary to accomplish these goals. She wants a smooth-running home with conveniences and beauty, a home that will serve the family well. She wants good health and opportunities for the children and many more things that make a happy home. She also has personal needs and rights. Filling these needs is an integral part of her life. But she is at the mercy of her husband. She is dependent on his understanding, his unselfishness and consideration. She is dependent on his cooperation in reaching her objectives. He holds power over her, over everything she holds near and dear. Every desire of her heart is tied to him and his rule over her.

When a woman marries, she puts her faith and trust in her husband. She gives up her freedom and moves into his camp. When he denies her what is rightly hers, serious things can happen. Love is apt to disappear, for love vanishes when selfishness and inconsideration enter in. Strange things also happen when a woman is so abused.

Suppose she orders a new type of linoleum or floor covering for her kitchen. She immediately realizes it is a poor choice. Her husband says it is fine and she will get used to it. But as the months roll on, she finds it more and more difficult to live with. An attempt to explain to her husband is futile. He will raise his voice and tell her that's the end of the matter.

When a woman's rights are so easily put down, she may resort to strange behavior. She may develop a desire to move to a new community. (He would never consider a move to a different house in the same city.) As her desire grows, she hints of it and he ignores her. Finally, she develops asthma, or some other reason develops where a move is necessary.

The same strange action may be noted in other situations wherein a woman finds herself trapped. She may want a doorway cut between the master bedroom and the hallway so she can hear her children at night. She may want a fireplace in the living room or some other desire that a man can not understand. She may have made a mistake in selecting paint, furniture, drapes, tile, or carpeting, which she has difficulty living with. She tells herself again and again that it is of no consequence, but she is continually disturbed by it and frustrated in being unable to make changes.

It is well to recognize the effect of color and design on some people. The problems created by lack of harmony in our daily environment are marked and cannot be ignored. They are not whims. These are real problems, and strange and unpredictable behavior occurs when one is trapped in such a situation.

A woman is not always honest in her dealings with her husband. She can't be. This is because of her subordinate position. Often she must say *no* when she means *yes*. She may concoct reasons for her action, untrue justification for her desires. A man, she may reason, will never understand. She has no power to meet her needs.

A wise leader can change all this nonsense. If he will understand her subordinate position, he can end his problems and hers. He certainly does not have to give in against his judgment, but he can be as fair with her as he is with himself. When a man makes a mistake what does he do? He changes things. If he buys a new car he doesn't like, he turns it in on another model. He may consult his wife, but with the power of decision, he can make the change. Not so with a woman. She must go through official channels. She is dependent on her husband for changes.

When a man understands the sensitive position his wife occupies and her vulnerability to neglect and abuse when he is insensitive or selfish, he can appreciate why she reacts as she

76

does. The hard and embittered attitude of some women crying for *liberation* can be understood.

In man's leadership it is plain to see there are many things to consider. Sound instruction is needed, encouragement and understanding offered, human rights respected, and justice and mercy exercised. The responsibility is great, extending for a lifetime, for even when sons and daughters marry, they need their father's guidance. If he has given wise leadership in their youth, they will turn to him for his guidance along life's path.

But this responsibility, great as it is, is not beyond the capacity of man to do, and to do well. He need only apply the principles of good leadership, as have been outlined, and seek divine guidance in his calling.

Principles of Good Leadership

1. Assume the responsibility as a sacred calling.
2. Instruct family in good principles to live by.
3. Provide a sense of direction.
4. Display confidence.
5. Seek knowledge before making plans and decisions.
6. Consult family members for their viewpoint.
7. Be decisive.
8. Allow for your mistakes.
9. Win their support.
10. Sometimes keep reasons confidential.
11. Be consistent - follow through.
12. Listen to family ideas and suggestions.
13. Listen to and consider requests and desires.
14. Listen to problems, offer solutions or sympathy.
15. Listen to objections, complaints, dissenting voices.
16. Hold to your convictions.
    a. Don't be pushed around.
    b. Don't be pressured against your better judgment.
    c. Don't compromise.
    d. Have the courage of your convictions.
17. Seek God through prayer.

5

The Protector

Another area of masculine service is the protection of women and children, especially members of one's own family. This is another of the God-assigned duties given to a man. Consequently he was created with a body which is physically stronger and of greater endurance than the woman's. God also placed within him a natural courage that women do not have and implanted in his nature an instinct to defend and shield from harm those who need such care.

The role of the protector is more than a responsibility - it is an opportunity to grow. To shield women and children from the hardness and difficulties of life develops strength and manliness. To be robbed of this opportunity is to be robbed of manly growth. In other words, a man suffers personally when he is unable to serve in this way.

Life in today's world is in strong contrast to earlier times when protecting one's family meant conquering the elements, building a shelter, finding or growing the food for the table, preserving life in an environment where effective government did not exist. Failure to meet these needs meant destruction. The male role as the protector was a dominant one, clearly seen and appreciated.

To meet these needs today a man adjusts the thermostat, makes a trip to the market and votes for the government he wants. Courage, physical strength and endurance are not seen as part of the picture. But the need for protection is still a vital concern. In some ways it is more urgent than before. Women and children are exposed to hazards which are sinister and threatening. Providing a shield against these hazards demands that a man recognize the full measure of the threat they impose and then take the action required. The dangers I wish to emphasize fall into three groups:

Protection from Dangers

1. Sexual assault: The general lessening of moral restraints has contributed greatly to this problem. Sex is spoken of lightly and casually. It is often the main theme in movie and TV productions, and usually done in a way of cheap humor or violence. It is commonplace conversation in the schools. Premarital sex has increased enormously and is spoken of without shame. It is discussed as a fact of life in which everyone is involved. Homosexuals are fighting for their *rights*.

Sex is constantly before us. With this comes the abuse of alcohol and other drugs to further reduce inhibitions that would otherwise restrain one. In this environment is it any wonder sexual assault is commonplace? In fact it is so commonplace that many times law enforcement officers cannot be sure when there has been an assault.

The likelihood of assault is increasing. As the protector, a man is responsible to do all possible to avoid such a catastrophe. This means seeing that your wife and daughters understand the threat and are prepared to avoid situations that would make them vulnerable. This means the elimination of trashy movies, literature and foul language in the home. First by your own example. The home should not be the seedbed of the problem. There must be constant reinforcement by teaching strong morals, providing love and encouraging openness for communication between parents and children.

Women and children should not be permitted to go places alone at night or to enter questionable environments or be escorted by persons not entirely trustworthy. Girls should not be permitted to hitchhike. This is an open invitation to assault and a threat to life. The fact that they put themselves at the mercy of someone whose character they do not know shows a naivete which is alarming.

Women sometimes willfully go their way unprotected.

They are likely in pursuit of the routine duties of life and do not know the risk they are taking. Others deliberately discourage the protection of a man. Many, however, appreciate male concern and smile with gratitude when they receive it.

2. *Evil influences:* The Protector is the watchdog who guards against any influence which would corrupt the mind or spirit of anyone in the home. This is not only the elimination of the obvious trash so easily identifiable, but includes negativism, disorder, slovenliness or anything which is an interference to high performance or to calm and emotional peace. The home should be a place of tranquility where people speak with respect, and where good manners and courtesy are the rule. Instead, the typical home is a place of disorder, confusion and loud voices - a place that invites an evil spirit to prevail. And this sad state is joked about and accepted as inevitable.

3. *The hard elements:* Women and children need protection from the hard elements of the world - the cold, the wind, the rough terrain, heavy traffic, heavy equipment, lightning, thunder, and even dogs, spiders, and mice. It may seem strange that women need protection from such things as spiders and mice. The truth is that whether the woman actually needs this protection is not so important as the fact that she *thinks* she needs it. If her fear is apparent, if she is trembling at the sight of a shadow in the dark, her fear is just as real as if she were frightened by a tiger. It is comforting to have a man calm her fears and place himself as a barrier against the dangers.

Protection from Strenuous or Masculine Work

The need persists for women and children to be protected from strenuous work which produces undue physical strain. Working with heavy equipment, lifting boxes, moving mattresses, hauling rocks, etc. are masculine chores and are difficult for most women. It is true they have the capacity for some of this work, but it is an assault on their femininity to have to do it. It is also an affront to the dignity of one whose best interest a man is entrusted to preserve. In preserving and protecting the delicate natures of women and children a man enhances his masculinity. Because this is an acute problem we shall deal with it in more detail later in this chapter.

Lack of Protection Today

There is a noticeable lack of feminine protection today. Women are seen everywhere with no concern for their safety. They take long distance trips alone and walk unguarded down dark streets. We find them doing all kinds of masculine work - lifting heavy bundles, fixing the plumbing, repairing the furnace, working with heavy equipment, and doing other difficult tasks. This problem is compounded because of the false teachings of the feminist movement that would have women believe they must move into every masculine field and perform just as a man does.

Several years ago I had an experience which saddens me as I recall it. I rented a trailer from a man to do some light moving. When I returned the trailer his wife was on duty. She was dressed in heavy work clothes, wore shoes which resembled army combat boots, and wore a man's cap. At first glance I thought she was a man. As I tried to unhitch the trailer, she moved in with a large wrench and said, *Here, let me take care of this*. She was competent and knew just what to do. When it was unhitched, I started to push it to the spot it had to go, but she said, *Let me do that*, and she pushed me aside.

I don't know whether her husband placed her in this position, allowed her to do it, or whether she willingly assumed this manly task. But I do know that if he were a real man, he would not allow his wife to present herself to the world in this unfeminine way. He allowed her to be stripped of her femininity in public view. How would he like to be stripped of his masculinity in such an unseemly manner? This lack of chivalry is a public embarrassment.

I recall another disturbing experience, this time in the Far East. To me the Oriental women represent something special in femininity. Their features are small and delicate, and they seem to be soft and dependent. Traveling in Hong Kong I noticed the construction of a multi-storied hotel. There was a line of several dozen women carrying mortar in a hod to the masons. To see these gentle little women bending their backs to carry a load such as this in a masculine trade was enough to bring tears to the eyes. Where were the men who should have been doing this? I am not presuming to analyze the hard economics of life in their part of the world. I can only say it seems pathetic that any of the lovely ladies of our world must serve in this manner.

Certainly women are somewhat to blame. Many of them have by choice taken over masculine work and sought positions in army combat, fire fighting, highway construction and law enforcement. But in a majority of cases men are to blame. They sit back and allow women to lift heavy objects and struggle with many masculine chores. Women may at first request manly assistance, but they do not get it because of laziness or lack of concern. They are forced to do the man's work because he will not do it. To keep peace in the family and avoid friction, they do it themselves.

Children also are often unprotected. A young woman told me that when she was sixteen her parents sent her alone with strange people to travel to the East. She had never met them before, but to save money the parents paid strangers for her transportation.

In another instance a young woman was sent to a large city alone to find a job. She was only seventeen and arrived at the train station with no one to meet her. She had to find city transportation to a prearranged place. She sought work by herself, solved her own problems, and fought her own way in life. One may rationalize that it is good for young people to meet such situations, but the dangers involved are too great. Plenty of legitimate situations later on will provide opportunity to learn the lessons of independence.

Some children are allowed to do heavy work far beyond their capacity. Although it is developing for them to do hard work and learn responsibility, it should be limited to the capacity of their years.

Harm in Lack of Protection

Harm to the woman: Lack of protection diminishes femininity. In taking on themselves masculine activities and assuming burdens beyond their normal capacity, they acquire masculine ability. This is a point I keep emphasizing, because I rarely find that people understand that this is what happens. They may not only acquire the ability but also the mannerisms.

Many women have become competent in masculine tasks. They paint with skill, are adept at repairing a machine, and are able to lay cement. They fight their own battles and make their own way. But the important thing is that as they become competent in masculine labor, they lose some of their womanliness. They need a man less. Let me refer you again to the lady who unhitched the trailer. As she moved into the man's world, she did so at the expense of her femininity. She was trying to be of assistance to her husband, and helpful to me, but at what price? I could not regard her as a woman. She was repulsive and awkward in her dress. I had sympathy for her and compassion. But I did not feel I was in the presence of a real woman. I could see that she could have been a real woman. She could have been feminine and charming.

A woman dressed as a man and working in a man's job is a striking example I wish to make. Other examples are more subtle -consequently more dangerous for a woman who can be ensnared with no awareness of what is happening to her.

I was once being interviewed on a TV show where this subject came up. The host had invited three women to appear with me to get their opinions. Sitting next to me was a woman dressed in a feminine, even frilly manner, perfumed, her hair perfectly styled. She spoke in a soft and restrained way. A little later in the conversation I learned that she was the manager of a large and successful business in her community.

She seemed agreeable to the philosophy I teach until I mentioned that a woman who gets into masculine work takes on masculine mannerisms. At this comment a Jekyll-Hyde transformation came over her. Her tone of voice became harsh and demanding. She shifted her seating position so as to look me in the eye and said, *What you say is not true. I have worked for several years in my position and it hasn't affected me one bit!*

I said nothing, but the visual aid she had supplied was so striking that no one on the panel had anything to say. The host discretely brought up another subject. I bring up this incident at this time because here was a hazard her husband might have protected her from.

A woman functioning in her natural sphere, surrounded by her feminine tasks, moving in her domestic world with her natural adaptability to her sphere is a delight to see. Here is heaven's creature, born to be vastly different from man. She has a charm, probably unknown to herself. But this charm is lost, and what a loss it is, as she moves in the man's world.

Lack of protection can also cause a woman to develop a *resentful attitude* towards her husband. If she asks for help and is ignored or refused, she may respond in several negative ways. In the first place, the refusal is an insult to her femininity. She may not consciously realize that this is the case, but in a subtle way she feels it. She may feel that her husband does not love her. His refusal to perform is no credit to him either. Instinctively most people have a sense of what is appropriate behavior for men and women in relation to one another. If out of necessity she must do the job, she will likely feel deserted and imposed on. Women desire and expect chivalry from men. When denied, their feelings suffer.

Harm to the man: A man suffers a loss of masculinity if he fails to perform his rightful duties. This loss is more detrimental than he realizes. He will not feel good about himself. This is not a case of just an opportunity lost, but losing a little bit of something he previously had. Each day we make decisions which move us forward or backwards. Many of these decisions do not seem of much consequence, but they have an effect. It is impossible to have a feeling of well-being without assuming the burdens that are ours.

Harm to the household: The man's failure to perform his household tasks is the cause of much discord in many homes. The subject is much discussed and even thought to be humorous as a man fails to fix the leaky roof, wash the car, or cut the grass. His wife who has waited until Saturday for him to do these jobs finds he is either watching TV or reading the paper or has sneaked away to play golf with his buddies. She began with polite requests, then reminders, finally harping and nagging. She has been brought to this unhappy position through no fault of hers. The husband has brought discord into the home.

Harm to children: Children are greatly harmed by the lack of protection from dangers. They may develop self-reliance out of necessity, but at some point will realize that their parents were neglectful and unconcerned. In the eyes of the child he may feel unloved or unwanted. He needs to be treasured.

The value one places on any object is clearly discernible by the care he takes to preserve it. A child is entitled to feel that he is of great worth. He is benefitted by obvious acts which demonstrate the value his parents place upon him.

If children are given strenuous work beyond their normal capacity, they may carry their burdens without complaint but not without injury to their feelings. The injustice of it will be felt and there will be unfavorable consequences. The greatest need children have from their parents is to be loved and treasured and understood. This does not mean spoiling them with extravagant indulgences. Love and understanding bridge the generation gap.

Protecting Woman from Strenuous or Masculine Work

Many duties around the house are too strenuous for women and therefore belong to the man. Many men feel that any work that is associated with the home falls into the wife's category. Whether any of it is beyond her strength or is too dangerous, such as climbing ladders, may never enter his mind. He feels he has done his part by bringing home the paycheck.

For the jobs that are obviously his, he will expect to do at his own convenience. Most men do not put these jobs in priority. The fact is that if this work is not done systematically, disorder comes into the household. Either his wife will be doing work detrimental to her or a backlog will be building up. If it is beyond her strength or ability or is of a masculine nature and therefore not proper for her, he must do it. Solutions are simple. A suggested outline is given here.

1. Divide household responsibilities:

a) Her work: Cleaning the house, cooking, shopping, care of the children, sewing, washing, ironing and transporting children.

b) Your regular home duties: Cleaning the garage, doing the yard work, washing the car and seeing that it is filled with fuel, (Is it fitting that she should wrestle with gasoline hoses and lift the hood to check oil level?), keeping the house in general repair, changing the filter on the furnace, putting salt in the water softener and organizing the basement.

c) Your occasional or emergency duties: Moving furniture, repairing equipment, lifting in heavy groceries, building shelves, etc.

First, divide responsibilities so that they are clearly defined, and there will be no misunderstandings. Discuss it together in detail and come to a mutual agreement on each duty. In discussing it be sure to be her advocate and see that she does not volunteer for more than she should be doing. Some jobs can be done by either, such as transporting the children to music lessons or doing the grocery shopping. The important thing is to have a clear understanding of who is to do the job.

2. Getting your regular home duties done: It is important to place these home duties in proper priority with your other activities. They certainly do not take preference over employment, but they are in priority over sports and entertainment. This is a touchy spot for many men who feel that recreation and commitment to friends is of prime importance. But consider it this way: A man who does not place these home responsibilities ahead of his own pleasures is not setting a proper example to his family. He can hardly complain if his wife fails to have meals on time because she was visiting on the telephone, or his children fail to do their job because they were too busy playing.

Once you know what you must do, set a particular time during the week to do it. Early morning is excellent as it is usually free of interruptions. You will find satisfaction in getting these jobs done quickly and regularly and will soon form the habit.

In work such as yard work, painting, and cleaning the garage, children can be assigned the duty, or can work with you in it, or the job can be hired out. The important thing to remember is that it is your job and your responsibility to follow through and see that it is done. Do not expect your wife to worry about it.

A major part of any responsibility, and sometimes the most aggravating and time consuming, is *seeing it gets done*. There is nothing so disheartening to a woman as to hear her husband say, *All right, children, get the weeds pulled and the yard cleaned up*, and then leave it up to her to see that they do it. She may as well take over the job herself.

If a woman has been used to worrying about a man's job, she may find it difficult to let go. She may remind her husband frequently to get the job done, a habit which can be very annoying to him. The solution lies in his letting her know that he accepts the responsibility and she is not to worry about it. He should tell her that whether he does it or neglects it is his concern, and in any case she is not to remind him or be concerned about it.

3. Facing the occasional or emergency duties: These are the jobs that are not on the regular schedule. They are unexpected or may require immediate attention. Sometimes you may not be aware of them unless your wife points them out. They are a source of contention in many families, since the wife must ask her husband to do them. This is nagging.

When such requests are made, a man is usually not in the frame of mind to respond. Something is already on his schedule. These jobs are not in his plans. If he is thinking deeply on something it is irritating to have a change of focus.

Not wanting to be bothered, he ignores them, hoping they will go away.

Since they do not go away, he finds himself being reminded again and again, which only builds up the more resistance to doing them. Finally the frustrated wife gives up, calls a repairman or does the job herself. The trouble is that now she has a resentment towards her husband and he may also have one towards her. This painful problem can be resolved in the following ways:

a) Face the responsibility as yours, not hers. She is not asking a favor. You are part of the household too.

b) Get the job done immediately and out of the way if possible.

c) If you can't do it immediately, tell her you will do it. Add it to your notebook of home responsibility. Arrange a definite time to do it or hire it done.

d) Most important - let her know you understand that this is your job, you are concerned about it, and she has no further worry.

When the job has been taken care of, do not act like she is now indebted to you. If you really want to surprise her with something she least expects, tell her you are happy you had the chance to do the work. She will probably appreciate it and be grateful, but the job was yours and should be regarded as such. There is no way you can avoid it. Under such circumstances, if you are happy you get a benefit with no extra effort.

Any job requiring masculine strength or ability belongs to the man and not the woman. It seems trite to have to dwell on such simple problems which have such simple solutions, but the sad fact is that they are a major source of friction. A man who willingly performs these duties will be greatly appreciated.

The joy of living is greatly increased when a home is kept in good repair. It is wiser to live in a smaller, less expensive home which is well cared for than to live in more luxury where things are falling apart. A well kept house is basic to good living and a marvelous example to the children. Whether the house is humble or not is of no matter. In establishing these priorities, a man may have to adjust his values and use discipline, but it will greatly aid him in his overall responsibility and bring harmony into the home.

4. Preparation for home duties: Some men are inadequately prepared for their work in the home. Despite training in a specialized field in which they are highly educated and skilled, they may know little or nothing about repairing a toilet, planting a lawn, carpentry, or fixing a motor. No one likes to take on a job for which he feels incompetent, so he has no choice but to hire it done or learn the rudiments of handling it.

Again, it is not the wife's responsibility to acquire this knowledge. If a man does not know, he is expected to learn. Although one may find it easier to hire these chores done, there is satisfaction in learning to solve household maintenance problems. When emergencies arise, family members look to the father for solutions.

Fortunately much information is available.   Adult education sometimes offers courses. The classes are given at a modest fee. Books are available as well. Another good source are friends and acquaintances who are not so inept as we may be.

When acquiring knowledge, do not do it as if it were a hobby in which you are expected to have a natural interest. Accept it as a necessary responsibility just as you would learn to read or write, earn a living, or do anything which is a preparation for life. When a woman marries, if she does not know how to cook, sew or clean, she must learn. If she does not know how to make beds, change a baby's diaper or clean a home, she is expected to learn. When she acquires this knowledge, she does not do it as if it were a hobby to satisfy her own interests. It is part of her work and duty. Our responsibility is obvious.

One can acquire competence in such duties without expecting himself to have the art of the professional or the skill of the tradesman. One need learn only enough to fulfill the essential needs. Of course there is more satisfaction if we learn to perform a job well.

In summarizing man's protection of women from

strenuous or masculine work, keep in mind that one will solve his problems by dividing responsibility at home, outlining those duties which are his and either doing them or seeing that they are done. When emergencies arise, we should willingly take care of them or assure our wives that we will as soon as possible. A man should always give his work at home proper priority and regard it as his responsibility, not his wife's. If he lacks knowledge or skill he should learn so that he can fill this important need.

Protection From Difficulties

Women and children need protection from certain difficulties. These include problems which require masculine fortitude, problems which otherwise would produce worry and strain beyond their capacity. They need to be protected from situations with troublesome people where they may be insulted, imposed upon, pressured, taken unfair advantage of or misused in any way. Women, especially, are inclined to be subjected to such misuse unless protected by a man.

For example, a relative or friend may impose on a woman. Perhaps special favors or considerations are expected, and she is overpowered by these requests. Accommodating by nature, she may not have the strength to refuse or know how to deal forcefully with the matter. She may be pressured to take on burdens she may not want to have. Rather than criticize her for taking on more than she can handle, help her reduce her commitments and become uninvolved.

She may be pressured to buy something she really does not want. She signs on the dotted line and finds herself committed before she realizes how unhappy she feels. Now she needs relief. You can be her hero by stepping in and getting her out of it. Whatever you do, do not complain about it. Tell her you are happy you can help.

If she has an accident with the car, or gets into financial entanglements with her checking account, she needs a sympathetic husband to pull her out of it. She has no one to turn to but you. Remember, no matter how angry you are, the fact is - it has happened. Nothing will change that. You have ✓ *everything to gain* by helping her with patience and love. She may remember it all her life. At a time when emotions are not high give her the counsel she needs.

Tender women are injured by harsh criticism. Any circumstance where she is brought into heavy negotiations because of business arrangements or misunderstandings about purchases or warranties should be handled by her husband.

In summary, remember that women and children need protection in three ways:

1) Protection from dangers.
2) Protection from strenuous or masculine work.
3) Protection from difficulties.

Rewards of Chivalry

In reviewing the role of the man as the protector, let me assure you this service is greatly appreciated. Your wife and children may take for granted your role as the guide and provider of life's necessities, but when a man steps out to defend and shield those who are less able to do so for themselves, he becomes a hero.

The story has been told for generations of how Sir Walter Raleigh placed his cloak over the mud for Queen Elizabeth. So great was her appreciation that she made him a knight. Did she do as much for the soldiers who fought valiantly for her? Women and children will not forget the acts of chivalry. Such protection is in reality a velvet trait, but because it requires a man's strength, ability, and courage, we have studied it as a steel trait. Chivalry is, in fact, both steel and velvet which is ✓ why it is so appealing to women.

What it does for a man has already been explained as an opportunity to develop courage and forcefulness. It solves problems and brings love, peace, and harmony into the home.

6

The Provider

In the sweat of thy face shalt thou eat bread,
until thou return unto the ground. (Gen. 3:19)

We have already learned of a man's sacred responsibility to rule the family and protect them from the hardness of life. His obligation to provide the living is just as sacred, for in the beginning God said, *In the sweat of thy face shalt thou eat bread, until thou return to the ground.* We need to remember this command was not given to the woman, but to the man. This he must do regardless of the struggle involved or the diversion of other interests that may be uppermost in his mind.

When God placed man in the world and gave him the divine command of earning his bread, he cursed the ground with noxious weeds, thorns and thistles. This action was not entirely punishment, however. It was a blessing, for He said, *I have cursed the ground for thy sake.* The thorns and thistles were given as opportunities for growth. All the struggles, burdens and difficulties men face in earning a living are for a divine purpose and should be regarded as opportunities for growth.

In present times there a disregard for this sacred and traditional role. Efforts to change the law would remove a man's obligation to pay alimony in the event of divorce. The proposed laws would place an equal burden on the woman for the support of the family. Many feel the man's role as sole provider is unfair, that it overtaxes him and may be injurious to his health. They advocate an equal sharing of this burden. In return he is expected to share equally in housework and child care. Some advocate the government also share the responsibility. When a man's load grows heavy, he is entitled to assistance. It has been suggested he draw *unearned income* should his regular income drop to a certain level. This is a far cry from God's command and has led to unexpected difficulties.

Trends and laws do not establish correct principles. There is a consequence for disobedience to eternal law. Man's responsibility to provide is a fact of life. A failure on his part creates serious problems. In the New Testament the Apostle Paul warned, *If any provide not for his own, he hath denied the faith and is worse than an infidel.* (I Tim. 5:8)

The responsibility to provide the living should be in top priority in a man's life - his first and foremost obligation. He may be consumed with personal ambition which, of itself may be worthy. He may want to *leave his footprints in the sands of time.* But noble as these goals are and important as they may be, they are secondary to his responsibility to provide the living.

Not only is his a sacred responsibility - it is a moral one. Each man has this obligation to care for himself, his wife and children. A man who does so is a gift to society. The man who does not is a burden. Because of his failure, others must sacrifice to carry a responsibility that belongs to him. In this failure he has failed as a man. He does not have strength but weakness. This is the most fundamental area in which he must function. *The man who does not provide for his own is not a man.*

What A Man Should Provide

Simply stated, he should provide the necessities. This means food, clothing, and shelter, plus a few comforts and conveniences. Through all generations of time it has been recognized that when a man marries, his wife and children are entitled to his financial support. Failure to meet this obligation has been just cause for divorce, and even after the marriage separation, a man is still under financial obligation. Financial support, and along with this, *fidelity*, have always been the two main entitlements for a woman in marriage. But whether these laws remain in force or not, the moral and sacred obligation is just as binding, the need just as great.

93

It is important that a man provide a shelter separate from anyone else. This is important for the sake of privacy and giving the wife the opportunity of making her house a home in her own way. Perhaps this is why a special instruction was given by God, in the very beginning: *Therefore shall a man leave his father and mother and cleave unto his wife.* (Gen. 2:24) Under stress of circumstances there may be occasions when a man must move his wife and children into another household. Although there may be justification for this temporarily, it is contrary to the divine plan and unfair to the wife if this situation extends for any time beyond a brief emergency.

Although a man has a sacred and binding obligation to provide the necessities, he is under no such obligation to provide the luxuries. His dependents are not entitled to ease and luxury, to style and elegance. His duty is not to provide a costly home, expensive furniture and decor. Concerning the education of his children, he has an obligation to provide a basic education, but such a binding obligation does not extend to a higher education, music lessons, the arts and cultures. He may wish to provide these, and it may bring him much pleasure to do so, but it is not mandatory.

In providing a high standard of living, some men make near economic slaves of themselves with great disadvantage to themselves and their families. Too often a man is so consumed with meeting increasing demands, not only by his family, but by himself, that he does not preserve himself for things of greater value. He has little of himself to give - time to teach the values of life, how to live, standards to follow, and time to build strong family ties.

A man is also entitled to time for himself for recreation, study and meditation. He has a further need to be of service outside his own circle, a commitment to society, as we shall see later in this writing. Church service is an important part of this as is civic responsibility. Men have talents which need to be shared, ability which could be developed to make the world a better place. *It is not right for him to spend his entire time and energy to provide luxuries for his own family circle.*

Let us examine how God has prepared man to meet his responsibility to provide. His preparation includes physical, emotional, and temperamental qualifications.

A man who has preserved the body God has given him is a perfect specimen for his work. He has a strong body which functions beautifully under normal strain. To see a man at his work, his muscles flexing in beautiful coordination, is to see the handiwork of God. He has physical endurance, taking day-in and day-out toil which extends for a lifetime. He enjoys the flexing of muscles and the habit of work.

He is blessed with the emotional make-up to endure the demands of his work - the stresses and strains of the marketplace, the roar of industry, the uncertainties of the crops in the field, and the financial challenges of the office. He can endure worry and has the capacity to overcome obstacles, solve problems, and succeed at his work.

He is competitive in temperament, a characteristic fitting him to gain his place in the world. He is aggressive, decisive, and possesses the qualities necessary to deal with perplexing problems in a challenging world.

There are, of course, many men who succumb to the pressures of the working world. Statistics point out that the competitive business world is killing our men, since his life expectancy is less than the female. His arduous life style is said to be destroying him.

Men do not die so much because of their work as because of other things. Faulty diet, little exercise, use of drugs, alcohol and tobacco all take a toll. Frustrations caused by emotional turmoil at home, misunderstandings and unreasonable family demands bring discord that cause strain. Bad habits and unrepented sins create serious debilitation. Further frustrations occur because he has not understood his rightful place as leader and the consequences of an off-balance leadership arrangement.

He may be working too hard and too long in providing luxuries for his family. This emphasis on superficial values does not bring the internal satisfaction expected. Hard work usually is an advantage, but misdirected hard work is destructive.

Any normal man who has properly cared for his body and is in good health has the capacity to provide the necessities of life with reasonable ease. In addition he will have a reserve capacity, allowing for responsibility beyond his home as well as time for personal pursuits. God has blessed him with greater capacity than most of us suppose.

Pride in his Responsibility

There is masculine pride in connection with providing his living which is inborn. He accepts this obligation with a willing spirit regardless of the difficulties encountered. He is not a leaner; he is not looking for someone to carry his burdens or do what he is charged with doing. This natural instinct is not a vain weakness, but is implanted in him by God for a divine purpose - to assure that families will be adequately cared for.

For him there is satisfaction in knowing he has a niche to fill which is vital. He realizes that within his family, no one is so well suited to meet this need as himself, and he sees the benefit to himself and his family as he functions in this important role. Security comes to all family members in seeing their leader struggle with difficulty, solve problems, and cope with the challenging circumstances that confront him. Confidence is focused on the individual rather than on the things that he provides. They see that he is adaptable to the many unexpected and unpredictable events he encounters.

A lady once told me that during the early years of her marriage her husband lost his job, as did many other men, when a financial recession struck their community. Many men were overcome with a defeated attitude. Her husband set out to find another job and would spend the entire day away, walking the streets, seeking interviews and doing everything conceivable to find a job.

Eventually he found work and during these years of recession made a living. Circumstances improved later on, but this woman recalled these difficult years as the time when her husband really proved his adequacy as a responsible provider.

So great is the feeling of masculine pride that some men suffer distress if they are unable to provide for their own. A man of my acquaintance had been a good provider until he had a serious illness which made him bedfast. His illness persisted for years with a gradual deterioration until it became apparent he would never work again.

During this time his wife provided the living. She took care of the needs of the family and had his care to shoulder as well. This man suffered tremendously because of this reversal of roles. No justification for his predicament could ease the pain in seeing his frail and feminine wife shoulder the burden he felt was his. Great sadness overcame him day by day and he slipped, not only in body but in spirit.

Although this man failed to adjust to unavoidable circumstances, he is to be admired for his keen sense of responsibility. He obviously had a case of unjustified pride. I am certain that when God placed pride in a man's heart, He did not intend that he never turn to others for assistance, or that there is disgrace in accepting the benevolent kindness of those who care and *should* assist. But it is clear God intends a man not lean unless absolutely necessary.

Failures to Provide

There is, unfortunately, a failure with some men to be responsible providers. This is illustrated in the pleading letter of a young woman who wrote:

I cannot seem to accept one thing in my husband. He does not seem to care whether or not he provides for us. He was in the insurance business where he did very well, but quit because he wasn't happy in it. He now sells brushes which he says he likes, but only spends four hours a day doing it. Consequently we are desperate for money. We have been living with his parents for the past seven months and it doesn't even look hopeful that we might possibly have our own place to live. I am losing all respect for my husband and without respect there is not real love.

97

My husband's parents tell me that he has never been a responsible person and that they were hopeful that our marriage would change this. They sympathize with me. What makes things worse is that I had to be very independent and responsible as a child and teenager; thus it is hard for me to unlearn these qualities. If my husband had these qualities, it would be easier for me to unlearn them.

This man has failed on several points. Not only does he not provide an adequate living with a home of his own, but he is not bothered or worried about it. There is no evidence of remorse or suffering for this situation. He offers no hope of a better future. Just because his former employment was not to his liking is not justification to leave it for a lesser job, no matter how much he enjoyed the new job. Whether a man likes his work is important, but it is secondary to its being adequate to provide a living.

Another situation concerns a young couple with three small children. They were a beautiful pair, both handsome and intelligent. The husband had the misfortune of losing his job. He made an effort to find work but jobs for which he was trained were very difficult to find. In the process of deciding how to best solve his problems, he approached his wife with the suggestion that she find a job. He offered to remain at home and care for the children as he felt she likely could find employment sooner than he could.

His wife was shocked and crushed at this suggestion. In pouring forth her heartfelt feelings and seeking advice as to how she should react, deep feelings were expressed:

1. She loved being with her children and cherished her time with them. She felt a duty to guide and train them and never dreamed of leaving this responsibility. To do so was a great personal sacrifice.

2. The husband's situation was not a desperate one. Several jobs were available, but he wanted to wait for something more in line with his training. She felt this demonstrated a poor sense of values.

3. She was suffering an emotional adjustment towards her husband, a disillusionment stemming from his failure to feel

responsibility, his lack of manly pride in his duty to provide.

Instead of lifting the burden, he was turning to her to do it. Her feeling of security in him was threatened. The romantic feeling was disappearing. Many men do not realize this strong emotional feeling in women wherein they yearn to be protected by the man they love.

In contrast we will consider another case. A man had also lost his job. He was a highly skilled technician and also could not find work in line with his training. His circumstances were just as desperate. But instead of turning to his wife for the solution, he took a lesser job. The only job he could find was working as a farm laborer in the fields. This meager work was tiring and poor pay, but it solved his problems.

Some would have said that this man lacked pride in accepting a job beneath his level of training. I say the opposite. He had genuine masculine pride in his responsibilities. He was willing to do whatever was necessary in order to fulfill an obligation that was his.

Many men lean on the state to provide when there is no justifiable reason. They may feign an illness or pretend to seek work, but deliberately fail to find it. This is a deliberate side-stepping of responsibility. In deceit and weakness they force others to carry the burdens God has given them. These men becomes leeches on society - lambs, doves, kittens, but not men of steel.

The Working Wife

Millions of working wives are in the marketplace. In reviewing the sacred principle of the man providing the living, it appears we have gone far afield from God's command. Certainly there are emergencies when a wife must work, but the majority of these cases are not justified. There are, however, individual circumstances where the earning of money to provide the basic living is not the motive. Consider the following reasons given for the working wife:

1. Easing financial burdens: Often a woman will offer to work to ease her husband's load. He may be under such financial difficulty that she fears for his health. She may prefer not to work, but is willing as a sacrifice to ease his burdens. This is very noble and unselfish, but unless it is absolutely necessary her husband should decline her offer by saying, *No, I will not allow you to work.* Women love such a firm refusal. There is nothing a domestic, feminine woman delights in more than not being allowed to work. It is something she will likely boast about to her friends. Together they can solve their problems by reducing their standard of living and employing principles of thrift and resourcefulness to preserve the husband's right to be the sole provider.

A contrasting situation occurs when it is the husband's idea for her to work. He may not only suggest she work, but urge her, literally shoving her into the working world against her will. I know a husband and wife, both school teachers, where the wife has been compelled to work over the years. Her husband allows her only three weeks for a baby. His justification is that they need the extra money. Her working clearly is his idea. Surely there must be an alternatives to such heavy dependence which deny her the right to serve in her feminine world.

The working wife may not actually earn as much as supposed when one considers the extra expense demanded by her working, such as extra clothing, transportation, baby care, etc. But this is a side issue and not pertinent to the principle.

2. *Working for luxuries*: In the majority of cases women work for additional luxuries or conveniences, whether they admit this truth or not. It may be that she has a drive to meet the standards of friends and is overly material-minded. If her husband tries to discourage her from working, she resists. In this case, as in any other where she is not justified, her husband should exercise his right to insist she not work. She will probably resent it temporarily, but will one day come to see that she has lived a better life than the woman who works for luxuries. This man has a difficult situation to cope with, for he must inspire her with a greater sense of values. She must realize the value of her presence in the home. She should further understand that in protecting his wife a man is

demonstrating his love. Some women have never understood these fundamental principles.

It may not be the woman, but the man who has the desire for luxuries and suggests his wife work. I know a man who sent his wife to work so he could have a cabin in the mountains. The next year he wanted a boat to go with it. Without her supplemental income these pleasures were impossible. She complied, and perhaps they did receive pleasure from these material things. But there is a price to pay for such a decision, as I will explain later.

3. *A broadening experience and greater fulfillment*: This rationale is frequently used as justification for a woman working, both by herself and her husband. They feel she will be a more interesting and happy person if she leaves the confines of home and finds an outside career. Some feel that tending children and the monotonous duties in the household limit a woman. She needs to get out where she can utilize her talents, intelligence, and gifts for not only the betterment of the world but of herself.

Although this sounds reasonable on the surface, some fundamental principles are being ignored which can not be disregarded without serious consequences.

Harm in Women Working

1. *Harm to the woman:* When a woman shares the burden of earning the living, she loses some of her femininity. Notice that the emphasis is not in her working, but in earning the living. In her home she has her best opportunity to acquire the charm of true womanliness. Here she develops love, patience, and the feminine arts and skills; she acquires a charm that makes her distinctly different from a man. When she rejects this role for that of the man's world, she loses some of the luster and charm which is her natural inheritance. She takes on masculine characteristics to succeed in his world.

Another harm is this: When a woman divides herself between two worlds, it is difficult to succeed in either. In her world alone she has challenge enough to achieve the domestic excellence she desires. Here she is the understanding wife, the devoted mother and homemaker and gains great satisfaction from a job well done. This takes great effort. To divide her time and interests between two worlds makes success in either difficult. It is terribly unfortunate that among many people there is a belief that a woman's duties at home require little skill or talent and can be done with a half-hearted effort.

Even if she rejects her home sphere and turns her heart and soul to the working world, she will have difficulty. In many jobs she will have a natural disadvantage. She will not meet man's excellence in his world, but will always be secondary to him. So she wanders between two worlds, having rejected her own where she could be superior and build a career with *guaranteed* lasting satisfaction and chosen another where she will never be anything but a second-rate man.

I know when I say this some people will think me chauvinistic and arrogant, cold and unsympathetic. But this point is so important that it needs emphasis.

When a woman works because it is her husband's idea, an even greater harm comes. His suggestion that she work casts doubts in her mind as to his adequacy as a man. If he must lean on her, she will question his ability to solve his problems and face responsibility that is his. This brings insecurity.

It is common among men anticipating marriage to suggest that his bride work. They often make their plans anticipating the incomes of both. If they accept as inevitable that each must work throughout their married lives, they acknowledge that their children, if they have any, will spend much of their infancy and youth in day care centers.

The advisability of this requires much thought. The long range effects upon children who spend so much time away from home are very suspect. Many adverse effects have been noted. In attempting to solve such problems many parents find themselves in a tangled web they would give anything to have avoided. At best, it is far from ideal and is an invitation to disappointment. Plan in the beginning to make the adjustments necessary to live on the husband's income. At some point the focus of the problems resulting from a wife having to work will rest on the man. After all, this is the area of his responsibility.

Still another harm to consider is the woman's relationship to her employer, especially if he is a man. She is accustomed to looking to her husband as the director of her activities. When she finds herself taking orders from another man, it is an unnatural situation. She owes him obedience as her employer, and in countless hours of close contact may find herself physically attracted to him. Seeing him at his best and perhaps as a more dynamic and effective leader than her husband, she makes comparisons unfavorable to her husband whose faults and failings she knows all too well.

If her employer is calloused and does not regard her with the measure of dignity she deserves, he may require of her work that is beyond her capacity or otherwise negative to her best interests. He may take unfair advantage of her, being aggressive or even demanding. He may be insulting or offensive.

So rampant is this problem that it has become a national issue. Harassment of women in the marketplace is commonplace in highest levels of government and industry. Regardless of her situation in the working world, a woman is out of her natural sphere when she is taking direction from anyone other than her husband. A man with a keen sense of responsibility and love for his wife finds such a situation abrasive and will avoid it if possible.

2. *Harm to the man*: When a man discovers his inadequacy to provide, he loses a measure of self-respect. He was born with masculine pride, and this is an affront to it. He begins to feel he is less of a man than he wants to be.

His feelings towards his wife may suffer. An important principle to recognize is that masculine men have a protective feeling towards women - an inborn desire to protect and shelter them. In fact a man's feeling of love and tenderness towards a woman is very closely tied to his desire to protect and shelter her. When she joins the working world, she proves she can get along without him. This is a very disturbing situation for both of them.

A man may not realize the pride and tender feelings he is robbed of when his wife works, especially if she has worked a long time. He becomes desensitized to the abnormality of his situation. So many others are involved in the same arrangement that it has probably never occurred to him that it is anything but normal or even ideal. He may be unaware of the marvelous feeling of well-being in knowing he has measured up in the most important role he has, or that tender feeling as he protects his family from hunger and want.

Having a wife in the work force adds another complication to the balance of family management. A man loses a measure of flexibility in his work, especially in making decisions which he feels is for the best interest of the family. The outside obligations of his wife's employment may be the one factor that upsets everything.

3. *Harm to the children*: When a mother works due to a compelling emergency, children adjust to this situation. They are able to understand when a genuine emergency exists. They may suffer neglect, but do not feel lack of love or concern.

When a mother works by choice, great harm can come to the child. When he realizes she prefers to work instead of taking care of him, that she places her interests, or luxuries ahead of his needs, this raises doubt about her love. He does not occupy the first priority place he is entitled to have in the home of his parents. The full force of this situation may not hit him until he is an adult. But it will certainly come at some time.

The children of working mothers usually suffer considerable neglect. Not in all cases, but in most. The woman who works must dedicate herself to her job in order to succeed and justify her pay. During the working hours her job is a priority. At times it will be demanding. Her children are less demanding. They are naturally the ones who suffer.

Suppose a woman with an outside job were to decide she wants another full time outside job as well. How do you suppose either employer would feel. Knowing what their expectations are for her time and commitment, it would be unlikely either would agree. But the fact is, she does have another full time job. By implication both the employer and working woman agree that her job is the priority rather than the family.

4. Harm to society: The trend for the mother to be out of the home is a pattern of living for many years in America, since the emergency of World War Two took millions of them into factories. It has been during this time that we have developed some of our most threatening social problems: marriage problems, divorce, violence in the streets, drug abuse, rebellion against social customs and moral standards. Many of these problems can be traced to homes of working mothers. Children are neglected and do not receive the attention and training from their parents they deserve. Some have reading disabilities and other learning problems. Some have mental maladjustments or develop into mental cases, or fail to find purpose and happiness in life. They turn from the standards of their parents and seek new ways.

Dr. David V. Haws, psychiatrist, has said, *Mother must be returned to the home. The standard of living is a fictitious thing. It's a woman's primordial function to stay home and raise children. She should not join the hunt with men. A man, too, feels less of a man when his wife works. If you don't leave a* √ *family of decent kids behind, you have left nothing. The footprints we leave on the sands of time are soon blown away. Basic to the solution of adolescent problems of any generation is an intact home.* The problem of the working wife cannot be ignored as a prime contributor to trouble in society.

Because we have not lived these concepts we are reaping the effects. Homes are mismanaged and neglected. Fathers do not lead, teach and inspire. Wives are away in the work place. Children are undisciplined, irreverent and rebellious - addicts to TV, fast foods, designer clothes and self-indulgence. Failure in the home is the cause of most of our national problems. *Massive grants for child care will not solve these problems.* Trying to relieve parental obligations for the upbringing of their children will only worsen the problem.

What is the solution? *Bring mothers home to do what they* √ *can do better than anyone else - what no one else can do.* Each father should make a solemn commitment to solve his part of this problem. This means, if your wife works out of the home, get her back as soon as possible. This is more important than saving the planet, important as that is. Desperate times require desperate solutions. Public sentiment rallies to fever pitch to save a child in a well. Millions of children need saving by their parents.

Preparation for Role as Provider

In planning his life's work, a young man should first try to get a wide scope of the possibilities. Too often he limits his consideration to work he is familiar with: the professions, school training, or work his father or relatives engage in. Such a limited choice may exclude talents and interests for which the young man has talent and adaptation.

One good resource for information on job opportunities is a book published by the Department of Labor called *Educational Outlook*. This is an annual publication and can be obtained at the library. This book lists every conceivable occupation a young man would be interested in. After you have researched the possibilities, consider the following priorities:

1. Providing an adequate living: First consideration is that the work provide an adequate living. Any job that fails on this point should not be considered. It will be necessary to consider the future and the number of children you hope to have. You will have an obligation to provide them with the necessities, some comforts and conveniences, and keep them from financial worry and distress. You alone will be responsible to meet these needs. You cannot trust to luck or circumstances to see you through. Consider the needs of your wife and the standard of living she expects. What are your aspirations for the future?

There will be a temptation to place other things ahead of this priority. A man may want to develop a talent or seek a job that is exciting or will bring notoriety. Maybe he envisions himself as a benefactor to mankind. Important as these altruistic aims are, if their pursuit jeopardizes his ability to provide an adequate living, they are not good goals to consider. Reformers have been known to allow their families to suffer hunger and privation while trying to cure social ills. Artists have justified their efforts as a noble work while their families were neglected. The man who is a man assumes his God-given ✓ role as a provider and places this as his first and foremost obligation in life.

In addition to the necessities and comforts, he will want to provide more. It is good to attain a standard of living beyond the necessities when this is done in balance with other requirements. There is nothing wrong in desiring a large income if one has legitimate objectives.

2. Ability to succeed: Next, a man will need to consider his ability to succeed in his chosen field. Do you have the talent, adaptability and capacity for the job? Counseling is sometimes helpful in making this determination. There are departments in both high schools and universities that have this service.

It is very disturbing to be tied to a job where one has difficulty performing well. Better to direct yourself into a job where you can give an adequate service competently. You must, of course, consider your personality. Are you satisfied with mediocrity or will you never be satisfied unless you reach the top of your field? If not, then do you have the capacity to reach the top?

3. Work you enjoy: Of important consideration is that you enjoy the work you have chosen. The entire family is benefitted when the father is happy in his work. A man who looks forward to his daily work functions better and accomplishes more in every aspect of his life. Men are created with different interests and capabilities. For a man to find himself in work that he does not like can make him miserable. Sometimes a man in the midstream of life learns he is in the *wrong field*. Making a change at this time usually results in severe adjustments.

4. Is the work a challenge to your ability or capacity: A serious mistake is to choose a field that is too easy. It is a temptation because preparation will take less time, energy and perhaps money. A person needs a goal that will challenge the best that is in him. There is satisfaction in reaching upward.

5. *Is the work conducive to good family life?* Questions to ask yourself are: Will the hours be conducive to good family living? Will I have to be out of town frequently? Will my work require Sundays, the day I should devote to the spiritual welfare of my family? Will the work be demanding in such a way that it will interfere with my family life?

Another point is the location of your job. Will it be in the city or the country, a metropolitan area or a suburb? Although this need not be a determining factor necessarily, it is well to consider that children are helped by being next to the beauties of nature. It helps develop a faith in God and will assist in character development, especially if they have the opportunity to work in the soil.

6. *Financial means for preparation:* Next to consider is your financial situation. Do you have the means for the education required? Some of the professions are very costly and beyond possibility for many young men without outside assistance. This will have to be considered along with your desire and adaptability.

7. *Service to humanity:* Consider the worth of the job itself and its usefulness to the world. It can be disheartening to spend years of time and toil in a work that is of no real consequence or, worse still, is injurious. The manufacture of products which are harmful and the encouragement of activities which are destructive can plague a man's conscience. He may be so depressed as to search for a way to redeem himself. This may mean a change of jobs at a sacrifice of considerable money.

A man's job should be important work, work upon which the success of the world depends. It need not be spectacular or revolutionary, but it needs to be essential. Participating in work that helps make the world better will bring a man a feeling of well-being, a feeling of contributing something in addition to supporting his family.

7

Family Finances

Few families are free of anxieties and contentions in the matter of family finances. To some it is a matter of such major importance as to be an ever-festering sore, never healing and continually thwarting the happiness of the home. As a factor in marital breakup, it is a major cause. Problems arising from debt, selfishness, unwise use of money, and conflict in values are sources of contention. Here are a few facts which, if recognized, will aid in the solution to these problems:

The Man's Responsibilities

There are three major areas of responsibility that fall to the man in money matters:

To provide the money
To manage the money
To do the necessary worrying about the money.

We emphasize continually that it is the man who should provide the income. Unfortunately many men think this is the full scope of their obligation. It is certainly a most important part, but by no means the total. What about the management of the money? Without wise direction, the money earned may not meet family needs.

As *the manager of finances,* the man will manage the entire pay check. He is responsible for house payments, car expense, insurance, taxes, medical bills, yard and house maintenance, and an allotment to his wife for household and personal use. He will pay the bills, and if there is not enough to cover expenses, he will face and solve this problem. He will not expect his wife to take over. He will, of course, expect her to cooperate and cut expenses when possible, but the overall role in money management belongs to him.

In the ideal home the man will also do the necessary worrying about money. He will face the unpaid bills, insufficient funds, and creditors. If there is not enough money to cover expenses, this is his concern. He will ponder the problem, struggle with the difficulty, and seek solutions. If additional income must be secured, he will consider a second job. He will not allow his wife to worry, but will protect her from it by his concern and action. He will explain that he is giving careful thought to their problems and she has no need to worry.

As the money manager, a man must maintain his position as leader with the power of decision. Let me explain why this is so important:

In solving financial problems, a man may have to make major changes - a change of jobs, move to another community, change to a less expensive residence, sell one car, or in other ways reduce costs. To make these changes it is essential that he have power of decision without resistance. If he is to make the living and manage the money, he must have the power to solve his problems.

This makes it clear why it is such a mistake for the wife to manage the money. She does not have the power of decision. She cannot make major changes to solve financial problems. It would be grossly unfair to expect a woman to manage the money unless she also has the power of decision. The role of the leader and money manager are inseparable.

The Wife's Responsibilities

These responsibilities are clearly defined and just as essential as a man's. These are feminine duties and often make the difference between success and failure. Both wife and husband must clearly understand this interdependence which exists between them:

110

To *cooperate* with her husband's plans and decisions in solving money problems or reaching financial goals.

To provide a peaceful home atmosphere.

To make a dollar stretch in the money allotted her.

1. Cooperate with husband's plans: The wife will be expected to cooperate in any changes he must make in solving financial problems. If she will accept a reduction in the standard of living and adjust to changes which require sacrifice, without complaint, she can make *all the difference* in his efforts to manage their finances effectively.

She is also expected to cooperate in her husband's goals to get ahead. The entire family may be required to sacrifice things they need or want. The wife is the key in setting the proper attitude of complete cooperation. If she will not cooperate and willingly go without when necessary, she may derail the plans. Her support is indispensable.

2. Provide a peaceful home atmosphere: This can not be over emphasized. A wife sets the tone in the home. When there is peace there, a man will be more successful. If he has financial problems, they will not be compounded by the pressures of home life. He will be able to think through his problems and reach solutions. Otherwise, under continuing stress at home, he may wonder if the price he is paying is worth it.

3. Make a dollar stretch: The wife plays a major role in her husband's financial success or failure. Her prudent use of the funds for which she is responsible, is an example to the children and shows respect for her husband's efforts in providing them.

Two families with identical incomes and similar needs may show one living in comfort and the other in poverty due to the wife's ability or inability to manage money. She is expected to be economical, resourceful and discriminating. A woman able to handle money wisely is a prize indeed.

111

A prerequisite to an understandable and workable relationship between husband and wife in handling money matters is the wife's budget, which should cover the following:

1. Food
2. Clothing for the family
3. Household expense
4. Her personal expense (clothing, cosmetics, etc.)
5. Miscellaneous family expense (music lessons, school supplies, etc.)

The budget should be based on needs and how much the husband can afford. It should be sufficient to provide an excess if the wife is careful. This excess she should be allowed to keep as a reward for thrift. This is money she is not accountable to you for. It is money with *no strings attached.* Her budget should be a definite amount to be paid on a specific day of each month or week without any need on her part to ask. She is not receiving a gratuity. This is not an amount which must be justified each week or month or brought up for negotiation. As her husband you are expected to respect the priority her position deserves. Her needs should be your first consideration.

The dignity of women is often offended by selfish or thoughtless husbands who do not realize that their wives are entitled to a portion of the family income for their own use. This is money in excess of what is needed to operate her part of the family budget. It is no wonder that eventually many of them are forced into the working world to preserve their self-respect.

In realizing the value of a budget, remember that the only money she has comes from you. She is dependent. She must ask or go without. Many women would rather go without than ask too often. Despite the fact that many states have community property laws based on the premise that half the husband's earnings belong to his wife, many wives feel reluctant to ask for their allotment and feel the husband has full claim on the income he earns. It may be up to you to assure her that she is entitled to a fair portion of the family income. Be happy to share it with her. Make her feel comfortable about the situation, and remind her frequently that her part is as important as yours is.

Problems in Family Finances

There is a great deviation from the ideal I have just described which works to the detriment of many families. Let me name some of these mistakes.

1. The working wife: The wife who must share the burden of earning the living is leading a double life. She is not free to meet her part in the arrangement just described. After a day away from home, she may find it difficult to provide a peaceful home atmosphere and make a dollar stretch. She will, in fact, find that *she must be more extravagant with money as she is more conservative with time.* She will not have time to shop for bargains, sew, re-cover the sofa or cook economy meals. She will be denied the satisfaction of being thrifty by making something useful from very little. Instead of a contribution in making the dollar stretch, she shares in her husband's masculine duty of earning the living.

2. Wife manages the money: In millions of cases men come home at the end of the work week with a check which they hand over to their wives. They may ask for the return of a small amount for pocket money, but she is expected to manage the rest. Now she steps into the masculine role. She will pay the bills and meet all expenses. Being so involved, she will consequently worry. If the money does not cover expenses, she will struggle with it, weighing one value against another. If she finds solutions, she may come to her husband for approval. He may not be that concerned. How can he be? He is too far removed from the problem. An actual case will illustrate.

The husband gave full responsibility to his wife for the management of their money. As their family increased, she

113

became more concerned as she had difficulty in covering all the expenses. While searching for a solution, her husband was offered a transfer to another city where his salary would be increased substantially. The job was tempting but the city was not. They were residing in a peaceful community where he was completely satisfied. Fishing in mountain streams was available nearby. The city to which he would be transferred was crowded and far removed from the streams and lakes he enjoyed so much. He rejected the job offer, much to the distress of his wife.

The problem in this case was that he was so removed from their financial difficulties as to feel no urgency. Yet he held the power to decide. His wife shouldered the burden of money management but was denied the power of decision. This unfair arrangement naturally leads to misunderstanding and recriminations.

Much harm results when a wife is placed in this unfair position. The results are not dissimilar to those occurring when she moves into other areas of a man's responsibility. She loses part of her glow, her distinctive feminine nature, and is usually not as successful as he would be in the same capacity.

This is logical, for she is functioning in a man's job for which she will likely not have an adaptation. If she is required to handle money matters that belong to her husband, she will find herself *wearing the pants*. This is a frustrating position, particularly if her nature is to want to be feminine.

We continually hear the argument that many women are better equipped to handle money than are some men. This is obviously true. But her talent will not be lost if she is second in command with the responsibility for the household budget. I have seen many women who handle all family finances, and the results are never ideal. They may do a remarkable job so far as the money goes. But there are other issues at stake. Problems centering around money management are common in the husband-wife relationship. She rightfully feels that he is not fulfilling his responsibility, or perhaps she feels he is incompetent. In either case it introduces feelings which should not exist between them.

Many women suffer severe strain when given such responsibility. They experience nervousness, hypertension, and even sexual frigidity. Being more delicate than men, they find themselves the victims of these negative reactions without understanding the cause. The strains of money management interfere with a woman's duties in the home and may result in complete demoralization.

I saw this happen to a family I knew well. The wife was managing the finances when the husband began to have serious difficulties in his business. The family was plagued with debts and heavy obligations which they could not meet. Knowing of these problems was bad enough for the wife, but she had to face irate creditors and attempt to explain the difficulties in which her husband was embroiled. As this went on, her worries became so severe and all-encompassing that her children were neglected and her house was in disorder. She lost all interest in her home life. She had no spirit to give beyond the trying hours she spent in a hopeless situation that finally resulted in bankruptcy. This dire neglect at home was foreign to her nature, for she had formerly been a neat and organized housewife and dedicated mother.

3. *Husband fails to do the worrying:* Sometimes a man fails to worry about financial problems, or at least appears not to be concerned. He may disregard the house payment or let bills accumulate. Despite these debts, he may not be making plans to pay them. His wife sees that he is not concerned. This brings her into a distressing situation causing anxiety. If he does not worry about the debt, she wonders how it will be paid. She will regard him as irresponsible and worry more over the man than the obligation. Her feeling of security is threatened not so much by the debt as by his lack of concern.

In reality he may be greatly concerned and is only trying to shield her from worry. But he must realize that as long as she is aware of their difficulties, his silence may be misinterpreted as lack of concern. Her mind is put at rest only when she realizes her husband is concerned and is making plans to solve the problem.

The only way a woman can be completely protected from

worry is to know nothing about the problem. This is seldom if ever advisable. She is certain to detect, either through circumstances or through his attitude. There is a further threat. Through her husband's death or incapacity the entire burden would suddenly fall to her and she would be completely unprepared to cope with it. The safest rule is that she knows the truth and realizes her husband's feeling of responsibility for its solution.

4. Wife's opposition to financial plans: Great difficulty occurs when a wife will not go along with a man's effort to solve his financial problems. If he is cutting expenses or making major changes, she may resist. While this is extremely frustrating to him, it is well to recognize her situation. Unless she is fully aware of the entire situation, she may find it hard to understand why drastic reductions are necessary. She is expected to trust his judgment in plans which may not seem justifiable.

If you are in such a situation as this, employ the principles of good leadership explained in a previous chapter:

a) Seek her viewpoint before plans are definite.
b) Consider her feelings and express a sympathy for them.
c) Try to win her support. Explain to her that you need her support.
d) Make certain that you are sufficiently convinced of the step you are recommending and that you will have the courage to follow through firmly.

If this action is taken, women will usually make the adjustment. When they fully understand, they may be quite willing to make sacrifices beyond what you would expect.

5. Extravagance and living beyond one's means: Husband or wife or both may be guilty of this grievous fault. If both are guilty there is no hope until a remedy is found. It is the cause of most financial troubles. Financial difficulties would be minimal if families purchased only those things they could comfortably afford.

To solve this problem, a sound philosophy must be

developed in which there is the definition and establishment of proper values. Material possessions, luxuries, comforts, and pleasures mean very little when weighed against the peace of mind one can know when he is living comfortably within his means. Great as may be the pleasure and joy of elegant furnishings, expensive art objects and fine clothing, these should not be valued more highly than the health or mental peace of the father who must provide these luxuries. There is no way to measure the happiness that is lost through financial bondage when people succumb to the allurement of extravagance. To follow a plan which frees one of this bondage is worth more than gold.

A major cause of extravagance is the desire to impress others. This is a useless effort. True friends are not dependent upon what we own as a measure of the value they place on us. They are impressed by our kindness, character, and the worthiness of our lives. We may be trying to impress ourselves by thinking our possessions are a measure of our worth. This self-deception is dispelled in a moment of serious thinking when we realize we can comfortably live with ourselves only as we contribute something of value to others.

Self-control is the answer to overcoming extravagance. This means a strict rule to avoid buying that which one can not afford. Years ago I learned an excellent guide in wise buying: When considering a purchase, ask yourself these questions:

   a) Do I need it?
   b) Can I afford it?
   c) Do I need something else more?
   d) Can I get by without it?

This latter question is the supreme test, for if one thinks he needs it and can afford it but is willing to get by without it, he is developing a spirit of thrift which will overcome extravagance.

6. *The husband who is tight with money:* Many wives complain that they are living with a miser who will not allow sufficient money to even purchase adequate and wholesome food. The children are never allowed to go to the circus or for a pony ride. The little girls are denied hair ribbons and other

things he could well afford but thinks are senseless expenditures. At the same time he may be buying expensive cars and sports equipment. One man I know purchased an airplane for his private use while his wife was on a household budget so strict she could hardly get by.

One would suppose that such a man feels his income is his own and that the services of his wife count for nothing and that his children have no claim on him. Such selfishness usually brings on serious consequences, for no one can live under such despotic treatment.

We have reviewed many of the problems involved in family finances and pointed out solutions to help. The following suggestions are given to assist in money management.

Success in Money Management

To be wise in the use of money is of greater consequence than the ability to earn a larger income. Too frequently there is no correlation between the amount of money earned to one's competence as a provider. A national magazine carried some case histories of various families in certain economic levels showing their incomes, budgets, and debts or savings. It was interesting and startling to note that some families with an income of one hundred thousand dollars per year or more were on the brink of financial ruin. In one case professional counselors were called in to take over the income completely, allowing a limited amount to the earner for pocket money.

A medical doctor of my acquaintance with an income of one hundred and fifty thousand dollars per year (he had earned this amount for several years) decided to return to a university some distance from his home for further training. He had to borrow money to make the trip and get settled.

Developing the wisdom to manage money wisely is an ability which can be learned. One has but to follow certain guidelines and rules. The following ideas are given as suggestions:

1. Save money: A penny saved is a penny earned is an old adage. From this, one might reason that $100 saved is $100 earned. If one needs $100, there are two ways to get it: *Earn it or save it.*

To have an additional $100 from earnings, a man will likely have to earn $130 or more, depending upon the amount he pays in taxes after deductions. If you save the $100, you will need to save only $100.

Considering this, each dollar saved would be equivalent to $1.30 or more earned. It is as though you were earning interest by saving the money rather than working for it. Any investment that would pay such a high return would be considered phenomenal indeed. The old saying is not so true, for a penny saved might very well be as much as two pennies earned.

2. Avoid a second car: One of the heaviest drains on a budget is an automobile. Granted that in most cases one is a basic necessity, most families now have two or more. An automobile frequently results in a greater dollar drain than housing, a college education, or food requirements for a small family. Nothing depreciates quite so rapidly with such constant demands for operation and maintenance. Families have been known to solve critical financial problems by selling one car.

You may feel it impossible to get by with one car. Financial advisors point out that in most cases it is easily possible. The second car is purchased mostly for occasional use - usually not for more than once or twice a week. The use of municipal busses, even a taxi, is less expensive than owning a second car. Second cars also encourage other expenditures since they make a family more mobile.

3. Preserve health: This is probably the single most important means of preserving wealth. Many years ago the highly respected financial advisor Roger Babson was asked, *"What is the safest financial investment a man can make?* Mr. Babson, accustomed to offering advice about the stock market and other business investments, offered this surprising but valuable advice. *The safest financial investment a man can make is in his health.*

When health is disregarded, and one's body is neglected or abused with tobacco, alcohol, or other stimulants, not only will money be wasted on their purchases but on the breakdown of the body and disability which follows. When Mr. Babson gave this excellent advice, he recognized that the body is the machine whereby a man makes his living. To preserve this ability to provide, one must also preserve the machine which makes this possible.

4. Avoid time payments: Almost anything now can be bought on time payments - furniture, automobiles, clothing, appliances, jewelry, and even vacations. One of the great shocks of my life was an occasion when I took my wife out for an ice cream cone and was asked if I wished to put it on my credit card. With the exception of buying a home, time payments are almost always foolish, for two sound reasons:

a) If you cannot afford to pay the cash, you should not afford the item.

b) High interest rates greatly increase the cost.

The high interest rates used to be somewhat obscured from the customer and thus many people were innocently led into unwise financial obligations. But now, strict regulations inform the borrower of the actual rate of interest. We can see clearly the additional costs we are getting into. Avoiding this costly expense is one of the keys to sound money management. One financial counselor summed up rather succinctly his thoughts on time payments: *There are two kinds of people - those who don't understand interest and pay it, and those who do and collect it.* This is often the difference in principle that makes one man poor and another rich.

5. Avoid borrowing money: In addition to time payments, men sometimes borrow from loan companies or individuals for unsound reasons. Although it may be sound to borrow money for an education, or to increase one's business opportunities, most loans are painful mistakes. Those to avoid are - burrowing money to live on a higher plane, to go on a vacation, or to have conveniences, comforts or luxuries.

It is impossible to measure the anxiety, sleepless nights and heartache caused by debt. Money is so easy to spend and so difficult to save, especially for paying off debts. Ordinarily men do not worry so much about debt as women. The natures of men and women are so different. The nature of man is to struggle for his place in the world. He may even consider debt as a challenge, or a part of this struggle. He is not so security minded as to let a good opportunity pass him by just because it involves borrowing money. But the woman is different. She looks to the man for security and protection - to provide a safe place for her and her children. Debts stand as a barrier to this feeling of security. Facing this fact, a man should consider feelings and avoid debt for her sake, if not his own.

One of the greatest disservices of our day is the bombardment of enticing advertising urging people to spend now and pay later. A vehicle for this may be to further mortgage a home which has appreciated in value to buy products which are pure luxury. This concept is morally wrong and engenders habits which are destructive to sound and happy living. Carelessness with money becomes an addiction wherein people have no will. My personal opinion is that persons and financial institutions which encourage this practice are getting close to those who traffic in drugs. Nothing good is ever gained in developing an addiction. Easing the burden now cannot possibly make it easier later when you have to not only pay the debt but also the interest. I have known men to make an iron-clad rule to *never borrow money unless in urgent emergency*. This is a sound rule for a wise money manager.

These are only a few of the most fundamental rules in managing money wisely. Other things might include a policy of canceling all charge accounts, use credit cards for credit reference only, and go on a cash basis. It is not so difficult to earn an income sufficient to meet family needs if we know how to spend it to greatest advantage.

Of the utmost importance in money management is an abiding feeling of responsibility to pay one's bills on time and meet every financial obligation. If circumstances require an extension of time, one should face the problem immediately with the creditor and work out arrangements. It is easier to face an embarrassing situation such as this in the beginning.

I have discovered also that an excellent way to be successful financially is to be honest with the Lord by paying a tithing, which by definition is ten percent of one's income. Read Malachi 3:8-10 and note the generous promise for obedience. I have never seen another promise more explicit, nor made by One so capable of paying.

Investments

The purpose of this study is not to attempt a comprehensive analysis of such a complex subject but merely to point out a few helpful guidelines to assist in averting some common problems.

A sound investment can ease the burden of making the living by providing a supplementary income. If a man works reasonably hard, is careful and saving with his money, he should be able to set aside money each year for this purpose.

Some investments are very safe. Savings accounts are of this type and offer liquidity and provide an immediate return on your money. The interest rates are low, but if money is deposited regularly, it can prove to be an investment free of worry, bringing security and satisfaction to you and your family. Thrift is a virtue which produces rewards other than financial. As a guiding principle to live by, it is an aid to character growth and an enhancement to self-esteem.

Among the varying types of investments, there are those which are moderately safe but not liquid; others are very safe but tie one's money up for an extended period. It would take a special study to review the many types of investments available and the merits and demerits of each. I would like only to issue some special warnings.

Investments which show promise of high returns are invariably filled with risk. Sometimes they turn out well; other times they are sad and shocking mistakes. There is an element of chance in investments which even the more knowledgeable men may not be able to accurately assess. With all the facts at their disposal, most investors discover that there are too many undetermined factors to make a clear, safe judgment. Therefore, the most shrewd businessmen acknowledge the risk attached to investments promising high return.

Unwise investments have caused bitter disappointment, a spirit of defeat and even suicide. Although some of the brave ones come out of the fray better men and gain a certain amount of valor in the financial battle, it is not a road which is desirable or recommended as the good life.

No one can provide absolute rules to follow in making wise investments, but we can rely upon some definite guidelines which will free you of painful and distressing experiences:

1. Never borrow money for investments: It is not wise nor morally right to risk money that does not belong to you for use in speculation. Invest only money you already have or is surely committed to you.

2. Never mortgage your home to secure money for investments: Every family would be greatly benefitted if they had a home free of mortgage. Although you may be forced to buy a home on the time payment plan, which is what virtually all families do, yet it would be prudent to pay off the obligation as quickly as possible. Money for investment is not justification for mortgaging the family home - the return seldom justifies the risk.

But when you make payments on the outstanding obligation, you are earning for yourself the rate of interest you are being charged. This is a better return than you would ordinarily find. When obligating yourself to a mortgage, be sure you are able to prepay without penalty.

3. Never invest more than half your savings in a risk venture: This rule diminishes the risk and disappointment should the investment fail to meet expectations. One must believe in any venture if he is persuaded to risk any amount at all. So the temptation may be overwhelming to invest all funds available in something one has confidence in.

4. Risk only those funds which, if lost, would not disturb the normal routine of family life: If you follow the above rules you will more easily gain the support of your wife. Women are usually very much afraid of investments and will tend to oppose anything which contains an element of risk. If you can assure her that the investment will not endanger her security, that funds are available to meet current obligations, she will likely have an open mind. Also, if you are a man who has proved his financial reliability by keeping bills paid and all obligations under strict control, her confidence will be much stronger. Beyond that, she must realize that it is your prerogative to make investments which you think will assist you in meeting your obligation as the provider.

Before committing himself to any investment, a wise man will again employ the principles of good leadership in first, consulting his wife; second, considering her viewpoint; and third, trying to win her support. She is not so likely to condemn an investment if she has been permitted to express her feelings beforehand. She bears a responsibility along with you, and should she be left a widow, would have to live with it.

It is surprising how many investments are made on hunches or questionable recommendations in a spirit of gambling. The least that can be said is to learn as much as possible before making the decision. Classes are available and good books as well as qualified men who have no selfish interest in your investments.

Summary

We have talked at length of the man as the leader, protector, and provider. While much can be said in each of these categories, there is a strong correlation which tends to fuse them into a single function and responsibility. A man cannot measure up to his full stature as a provider and ignore his duties as a leader and protector. Some men assume that if they provide adequately the physical needs of their dependents, they are accountable for no more. The folly of this assumption is revealed on all sides and particularly in the youth rebellion which is an outgrowth of the need for leadership and example.

Happiness is not to be found outside the acceptance and performance of one's duty. Certainly man's chief duty to himself and others is to learn to understand the nature of his responsibilities and become as effective as possible in their performance. The rewards far exceed the sacrifices required.

8

The Builder of Society

Beyond his role in the family, a man has an additional role as a builder of society, to correct social ills, solve problems, and make improvements which will make the world a better place for all. We enter this world as beneficiaries of countless benefits wrought by the labors of others. We do not start at ground zero. Each of us has an obligation to give of himself to create a better world than has been before, to add something to the accumulated inheritance of mankind.

Man's most important contribution is achieved in building a happy home which is free of problems. If his marriage is intact, his children well-adjusted, if family members are lifters rather than leaners, he has not created problems for others to worry about. Over-burdened public agencies will be spared an additional hardship. His success gives him additional incentive to help others. One who is burdened with difficult personal problems will be stifled mustering the spirit to enthusiastically extend himself to others.

Problems of Society

We have inherited a society which is a combination of marvelous advancements but gross weaknesses. People of great wealth a generation past would have had no way to obtain the conveniences now available to average people. Persons classified as below the poverty level usually have a TV, reasonable home and furnishings and an automobile. Our technology spreads benefits to everyone. No one is excluded from public parks, libraries, roads and service agencies which provide invaluable service to all. But with all we have, we are in serious trouble.

Mental illness is more prevalent than at any time in history, as is domestic violence, troubled homes and youth problems. Crime on the streets is endemic. Most people will say they are not happy, but are plagued by anxiety. How to find happiness is uncertain. What reliable guides are there to teach one how to live?

The emphasis is on materialism and pleasure. How can we have more fun and how can we avoid work and pain? And how can we get more of the good things, i.e. possessions? The drive for luxuries is causing many women to leave their households in search of something of lesser value.

Alcohol is numbing the minds of our nation's population so that it is impossible for them to be directed by conscience, or to think clearly through problems or discern correct principles. This has led to a weakening of standards, the most serious being sexual immorality and various types of perversion. This is our number one threat.

The greatest problem in our country is not poverty, disease nor international strife, but immorality. The most alarming part of this is that it is not looked upon as a problem. The consequences of immorality bring problems, such as unwanted pregnancies, venereal disease and disillusionment as confidences are shattered. But the fact that immoral behavior is destructive to the integrity of the individual bearing an accountability to God is not usually viewed as a problem. We have only to look at the downfall of great nations to see the spiral downward when immorality becomes a way of life.

Perhaps the most frightening problem is the loss of faith in people generally and in the government specifically. Our country is not as it was when founded by brave and valiant men. The expectation is that anyone with an opportunity to dip in the public treasury will. People are being brought into bondage through oppressive taxation and dependence on government.

We are becoming a *godless* society with religious principles questioned and reverence for God removed from our public schools and universities. Whereas our country was formerly a

126

God-fearing nation, based on the statement *In God We Trust* it is fast rejecting religion as a vital part of both government and country.

Besides these spiritual and moral issues, our physical environment is deteriorating. Although we have an abundant food supply at present, it is grown on deficient soil, robbed of vital elements and contaminated by pesticides and chemical fertilizers. Our food is not of the nutritious quality it was a few years ago. The air we breath and our water systems are polluted. All of these things threaten our existence and survival as a nation.

How great it would be if these problems did not exist. We could then build society in a positive way by the creation of fine literature, art and music, could build beautiful cities and parks. But these high goals may have to wait until we have rescued our dwindling society from disaster.

We need not lose hope because of these problems. Faith must be implanted in the hearts and minds of our people that with God's help there are solutions. The key is *with God's help*. Otherwise there is no solution based solely upon the strength we cumulatively possess as individuals. Valiant men with high purpose and the strength and support of God, will be the instruments through which the needed corrections will be achieved.

Each man, for his own peace of mind, must come to realize that he has a personal responsibility to help solve the world's problems. This is not a presumptuous idea. God will not miraculously lift us out of our troubles without our effort to assist. These problems are solved through people. We must develop a feeling of obligation to society, a consciousness of a debt we owe for the precious gift of life and for the inheritances we have received from the past. When we do not have this feeling, but focus all our energies on ourselves, we create an imbalance in the spirit that will invariably lead to emotional distress. This fact is recognized by Dr. Max Levine, M.D., a psychiatrist associated with the New York College, in the following statement:

I speak not as a clergyman, but as a psychiatrist. There

127

cannot be emotional health in the absence of high moral standards and a sense of social responsibility.

This may explain in part the severe and widespread incidence of mental disorders. People who do not give of themselves to society or think of the needs of others are often consumed in their own concerns. They suffer inwardly the turmoil which stems from neglect of duty.

Self-Centeredness of Men

Men are too consumed with their own problems, pleasures and desires to be concerned about others. Self-centeredness is the underlying fault in his neglect of duty to others. We shall consider examples of this widespread practice.

1. Many men spend their spare time in pleasure and amusement such as following sports events, hunting, fishing, camping, boating, riding motorcycles and visiting friends. They may spend additional time polishing their guns or keeping their sporting gear in order. And we must consider the many hours worked to pay for their boats, trailers, camping equipment and motorcycles. Wholesome as these pleasures are and entitled to them as we may be, they consume a tremendous amount of time. If men are to assist in solving the world's problems, there must be some fair sharing of time with society.

2. Most men waste time in which no one is benefitted - time spent loafing, in idle talk on trivial matters, or attending movies of questionable worth, playing cards, and other useless pursuits. Many persons return from work and flop into a chair to be passively amused by whatever happens to be on T.V. Although we recognize a man's need for diversion, he should divide his time between activities which are a wholesome benefit to himself and to others as well.

3. The disposition of many men is to live entirely for their own family and friends in their own little sphere: A man of this disposition appears to be an ideal citizen. His home is in good repair and his yard neat and clean. He probably spends his weekends in gardening, lawn care, and keeping his cars

polished. He provides his family with the material things they need and, aside from an occasional parking ticket, is never at odds with the law. He is not a burden to society, but neither is he building it. He is living for himself. His concern is for *his* home and *his* family. *I'm doing my share; let others do theirs* is his motto. His children may not have problems, but what about other children? Does he ever think of them? His is pretty much a sterile concern for anyone other than his own.

4. Many men make a small contribution and feel they have done their part: A man will occasionally make a donation of fifty dollars or so to a charity. This is a good step, but is a small part of what needs to be done. He may help a neighbor in difficulty or assist in a community project. These acts have merit, but much more than this is needed to make a dent in the world's problems. These small acts can hardly discharge a man's duty to his fellow men. Acts such as these do not require *sacrifice.* One can be sure that if he is doing something of real merit *there will be sacrifice.*

Type of Men Needed to Build Society

The qualities of true greatness are required of men to build society in the most beneficial way and include these listed below:

1. Men who can recognize needs: First, we need men of vision, men who have a broad view of the world's problems, who can see the crying needs of the multitudes. They are capable of evaluating present conditions against an idealistic picture of what the world should be. And yet they have an intimate perception, can recognize the needs of a small child nearby, notice the downcast eyes of a teenager in trouble, and are sensitive to the needs of those who so closely surround them. They do not have to be told in which ways the world needs to be built - they are aware of the needs.

2. Men of compassion: These men are moved with deep emotion when viewing the aspirations and struggles of their fellowmen. They value life, single or in the thousands. They are moved to action when they see people who are oppressed or discouraged. This was the quality of the Good Samaritan who, seeing a stranger in trouble, came to his aid, a compassion sadly lacking in the priest and Levite who passed by on the other side. Compassion is the quality of velvet necessary in man to build society.

3. *Men of responsibility:* We need men who view themselves as a solution to a need. They don't turn away, imagining someone else will do it. When the church calls for help, or the community, or when an important petition must be circulated, they respond to the call and feel an obligation to help. They don't ask *Do I want to do it, but Had I ought to do it?* They are not afraid of responsibility, nor do they feel above the most menial tasks if these must be done to help others.

4. *Willingness to sacrifice:* As mentioned previously, with all responsibility, and especially great responsibility, there must be a willingness to sacrifice whatever is required to achieve the goal - time, energy, comforts and pleasures and often our money. The great social needs we are discussing are not to be solved with minimal effort.

5. *Men of wisdom:* Society needs men of wisdom and knowledge, men who seek truth diligently, who are willing to abandon preconceived ideas if they prove to be faulty. They treasure knowledge, and are generous in sharing what they have learned with others. They have something worthwhile to contribute. They are willing to accept the criticism of the arrogant and close-minded, risk falling out of favor if their wisdom is at variance with others. They know the value of their experience and knowledge and feel a responsibility to share it.

6. *Men of determination:* The problems of our world are challenging and discouraging. There have been many men who started out with a plan which would have been of great benefit, only to give up because of discouragement. The world needs men who are not quitters, men who have determination and have the drive to follow through, regardless of obstacles. Men of determination see only the object; the obstacle must give way. They are unyielding and uncompromising when they have an objective.

7. *Men of courage:* We need men who have both physical and moral courage. Physical courage is the willingness to face dangers and take risks, even the risk of life for a worthy cause. This was Patrick Henry's spirit of *Give me liberty or give me death.* We need men who are motivated, not for their own benefit, but for others. The real heroes have not risked bodily harm for some advantage to themselves, but for the benefit of others. Such were our revolutionary forefathers.

While it is stirring and inspiring to witness feats of physical courage, there are probably more opportunities for moral courage when valor is required to defend a cause you know to be right and which is unpopular. The firmness and conviction to stand alone in defense of those who cannot speak for themselves marks a person of courage. Moral courage is to do what is right, even in the face of criticism, humiliation, or personal disadvantage. Courageous men are not afraid to appear foolish in the eyes of others. They do what is right and let the consequences follow.

How to Help Build Society

1. *Preparation of self:* If we are to be of assistance to others, it is first necessary to prepare ourselves. especially in the seven basic ways just stressed. It is important to gain knowledge and wisdom. It is necessary to develop compassion and a sensitive perception so that we are able to recognize the needs that surround us and help in a beneficial way. We must understand other people and realize that there are a multitude of circumstances peculiar to them alone. They may have unique needs. A person who has had the security of a congenial and happy background may find it difficult to appreciate the traumatic adjustments of another who has never known such security. One who has enjoyed love and respect may not easily sympathize with one who has been deprived of such basic needs.

It is essential that we have a feeling of self-worth. We must trust in our capacity to grow to do whatever is needed. This trust in self is beautifully described in the following words

131

by Ella Wheeler Wilcox:

> Trust in thine own untired capacity, as thou
>   wouldst trust in God Himself.
> Thy soul is but an emanation from the whole.
> Thou does not dream what forces lie in thee,
> Vast and unfathomed as the boundless sea.
> Thy silent mind o'er diamond caves may roll,
> Go, seek it, but let pilot will control those
>   passions, which thy favoring winds may be.
> No man shall place a limit in thy strength!
> Such triumphs that no mortal ever gained may yet
>   be thine.
> If thou wilt but believe in thy creator and thyself.
> At length some feet will tread all heights now
>   unattained.
> Why not thine own? Press on! Achieve! Achieve!

God has endowed each of us with a unique individuality and a capacity far beyond what most realize. If we but trust in this divine inheritance, we can serve in a way that may greatly alter the course of history.

I am reminded of the lasting influence of Mohandas K. Gandhi on his nation and the world. In his youth he was an ordinary young man with many weaknesses. No one could have guessed he would affect for good the lives of millions of people in India. And yet this young man with frail body and unimpressive voice had something great to give. In his desire to serve and benefit mankind, his unique gifts came to light and he achieved a miracle by bringing the greatest nation of his time to its knees.

The secret of Gandhi's greatness was his goodness, his faith in God and his desire to serve. He also had a pure motive in serving, placing the needs of his countrymen first.

2. *Observe what needs to be done:* As we develop a sensitive perception, we become aware of how best we can serve. Generally speaking, society is built in two ways: solving difficult problems and advancing society in a positive way.

a) Solving difficult problems: These are divided in the following categories, although they are interrelated. They can best be observed separately: *(1) Social problems:* These include marriage problems, divorce, youth problems, crime, drug abuse, alcohol, violence, race problems, and others. *(2) Mental and emotional health:* Many suffer from severe mental illness. The lesser forms are emotional turmoil, nervousness, uncertainties. insecurity, and unhappiness. *(3) Lack of morality or spirituality:* There is a general rejection of moral principles; We are troubled by immorality, dishonesty, pornography, homosexuality, etc. *(4) World affairs:* This includes problems within our country and international problems. *(5) Health:* This includes depletion of food and soil and pollution of air, water, soil, and foods.

b) Advancing society: This includes advancements in industry, medicine, food production, education, the church, and in creative work such as music, art, design, architecture, literature, entertainment such as movies, T.V. and others.

3. Search for solutions: When one considers the difficult problems, he is apt to expend most of his energy complaining. There are more people than we need who are competent to list all the ills we face. They can go through them one by one and with deep emotion enumerate the pains and grievances and threats to nearly everyone, leaving a feeling of despair and helplessness. It is safe to say we are not so much in need of an elaboration of the problems as we are for constructive solutions, even though the part we play may be minor.

These solutions can come from a study of the information already accumulated relating to the problem, and also from one's own insight, perception and experience. When one searches his mind it is amazing the flow of ideas that come. Especially is this surprising in a society so sophisticated that one would think all the answers would have already been found. Relating what one knows to the insights of others often results in startling opportunities.

The greatest source of truth is often the last to be tried. God, who is the fountainhead of truth and consequently knowledge, has said, *Seek and ye shall find. Knock and it shall be opened unto you. Ask and ye shall receive.* This is a definite and straightforward promise to all who will study God's word and ask in faith. If one's purpose is single to the end of doing good, the plea to God will not be denied. Knowledge from God may come as something completely new, direct inspiration, or it may be a recollection of information already known.

4. Avenues to serve: Many men will be able to build society directly through their daily occupations. If they are engaged in work which is important, any efficiencies they effect is a worthy contribution. In fact, most of the major improvements have been accomplished along with a man's earning his daily bread. However, you may have some unique insight into a problem which is entirely out of your field. If so, follow your interest. You may be guided by a greater power than your own.

Whether a man serves in his work or aside from it, there must be a dedication beyond the desire for money. Horizons for human betterment extend beyond the *nine to five* commitment of most employment. It involves a state of mind which one adopts as a permanent part of his being. It becomes ingrained in his make-up until his desire to serve is not an obligation accepted because of duty, but rather because of desire.

It is important to stress that society must be built in the right way. Some things man has created are detrimental to society. Not all technology or scientific changes have accrued to his benefit. We need those changes which will benefit people. This is not necessarily the easier way, a more comfortable way, or luxurious way or convenient way, but a way that will make men happier and better.

Consider the power of example. The power of a single individual such as Sir Winston Churchill during World War Two was phenomenal. When England and the free world were in deep gloom as totalitarianism was sweeping a mighty tidal wave, destroying every obstacle in its path, Sir Winston stood in the rubble of London with his fingers extended in the victory sign, promising his people that despite all hardships, they would *never surrender, never, never.*

Such unyielding confidence fired a people to hope when all such hope would normally be gone. No matter who we are, we are creating an influence which is felt by others. They may not know us, but our respect for law, our attitude towards life, our enthusiasm or negativism are felt by others. We build or destroy society in our own way by how we live and think.

Motives for Building Society

There are two motives for public service: Let us consider these two motives.

1. Desire for acclaim: Inborn in every man is a desire for status or acclaim. This instinct is noticeable in all males of the animal world from the lion, the bear, or sea walrus to the pecking order of the barnyard. There is always a jockeying for top place.

The human male possesses desires to achieve and win positions of leadership and distinction. We find ourselves as participants or shouting observers at tournaments and contests to match skills for top honors. Sports of all kinds are big business where winning is the objective. In a vicarious way a man sees himself as the victor when *his team* or *his man* wins. It is to be expected that men will direct their energies into activities to bring fame, recognition and prestige. They want to stand above other men.

Reasonably controlled, this is a virtue which gives impetus to a man, providing him with that extra drive to succeed. Without it he is not quite the man he could be. Its complete absence leaves something less than a man.

On the other hand, when this drive is exaggerated and becomes the most important reason for achieving, superseding things of greater value, it is an evil which is destructive to the man professing to do good. Similar to the lust for money, the drive sparks negative traits causing one to lie, cheat, or steal or take unfair advantage. He may push others aside in his lust for honors. He may discredit another whom he considers a threat. Because of his unrelenting thirst for recognition, he may neglect his job and family. He is the victim of an addiction.

135

Although his objective was intended to build society, on the route he destroys it.

2. *Desire to benefit mankind:* In contrast, consider the man who is building society solely for the benefit he can do for others. He may be developing medical cures or advancing ideas to end erosion or pollution or writing a book which he hopes will bring reforms. He may be a politician altruistically motivated to promote justice or a scientist dedicated to technological improvements to save time and ease life. Many men seek leadership in service clubs, the church, or public office to benefit others. Whatever his work, he has as a prime objective the benefiting of his fellowmen.

Such benevolence has many rewards. It is moved by love, compassion, concern, unselfishness, and a spirit of self-sacrifice. He will not care who gets the credit. If someone else comes along with an idea greater than his own, he steps aside and supports and applauds the other man's contribution. If someone beats him to the mark and reaches the same objective he sought sooner, he is happy the benefits came sooner than expected. If another is better qualified for a job than he, he supports that man who has the greatest talent.

Many inspiring examples of such dedication to public concern are before us. Men spend countless hours, sometimes a lifetime in altruistic service with no thought for acclaim. Frequently men work cooperatively to accomplish their objectives with greater speed and efficiency. No one really knows who came up with the genius. Who, for example, invented the jet engine? Who invented the automatic clothes washer? Who is really responsible that a few remarkable men have felt the elation of watching the earth to which they are tied revolve in a course completely independent of themselves as they watch from a vantage point on the moon? Countless men contributed their ideas, but we can be certain the original ideas were not miserly kept secret by one who hoped to do honor to his name. The motive must certainly have been for the benefit of mankind. Remember: It is difficult to measure the good one can do if he doesn't care who gets the credit.

One of the revealing signs of a man who is moved by the

right motive is that he does not focus attention on himself or his work. He does not boast about his achievements or *sound a trumpet* before himself. He follows the precepts taught by the Savior:

> *Take heed that ye do not your alms before men, to be seen of them: otherwise ye have no reward of your Father which is in heaven. Therefore when thou doest thine alms, do not sound a trumpet before thee, as the hypocrites do in the synagogues and in the streets, that they may have glory of men. Verily I say unto you, they have their reward. But when thou doest alms, let not thy left hand know what thy right hand doeth: That thine alms may be in secret: and thy Father which seeth in secret himself shall reward thee openly.* Matt. 6: 1-4

Should Women Be Builders of Society?

There are some who feel that women should build society in the same way men do. A well-known politician made a plea before the Senate of the United States for women to join forces with men in advancing society. He said, *One of the untapped resources of this country is woman power. We need them in science, medicine, engineering, politics, education in all endeavors.*

Many young women are heeding such calls, feeling they have a great responsibility to make the world better. *Women are needed to build society, but not in science and industry.* Our deficiency is not a technological one. Our scientific strides have been phenomenal and are going forth with such acceleration we wonder if we are going to trip over ourselves. We are not short of working personnel. The work week has been continually lessened until now we hear proposals that no one work over thirty hours, that people be allowed as much as twenty-five weeks during the year as vacation. There is no conceivable way an assertion can be substantiated that we need more women in the working force to advance society. There is sufficient male population for that.

Women are misled if they feel they will best achieve their duty to mankind by becoming a figure of renown in politics,

137

science, and industry. Although they are capable enough, they can render no service of greater consequence than to establish an ideal home. Theirs is the prime opportunity to prevent and *correct the great social evils in the place most of them start.* There would be an absolute minimum of social problems if our homes were in order. Too much emphasis cannot be given in reminding our girls and women of their vital role in the well-being of society. Theirs is a role that cannot be shifted to men. Although often willing, this is not a position men can handle as a woman can. The shaping of the lives of children is of such magnitude and consequence as to be incomprehensible. These values are realized not only here but extend into eternity.

If men cannot solve problems of government and industry, if we must lean on women for these responsibilities, then we have failed as men. Half the population is male. There are plenty of men to produce the material necessities, but not enough women to be good mothers. Men are not capable of being mothers. Being capable of doing feminine work is not being a mother. This shortage of good mothers is probably the greatest deficiency in our work force.

As with a man, however, a woman has an obligation to give of herself in humanitarian service after she has fulfilled her role in the home. Women are benevolent and are greatly enriched by unselfishly giving of themselves to the church, the community, and to individuals who are in need. In the home, and by giving benevolent service, women greatly build society.

Women who choose not to marry are in a different category, and obviously free to give far more time to others. They are greatly needed in the world as teachers, nurses and other feminine services vital to the national welfare.

Not having the responsibility of children as a priority they are free to enter the male world if they desire. Their liberty to do this should be maintained and their benefits fully comparable to that of men in the same service. *But be it forever remembered that for them to enter the masculine world they will lose some of their femininity.* Whether married or not, I would not think they would choose this option. As a father,

I would be sure to explain this to my daughters.

Rewards

Eye hath not seen nor ear heard, neither entered into the heart of man those things which God hath prepared for them that diligently serve Him. This reward is not withheld until we die and face our Maker, but is felt in good measure now. There is nothing that will bring peace to the soul in such abundance as to be in unselfish service of others. Jesus said, *Inasmuch as ye do it unto the least of these, my brethren, ye have done it unto me.* This being the case, God rewards such honest efforts with His spirit immediately.

So often one discovers that those things to which he has directed most of his energies crumble to dust. Where he felt he was building a monument, he finds nothing, for his efforts have been selfishly directed. One who has given much of himself in the service of others will not find when he comes to die that he has misdirected his energies. He will know that he has not lived in vain.

A man who will develop within himself a concern for others and proves this concern through constructive action brings benefits to his entire family. A woman's glory is in the success of her husband and the happiness of her children. Children are encouraged to greater strivings by the unselfishness and magnanimity of an exemplary father.

Summary

The responsibility of building our better society rests primarily on men. The function of women may well be more important, for they it is who shape the destiny of youth, establishing their aspirations and ideals. A woman is usually the motivation to a great man.

But it is the man who must take up the banner and move onto the stage and do something. Indicate by your attitude and actions that you expect a better world and are doing something to move it in that direction.

9

Masculinity

So God created man in His own image, in the image of God created He him, male and female created He them. Gen. I :27

It is significant that we are created as either male or female. Although we are born into the world as God's children, we are born as either a male child or a female child. Thus inherent differences distinguish us from one another. These differences are not only the obvious physical ones, but are emotional and temperamental.

Masculinity is that part of a man which makes him so distinctly different from a woman. By nature he is strong, firm, steadfast and unyielding, whereas a woman by basic nature is soft and yielding. As a man grows to be more masculine, these characteristics are more strongly solidified in his nature. As a woman develops her femininity, she loses any traits of masculine firmness or unyielding temperament. As we widen these differences between men and women, a woman grows more strongly feminine as a man becomes more strongly masculine. This is an instance when the development of separating differences works to the advantage of both.

It is important to dispel any false ideas about masculinity. Some think masculinity means to be loud, bullheaded, hardhearted, and unemotional. These are not traits to describe masculinity as God intended man to be. What is true masculinity?

The Masculine Traits

That they may be more easily understood, we shall discuss the masculine traits under three main classifications: the physical traits, the masculine traits of character, and masculine ability.

1. Physical Traits: A man may or may not be born with a large build, a deep-pitched voice, and a heavy beard. If he is, he can count it an advantage, but these characteristics do not necessarily identify him as a fully masculine man. Of more significance are strong muscles which result from hard use or his physical energy or endurance which is derived from a well-trained body and spirit. A real man is made - not born.

Of more importance than his physical make-up is his masculine manner - his heavy gait, the firm and decisive use of his hands, the masculine stance, how he moves his head, and the tone of his voice. The masculine manner comes, not out of practice as an actor learns his lines, but is derived from an inner attitude of manliness. If he thinks like a man, he will carry himself as a man.

A friend I have known for many years is slight of build, being slightly over five feet tall. His frame is not sturdy, nor is he physically commanding. But he is a disciplined and educated man who has successfully served his family and community. He is easily recognizable as a manly man, even by those who barely know him. His bearing and self-confidence leave no doubt.

2. Masculine traits of character: Traits which are strongly masculine include aggressiveness, drive, decisiveness, firmness, determination, resoluteness, unyielding steadfastness, courage, fearlessness, independence, and competence and efficiency in the masculine world. These will be considered in detail shortly.

3. Masculine ability: This is defined as the knowledge, skill, and ability required in any masculine role, such as the ability to earn a living or the ability to perform a skillful work as a carpenter, bricklayer, plumber, office worker, financier, or medical doctor. It is exemplified in the leadership ability needed to guide the family or succeed in some phase of work. A man typifies such ability by possessing the knowledge to build his own shelter, grow a garden, or otherwise protect his family from want. The skill may be inborn or acquired by education or specialized training. Masculine abilities are those adaptable to the man's role as the guide, protector and provider and as the builder of society. These abilities are the means by which he solves his problems and reaches his objectives and fulfills his responsibilities.

Returning again to the masculine traits of character, it is well to devote time to them for they are the least understood. The words have a definite meaning to all of us, but we shall now consider them as relating in a positive way to masculinity.

Masculine Traits of Character

1. *Aggressiveness:* This is a self-asserting, pushing, or enterprising quality. The aggressor does not wait for things to come his way - he goes out to meet life, to get what he needs or wants, often in the face of opposition. This quality is of special value to the salesman or any man who is trying to reach the top of his field or advance in his work. He does not leave a stone unturned to achieve his objective. Used excessively, aggressiveness is negative in that it causes a man to push others aside for his own selfish interests; but when this extreme is avoided, aggressiveness is a positive force in achievement.

The opposite of aggressiveness is lack of initiative in getting what you need or want. This quality is frequently found in the feminine woman who would rather *go without* than push too strongly for what she needs or deserves.

2. *Drive:* Those who possess *drive* have abundant energy for accomplishing their objectives. Drive comes not so much from the physical source as from the *spirit* which carries one unrelentingly towards a goal. This quality is well described in the following verse:

The Champion

The average runner sprints
Until the breath in him is gone
But the champion has the iron will
That makes him *carry on.*

142

For rest, the average runner begs
When limp his muscles grow
But the champion runs on leaden legs
His spirit makes him go.

The average man's complacent
When he does his best to score
But the champion does his best
And then he does a little more.

Author unknown

Thomas A. Edison was a remarkable demonstration of drive in action. He was tireless in his objectives and took defeat as a further challenge. He said his drive was a result of his emotional self-mastery. Hard work does not drain off energy so much as emotional upheaval, which can be so debilitating as to make physical exertion impossible under extreme conditions. Emotional health, then, is fundamental to the quality of drive.

3. *Decisiveness:* This consists of the ability to make decisions promptly and firmly. A decisive person reviews the facts, comprehending the consequences of various alternatives, drawing a conclusion without undue struggle or vacillation. When he has made a decision he is confident in his judgment and does not weary himself with anxiety. He has a positive approach to the outcome. Obviously he will not always make the best decision, but he is more likely to make a good decision than the person who wearies his mind jumping back and forth. When the decision is made, action is taken without undue delay.

Feminine women are inclined to lack decisiveness. When they make a decision, it is never quite final. They often think they have decided for sure, but then change their minds. (Ask any building contractor who has built a custom home.) If an excuse can be found they will postpone a decision, sometimes indefinitely. In women this quality is part of their natures and may be attractive, but not so with men. Decisiveness is a male

143

characteristic which inspires confidence.

   4. Firmness: Firmness is the ability to remain constant, steady, or the same. The man of firmness is not easily moved or shaken from his convictions or decisions. He does not succumb to pressures when in his own mind he is confident he is right. This is an essential quality for success in leadership.

   This virtue is important for women also, especially in their dealings with their children as they hold to ideals and principles. But truly feminine women are not so firm when it comes to activities away from home that do not involve moral issues. This seems to add to their womanliness rather than detract, as it does with men.

   5. Determination: A man with determination is not easily swayed or moved off course. When subjected to pressures he is not deterred from his goals. This quality is essential in masculine leadership and for reaching objectives.

   Christopher Columbus is an outstanding example of a man with dogged determination to pursue a goal which he reasoned was sound in the face of overwhelming opposition. Men serving under him were aware that a real man was in command.

   This virtue should not be confused with *will power* or *self-mastery*, qualities both men and women need in adhering to principles and standards. Women seem to have self-control superior to men. But when it comes to determination which does not involve moral issues, a feminine woman tends to lack this quality.

   6. Resoluteness: This quality is similar to determination, only stronger, since it is characterized by a decided purpose. Moved by a strong conviction or objective, a man carries out his decisions with a steadiness which is unshaken. There is a solemn will attached to the quality of resoluteness, which suggests that the issue at stake is a moral one. This is a quality needed to carry a man to his objectives in the face of intense opposition or even defeat.

   7. Unyielding steadfastness: The man with this trait does not give up, quit, relinquish, or surrender under pressure of individuals or circumstances. The test of this virtue is only fully realized in the face of opposition. It is like the heavy mast of a ship whose strength is not realized until it is subjected to heavy winds at sea.

8. *Courage:* Courage is a quality of mind which enables ✓ one to meet danger and difficulties with firmness and strength of spirit. The man with this quality will do what he believes in, in spite of the danger involved. The danger might be physical harm, abandonment of friends, or loss of prestige. A courageous man has the strength of his convictions, and will follow them despite the risk of criticism or failure. He will not avoid an action because it is fraught with problems or possible failure. If he believes it is wise and right, he presses on. Carried on by his convictions and objectives, he overcomes the fear of risk, defeat, or danger. Cowardice is the opposite of courage.

9. *Fearlessness:* Similar to courage, fearlessness is more ✓ intense. A man of courage may have fears, but will follow his convictions in spite of his fears. The fearless man is free from fear. This may result from experience or because of faith. Fear is, in fact, the opposite of faith, for where there is faith, fear vanishes.

✓

10. *Independence:* While we are all dependent upon one another and certainly upon God, yet independence is a virtue to seek. This independence is not an arrogant disregard of others, or a glorying in one's own strength. It is rooted in self-respect and a responsibility one feels to care for himself. An independent man makes every effort to be self-sufficient in earning his livelihood. Only in case of dire necessity would he rely on others for sustenance. Such a man looks to himself for the solution to his problems. It is important to him to avoid dependence, which in severe cases borders on servility and loss of self-respect. Masculine men are always independent as they can be.

Women have a special dependence upon men for their support. This is not degrading to them, but is attractive in a feminine woman. For a man to behave this way is decidedly unbecoming.

11. *Competency and efficiency in the man's world:* I am ✓

145

speaking here of a man's efficiency in running his entire life, not just his occupation. I speak of efficiency in directing his family, in handling the money, and in making wise use of his time. I also refer to efficiency in any phase of his work or in solving problems in his masculine responsibilities as the guide, protector, provider, or the builder of society.

Women may be efficient without being masculine. But this efficiency should be limited to their own sphere. They can and should be efficient in running a household, in the care and training of children, etc. But when a woman moves into the man's sphere and develops efficiency there, she takes on masculine qualities.

The importance of this point cannot be emphasized too strongly. Some people vigorously reject this concept and accuse me of saying women do not have the ability to be efficient in a man's world. Women certainly do have this ability, but remember, as they do, they tend towards masculinity.

When a woman takes over the leadership of the family or management of the money, or steps into the man's world to assist in earning the living, she must acquire traits which are masculine if she is to be successful in these jobs which are masculine. These traits are unattractive in women, which only verifies how admirable they are in men, since they are natural to his sex.

How To Develop Masculinity

1. *By serving as the guide, protector, and provider for his family:* If one accepts this role in good spirit and strives to his utmost to succeed in all three categories, masculine growth is inevitable. As a man wholeheartedly accepts the position as patriarch or leader of his family, ruling with firmness and fairness, he will grow in the masculine qualities of leadership. He will acquire the traits of decisiveness and steadfastness and become that strong leader he has set himself to be. Should he, on the other hand, allow his wife to lead or, worse yet, insist she lead, he will deny himself this growth and will actually

146

retrogress, becoming less masculine than he was to begin with.

As one protects women and children, shielding them from the hardness and difficulties of life, he develops manly chivalry, courage, and valor. As he strives to provide an adequate living, facing problems and heavy responsibilities, he takes on a quality of manliness that cannot be reached in any other way. When one truly understands this principle, it becomes clear that these male obligations or burdens are in reality opportunities which are highly desirable and essential to one's growth.

2. *By building society:* Further opportunities to develop masculinity and other desirable traits of steel come as a man projects himself beyond the interests of himself and his immediate dependents. This occurred to Moses as he assumed the burden of the multitudes in bondage and led them out of Egypt. He grew in courage, steadfastness, and every other masculine quality needed to accomplish this almost impossible task. Without this burden on his shoulders, he could never have grown into such a magnificent man.

Since Moses was already a member of the household of Pharaoh and in a position where succession to the position of pharaoh was a strong likelihood, one wonders why God did not allow natural events to take place and then instruct Moses to free the enslaved Israelites by decree. Rather, Moses was sorely tested and prepared through trials to increase in faith that he might become the man of strength that was required to not only lead the captives from bondage, but to guide them for years to follow.

3. *By developing the masculine traits of character:* We have already learned of the masculine traits of character such as aggressiveness, determination, fearlessness, and others. These are acquired by an inner attitude of pride in being a man and by a conscious effort to put these traits to use in daily living. These traits may be already present, even in the young boy, but an awareness of them can help him grow in manliness.

4. *By increasing masculine skill and ability:* A man gains further masculine development by increasing his skill or ability in any masculine field. This includes his own occupation or

any masculine work such as building a shelter, pouring cement, planting a garden, repairing a car, fixing home equipment, repairing a roof, painting a house, repairing plumbing and other things. All of these skills help to develop the man. We see clearly that masculinity is developed by doing the work which naturally falls to us. These jobs are therefore a blessing, essential to our well-being and happiness. Why, then, do we so often resist?

5. *By developing his physical capacity:* Physical work, exercise, and a well-nourished body result in the hardening of muscles, increased physical strength and endurance - a more perfect specimen of manhood. Proper nourishment and the avoidance of tobacco, alcohol, drugs, and destructive products and habits are positive ways to become more manly. It is ironic that many young men are introduced to enslaving habits by the challenge *to prove they are men* by using such products. Evil in any form diminishes manhood.

6. *By accentuating the differences between himself and women:* In developing masculinity, it is important to accentuate the *differences* between yourself and women. Avoid anything which is soft and yielding or otherwise feminine. Avoid hesitancy, vacillation, feminine mannerisms of speech and bodily movement, or any characteristic which is identifiable as more to the nature of women.

A common feminine characteristic is to primp before the mirror, being conscious that every hair is in place. While no one will deny that good grooming is important, a preoccupation with the subject is unnatural to the masculine nature. Some men take an inordinate interest in clothes, considering cut, style and trends. They are unduly concerned as to how people react to their dress. They may wash, dry, and set their hair as is common to women. Their manners are effeminate, i.e., use of the hands and manner of walk. These outer indications of a feminine nature should be avoided.

7. *By setting challenging goals:* As a man accepts challenging goals, whether it is in connection with his work or otherwise, he brings to himself opportunities to enhance his masculinity. In seeking the *easy road* and avoiding

responsibility he denies himself opportunities for personal development. *The pursuit of easy things makes men weak,* ✓ whereas the pursuit of challenging goals, great responsibility, and difficult paths strengthen a man. This is not to say a man does not deserve time for rest and relaxation, for these things renew the spirit and body; but it does mean that the general trend of a man's life should be away from easy paths and towards the higher, more difficult goals.

Challenging Goals, A Means of Developing Masculinity

So frequently men drift towards the jobs that are easiest. In school the *cinch* classes have the heaviest enrollment, and those vocations and professions which require the least in effort will be the ones selected. All too frequently the effort and discipline required to reach a higher objective will not be exerted if something acceptable can be found which requires less energy.

Generally there is a point of compromise at which parents, friends or family members will be satisfied, but the nobler self within will not be. To feel good about ourselves we ✓ must do our best. The real man will prepare himself to do the ✓ thing which is difficult. In preparing for a vocation, the young man who is interested in being the most he can be will accept the strongest challenge available. It might require more years in training and more sacrifice to master difficult subject matter. But to be true to himself he will reach for the upper limits of his ability.

Please note: This places no greater inherent value on any particular job. It is a matter of using one's available talents to the utmost, whatever category of work that finally puts him in.

Consider the conquests of some masculine men in doing things which might appear ridiculous to the fainthearted. What, for example, drove Admiral Richard E. Byrd to explore the wastes of Antarctica? Whatever else may have justified the venture, certainly one great motivation, if not the dominating one, was the desire to do a challenging, hazardous job. Not only those who go to such a wasteland experience this

149

challenge, but those who vicariously participate as they view the movies and read of the dangerous exploits. People like to be part of something requiring courage.

What real merit can we say there is in climbing the sheer wall of El Capitan in Yosemite Park? Consider the risk, and for what? Whether there is any value or not in such an exploit is not the issue. It is a masculine trait to face a challenge and conquer it.

There is abundant challenge for every man. Most challenges are not so dramatic as these. But they may be more of a test of real manhood since they require the courage to carry on when acclaim or recognition is lacking. But whatever the goal, known or unknown, dramatic or otherwise, we must fight the tendency to do the minimum. One decisively demonstrates his manhood by working at the peak of his capacity.

We have seen that in applying masculinity to the role of man, it is imperative to accept the role wholeheartedly and be firm in the pursuit of the tasks we face. These tasks are usually ordinary, but their pursuit in a courageous manner is not ordinary. A wise man once said, *To do well that which is the common lot of all is the truest greatness.*

Set Some Goals

Initially these might well be the development of something distinctively masculine, such as a program of physical fitness to harden the muscles. Perhaps it could be a project in the yard, basement or garage - some type of improvement, a job that your wife should not or cannot be expected to do.

Our specialized society has many drawbacks. Among them is the tendency to discourage masculine activities which had to be used a generation or two back just to survive. When a man had to physically build the shelter his family was to occupy, when he obtained food through hunting and gardening, and when he had to supply the protection from danger in order to survive, the emphasis was clearly upon these important qualities. They were recognized as essential and appreciated.

150

Unfortunately this definition is nearly unrecognizable now. The masculine traits will be seen in less obvious ways, but in ways no less important. But if emphasis can be placed upon the masculine by deliberately cultivating the outward manifestations, it is an aid in enhancing the differences in the masculine and feminine with great benefit to both sexes.

What Masculinity Does

1. For the woman: A masculine man stirs the heart of a ✓ woman. In Cecil B. DeMille's version of *Samson and Delilah,* the remark was made of Samson, *The man who can still the heart of a lion can stir the heart of a woman.* When a man displays strength, courage, or any quality of manliness, women are naturally and deeply moved. This can be true of all women who observe him, not just the one who may be emotionally involved with him. As a woman who is strongly feminine and delicate inspires and moves men, so does a truly masculine man affect women.

It was Petruchio's masterfulness that tamed the shrew, Katrina, in Shakespeare's play and brought her lovingly to his feet. His masterfulness, however, would not have been effective if he had not also been gentle and tender. Wherever men are masterful and also tender, women succumb to this manly charm.

As a woman observes masculine qualities, admiration is awakened. Every man desires to be admired, not for just ✓ himself as a person, but for his manly qualities. This admiration is deserved only as he serves in some manly capacity. When a man sets out on a daring adventure, or courageously pursues a difficult goal, people admire him. When he stands firm on a decision in the face of opposition, or takes off his coat for a shivering woman, she admires him as doing something manly.

He may do other things less masculine, such as helping with the dishes, shopping, helping a neighbor, or doing a thoughtful act for a child. These are important and will awaken in a woman a feeling of respect and appreciation. But

151

these are not acts which awaken the feelings of admiration of which I speak. This admiration that every man seeks can only be awakened when he serves in some manly capacity.

Important to remember is that manliness makes a woman feel womanly. This is important to her. In the presence of a strong, able and virile man, a woman feels, in contrast, delicate, soft and therefore womanly. This realization is one of the of the most pleasant sensations she can experience. She may therefore seek the company of such a man for the renewing of this feeling. This is one of the dangers in marriage, for a husband who lacks these qualities makes it easier for his wife to succumb to the attentions of another man who has them.

A woman can be quite unfeeling in the presence of ordinary men. If she is inclined to be slightly masculine, most men will do nothing to affect her feelings. But when a strongly masculine man comes into her life, she suddenly feels like a woman. She may never have had this feeling before.

Women in the working world are often subjected to this danger. Her husband may not be a particularly masculine man. In her working environment she may find herself associating closely with a man who is strongly masculine. Without realizing it, she finds herself attracted to him for now she feels feminine. This is not a feeling she seeks, but may be one hard to disregard. She needs to be home where she can achieve the maximum femininity, hopefully in the presence of a masculine husband.

2. *For the man:* The feeling of being masculine is one of the most pleasant sensations a man can experience. It sets him apart from women. This is one reason men strive for high honors - not so much for the honor itself as for the realization of the powers exerted in attaining the goal. An undeserved honor is an empty shell. It is not being a champion a man glories in so much as the realization of the masculine ability required to become one.

All men strive for fulfillment, but few realize what it is or how it is gained. There is a mistaken idea that it comes as a result of money or acclaim. If these goals bring fulfillment, it is because a man used his masculine abilities to attain them.

Inherited wealth brings nothing in the way of fulfillment, nor does undeserved fame. This is a reason why some men of wealth and fame become desperately unhappy and commit suicide. Money and fame satisfy the ego, but do not give lasting satisfaction unless there is growth in character and exertion against obstacles.

3. *Benefit to society:* When a man stands as the firm leader bringing security, strength and protection to his family, he presides in a home of *order*. This is of inestimable social benefit. This is the greatest need there is - to have a nation of well-ordered families. If this situation prevailed generally, what problems would we really have? Masculine men functioning in the areas discussed thus far in this book would solve our problems. Men who are weak, spoiled, pampered, spineless, soft and yielding have never done anything for the betterment of the world.

Masculine Pride, a Special Problem

Men are proud to be men. Unlike many women who deliberately turn from femininity and seek a man's life in a world foreign to their sex, men adhere more closely to that which is distinctly masculine. They may not be all that they could be, but like to think they have the inherent qualities of manliness. Even a weak man will rise to defend his manhood when threatened.

Men are proud of their special abilities, skills, achievements, muscular development, or any manly trait. There are both benefits and hazards to this masculine pride. In as much as pride is a part of his nature, we are assured that it serves a useful purpose. It is a two-edged sword, however, and can result in pain and injury when permitted to dominate or when it is trampled on by an insensitive person.

Since the integrity and preservation of the family is essential to the well-ordered growth of all, God placed in man a pride in his manly role. Born in him is a desire to achieve something of merit, to be productive and contribute to the welfare of others. A man has pride in his work and a desire to

153

excel.

Since this is such an integral part of his being, anything which depreciates the male ego usually encounters a vigorous, hostile or even uncontrolled reaction. As already indicated, even men who are effeminate hate to be told they have lost their virility. Men resent any inference that they are deficient in any trait which is distinctively masculine. Although few men qualify completely as being thoroughly masculine, to admit that they are anything less would be unthinkable. With this built-in sensitivity, he has a very vulnerable spot which is frequently injured.

Wounded Pride

A man's pride can be seriously wounded by *ridicule, contempt, or criticism.* In the keen competition of the business world, men often belittle one another. This is usually done by someone trying to bolster his self-esteem. Sometimes it is thought to be humorous. Even family members are guilty. Wives are often at fault, not understanding the sensitivity of the male ego.

One of the most common offenses is *indifference* towards masculinity. When a man excels in a way that is *masculine* he is pained when ignored. He is not wanting praise necessarily, but likes to feel his masculinity is recognized. Every man has had this experience. Knowing how it feels, why do we do it to one another?

I know a man who lost his job as an engineer after more than twenty years service with one company. Many engineers were unemployed in his area. When he went to the employment office for assistance, he was greeted with, *Boy, are you bad luck. I couldn't place you in a hundred years.*

What could prompt such an insensitive remark? It is a slam to be thought foolish in his vocational selection. Other unemployed men were told, *What's the matter with you? How can I ever place a man like you?* It is an inference he does not have what it takes to hold a job. Such callous inhumanity is not what is needed if we are interested in helping someone.

Wounded pride often causes a response far out of proportion to what one would expect. Wars have resulted when a man's pride has been offended. The more usual effect is cutting or humiliating pain. If this happens often, a man will withdraw from any circumstance which would cause a reoccurrence. This means building a *wall of reserve or going into his shell.* In extreme cases he will be unapproachable and quiet. He may talk on superficial subjects, but will *clam up* if the conversation is probing. He wants his feelings protected. This effect is serious because it cuts communication.

A man builds this wall of reserve because of fear. He wants no more humiliation. This is a block to progress. He may hesitate to think creatively or *go out on a limb.* This wall of reserve is not a pleasant experience as you may already know. A man needs to express himself with a free flow of ideas and aspirations. He wants to win approval and admiration. Nothing but the absolute certainty that his ideas will be met with appreciation rather than ridicule or indifference will induce him to come out of his shell.

When pride has been wounded extensively and over a long period of time, it causes a numbing effect or a dulling of the senses. This is a self-induced numbness which a man acquires unknowingly to stand the pain of humiliation. The harm is this: Although it reduces pain, it also reduces pleasure.

In Dr. Edrita Fried's book *The Ego in Love and Sexuality,* she speaks of this numbing effect and its danger. *We pay dearly for the self-induced numbness, for while it relieves our pain, it also reduces our ability to experience pleasant emotions and to respond to pleasant stimulation. Unresponsiveness, like an indiscriminate scythe, mows down the flowers with the weeds.* A man no longer experiences the pain, but neither does he respond to the beauty of the sunset, the laughter of his children, or the love his wife has to offer. This self-induced numbness can cause a man to be sexually impotent.

When a man's ideas have been squelched, his hurt pride can cause him to alter his life's plans or goals. He may lose heart in pursuing the goal he was planning with such dedication or give up the daring adventure he was so enthusiastic about. Much as he may wish to proceed, he will not risk the threat of further humiliation to his manly pride.

Eliminating Hurt Pride

1. Avoid belittling or humiliating other men: The common practice of belittling is often made in humor without meaning harm. Although a man may not show evidence of humiliation, he may still suffer emotional pain. It is not safe to risk a cutting remark even though made in jest. If one wants to use someone as the butt of a joke, he should use himself. Many emotional problems would be relieved or eliminated if men would offer appreciation to one another rather than ridicule.

There is a temptation to cut one another down because of jealousy. This stems from a desire to elevate oneself above another. To do so is entirely negative and should be recognized as a weakness to be overcome.

2. Heal the wounds of other men: To see a person in distress and provide relief strengthens both parties. We help ourselves in losing ourselves in the needs of others. Diverting attention from ourselves is good therapy.

We have opportunity every day to offer encouragement. We can always smile and be warm even under casual circumstances. Consciously ask yourself, *What can I do today to help someone?*

3. By growing in manliness: If you expect to always be appreciated as a man, it is essential that you do things worthy of that appreciation. Do things to be proud of! Eliminate softness and fearfulness and be a man! Build self-esteem within yourself. Then when men attempt to cut you down, you will have an inner defense - a feeling of worth to protect you.

Men who are soft and weak are easy targets for belittling. Can they expect otherwise? If a man has not measured up as a man, he can hardly expect to be regarded as one. He must do things deserving of appreciation, if he is to avoid constant humiliation.

4. By a sense of humor: Often slighting remarks are made with no ill intent and should be received in the spirit given. Even serious accusations are tempered when one will come forth with a direct admission, even an exaggerated one such as, *You are right. I'm probably the most stupid guy in the office.* The offender is disarmed immediately. Most people are not viciously anxious to offend. You can do them a favor as well as yourself through a sense of humor.

When a Man Faces Failure

1. Face mistakes, failure, and defeat with manliness: The German author Goethe has said, *You cannot always be a hero but you can always be a man.* Masculinity can be displayed just as much in times of misfortune as in times of success. In fact, times of trial offer an exceptional opportunity to prove manliness. In defeat a man has the opportunity to display courage, idealism, and an undefeated attitude - all masculine qualities of steel. He may win more admiration in times of failure than in periods of success.

Women are especially stirred to admiration when a man will struggle in the face of serious obstacles or defeat. This is illustrated in the case of a lawyer who had a good practice in an eastern state, but for reasons of health was forced to move to a dry climate. He came to California, but could not practice law, as he had not passed the bar there. Several months were required to do the additional studying and prepare for the examination. In the meantime he had to support his family, so he found employment in a grocery store where he did heavy manual work. His wife remarked that this was when she first really became aware of his undefeated attitude. The manner in which he faced his problem brought her more security and a greater feeling of admiration than in periods when he enjoyed a prestigious law practice.

Men who are not manly in times of failure shrink from their problems. With fear and complaints, they blame others for their situation. We do not admire them. We are disappointed at their lack of masculinity. If they would rise to the occasion with a manly spirit, we could admire them.

2. *Acknowledge mistakes in times of failure:* Although it is not necessary or even wise to acknowledge mistakes to everyone, it is important to confess them to those closely involved, especially your wife.

Because of a man's sensitive pride, he is reluctant to confess mistakes to anyone, especially those who are near and dear to him -his wife in particular. The natural tendency is to want her to see all the good points and none of the mistakes. When defeat comes, a man wants to hide his mistakes, sweep them under the rug, or obscure them in any way he can. Frequently he blames circumstances or *bad luck.* This effort to conceal failure is caused by the fear of humiliation. One cannot stand to face defeat in the eyes of those who mean so much to him. Acknowledging mistakes, however, can actually relieve the pain of humiliation.

Why is this so? It takes *courage* and *humility* to acknowledge mistakes. One who can do this wins admiration. We all know this is a hard thing to do. And we all know we have made mistakes ourselves. There is always a sympathetic feeling for one who is trying to correct a difficulty.

Confessing mistakes also gives others a chance to be forgiving, if this is required. Especially is this important in the case of a wife. She will have the opportunity to show her strength of character, her heroism, her love. She will have the chance to overlook the mistake, to minimize it and offer understanding and support. To deny her the opportunity to demonstrate strength of character is to deny her a benefit. Women love to heal wounds, to offer forgiveness, support and consolation in times of strife. Do not deny her this privilege.

Another benefit from confessing failures is that your wife will be made aware of the mistakes. This will ease her mind so she can forget the matter. She will be assured that if you have defined your mistakes, you have them clearly in mind and will not likely make them again. To hide them or minimize them gives her no such peace of mind. She may take it upon herself, for your sake, to inform you of your failures to save you from future trouble. This is doubly humiliating. To be so stupid that you do not realize your mistakes and must be informed by your wife is not the feeling you need.

If your wife is in the dark she may blame others for your failure. This, of course, is unfair. If she is a campaigner for justice, she could get herself involved someway, trying to right a wrong that will be embarrassing to everyone. If one has erred or is in the wrong the only policy that really works is to face it directly and make amends before things get worse.

Is There Masculinity Today:

There is true masculinity with some men. They are the strong men who are the builders of society, both in the home and in the world. They are the lifters who do more than their share without complaint. They are the men who meet every honest obligation and set a worthy example to their children. They try to be what they hope everyone else will be. They are proud to be men, proud of their masculinity and are trying to develop it.

But it is unfortunately true that there is a greater lack of masculinity than there is an abundance. This lack is at the root of more troubles than most men care to admit. Many men seek the soft and easy life. They shun responsibility or anything difficult. Their goals are easy goals. Their work is easy work. They want to be undisturbed, to rest, to *let George do it.*

Men lean on women. They do not stand on their own feet, but expect the strength, initiative, mental fiber, and even physical work to be supplied by women. They do not lead. They are wishy-washy and indecisive. They are easily pushed around by women and lacking in positive conviction.

There is a lack of chivalry. Men do not protect women nor do they understand them. They not only do not protect them from masculine tasks, but often force them into such tasks. Many men are effeminate in their mannerisms - the way they use their hands, walk, type of clothes, and interests.

There is a general lack of masculine skills and ability. Although a man may have a trade or profession, he knows little else. He does not have the skill to solve his problems.

The average man is not a builder of society. He is self-centered, does not want to get involved in outside responsibility. He has a spirit of apathy. He complains about the sad state of affairs, but does nothing to supply relief. He is apathetic.

Strong forces are operating which deny the male responsibility as the guide, protector and provider and the builder of society. A man of weakness might succumb to this philosophy, for in it, his weakness is justified. A constant barrage of false information is unceasingly broadcast by influential people who say that women can do anything men can. Many women encourage this by leaning towards masculinity. They openly resent their sex, envy men and adopt their habits. They see no conflict in this blurring of roles.

Under such conditions what incentive does a weak and lazy man have to protect and cherish a woman who knows nothing about being a woman? Many of them are badly victimized and used as pawns. Now is the time for men to help women realize who they are and to protect them from themselves.

There can be no argument in the fact that *God created man in his own image . . . male and female created he them*. This creation was for a definite and eternal purpose. These separate identities must be maintained and magnified. In review, remember these salient points in developing masculinity:

How to Develop Masculinity

1. Assume masculine role as the guide, protector, provider.
2. Help build society.
3. Develop masculine traits of character.
4. Develop masculine skills and ability.
5. Increase physical capacity.
6. Accentuate the differences between yourself and women.
7. Accept challenging goals.
8. Face mistakes, failure, and defeat with manliness.

160

10

Character

What a piece of work is man! How noble in reason, how infinite in faculty! In form and moving how express and admirable! In action how like an angel! In appearance how like a god! The beauty of the world, the paragon of animals.

— William Shakespeare

The supreme quality of manhood is the strength of a noble character. A man may have the strength of masculinity that adds substance to his life, but it will never be of maximum worth unless refined by a sterling character. Harold Bell Wright recognized this when he described the man of the early West, *and a man's soul must be as the unstained skies, the unburdened wind and the untainted atmosphere.* Shakespeare observed this when he depicts perfect manhood as being *in action like an angel, in appearance like a god.* A noble character is the most important ingredient in a man of steel.

Those qualities of character which relate to a man's steel side will be discussed in this chapter. There are others which are velvet traits; they will be discussed later. The steel traits which are most essential to strong character are the following:

1. Self-Mastery

He who rules within himself and rules his passions, desires and fears is more than a king. — Milton

The *foundation* of a noble character is self-mastery. It is the key to overcoming faults which prevent us from the perfection we have been commanded to strive for. (Matt. 5:48)

161

It is the means by which we apply truth to overcome weakness, conquer appetites and passions, and gives us the strength to devote ourselves to duty.

The goal of life is to become finer persons and eventually perfect beings. The Savior taught, *Be ye therefore perfect, even as your Father which is in heaven is perfect.* To reach this perfection we must acquire the virtues of love, patience, compassion, generosity, devotion to duty, and many other godly traits. We will need to spend our time, money and energy in useful pursuits. It Is essential that we respect our bodies, seeing that they have proper food, sufficient rest and exercise to function adequately as the residence of our spirits.

An enemy or opposing force constantly lures us downward and away from high goals. Inborn is the inclination towards evil. We are inclined to be carnal, sensual, lazy, irresponsible, selfish, and filled with fear. To overcome these weaknesses we must control ourselves. Reaching for higher ground is a constant battle of overcoming.

Self-mastery is the motivating force whereby we reach upward. Desire and willingness are not enough. Knowledge and insight are not sufficient, nor is an emphasis on priority. Suppose, for example, you would like to apply the knowledge of this book. You have the knowledge before you and you consider it important. You have a desire and willingness, but unless supported by a strong will, little will be accomplished.

As further examples, you may wish to improve your conversation, to guard against brutal frankness, bragging or harsh criticism. You may wish to conquer the habit of over-eating, smoking, drinking or other indulgences. With the knowledge and conviction and realizing the benefits you want to achieve, nothing will happen unless you exercise your *will*. This is the only way any change will occur.

Perhaps you have a worthy objective that would benefit yourself and others. You can be sure you will find that unless you overcome fear, laziness, or distraction by selfish desires no progress will be made. The matter of *your will* becomes the critical issue.

An interesting account is recorded in the scriptures of a

rich young man who desired to know what he should do to gain eternal life. He had lived a good life, could answer positively that he had kept the laws as he had been taught from his youth. Jesus, perceiving his principal weakness - a love of wealth - asked him to sell his goods and give to the poor and follow Him. Sorrowing, the young man turned aside, for the attachment to his wealth was greater than his determination to change his way of living.

Although he knew he should give up his riches, and much as he desired eternal life, yet he could not rise above the selfishness and pride required to follow these instructions. His lack of will stood in the way of eternal blessings.

In today's world there is a downgrading of the virtue of self-mastery. Some say it suppresses the emotions and that it is better for mental health to go along with natural impulses than to confront them with the opposition of one's will. Especially is this viewpoint applied to promiscuous sex. Some claim that denial of these urges leads to frustration and emotional turmoil. Those who advance this false theory do not realize that it is *sin* that leads to frustration and mental problems, not the control of impulses. *Subduing impulses results in growth.* The goal of life is to have self-mastery over our natural impulses. The basis of true religion is to do that which is counter to human impulse - to love your enemies, to do good to those who hate you, and to pray for those who despitefully use you. The natural tendency is to hate our enemies and curse them that abuse us.

Other teachings say that although we must seek virtue, self-mastery is too difficult and we must seek easier, more effective means of overcoming weakness. Self-mastery *is* difficult, and it is wise to use any means available to make it easier. We can acquire knowledge that will help us understand the cause of our weakness and in this way assist in overcoming it more easily.

We can adopt a positive habit to overcome a negative one or provide incentives, rewards, and reminders. But we must face the fact that we do not overcome weakness without strength - the strength of a strong will.

Self-mastery may be gained by:

a) Training the will
b) Prayer
c) Fasting

1. Training the will: As one continually trains the will in small steps by increasing self-control, discipline and restraint, one grows in self-mastery. The training of the will is a deliberate action, or preparation in advance, rather than waiting for a great need to arise. When the will is trained by a continual effort in smaller steps, we are fortified. We are strengthened to meet temptation and weakness in emergencies which might otherwise catch us unguarded.

There are some effective means of training the will, such as the following:

a) *Do something you don't want to do and do it regularly:* It may be something unpleasant, like taking a cold shower every day or getting at a job you have been avoiding. The purpose is to train the will. If you determine to do this, no matter how unpleasant, you will find that very soon it will not be unpleasant. The success of your endeavor will now be showing results.

b) *Deprive yourself of something pleasant:* Deliberately decide not to watch your favorite T.V. program, give up your favorite dessert, don't snack between meals, give up candy, soft drinks, coffee, smoking, drinking, or other habits. Although you may have other reasons for giving up these habits, in this case the primary purpose is to train the will.

c) *Demand definite quotas and performance of yourself:* For example, arise at 4:30 each morning, get a certain number of jobs done at a particular time, do physical exercise a specific amount of time each day, outline a definite program of responsibility and follow through consistently. Do this deliberately to train the will.

d) *Do something difficult:* Set a goal for yourself that is not out of reach, but difficult. Pursuing a difficult goal will train the will, whereas seeking an easy goal does nothing for it. Engage in work or responsibility that is difficult. Children especially should be given difficult things to do, if for no other reason than to train the will.

In each of these instances emphasis is upon training the will, otherwise you might be sidetracked. To illustrate, if you have decided to get out of bed a half hour early to do some extra studying, unless training the will is foremost in your mind, you might rationalize that you can study at another time under better conditions. The time studying is not as important as is training the will. Say to yourself, *I am doing this because it is difficult, and I will deliberately overcome the pull of the flesh in this way*.

2. *Prayer*: The goal of self-mastery is so difficult that it is not likely you can accomplish it by yourself. If you are to reach upward sufficient to conquer your passions, weaknesses and fears, or to reach high objectives, you must have self-control. Such a goal can only be reached with the help of God.

Alcoholics Anonymous recognizes the need for God's help in overcoming the enslaving habit of alcoholism. They realize the futility of their problem without divine assistance. They must, in fact, acknowledge their helpless dependence upon God before they can make any progress.

I recall talking with a man who had been smoking for forty years and had finally overcome the habit. He had tried again and again to quit, but was unsuccessful until he sought the Lord's help through prayer. *Then*, he said, *God took away my desire to smoke*.

High goals are often out of reach without God's help. This is particularly true when the goal has a strong moral value in it. The amount of discipline required may be more than we have. But fortunately we have a source for the strength we need.

3. *Fasting*: The most effective means of gaining self-mastery is by fasting. This is a religious practice consisting of abstaining from all food and drink (including water) for a

165

period of at least twenty-four hours.

During this time we humble ourselves before God in sincere prayer seeking His assistance. Fasting can be practiced in a time of urgency, when there is a particular need, or regularly as a means of gaining self-mastery. Fasting is a type of prayer, one in which we not only ask God for help, but demonstrate our intense desire by sacrifice of material needs.

Fasting with prayer is a powerful force in obtaining divine assistance. When one is willing to deprive himself of something he has every right to have, and do it voluntarily and deliberately as evidence of the intensity of his need of heavenly favor, there is a power set loose that works wonders.

Jesus Christ began his ministry by fasting. He did not attempt to shape the souls of other men until He first became master of himself. He left the crowded cities and went into the wilderness where He fasted for forty days and nights. His purpose was to overcome the powers of evil - to gain mastery over Himself. The scriptures describe His trying experience in being sorely tempted by Satan who promised Him the satisfactions which all humans seek. By rejecting Satan He proved Himself the master over the fleshly urges which enslave people. His mastery of Himself gave him power over evil.

Self-mastery is the highest goal of a noble life. It was said of Jesus, *He put all things under His feet.* And He promised us, *And to him that overcometh will I give the crown of life.* In the Book of Revelations we are promised the following: *To him that overcometh will I give to eat of the tree of life which is in the midst of the paradise of God.* The rewards of both heaven and earth await those who attain self-mastery.

2. Chastity

Chastity means to be sexually pure, or to refrain from sexual relations outside of marriage. It also means to avoid any perverse sexual activity in marriage or by oneself. Those who are not chaste are immoral, usually in the form of fornication, adultery or homosexuality. Fornication is having sex when unmarried, adultery while married with someone other than

166

one's wife or husband. Homosexuality is sex with someone of the same sex.

Pernicious theories claim there is no harm in sexual activity if these intimacies are practiced between two consenting adults who both receive satisfaction from it. They blame society for their feeling of guilt. God has placed a conscience √ in us. It is the *outraged conscience* which is offended by √ immoral practices. The guilt is a positive feeling, urging one to do what is right. When the offenders of God's law urge public acceptance of their actions, they are hoping to avoid the guilt which is inevitable when one sins. What is *right* is not determined by vote or by public acceptance. Neither is it determined by educators or students who attempt to rationalize a justification. The consequence of sin is unavoidable.

Why Be Chaste?

The first reason is that it is the command of God. The √ ringing command *Thou shalt not commit adultery* was given to Moses for his people. This instruction was written in tablets of stone and reinforced in scriptures many times. We read in I Cor. 6:9, *Know ye not that the unrighteous shall not inherit the kingdom of God? Be not deceived; neither fornicators, nor idolaters, nor adulterers, nor effeminate, nor abusers of themselves with mankind.*

Not only is chastity adhered to for reasons of obedience to God, but for a divine purpose in preserving the individual from deterioration. When practiced universally, immorality destroys civilization. Sexual sin brings with it injury to the individual and is corruptive to society in the following ways:

How Sexual Sin Corrupts Mankind

1. Distraction and deviation: Sexual sin is a consuming √ distraction to a man in his work and causes him to deviate from worthy goals. In focusing his interests and energies in an addictive life style, he loses perspective which eventually can lead to his downfall. It is difficult enough for a man to stay on the right track, moving forward towards his goals, and focusing on his daily responsibilities, but when he falls into immorality he can easily get sidetracked from the important things in life.

2. *Conflict in spirit:* The spirit of God strives in every man to lead him to righteous paths. When a man is immoral, he brings himself into conflict with God's spirit, or his own conscience, which produces a feeling of guilt. This guilt can cause emotional distress and mental illness. Immorality also destroys the finer or more noble things about him which emanate from a good spirit.

3. *Loses the spirit of God:* It is written in the Holy Scriptures, *He that looketh upon a woman to lust after her, or if any shall commit adultery in their hearts, they shall not have the spirit, but shall deny the faith and shall fear.* The spirit of God is greatly needed to guide a man to a successful life, to help him make wise decisions, lay sound plans, and use good judgment. When he loses the spirit of God, he is left to grope along life's paths with forces so bewildering and difficult that they defy solution. This brings failure, both in his family and in his work.

4. *Eternal punishment:* Those who commit adultery *shall not inherit the Kingdom of God* as has already been pointed out in I Corinthians. They will also be due eternal punishment. The initial day of judgment, at the Second Coming of our Lord Christ, *will be a swift witness against the adulterers and they shall be burned as stubble.* (Mal. 3:5) Why God has placed such severe punishment on this particular sin may not be entirely clear to many, but in His noble purpose, which is to bring about the eternal life of man, He follows undeviating principle.

5. *Downfall of nations:* The greatest threat of any country lies in immorality, and especially in sexual immorality. Like the columns of the temple of Gaza which Samson pulled down, causing the entire temple to collapse, so will immorality lead to the weakening and eventual destruction of an entire civilization. Sexual immorality was the principal cause of the disintegration of the Roman empire, Greece, Persia, Babylon, Sodom and Gomorrah, and others. It is the greatest threat in America today as well as many other countries and supersedes

all other problems. It does, in fact, create most other problems. If for no other reason than love of country and love of life should we avoid immorality and run from it as the greatest enemy of mankind. It will tear from us all that is near and dear.

What Chastity Does For the Man

In addition to avoiding the pitfalls which would destroy him, chastity brings strength, both spiritual and physical. That individual who will garnish his life with virtue provides for himself an armor of protection which will help him withstand other temptations. He will attain an inner strength of spirit which will help guide him to a more perfect life. In addition he will gain a bright countenance and wholesome spirit which makes an evil-minded person uncomfortable in his presence.

The morally pure person has peace of mind - a freedom from fear that some long hidden skeleton in the closet will be uncovered, that he will cross paths with someone with the ammunition to blackmail or embarrass him. In teaching chastity to his children, he can do so with conviction and power.

A man who is sexually pure will prolong his sexual function and health. Some have attempted to refute this fact and rationalize immorality with the claim that it is not healthful to suppress sexual desire. This is false teaching. Quite the contrary is true. Suppression and control brings strength and health to the individual and will prolong sexual function and satisfaction. One's sexual organs are not like muscles which must be flexed and used to avoid atrophy. Their function is enhanced under conditions of restraint, whereas promiscuity leads to debility.

It is well to note that one of the greatest frustrations of those who wildly and promiscuously vent their sexual passions is the loss of virility and a failure for sustained satisfaction. Bizarre aberrations are then indulged in which not only fail to quench the fire but add to it. As with drunkenness and other serious vices, the end is sometimes self-destruction as one realizes that he has pursued a path which cannot provide the satisfaction sought. Next to the gift of life, the greatest gift to man is his opportunity to participate with Deity in populating the earth. To make foul the fountain of life is a sin which is, in magnitude, next to murder.

Overcoming Immorality

For those who feel trapped in a life of immorality, be assured that a chaste life is attainable. Many thousands of people have achieved this goal, as attested by the virtuous lives they live. Don't be persuaded by the satanic teachings that say such a life is impossible. If you have made the mistake of pursuing an immoral course, determine to give it up and pursue a course that will produce lasting satisfaction. Few offenses are more difficult to overcome, and the strength given by God will be required to change the pattern. But an immoral life can be changed and the sins wiped out, if one's repentance is sincere and sustained. Any other choice will end in defeat and destruction of the soul. The steps to follow are:

1. *Recognize the sin:* The first step is to recognize the sin and its seriousness in the eyes of God, without an attempt to justify previous behavior. God already knows all the circumstances connected with your life, your opportunities and limitations. In a spirit of humility, determine to live a moral life.

2. *Approach God:* Come to God with humility, acknowledging your guilt with a heartfelt sorrow for your offense and a firm determination to avoid it in the future. Ask for forgiveness and assistance in living a moral life.

3. *Good works:* Get busy immediately on some completely unselfish project that will benefit someone in need. Give of yourself.

4. *Improve Yourself:* Avoid judgment of others, a critical attitude. Be patient and forgiving yourself. This is a key. God's forgiveness of you will be measured as you are willing to forgive others. This is a very sobering fact we must keep in mind. These steps provide additional strength in overcoming

your problem.

3. Honesty

We can best understand the principle of honesty by considering its opposite - dishonesty. The well-recognized forms of dishonesty are stealing, lying, and cheating. Men who claim character would not think of indulging in these forms of deceit, and yet these same men may be guilty of dishonesty in the more obscure forms. They may, for example, obscure the truth, or give a false reason for their actions, or blame others for their mistakes or weaknesses. They may exaggerate or deliberately make a false accusation.

Some Forms of Dishonesty

One of the most common failings of men is to obscure the truth. Notorious exploitation has occurred in the rate of interest charges, especially to those unfamiliar with certain business terms. A buyer may be told he is to pay six percent *add on* interest rate. He assumes that he is paying the borrowed money plus six percent *added on* as interest. But the truth is obscured. *Add on* is an ambiguous or deceiving term. In reality, *add on interest* at six percent is about twelve percent simple interest. Words are used which are technically not dishonest, but with intent to misrepresent, for they are not generally understood. This form of dishonesty has resulted in *truth in lending* legislation which has fortunately made it mandatory to disclose the actual rate being paid.

A common form of dishonesty is to use terms which attempt to gloss over the sin. For example, the term *gaming* is a cover-up for the word *gambling*, which has a well deserved negative stigma because of the abuses of this addictive habit. But changing the word does not change the consequences, as deceivers would like us to believe. *Life style* is another innocuous term used to gloss over many types of perversions such as homosexuality. Calling homosexuality a *life style* is a deceptive way of trying to cover up the evils of the practice.

171

Another example of dishonesty occurs when unsuspecting or credulous investors are sold franchises where an unrealistic projection of profit is given or where all the hazards are not disclosed. The product may be insufficiently tested or may have inherent weaknesses. Vital data may be withheld, since it would be unfavorable to the seller.

Flagrant examples of dishonesty are observed in specialized services such as automobile repairing, electrical repairing, plumbing, and many others. Unnecessary work is done and parts installed which are not necessary. There is no way the average man can detect this deceit.

Professional people are no less involved in such deceit. Doctors and hospitals often charge exorbitant fees or a weighted price if the payer is an insurance company or a government agency. Extra diagnostic charges are often included when the need for them is in question. This is a particularly reprehensible offense because the perpetrators have the protective shield of a degree, or a license to order services which no one is in a position to challenge. They charge *what the traffic will bear. Others get theirs; I might as well get my share* is the justification.

Dishonesty is so widely practiced as to make one feel that this is the way business is done. Defense contractors often bilk the government out of hundreds of millions of dollars. Congressmen accept perks without question, not minor amounts, but amounts to equal double salary perhaps. Opportunities to cheat and falsify occur in all businesses. These excesses are frequently brought to public attention. And because they are so commonplace, it is easy to justify dishonest acts.

God's spirit, through our conscience, warns us of these traps. Like any form of evil trying to erode our characters, there is the rationalization of public acceptance that tells us we are justified for reasons of self-preservation. If we are being cheated we reason we must cheat also. In all this there is a temptation to justify ourselves if there is any element of truth at all behind which we can hide.

172

Why do men who claim to be honest engage in these forms of deceit? They are moved by the same reason that any man is driven to lie, cheat, or steal. The reasons have their roots in human weakness which are described here:

1. *Love of money and material goods:* This human weakness is the number one reason men rob banks, steal furniture and jewels. But it is also a reason behind the more obscure forms of dishonesty, such as those just described or other acts such as taking a small item from a store without paying for it, failure to return an overpayment, lying about a child's age to buy a ticket for half fare, buying goods wholesale under deceptive means, and lying to avoid paying income taxes. Some men have been known to switch price tags, to take lumber from a building lot, or help themselves to produce in the fields without paying for it.

All of these acts have to do with money and material goods. Perhaps this is the reason the Apostle Paul made the statement *The love of money is the root of all evil* - in that it leads to so many forms of dishonesty and vice.

2. *Fear of criticism or humiliation:* This is the reason a person will cheat on a test - to avoid the humiliation of a failure. It is the reason we blame someone else for our mistakes or grievous circumstances.

I recall the experiences of a man who had always been quite well-to-do. Because of unusual circumstances his business failed and he found himself in a humble situation. To save face in the eyes of his wife, he blamed someone else for his loss, a man who was innocent. His wife brought untrue accusations against the innocent man which caused more trouble for her husband.

Fear of criticism is the reason we make excuses and obscure the truth. Always there is a fear that if the truth is known, it will put us in a bad light. A man may make a poor business investment. He may have known the facts when he entered the venture, but to save face he may say the seller deceived him, misrepresented the investment, or made promises which did not materialize. The real reason, which may have been poor judgment or even foolishness or greed, is covered over because of the fear of humiliation.

It is not necessary to reveal our mistakes to others. Certainly these errors in judgment are personal matters which we have every right to keep to ourselves. But it is dishonest to make statements or accusations to *save face*.

3. Desire for acclaim, praise. or honor: The desire for acclaim is strong in men as we have already learned. When a man desires a particular advancement or position, he may defame a competitor by downgrading him or accusing him unjustly. By depreciating the other man he may rid him from the competition and win the honor himself. Men will also steal an idea or claim another's work as their own. This practice begins early in the school system.

My little daughter related the following experience: She had drawn a picture of a dragon. After school the boy who sat next to her erased her name and wrote his on the picture. When she confronted him with the matter, he said, *Oh, you can draw another. I had to do it for the teacher and my mother.*

If this practice is not stopped early in life it can lead to similar dishonesty in adult life. Often men will create original ideas only to have them stolen by a competitor. In many cases ideas cannot be protected by a patent. But it seems that although legal protection is not possible, there would be integrity which would prevent us from taking something that does not belong to us. It might be legal to do something. Things are often technically *legal*, but not ethical or honest. Honesty and integrity are really beyond enforcement. To be strictly honest often requires the greatest soul-searching.

Another form of dishonesty due to desire for acclaim is bragging or exaggerating. It is common to brag or stretch the truth to elevate ourselves. It may seem harmless, but it is not honest.

4. Laziness: Many people who would not think of stealing money or directly telling an obvious falsehood will steal just as surely by failing to perform diligently and adequately on a paid job. While accepting pay for their time, they idle away sometimes hours each day in slothful and half-hearted effort. In a very real sense, what was once their own time is no longer theirs, for it has been purchased for a price. To idle it away while on a job is therefore stealing just as it would be to take money from the till.

5. *Drugs, alcohol, and other enslaving habits:* We must not fail to recognize the above motive for dishonesty. The craving for drugs will drive a man to rob and steal, even at the risk of his life. It is pathetic that men who have already degraded themselves must further their downfall by stealing. This is an illustration of the pathetic situation a person may get into when he has had his *will* destroyed by an addiction.

The reasons for dishonest acts are principally a desire for money or possessions, fear of criticism or humiliation, desire for acclaim, laziness, and enslaving habits. If we can rid ourselves of these weaknesses, we will find it easier to be honest.

It is the more obscure forms of dishonesty the average man must constantly guard against, acts such as falsely blaming others, accusing, justifying, exaggerating, and concealing the truth. We should strive to be overly honest, if this is possible, that we may be assured of always being honest.

In the ideal man I describe, honesty is not enforced through outside measures nor is it practiced through fear of detection or punishment. His integrity is not weighed out each night or at every critical period of testing. Honesty is an integral part of his being and comes automatically. Such a man is not governed by law so much as he is governed by conscience. The fear of violating his own integrity provides the greatest deterrent to any act of dishonesty. His honesty provides for him strong guidelines of behavior which can be relied on with certainty.

Karl G. Maeser illustrated this principle by suggesting that a truly honest man when placed in a confined area bounded by a chalk line, and giving his word that he would not go beyond that line, would be more solidly contained than a man locked behind steel bars supported by a ten-foot-thick stone wall, with no such promise.

Honesty is not only the strength of a good man's life, but a principle of success which will help him in all his activities - with his family, friends, and especially in his work. Dishonest men violate principles which result in failure. This includes failure in a material way. However, the greatest reason for living an honest life is that it is a command of God, who said: *Thou shalt not steal, thou shalt not bear false witness.*

4. Dependability

Dependability means to follow through on a job, a responsibility, obligation, or promise. It means reliability, wherein full confidence can be placed in you to get a job done according to instructions, and at the time expected, and that you will not let other things interfere with the objective. The guide to acquiring this virtue is a simple one: *Do the thing you are obligated to do, at the time it needs to be done, whether you want to do it or not.*

Dependability means you will keep your word. You will do that which you have said you *will do* and *not do* that which you have promised not to do. It means you will keep commitments and respect confidences. It means your word is sacred to you and can be solidly relied on.

One often marvels at the simplicity and homeliness of the greatest virtues of mankind. Dependability is certainly one of them and one which is within the grasp of the most humble and least naturally endowed with talent. *But it is rarely found.* Instead, there is a great failure to follow through, with a rationalization of unforeseen circumstances, interruptions, demands, and other distractions that serve as excuses. There are, of course, legitimate emergencies that interrupt a schedule, but most often laziness or a lack of responsibility is to blame. There are two general areas of a man's life wherein he must be dependable if he is to succeed.

1. On the job: Other than basic integrity, the most fundamental quality for a man's success is dependability. It rates higher than talent, training, or experience. Talent is greatly appreciated, but is of little value without dependability.

176

Training and experience are invaluable in qualifying a man for a job, but are of little worth without dependability.

Who of us in selecting an employee would not rate dependability as one of the most essential qualifications? I once heard a man say, *Give me an untrained man who is dependable any day over a trained man who is undependable. I can train the dependable man and he will be a valuable employee, but I can do nothing with the undependable man.*

2. *In the family:* Being dependable as a provider brings security to the family. The security of each family member lies more in the dependability of the father in earning a living than in the money itself. A father who receives money suddenly or by some spectacular means will not provide security as much as a father who has consistently worked through the years and proved his dependability.

The father must be dependable as the guide and follow through with plans, promises, and family obligations when this is at all possible. This will build trust in his word, prove his dependability, and bring security to the family.

Lack of dependability is selfish. One will set aside a commitment to follow a pursuit more convenient to himself. Dependability shows a concern for the interests of others. Especially is it important to be dependable in the daily tasks and obligations which are the common lot of all and which are often considered trivial. To perform these tasks faithfully and well, without complaint, is an evidence of true greatness.

5. Fairness or Justice

This means to strictly render that which is due, whether it be reward or punishment, and do it with impartial or unbiased judgment. This subject can best be understood by first considering unfairness and injustices.

1. *Unfairness in giving pay or rewards:* Sometimes an employer will extract everything he can and pay as little as required by law. He could argue that he is doing nothing illegal. Whenever I hear a man argue that what he is doing is not illegal, I know there is a problem. He is wrestling with his

conscience. His disposition is a selfish one and his conscience is bothering him.

It is also unfair to pay more than what is justly due. A generous father may overpay a child. He wants the child to get ahead and subsidizes him. This is belittling to the child and creates unreasonable expectations. He has an inaccurate measure of the value of his labors.

Unfairness exists in showing favoritism. Two men may render equal service, but one granted special privileges or advancement. Racial, religious or personal biases are often seen. There is also occasions when an employee will ingratiate himself seeking special favors. Obviously, he is entitled to nothing extra for this.

It is easy for a father to be partial to one child, often the oldest, youngest or cutest. He would probably never admit this, but it is a common failing.

2. *Equating rewards:* There is a tendency to reward people equally whether they deserve it or not. One of the reasons for this is that it is easier to do - it avoids explanations. Sometimes a faulty philosophy exists. Justice and equating are synonymous. Everyone gets the same. The idea of socialism follows this concept. But it does not work and it is not fair. Men must be rewarded for their efforts and are injured, not helped, when they receive something for nothing.

Sometimes a man equates rewards in his family. He loves all of his children the same and does not want to see any of them disappointed. I recall a painful example of equating in a family. One of the daughters wanted a cedar chest. She saved her money for many months, denying herself entertainment and pleasures that she might have the cedar chest. When she bought it, her younger sister, seeing the chest, also wanted one. But she had not been frugal. She spent her money on ice cream, candy, and pleasures. But her parents, in their desire to see both girls happy bought the second girl a similar chest.

This was a great injustice to the daughter who had earned her cedar chest, and a detriment to the spendthrift who didn't earn or deserve hers. There are times when the only way a lesson can be learned is to suffer the consequences. A word of caution: This is no time to tell the prudent girl that if she loves her sister she will be happy to see her have a chest too. This would be a serious mistake, and grossly unfair.

This same equating is often observed at birthday parties. The children engage in games and contests where a prize is offered the winner. But the hostess, in an effort to see that no one is disappointed, rewards each child with a prize. In so doing, she gives an incorrect picture of life. Children must be taught by experience that rewards are for those who earn them and that those who do not go without. They must learn to enjoy another person's success and endure their own disappointment as a normal experience. This is important training in character growth and learning the lessons of life.

There is harm in equating. It destroys incentive to strive. This is the failure with socialistic governments which take from the rich and give to the poor. They destroy a man's incentive to dedicate himself to a goal, to work long hours on a project where he hopes to realize an extra benefit. One may feel that a righteous man would strive for worthy objectives without material rewards. But when such a man realizes that part of the money due him is used to give to another who has not put forth effort, there is something within him that cries out *injustice*.

The world has witnessed a spectacular failure of this concept. Communism has been unmasked and stands naked as a system unable to meet peoples needs. It cannot support itself. On an individual basis we need to remember these lessons.

In reviewing justice it is well to note that money and goods which are inherited are not in the same category as the injustices just described. Those who inherit wealth are not being paid for services. Inheritances are gifts, a tradition in which a father leaves his family that which he has accumulated, with the thought that they are to become stewards of family possessions. There may be problems attached to this tradition, but it is not injustice.

3. *Justice in rendering punishments:* Justice is to render

179

punishments according to that which is due. Let us review circumstances. Suppose a child has been disobedient, or has injured another child. As the father, how can you bring justice to bear? First, *make sure you are in control of yourself.* Justice cannot be administered by one who is emotionally upset. Your leadership as a father and perhaps as an employer places you in the position of rendering judgments in which you are emotionally involved. You must keep control of yourself.

Second, get the facts. Make certain the child understood what was expected. It is so easy for some one to think he has put over his point, but from the viewpoint of another, especially a child, it may not have been clear at all. Now there is a problem, and it will take patience to clear the air and make certain the child understood instructions or what was expected.

Third, be sure you are free from any feeling of partiality or prejudice toward the offender. A particular child may be the one who seems to always misunderstand, or may be the *clumsy one.* In our legal system great care is taken to insure that people called to jury duty have not been prejudiced. This is a good point for a father to remember.

Fourth, be certain you have been fair in your expectations and not required something beyond the capacity of the child. To dress a small child in his Sunday Best and allow him to go outside after a rain and not step in a puddle is expecting the impossible.

Whether dealing with a minor problem or one with long term serious consequences, the procedure is the same. A man must learn the facts, free himself of prejudice and determine if his expectations are fair. With a child, particularly, do not expect behavior beyond the capacity of his years. Do not expect better performance than you would have expected of yourself.

The punishment may be only a stiff reprimand or it may be the denial of a privilege. You may assign extra work or responsibility or in some cases inflict physical punishment as is sometimes necessary with disobedient or impudent children. But whatever the punishment, justice requires payment for the deed. If a child steals something, even if it is of little value, he should be required to return or replace the article and be reprimanded for violation of a serious principle. If a child is guilty of a civil offense where punishment of the law is required, he should take the full force of it. Parents should not step in and attempt to spare punishment or in any way interfere with justice.

When it is necessary to mete out punishment or a stern reprimand, it is essential to follow up with acts of love or kindness towards the offender. If it is a child, he must know that you are not an opponent or enemy who wishes to do him harm, but are moved by love and concern for his welfare. Explain the principle of justice and that you are morally bound to exercise jurisdiction and punish when it is due. This principle applies in dealing with employees.

Some men are too firm and unrelenting in rendering punishment. This is often due to uncontrolled anger which causes a loss of judgment. Punishment given at a time of uncontrolled anger is often fearful and cruel. This will undermine the confidence his children need to feel in the one who is their leader and guardian.

But there will be times when, without losing his temper, a man will be unduly severe, feeling the only way a child will learn is by having punishment so severe he will never forget it. Be extremely cautions in rendering punishment to children. Never give punishment which is greater than the crime, or more than the child deserves. If you do, it will be felt as a painful injustice. Even a small child has a keen sense of justice.

In his novel *Great Expectations*, Charles Dickens makes an astute observation about the feelings of children concerning injustice:

In the little world in which children have their existence, whosoever brings them up, there is nothing so finely perceived or so finely felt as injustice. It may be only a small injustice the child can be exposed to, but the child is small, and its world is small, and it's rocking-horse stands as many hands high, according to scale, as a big-boned Irish hunter.

The prevalent attitude of so many men is towards

softness in discipline rather than *firmness*. This is occasionally seen in the working world where a man thinks he is too busy to deal in complete justice. It may be difficult to discover the facts, or he may fear losing favor.

If an employee is slothful or otherwise ineffective, a man may find it difficult to correct him and would rather dismiss him in as polite a way as possible rather than discipline him. A man who might otherwise be brought to more efficient and productive labor is denied the benefit of training which would be invaluable to him.

Because of love or tenderness, a man may be too soft in dealing with his children. Such emotional feelings overlook the child's errors. When the child is involved in a conflict with other children, he is usually innocent in his father's eyes. At school there is a disposition to blame the teacher or the other child. If such a father does acknowledge his child's offense, he may overlook it or let him get off with a minimum punishment. This softness can injure a child permanently and make him unprepared for the firm life ahead where society will deal justly with him in less favorable circumstances. It is the *right* of the child to be punished in justice for his offenses by someone who loves him.

Some may justify softness by calling it mercy. Because they do not understand this principle, they feel they are obligated to be lenient in punishment, if not to forego it altogether. This may be right if the mistake was made in innocence, or if the offender is sincerely repentant, acknowledges his mistake and asks forgiveness. But this is not so often the case. Usually there is justification for actions, a defense and tendency to blame others. If the offender is not humble and repentant, then justice must bring him to task. Mercy cannot rob justice, and there are many offenses for which one must make recompense even in the face of a sincerely repentant attitude. One can readily see that the leader of the family must understand this principle thoroughly to administer justice correctly.

The following are guidelines to rendering just punishments.

1. Make certain the guilty person understood what was expected of him.
2. Discover all of the facts relating to the offense.
3. Free yourself of partiality or prejudice towards the guilty person.
4. Make certain you have not expected more than is fair.
5. Make a fair judgment and render punishment due.
6. If your punishment must be severe or firm, follow up with kindness, love, and an explanation of your purpose in bringing justice to bear for his benefit.

Especially in the home we see justice on trial. It is here children first learn by personal experience. If the father is just, they will be benefitted; if he has been unjust, they will be injured. Children have a keen sense of justice which is why they are so sensitive about being treated fairly. The man who is firm but fair will serve his family well and gain their love.

6. Unselfishness

There is a natural tendency in man to be selfish, beginning in infancy. We observe this trait in tiny children who take things away from one another without a tinge of conscience, or cry to have their way in spite of inconveniences to others. In infants such behavior is not objectionable. Children tend to outgrow this self-centeredness quite readily, partly because of the teaching of parents, but more because of their experience. They soon realize they must lose their selfishness if they are to get along.

The problem is that most people lose only the amount of selfishness necessary to get along. They do not grow beyond this point since there is not a reason compelling them to. They have not arrived at the point of realizing that selfishness is a serious character defect which must be overcome. They do not realize that to be truly unselfish is a goal for which we should all be striving. The point is: Spiritual growth is in *direct proportion* to our unselfishness. There is no way a person can grow spiritually and be selfish. Unselfishness puts the focus of one's life on others. This is contrary to our natural disposition and is therefore painful. If we are growing to be more and more unselfish, we are growing in spirit; if we retain our self-centeredness, there is no spiritual growth.

Unselfishness and Spiritual Growth

Unselfishness is a willingness to give up one's own comfort or advantage for the benefit of someone else. There must be an element of *sacrifice* in a truly unselfish act. This means giving up some pleasure, comfort, material thing of value *to you*, or going to some trouble, risk, inconvenience, or out of your way for the benefit of someone else. There are some acts which are termed unselfish which in reality are not, such as giving away something you really do not want or need, doing something which is little if any trouble, or giving a small donation you hardly notice. These are acts of kindness, but are not unselfish since they require no sacrifice.

To be unselfish we must *lose our self-centeredness*. We must learn to think less of ourselves, our comforts and conveniences and advantages, and think of others. This is a genuine transformation of spirit and has nothing to do with a superficial act.

How A Man's World Encourages Selfishness

A man's world is one which encourages and cultivates selfishness. He is constantly faced with responsibilities to provide for his family. The demands are ever increasing and not wholly predictable. Despite careful planning the need for money is ever-pressing. With the greater portion of his time allocated to earning the living, this emphasis may be so strong as to distort his vision. The only way this problem can be relieved is to avoid a standard of living which makes too many demands. There must be room to grow spiritually.

The keen competition of the business world also encourages selfishness. The slogan *every man for himself* seems the only way available. With the pressure and incentive to watch out for one's own interests, it requires great intellectual integrity to decide what is selfish or not in business relationships.

I observed a lack of integrity in a man who was describing a scheme of raw land promotion to a group of prospective salesmen. He was at a high peak of enthusiasm as he described how they could sell land which had cost only three hundred dollars an acre for as much as four thousand dollars per acre. Someone suggested that perhaps the deal was weighted too heavily in their favor with insufficient consideration for the buyer and his opportunity to profit from his purchase. His comment was, *It's obviously better for us than for them*.

If we are to have integrity, any business arrangement should be as nearly equal as possible, considering costs, risks and effort of each contributor. It need not be a fifty-fifty deal, since both parties may not contribute the same, but for that which is contributed the chance for each to profit should be commensurate. Unless the deal is good for both parties, it is not good for either. This is not only a principle of integrity - it is a principle of success.

Sometimes we hear of legislators who feel it their duty to bring special advantages to the community they represent, regardless of the disadvantage other communities sustain. While urging economy generally, they may push for the continuance of a project in their area which may not actually be productive enough to justify its existence. At the same time they will oppose a similar project in another area with which they are not greatly concerned. Such an attitude is hypocritical, for one will not apply to himself the same criteria he would apply to others. It is so easy to give *lip service* to a principle which is remote, and expect others to do that which we cannot do ourselves. In this hypocrisy we find the seeds of many of our social problems.

The man who selfishly thinks of ways to enhance his position may be sorely tempted to use any means regardless of the legality or ethics involved. Thus, his selfishness has driven him to other evils. A constriction takes place in his personality, a narrowness of viewpoint, diminishing his power to be effective. It is ironic that in his selfish drive for advantage, a man sets in motion forces which make him less capable of attaining his goal. The selfish man adopts traits which lead to failure, whereas the unselfish man applies principles which lead to success.

If a man is to be successful in the leadership of his family, it is essential that he govern with unselfishness. If he is not unselfish his family will follow him only out of duty. An unselfish leader builds trust in those he leads.

A man should also unselfishly give of his time for the benefit of his family. He may reason that when he has earned the living he has fulfilled his obligation. He may feel justified in spending the remainder of his time in his own interests and pleasures. The family may seldom see him, except at dinner and when it is necessary for him to be home.

True unselfishness means giving, not only of material goods, but time and energy. This was the principle in the instruction given, *He who loseth his life for my sake, shall surely find it.*

7. Moral Courage

Moral courage is the courage to do that which is morally right or to follow correct principles at the risk of consequences. These consequences are usually the following:

1. Loss of money, or the opportunity for money.
2. Loss of prestige or acclaim.
3. Criticism or humiliation.
4. Loss of friends.
5. Loss of an advantage or position.
6. Physical harm.

One of the most common needs for moral courage is when we are faced with the possible loss of money if we do what is right. An example is the tobacco industry. Evidence is beyond controversy that their products are addictive and bring sickness and premature death to millions. Government figures show that for the year 1993 in the United States the injuries and costs coming from tobacco were fifty billion dollars.

One would think this knowledge would impel those involved in the business to get out of it, regardless of personal consequences. Rather, weak excuses and hypocritical arguments are used. The fear of loss of revenue makes honesty impossible. The measure of one's character and integrity are brought into public view. The weak argument that people who use tobacco are free not to can scarcely atone for the damage done.

The liquor industry is bringing destruction *worse than death* - the degradation and spiritual downfall of millions. Producers of alcohol are well aware of these evils. Alcoholics Anonymous is a reminder of the effort others are making to restore the damage brought on by alcohol. Yet, because of money, people in these industries encourage the use of their products. The same can be said for gambling casinos, the manufacturers of pornographic literature, obscene movies, or any industry which is destructive to mankind.

What about persons whose incomes are derived from the production and distribution of these damaging products. *At what point, one might ask, am I personally responsible for injury to my fellow men? Am I such a small part of a great system that my individual responsibility is lost?* Greater moral courage may be required in this instance than in the first, where the ill effects are direct. Imagine for a moment the effect if employees in these industries had the moral courage to leave their work. Such a mass demonstration of integrity would revolutionize the moral character of society. So it is not only the manufacturers of destructive products who are to blame. Everyone involved in the distribution bears a responsibility.

Persons in these industries must have feelings of guilt, for many of them attempt to clothe themselves with respectability by associating themselves with a worthy endeavor. Supporting a charity or providing scholarships, for example. Shamefully, a number of states have legalized the lottery which saps millions of dollars from the weak with the excuse that the funds will go to education. (Is it not an aim of education to encourage people in establishing sound moral values and habits?)

Moral courage is required in political life. One would suppose that men in politics would be thoroughly familiar with the Constitution, as it is the yardstick by which legislation should be considered. It is a magnificent document designed to preserve the interests of everyone, with special emphasis on the protection of the minority. Yet many politicians lack the moral courage to stand in defense of these principles if their prestige or job would be jeopardized.

It takes moral courage to defend a principle when one's friends would be offended by such a stand. If your neighbor operates a theater where undesirable movies are shown, it might be more convenient to let someone else initiate action to correct the evil. It is not easy to remember that one should be on the side of *right* in every instance. One is reminded of the story of Abraham Lincoln when a friend remarked to him that the Lord must surely be on his side. The wise Mr. Lincoln replied, *I'm more concerned about being on His side than having Him on my side.*

Inspiring examples of moral courage are contained in the scriptures. We read in the thirty-ninth chapter of Genesis that Joseph, who was sold into Egypt, won favor with Potiphar and was given authority over his property and business. Potiphar's wife tried to seduce Joseph. Rather than yield, he fled her presence, but not before she had torn his coat from him. With this as evidence, she blackmailed him and he was sent to prison. Despite this horrible injustice, he remained faithful and was, in time, able to redeem himself. He became the second man in authority in all Egypt, Pharaoh only being greater.

In ways great and small we are all challenged in a test of our moral courage, our commitment to do what is right in the face of strong desire or pressure to compromise.

Self-dignity is a dignity of spirit. With this virtue we rise above unkind remarks, criticism, abuse, or attempts to degrade or debase our character. Others may try to damage our reputation, but we maintain a kingly composure. This dignity of spirit is not something one superficially achieves by deciding he is going to respect himself, but arises from a genuine feeling of worth.

Men who are competing for position in the business world sometimes downgrade one another by spreading negative information. This is done in the hope the competitor will be eliminated from the competition. When an innocent man becomes a victim of this treachery, he will likely become angry and seek revenge. He may fight back viciously, displaying character traits as negative as those of his defamer. If he does, he lowers himself to the level of his abuser.

To attain self-dignity, it is necessary to restrain and control the emotions. It comes from developing the strengths of character just mentioned. We must be the genuine article ourselves. For this reason, self-dignity was mentioned last. It is the crown which rests on all other virtues.

The Need For Men of Character

We desperately need men of character in these troubled times. They are needed in the affairs of the government, in science, in the communications system, in industry, and in the business world. They are needed in all departments of education, at the printing press, in the fields, and in all endeavors. Men of character have always been the bulwarks of society. Honest men have been the builders of civilization, whereas men who are dishonest, unjust, and otherwise evil have destroyed it.

And what are men of character needed for? To advance science, technology, or to create inventions and useful ideas? Yes, but this is not the greatest need. We have made rapid progress in science and industry. *The urgent need is not to*

189

advance technology but to advance spirituality. Our greatest need is not to find a cure for cancer or an end to disease - *For we wrestle not against flesh and blood, but against principalities, against powers, against the rulers of darkness of this world, against spiritual wickedness in high places. Wherefore, take unto you the whole armor of God, that ye may be able to withstand in the evil day, and having done all, to stand.* (Eph. 6:12 and 13)

We need a *special kind* of men in our urgent times. Masculine men? Yes, those with great courage and determination. But this masculine nature must be refined by a noble purpose so that the motivating force is for public good and not for selfish advancement. We need men with the virtues explained in this chapter - the kind of man described by J. G. Holland:

God Give Us Men

God give us men.
The time demands strong minds, great hearts,
    true faith and ready hands;
Men whom the lust of office does not kill
Men whom the spoils of office cannot buy;
Men who possess opinions and a will;
Men who have honor, men who will not lie;
Men who can stand before a demagogue
And damn his treacherous flatteries without winking;
Tall men, sun-crowned, who live above the fog
In public duty and in private thinking!
For while they rabble with their thumb-worn creeds,
Their large professions and their little deeds,
Mingle in selfish strife; lo! Freedom weeps!
Wrong rules the land and waiting Justice sleeps.

- J. G. Holland

How to Attain A Noble Character

Attaining a higher, more noble character is difficult for everyone. This is because we have natural tendencies to weakness and evil. Men are by nature carnal, sensual and devilish. There is an inborn selfishness is us, a striving for comfort and self-protection. Even within our family circle the tendency is to pour out our love and concern for our own - without too much thought for those outside. The focus is on us, on our needs and desires. When we reach to higher heights, we are bound by our selfishness; and when we seek to overcome the weaknesses of the flesh, the appetites and other indulgences, we must struggle against a carnal nature.

Only by turning to God can men reach a higher plateau of character. The strength which comes from God made David, the young shepherd boy, into a great and noble king. And it was he who so poetically declared the source of his strength: *The Lord is the strength of my life . . . The Lord is my rock and my fortress and my deliverer; my God, my strength, in whom I will trust; my buckler and the horn of my salvation and my high tower . . . Yes, though I walk through the valley of the shadow of death, I will fear no evil; for thou art with me: thy rod and thy staff they comfort me.* Psalm 27:18, 23

Rewards of a Worthy Character

The special reward to those who attain a worthy character is peace of mind or inner happiness. A most fundamental principle of truth is, *The good life promises the happy life.* This is not necessarily a life free of problems, nor one of ease and comfort, but it is a life free of inner turmoil and emotional disturbances.

Spiritual growth means mental health. These two parallel one another. Only as we overcome, only as we lose self-centeredness and self-indulgence and grow in the grace of a noble character, can we gain peace of mind. This truth is supported in the most advanced knowledge of mental health. I would like to again refer to the statement by Dr. Max Levine, psychiatrist. *There cannot be mental health in the absence of high moral standards and a sense of social responsibility.*

Another psychiatrist, Dr. Richard R. Parlour, has written: *Much of what has been called "mental illness" by psychologists should more properly be called "spiritual illness" or better, "spiritual deficiency." The aspect of personality predominantly influenced in the process of psychotherapy is the "belief system" or in other words his religion . . . The field of clinical psychology, especially, is far closer to the field of religion than it has wanted to believe, and failure to see this kinship has hindered the development of clinical psychology.*

And from the Book of Psalms come these inspiring words which remind us of the source of peace and happiness:

> He who hath clean hands and a pure heart;
> Who hath not lifted up his soul into vanity
> Nor sworn deceitfully. He shall receive the
> blessings of the Lord. - Psalm 24:4, 5

11

Self Confidence

A self-confident man believes in his ability or competency and does not have undue barriers or feelings of inadequacy. There is something appealing about a confident man's manner, the way he stands with head erect, chest up and legs slightly apart. He walks with a positive assurance that he knows where he's going. Confident men use their hands with self-assured motions. There is an impressive tone in the voice which relays an abiding confidence within.

It is easy for others to believe in a confident man. Because of this, confidence is an essential quality in leadership. This is as essential whether a man is leading an office force or a family.

Besides being a leader ourselves, we are also followers in one capacity or another. We know from our own experience how difficult it is to rally behind a person who lacks confidence. Ineffective leadership makes any project difficult, if not impossible.

Lack of confidence afflicts most people. Negativism is everywhere. Staying uninfected requires an awareness of the problem and a determination to combat it. It is easy to feel inadequate when comparing ourselves to others. We may want to reach for a higher objective but lack the confidence to set out. Often there is something a man would very much like to do, and should do, but because he feels inadequate, he puts the idea aside. And yet, confidence can be built. Here are some suggestions.

The first step is to take on an air of confidence or, in other words, act confident. Walk with a firm step and speak with a steady, confident voice with head raised high. Give the impression you know what you are doing and are qualified for the assignment or responsibility at hand.

If necessary, face your tasks with at least a pretended confidence. Hide feelings of uncertainty or unpreparedness. If you are called on to speak, never apologize for your fear or lack of ability or unpreparedness. Be an actor, if you must, but *act* confident. Don't rationalize that you would feel deceitful. This kind of *deceit* helps everyone. This air of confidence is an essential part of confidence itself. Using this suggestion will bring results quickly.

This positive air of confidence is important for the security of people you are leading. I am thinking of a young mother who was left a widow with six children. These children looked to her for strength and security to fill the gap left when their father died. She felt unprepared for the task, but did not reveal this fear to them. Her confidence not only strengthened the children, but strengthened her.

Confidence is closely allied with *faith*. And faith is important in getting God's help in the solution of personal problems. When one is working diligently to be successful in an assignment for which he is responsible, such as his role as the leader, he can confidently expect divine help.

In contrast, I think of a young man, recently married, who needed to find a job. This was not an easy thing to do, especially since he was lacking in experience and filled with doubt. To bolster himself he asked his bride to accompany him as he made application at several places. I sympathize with his lack of confidence, but had he been able to assure his bride he was confident he could support her, both would have been helped over a difficult place.

Many men are not nearly so confident as they would like to be or need to be, but they give the impression they are. I have met some supposedly self-assured men who display great confidence, only to have them confess they suffer the same feelings of inadequacy other men do. But, because they *act* confident, others trust them and cooperate.

Consider the general who is leading a battalion of men in battle. He is certain to feel the stress of his difficult assignment. The physical danger and responsibility for the lives of his men would bring fear and anxiety to the strongest of men. How could he possibly prepare for *all* the contingencies? His position *demands* that he appear confident, regardless of how he really feels. Any doubt he must conceal. His men depend on him for strength and assurance and are putting their lives on the line. He probably reasons, *I am not fully capable, but what man is under these circumstances?* So he faces the challenge, and in a miraculous way his confident attitude brings forth hidden ability and he is able to meet the challenge more adequately than he thought possible.

This same attitude can be applied when a man is leading a family. He is painfully aware of his heavy responsibility to lead them safely and securely and wonders where the strength and talent to do it will come from. The last thing he wants is to worry them about how he will do it. He *acts* confident which inspires trust in him.

This *air of confidence* is not to be confused with *hot air* shown by the man who resorts to bragging and exaggerations in an effort to impress. One easily sees through this phony and overbearing demonstration which is actually lack of confidence. An *air of confidence* is positive and may not require that anything be said. It is rather *a manner a man assumes* that gives others confidence in him.

Avoid Failure Patterns

1. At work: In developing confidence, it is essential to avoid those things which destroy confidence, such as repeated failure at work. A man may drift from one job to another, each time being unsuccessful. Instead of his work building confidence, as it should, it destroys it. Each failure reinforces the negative pattern.

If a man has been unsuccessful in his work, the solution lies in discovering his talents and locating a type of work where he can adapt these talents. Every man has ability which will lead to success if he will discover it and put it to work. However discovering one's ability may not be easy. In solving this problem it would be helpful to have an aptitude test. Many men who have been unsuccessful find success when relocated in jobs for which they are adapted.

2. *In other activities:* Avoid failure patterns in everything you do. These might include sports, music, art and public speaking.

It is obviously not expected that a man is going to be the *top runner* in everything he does, nor is this desirable. Many of these activities are done purely for fun and not in a spirit of competition where achievement is measured. But if a man does engage in these activities with a desire to achieve, it will be undermining to his morale if he continually fails.

It is true that one improves with practice and should not give up merely because he is not good to begin with. But I emphasize that, although each man has talents, he invariably has limitations. If he wishes to excel in an activity, he would be wise to concentrate on things he can do well. He should avoid those areas in which he can never be anything but mediocre.

I knew a man who was determined to sing. He practiced many hours for several years and tried again and again to perform publicly. Each time his performance was weak. So weak in fact that many of us in the audience suffered unnecessary anxiety in his behalf. I often wondered why he wanted so very much to be a singer. Perhaps in his youth a great singer had inspired him. But I also wondered about his misdirected energy and how it could have been used to develop a talent to bring him both satisfaction and confidence.

If I had a child who was not as keen academically as he should be, I would not encourage him to be a top student, unless this was *his desire*. Instead, I would encourage him to be outstanding in wood work, mechanics, sports, or anything in which he could excel. As he succeeded in these fields, his confidence would expand and he would be more apt to do

196

better in his studies. That student who appears dull may suffer merely a lack of confidence, and when he realizes he is gifted in other things, he may well move to the head of his class.

Many failures are not the result of lack of ability, but lack of confidence. When we avoid failure patterns and concentrate on our abilities, confidence grows in everything we do.

Avoid People Who Undermine confidence

There are none of us so strong that we are not affected to some extent by the people we associate with. Hopefully our associates will be people of understanding and warmth who encourage us to be the best that is in us.

Unfortunately this is not always so. There are some people who delight in tearing others down. They do this to justify their own inadequacies or laziness. This may come from people who want to be your friend, but are worried that they will look bad if you succeed. Or they are afraid you will ignore them if you move out of their level of mediocrity. Many have negative patterns in thinking or flaws in their character.

Jealousy can cause a person to downgrade another for the feeling of self-importance he gets from appearing to be in a superior position. Acting as a critic, he is in a neutral position, not vulnerable to any consequences directly. It is a temptation to make ourselves look good by showing the faults of others.

Avoid associating with such people if possible. When you have sufficiently established confidence, you can cope with them on their own ground. But while confidence is growing, it is best to avoid their company. If you find you cannot avoid them, face them head-on. Tell them that although you have weaknesses, you would prefer to be reminded of your strengths. Let them know that their remarks are destructive to your confidence and that you would rather have their help than their hindrance.

Allow For Your Mistakes

Frequently a man's own belittling or critical attitude undermines his confidence. The business man who loses money in a venture into which he has put his best effort and thought, the athlete who loses an important contest, the singer who hits a sour note, may feel unqualified for the work he is doing. The greater the aim, the more a man is inclined to be critical of his mistakes. This self-depreciation is the most destructive of all.

It is the worst because we program our minds to accept these negative thoughts as facts. Countless studies show beyond doubt that what our abilities actually are do not affect us so much as what *we think they are.* If a man constantly feeds on negative thoughts he is actually *poisoning himself.* It is a form of suicide.

It is impossible to avoid all mistakes. We are human beings prone to error. We will not meet success on every turn, nor will we find it with every effort into which we put our best thought and skill. Our lives will be spotted with error and failure. The cabinet maker will make an error that will cost him a day's wages, and the athlete will not always win the game.

To maintain confidence we must allow for mistakes and tell ourselves that a natural part of life is failure. *The road to ultimate success is always strewn with failures.* Failure is, in fact, an inevitable part of eventual success. To expect perfection is unrealistic. Fretting over mistakes can undermine confidence and bring on additional failures. Allowing for mistakes, on the other hand, helps maintain confidence and therefore encourages future success. We must accept ourselves as human beings and allow in advance for our share of mistakes.

Overcome Inferiority Complexes

Often it is a deeply rooted feeling of inferiority which destroys a man's confidence. He probably has ability or skill equal to any man, but because of an unwarranted feeling of inferiority he does not feel equal.

To overcome these barriers, it is important to understand how futile they really are. The following are some of the common ones:

1. Complexes due to lack of money: Ours is a materialistic culture which places tremendous emphasis on money and tends to equate it with the worthiness of the individual. If one accepts this concept, he would feel uncomfortable in the presence of one who has greater wealth, feeling this person to be of more importance or worth than himself.

The truth is that people of wealth are not deserving of honor just because they have money. A person should be respected for what he is, rather than what he has. Like everyone else, people of wealth are both worthy and unworthy, depending upon their use of their money and the character they possess. Such a person should be respected for what he is. His wealth is incidental.

Money is not an indication of superiority. Some inherit it or gain it by more fortunate circumstances than others. Others have wealth through devious and illegal activity. Some have it by compromising their standards. Most people of wealth probably have it because of diligent effort. If this is the case, then this man is to be admired for his positive traits, but not for the money itself. Another man who has put forth equal energy in another direction, but one which is less financially fruitful, is not inferior.

Sometimes our mistake is not in regarding the person with wealth as superior, but in fearing he considers us inferior. This fear may cause a man to hang his head and act awkward and uneasy.

A revealing fact is that people with wealth are not inclined to regard those with less money as inferior. They are likely, however, to sense this feeling of inferiority in the other man which makes communication between the two of them difficult. It is repulsive to see anyone devaluate himself in a sheepish manner. This is a sure indication that such a man, if he had wealth, would consider those less wealthy as inferior.

199

So we see that this attitude indicates a flaw in his character. A person who respects another because of his worthy accomplishments and strong character marks himself as a person with sound values.

A person with a childhood background of poverty may have deeply rooted complexes, depending upon how his parents regarded their situation. If the parents were ashamed of their poverty, it is likely the child will be also. As he grows to adult life, he carries this feeling with him. As an adult he must develop a value system to override such unwarranted feelings.

The greatest danger is that people who feel inferior due to lack of money also feel that money would improve their self-image. Moved by this distorted viewpoint, they direct their energies to the accumulation of wealth, using any means to get it, sure this will solve all their problems. But, like the gold at the end of the rainbow, the possession of wealth will never bring the feeling of self-worth they seek. Self-worth comes when a person develops those qualities of character which build self-worth. He then knows himself. He knows that he is honest, virtuous and true.

2. Complexes due to lack of education: Nearly everyone has at least a moderate education. And yet some men feel inferior to others. A man with a moderate education may feel at ease around persons of similar status, but in the presence of more highly educated men he feels inferior especially if they have titles.

There is no justification for feeling inferior to a man because of his greater education. As with money, education does not make a man superior. He should be measured in terms of what he is, rather than what he knows. The mere acquisition of knowledge is not what counts, but how it is applied. That man who has trained and disciplined his mind is probably a better man for it. If so, he is deserving of recognition. But even so, this does not justify a man in feeling inferior. Education is not measured only by degrees. Skills and experience may be even more valuable.

It is likely the man of letters will not regard other men as inferiors. A truly educated man develops humility along with his scholastic attainments. He learns how little he knows in comparison to the vast store of knowledge which is available. He also knows that every man has gifts and special qualities and also limitations. We are all both ignorant and learned, but on different subjects.

Albert Einstein, acclaimed as a genius, was known to possess this humility despite the adulation accorded him. It was only in specialized learning that he was superior to other men. He was known to seek the advice of others on subjects he knew little about. He often made inquiry of the most common and ordinary of people. If the highly educated do not regard men of lesser education as inferior, there is no reason for the less educated to so classify themselves.

3. Complexes due to a lack of talent or accomplishment: ✓ When we are around someone who has developed a talent which makes our efforts seem commonplace, we may feel inferior. A famous actor, sportsman, musician, artist or public figure has achieved his place for deserved performance. You may have made a few strides to develop your gifts, but they seem insignificant by the unusual achievements of another.

There is no reason to feel inferior just because of his accomplishment. He will be judged for the man he is, not only for his special achievement. As an overall person, he may be inferior to you. You may have put more energy into those things which make a worthy life than he has. If he is a talented person and also a fine individual, he will be appreciated for the total of what he is.

We must appreciate, of course, that achievements usually ✓ come because of tremendous effort. Such persons often spend many years in practice, suffering periods of discouragement, even humiliation the public knows nothing about. He will have made many personal sacrifices for the sake of his talent. Few people realize the amount of dedicated effort which goes into the accomplishment which now seems so easy. We should always appreciate this effort as part of a worthy character. If a man has not measured up on all points, at least he cannot be counted as lazy. He is to be admired for his dedication and sacrifice.

With this thought in mind, you will likely conclude that your talent may not be so much less as perhaps your effort. Had you put forth a comparable amount of toil, sacrifice, and dedication in developing some of your talents, you may well have achieved as much or more than he. You are equal to other men. You need only to work as hard as they have.

4. *Complexes due to physical defects or handicaps:* Sometimes men are faced with physical defects such as a large nose, large ears, small build, or they are not particularly handsome, at least in their own estimation. They may have more serious handicaps such as a missing limb, loss of hearing or may be blind or crippled. It is difficult for such a man to feel equal to men who have no such disadvantages. They may feel that if they were whole and handsome they could accomplish anything.

Again I must stress that it is not what a man has or what he appears to be that really counts. It's what he is. A man who is completely whole physically is not a superior man to one who is handicapped if both have made the best of their circumstances. The man in the wheelchair may be more courageous, masculine and worthy than others. Each must be measured by what he really is, rather than what he appears to be.

I met a man on an airplane who was in a wheelchair. He had lost both arms and legs in an industrial accident. After living a vigorous outdoor life, one can imagine the trial he had in learning to use mechanical limbs. But he had learned to do this to a fair extent and had the courage to travel. He said he visited friends periodically and had no one to accompany him, so he went alone. Besides this, he had a schedule for several months each year when he would visit hospitals and train other amputees to use an artificial arm or leg. He was in worse shape than any he trained, but yet had the confidence to cheer them up and help them fight their feelings of inadequacy.

Another great man was Glen Cunningham who, as a young boy, was so severely burned he was told he would never walk again. Yet he overcame this handicap and became a champion runner. This tremendous will to amount to something has caused others to use their handicaps as a stepping stone to greatness. Jimmy Durante found that he would never be cast in the leading romantic role because of his large nose. So he exploited this disadvantage, exaggerated it, and made a fortune. He turned a lemon into lemonade.

In summary, we can say that each man must be judged according to what he really is, and not according to what he has. A man who strives to do his duty, to develop his character and be a worthy man has no reason to feel inferior to anyone. His confidence will grow because of his day-by-day efforts to live a good life.

If, however, a man is lazy, indolent, slothful and does nothing to improve his time and talents, he has reason to feel inferior. Unless a person is exerting himself to accomplish something worthwhile, he will never feel good about himself.

Do Things to Build Confidence

Confidence is built upon the qualities which make a worthy life. If a man is faithful to duty and earnestly strives to be a better person, to reach higher objectives, confidence will follow. If he is lazy and irresponsible and is content to be an inferior person, he should not be surprised to lack confidence. He cannot expect to gain confidence if he does nothing on which that confidence can be built. The following are measures that a man can take to build confidence:

1. *Discover your unique gifts, talents, or abilities:* Confidence will grow when a man discovers his special abilities and concentrates on making a success of them. Most men have talents which they ignore and never develop. These include special insight, even genius which the world sorely needs. He may have a faint reflection of these gifts at times, but usually disregards them. To discover these talents and make use of them becomes his sacred responsibility. If God has placed them within man, He also expects them to be used for good. By developing such talents, a man makes the world a more beautiful or pleasant place and advances mankind and himself as well.

2. Increase your knowledge and improve your skills: If you will learn to do things well, improving your skill and quality of work, confidence will increase. There is no satisfaction in doing a mediocre job.

3. Build success patterns: Strive to build success patterns in your work. If you meet with success in the beginning of a project, it will build confidence which will encourage another success. With this first success begin immediately to push forward. It is like a spiral upward.

To illustrate: An inexperienced salesman aims for success in the beginning by preparing himself as fully as he can. He wants to establish a pattern for success as soon as he can. This will give him greater confidence for the next. If this meets with success, he will have further confidence. He builds a success pattern that encourages both success and confidence.

But if, on the other hand, he were to say, *I have plenty of time, I don't care if I lose this first sale,* he is likely to fail. His failure undermines his confidence and encourages other failures. Or if he were to make a sizeable sale and decide to relax, he would drop into a down trend. In the absence of a positive factor, the trend is always downward rather than up.

Apply this principle to other activities, such as sports or public speaking. If you are called on to give a talk, do all you can to make it outstanding. This builds confidence which leads to future success. The trend is upward. Do not succumb to the temptation is accept a mediocre effort by saying, *My part is not very important.* It may not be important to anyone else, but it is extremely important to you. Fabulous careers often begin in the most unexpected ways.

This same plan should be followed in setting goals. Determine to leave no stone unturned to reach objectives. As you reach one objective, you will have confidence to reach another and another. If a young man will determine to reach the worthy goals he sets, he will develop a success pattern that will aid him throughout his entire life. If he does not, he will soon think of himself as incapable of reaching goals and will consequently not try.

4. Become a good conversationalist: Usually we are

inclined to think that to be a good conversationalist we must have a broad background of unusual experience, be an authority in some field or another, be colorful in the use of language, or have an acquaintance with many special subjects. This is not so. It is not difficult to be a good conversationalist. One need only have a superficial knowledge on a few subjects and speak the language reasonably well to converse with anyone. Here are a few guidelines.

a) Read widely: Know something of the main issues of the day. To help with this, read the daily newspaper, especially the main news items and the editorial page. Take a weekly news magazine. Read the scriptures fifteen minutes a day and read superficially on other subjects as you have the time.

b) Remember human interest stories: Develop a repertoire of experiences or human interest stories. This would include incidents you have read about, heard, or observed about people -something unusual, inspiring, or otherwise impressive. Also include humorous incidents, since people like to be amused.

c) Be interested in people: When you are conversing, be interested in the person - his life, his problems, his family, his goals, plans, and interests. Ask about these things and show a sincere interest as he talks. If he is enthusiastic, be so with him. If he is discouraged, show sympathy and understanding. Try to build his self-esteem. Give to him the things you would like to have if you were in his place. If he is excelling or reaching success, show appreciation for his success. It is seldom that men will be enthusiastic about another man's success. In such conversations as these you make warm friendships and leave both parties renewed.

d) Avoid the following: Avoid focusing the conversation on yourself. Although it is proper to tell interesting experiences about yourself, restrain from centering the conversation on yourself unless the other party shows an absorbing interest. Also avoid bragging, complaining, gossip, any attempt to demean anyone, coarseness, loud talking, vulgarity, profanity, or anything which would be offensive to the sensibilities.

e) Have a positive attitude: Present a pleasant, positive, optimistic, and enthusiastic attitude about life.

5. *Build character:* And last, if we are to build confidence, we must build character. This may be a new thought to you, but it is one of the keys to building an all-encompassing confidence. A man may have confidence in a specific ability or talent without this quality of character, but he will not have confidence in his total worth as an individual unless he has strong moral character. This is the kind of confidence which can be compared to steel.

In attaining character which leads to confidence, acquire the traits described in Chapter X, but especially the virtue of moral purity. This includes not only purity of actions, but purity of thought. God has said, *Let virtue garnish thy thoughts unceasingly and then shall thy confidence wax strong in the presence of God.*

To retain moral purity of thought, *avoid the very appearance of evil.* This includes pornography, trash literature, obscene movies or stage performances, or evil environments where obscene incidents occur. Reverence for the name of God is crucial if we are to enjoy his blessings. A contaminated mind kills out confidence.

12

Health

Let us turn again to the man of steel and velvet. We have learned that his steel side indicates strength, a strength which is derived principally from the firmness of his masculinity and the strength of his character. Completing this picture is a strong physical body, one which comes from good health.

What is genuine good health? It is not, as some may think, merely freedom from illness. The man with the strength of steel is in vigorous health. He has a strong body of remarkable endurance and well - developed muscles which are beautifully coordinated. There is life to his step and vitality in his manner. The vigor of his healthy body has, in a miraculous way, encouraged a vitality of spirit which increases his total liveliness. He has clear eyes, sound teeth, and a good color to his skin. We cannot help being reminded in seeing this wonderful specimen of manhood that *God made man in His own image,* and that man is, as Shakespeare declared, *in appearance like a god.*

In contrast, consider the man who is not healthy. He is not ill, as illness is generally defined; he keeps up the pace of life, but is not really healthy. He may have stooped shoulders, a sunken chest, weak muscles, sallow skin, and bags under his eyes. If he is overweight, his waistline is probably larger than his chest. He does not have vigor of spirit and manner, for his degenerate body lacks this vitality. He is not *in appearance like a god.*

Our modern life has sadly contributed to this degenerate condition. A man's work is apt to be confining, requiring a bare minimum of muscular endeavor. After work he goes from crowded offices into a heated or air-cooled automobile which carries him to a comfortable residence. If he engages in strenuous physical activity at all, it is only occasionally. In times past this situation was not nearly so acute. Life in the country demanded physical activity, and even in the cities men were forced out of doors at least part of the time, walking, riding horses or in carriages.

Our food supply is less than ideal. In plentiful America we have crops depleted of many of the nutrients they should have, grocery stores filled with artificial and processed foods, and an abundance of *junk* foods. Advertisements entice us to fill our bodies with alcohol, tobacco and soft drinks. The advantages of advanced medicine are largely canceled out by injurious substances we consume. We live in a world that invites death, not life.

A side effect of all this is that a sizeable portion of our population suffers needless or preventable deterioration and illness which could be avoided. There is great cost incurred as well. Not only are the resources of individuals depleted, but the government must provide benefits for those who are incapacitated in this way and are unable to solve their problems.

We can, however, take heart in the fact that good health is not out of reach for most of us, even in our advancing years. I have met men who enjoy good health into their eighties and nineties. But these are men who practice good health habits.

Fortunately there is a general awareness of the importance of health and a concern for the environment to see that optimal conditions are met. Many people take advantage of spas and exercise facilities and weight reduction programs. Education to discourage the use of tobacco and to limit its use to restricted areas is now the rule. Physical fitness is a way of life with millions. So these are encouraging signs. The following are basic principles to aid one in attaining good health:

Nutrition

Foods to eat: Wholesome foods fall into five categories:

Fresh fruit, fresh vegetables, nuts, whole grains and meats, which are to be used sparingly.

Here are some important guidelines to follow to achieve ✓ a balance in nutrition: Eat at least one yellow vegetable and one green leafy vegetable daily. Include some fresh and ripe fruit. Eat a third or more of your food raw (unless stomach trouble prevents this). Whole grains should be used rather than those which are refined such as white flour and white rice. Wheat was given to man as the staff of life and should be eaten daily.

Eat very little meat, if any, and avoid the fat of animals. ✓ Contrary to the teachings of the recent past, we learn that meat is not essential. In fact in the amounts consumed by most people in this country it is probably a health hazard. Milk and butter fall into this category. While we are still led to believe in advertising that these products are not only all right, but are critical elements for our health, we see strong evidence that they will become an *endangered species* if the present findings continue to hold up.

Be prepared for a vigorous battle by the vested interests who desire to market these products. Also beware of the temptation in yourself to deny the findings because you don't want to complicate your life with restrictions. Giving up the aroma of the outdoor barbecue will not be easy.

A guide to proper eating is to use fruits and vegetables ✓ as nearly as possible in the state God prepared them - apples, peaches, bananas, etc., as they come from the tree instead of in a rich dessert. Some fresh foods are available all year. Each season produces fruits, nuts, or berries and some fresh vegetables. Eat the foods which are in season. Grains remain fresh all year, so should be eaten at all times, as do beans and other dried foods.

The taste of food is not a safe guide to nutritive value. Bad foods often taste good. People acquire a taste for these foods through their use. Many foods which one would think should taste good do not taste good. I am referring to fruits and vegetables which are bland or tasteless.

The reason they do not taste good, in most cases, is

because they have been grown on depleted soil and have none of the flavor which should be present. It is my observation that God prepared food for us that is not only nutritious, but is delicious. If we had available food as it really should be, it is doubtful junk food would have the market it now has.

There are many people who have never enjoyed the flavor of a naturally grown tomato, as an example. To find such a tomato is difficult. Beautiful tomatoes full and plump in the market are enticing for those who know what they should taste like. But there is a disappointment awaiting if we expect them to taste like a tomato. This is the sad state of things for most fruits and vegetables.

I grew up thinking I did not like plums. While visiting at the home of a business associate I was offered a plum. *No thanks*, was my quick response, *I don't like them*. Not fearing to offend me, (we had had a business association for many years and he was almost like a brother) he insisted. *No thanks* was my continued reply. His persistence continued. *You've got to eat this plum*. I'm glad he insisted. For I then ate three of them.

What he gave me was a true plum, grown on organic soil and with the flavor our Creator had intended should be there. I have found this to be true for other things. Our Creator was overly generous in providing us the food we should eat.

Not only does He provide nutritious food, but it is usually in infinite variety. I was once going to plant some apple trees. The nursery to whom I wrote sent me a catalog listing one hundred and fifty varieties of apples. Just imagine! Apples in a variety of sizes and colors, some for cooking, some for eating *as is*. Some tart, some suited to a particular area.

What is true for apples is also true for other fruits and vegetables. Our available natural foods are also seasonal and adapted to the environments of the world's people - some tropical, some temperate. They are packaged for convenience in eating.

Oranges can be peeled and come to us with a separating membrane so we have bite-size. Garlic comes not only in a bulb, but can be separated into individual cloves. Notice how tight and secure the several membranes grow. Everything comes to us in a form for our convenience.

I am appalled at the arrogance of persons who feel they can improve on God's work. There is no way that baby formula is equal to mother's milk, for example. Obviously there are exceptions in particular cases of allergy or unavailability of the mother. But the exception does not change the fact.

The introduction of hormones or whatever stimuli to produce variations in our crops which offer a convenience to us is usually accompanied by a negative. These facts are becoming more clear all the time. I am not urging any one to become a *health nut*. What I am urging it that we understand the principle. The ideal way we might like to have is not usually available. But if we know, we can at least lean in that direction.

I have heard people argue that nutrition is not essential to health. To deny its importance is to reveal ignorance. For years it has been known that the growth, health, and quality of animals is directly affected by the way they are fed. The rancher cannot feed his animals inferior foods, or neglect and ignore proper nutrition without immediate harm. He has learned that he has only to apply the rules of nutrition to his stock to insure good results. Can a human being be less affected by his intake of food?

Foods to avoid: Our food supply has been contaminated by preservatives, refining, and processing which is harmful. Question all food which comes *packaged*. Read labels to see if they contain harmful preservatives. Prepared meats, such as wieners, bologna, and sausages usually contain several preservatives and are also about one-third fat. Avoid foods which are refined, such as white flour, white rice, white sugar, macaroni products, etc. Valuable food elements have been removed. Even when they are enriched after milling, they are inferior to the whole grains that God prepared for us. Avoid processed foods such as mixes, chips, and crackers. The rule is, eat foods as much as possible in the natural state.

Avoid overeating. In the world's highly developed

countries there are more people dying from over-eating than under-eating. Eating limited amounts of food is conducive to good health. (My personal opinion is that many people over-eat because of *hidden hunger* in not having the nutrients their bodies crave.) It is better to arise from the table not quite satisfied than to eat until all desire for food is gone. In an ideal situation it is probably better to eat two meals per day, rather than three. Simple meals are better than feasts. Time of eating is also important. It is wise not to eat late at night. Some serious students of the subject advise that one should not eat after 4:00 p.m. Certainly anything eaten later in the day should be light and easily digestible. Being overweight is a serious threat to health. Excess weight tears down the body and brings on ill health and shortens life. The extra burden imposed on the heart and other vital organs is too severe to go unheeded.

Exercise

There are many exercises which promote good health. These include walking, swimming, bicycling, weight-lifting, jogging, and athletic games such as basketball, handball and tennis. However, if you would like to achieve the maximum in abundant health, also include a complete program of exercise which will bring into play all the muscles of the body.

For a guide to such a complete program, I recommend you obtain a reliable exercise book. After establishing a daily exercise program, supplement this with vigorous outdoor activity such as jogging or swimming. The important thing is to engage in something which will cause deep breathing and bring you into the sunshine. Adequate exercise will reduce to some extent the damage caused by a diet lacking in nutrients. Some authorities feel exercise is more critical to one's health than nutrition.

Sleep

You will probably find that if you exercise regularly and

vigorously, you will need less sleep. But get sufficient sleep to feel rested. For best sleep it is wise to retire early and arise early. It has been said that an hour of sleep before midnight is worth two after midnight.

Provide yourself with a firm mattress. A good mattress is one of the best investments you can make. See that your children also have a firm mattress. It is unfortunate that so many people afford so many needless luxuries and deny themselves a good mattress.

If you have difficulty sleeping, try the relaxing method. First, think calm thoughts. Think of clear water, forests, birds, or a placid lake. Then begin with the top of your head and tell yourself to relax the skull, the eyes, the brows, the mouth, etc. If you think relaxing thoughts, your body will relax. Then do the same to your neck and shoulders, loosening up every muscle and joint so that they are limp and placid. Follow this same method with your chest. When you get to the abdomen tell yourself that your body is very heavy, very relaxed. Do the same with the legs and feet. When you reach the feet, think of your entire body as relaxed and heavy, sinking into the mattress. After this if you have not dropped off to sleep, begin the process again. Do it a third time if necessary. It is not likely you could remain awake longer than this.

Fresh Air

Fresh air, which until recent times was taken for granted, is now more difficult to come by. Awareness of this need is widely recognized. It is hoped this awareness will be sufficiently felt to correct the abuses of air pollution. Everyone is needed to contribute his part in keeping the air fresh.

Proper air supply includes both oxygen and moisture. Oxygen is obtained by circulation of enclosed air with that outside to obtain a fresh supply. Outdoor exercise is also important, for it causes deep breathing. The lungs contain thousands of little alveoli which need ventilation. Shallow breathing fails to bring the fresh air into these little alveoli which may remain closed and stagnant. The lungs resemble a balloon and should be inflated to full capacity to expel impurities and rejuvenate them with the purifying action of oxygen.

The lack of moisture in the air caused by inadequate furnaces results in much illness, including colds, sore throats, coughs, and even inflamed lungs. For solutions, install a moisturizer in your furnace or use a room vaporizer while the furnace is running. If necessary, hang wet bath towels in rooms you occupy or boil water. Ideally the furnace should be turned off at night and the windows opened for ventilation.

Water

All plant and animal life require sunshine, air, and water. Our bodies are made up predominantly of water, being more than two-thirds by weight. As water is required in bodily function, it must be used over and over. Essential to health, then, is a fresh water supply daily. Three quarts is recommended, which is probably much more than the average person drinks.

Mental Health

As with the other topics of health, we can only deal superficially with mental health in this writing. Most important is to stress the effect of mental health on the body. If the mind is at peace, the body responds better to food and exercise. If the mind is filled with turmoil, unhappiness or unrest, the body is adversely affected and may succumb to illness or death.

The source of mental health lies in attaining good character. We are promised in the scriptures, *The fruit of the Spirit is love, joy, peace, long-suffering, gentleness, goodness, faith, meekness, temperance* (Gal. 5:22) Anyone who has these virtues does not usually have mental difficulties.

Dr. J. A. Hadfield, one of England's foremost psychiatrists, has said, *I am convinced that the Christian religion is one of the most potent influences for producing that harmony, peace of mind, and confidence of soul needed to bring health to a large proportion of nervous patients.*

The fruits of a deficient character are negative traits such as worry, anxiety, hatred, envy, anger, greed, and fear. These traits induce mental turmoil. I would like to especially point out the harmful effects of anger and hatred as they cause disability to destroy the body.

The damaging effects of anger were dramatically brought to me by an experience of a friend who owned a dairy. He was short-tempered and impatient, but was otherwise an honorable man. One morning he arrived at his plant to find that someone had failed to assemble the bottling equipment properly, and the morning milk deliveries were being delayed by two hours. He became so furious that he felt quite ill and had to return home. On the way he suffered a fatal heart attack in his car.

Another example concerns a man who was swindled out of seventeen thousand dollars. His wife said that he was so overcome with anger that he would awaken at night and pace the floor. He also died of a heart attack.

We must recognize that anger afflicts nearly everyone. But this type of resentful anger is a weakness of character which is destructive to both body and spirit and must be overcome if we are to maintain peace of mind and health. We must develop strong character, learn the principles of forgiveness, patience, and humility, and overcome an over-materialistic nature by developing a sound sense of values. In this way we will control, if not eliminate, anger.

In summary we can say that good character leads to mental health. This in turn induces good physical health which is the physical health that provides the strength of steel found in the ideal man.

That good character can bring forth physical strength is difficult for some to believe. But, as in many eternal things, it is difficult to prove except by experience of your own. If any man will employ the principles of good health and develop a fine character, he will be able to see for himself what hidden strength it brings to his physical body. He will be able to say as Lancelot did in the Legend of King Arthur; *My strength comes from my purity.*

Work

There is something in one's make-up which demands that he be employed in useful work if he is to have continued good health. Perhaps this is the reason God cursed the ground for man's sake and commanded him to earn his bread by the sweat of his face. Sustained work, accompanied by a willing attitude, brings forth natural functions which rejuvenate the body. Many people who are in good health into old age attribute their condition to a life of steady work. I read an account of a ninety-year-old cowboy who was still riding the range. My next door neighbor who was ninety-five was still climbing trees, and I heard of a man of 113 years who was still gardening crops on a tractor. Work is a blessing, not a curse.

The benefit of work is not in physical exercise alone. If this were true, those who work at desks would receive little benefit. The greatest effects of work, especially demanding work, is the feeling of usefulness which it brings to the individual.

Retirement is often a grave mistake. Some men look forward for many years to the time they will retire and live a life of ease. But when the time comes, they find that the loss of physical activity and the realization that they are no longer needed in the world's important work has robbed them of a feeling of usefulness, and they degenerate. It would be wiser for one to cut down his work rather than retire completely.

Work, My Blessing Not My Doom

Let me but do my work from day to day
In field or forest, at the desk or loom,
In roaring market place, or tranquil room.

Let me but find in my heart to say,
When vagrant wishes beckon me astray,
This is my work, my blessing, not my doom.

216

Of all who live, I am the one by whom
This work can best be done in the right way.

Then shall I find it not too great or small,
To suit my spirit, and to prove my powers,
Then shall I cheerfully greet the laboring hours,
And eventide, to play and love and rest,
Because I know, for me, my work is best.

Relaxation

The body needs relaxation of three types: 1) Relaxation while working. 2) Relaxation through rest. 3) Relaxation by engaging in activities which are a diversion from work.

You may have wondered why some men can work for long hours and never seem to tire, while others weary at almost the beginning of a job. This may be due to the person's ability to relax while working. The muscles work with greater efficiency when relaxed than when tense, and thus have greater endurance. The pianist learns to relax while playing and is able to practice or perform for long hours without tiring. The public speaker learns that if he keeps his voice muscles relaxed, he can speak for many hours without tiring, but when tense, he may tire in thirty minutes. The laborer also can work with less tiring if he is relaxed.

A six year old boy had been playing hard outside all afternoon. After dinner he wanted to go to a friend's house who lived half a mile away. His mother suggested he must be tired and suggested he rest before going. He responded, *No, I'm not tired. I want to go now. Besides, I can ride my stick horse..*

Relaxing at work is accomplished largely by mental attitude. For example, when working at a difficult task, think of the word *relax*. Let your mind tell your muscles what to do. You will immediately find that you have mind control over your muscles and they will obey the command of the mind. When you tell your muscles to *relax*, there will be an immediate reaction felt.

Relaxing in activities is difficult for some. They find they become so wound up in a game that they are tense. This does not mean that one cannot be enthusiastic when playing a game. But play it so as to gain the maximum physical and mental benefit. Even the champion will often admit that being relaxed is the key to his doing his best.

In summary, we have reviewed briefly eight basic rules for good health. Although the knowledge can serve as a guide, only in application will the benefits be seen. Self-discipline is required to adopt new health habits when one is used to doing things a different way. This is not easy, but the benefits are tremendous.

As a suggestion, if you have been eating deficient foods, encourage your wife to begin your new program by removing all unhealthful foods from your shelves. Be determined to purchase only those foods which are nutritious. As she plans each day's meals, she will have to use more imagination than formerly to create tasty meals, but the results will be better nutrition. By following this rule, she will be forced to prepare wholesome meals.

If you have had little or no exercise, adopt an exercise program and practice daily. Doing it only occasionally will not bring the results you want. Use discipline, and exercise regularly. A good diet and exercise can transform a person's health so that he will feel noticeable effects within two weeks. Six months is required to achieve maximum results.

The rewards of good health are difficult to describe to someone who feels run-down. He has probably come to assume that he feels normal and about as he should. But there is a new life which comes into the body and a feeling of well-being which makes the effort worth it a thousand times over. It is safe to challenge anyone to a health program for six months with a promise that he will become a believer.

Part 2

The Velvet

We have discussed many of the steel qualities which provide the basis of character and dependability in a man - his firmness, sense of duty, dedication to responsibility, reliability in meeting tests and being strong in the face of adversity. At appropriate times we see sternness and immovability. Like the great raw buttresses providing inner strength in a building, such are the qualities to sustain a man in his trials and to instill confidence in those who follow his leadership.

But with these qualities alone, a serious lack exists, as with a building having no outside beauty. The velvet qualities we shall study in this section offer the softness, gentleness and tenderness, understanding and refinement of character which a man must have to round himself out as a manly individual.

There may be men who would resist some of these virtues as being unmanly or *sissified*. Perhaps standing alone this might be true. But as a thoroughly functioning building of maximum utility becomes a work of art by its design and outward beauty, the velvet qualities gives a man refinement that makes him a polished individual. These qualities of velvet cushion the steel so they don't sand forth in their sheer raw force to startle or frighten. It gives to the strong hand the gentle touch. To women this is indispensable.

In his classical novel *Great Expectations,* Charles Dickens gives a wonderful example of the velvet in a man. *Joe the blacksmith* was a true man of steel and velvet, but I will focus on his *velvet* side:

Pip, a young boy whose mother died when he was very young, was brought up by his sister and her husband Joe.

Later on Pip was offered a generous opportunity in the city by Mr. Jaggers, who represented an unknown benefactor. To accept this opportunity Pip must be released from his apprenticeship to Joe in the blacksmith trade. In the proposal, Mr. Jaggers offered Joe compensation. Joe responded with:

As compensation for what? Joe demanded, to which Mr. Jaggers answered, *For the loss of his services.* Then Pip describes the rest of the scene and his tender feelings for Joe:

Joe laid his hand upon my shoulder with the touch of a woman. I have often thought of him since, like the steel hammer that can crush a man or pat an egg shell, with his combination of strength and gentleness. Then Joe, an uneducated man who could not read or write added: *Pip is hearty welcome, to go free with his services, to honor and fortune, as no words can tell him. But if you think money can make compensation to me for the loss of the little child - what come to the forge - and ever the best of friends.*

Years later Pip reflects: *Oh, dear good Joe, whom I was so ready to leave and so unthankful to. I see you again with your muscular blacksmith's arm before your eyes, and your broad chest heaving, and your voice dying away. Oh, dear, good, faithful, tender Joe. I feel the loving tremble of your hand upon my arm, as solemnly this day as if it had been the rustle of an angel's wing.*

13

Understanding Women

In millions of homes every day there are men leaving for work who probably have as their last words, *Who can understand a woman? What makes her act that way?*

This lack of understanding between the sexes arises from the fact that women are not like men. They do not think as men do. They are different in temperament, characteristics, and needs. They have a different world of responsibility and therefore a different set of problems. They view problems differently.

And yet women can be understood. To gain such an understanding is to attain a liberal education - one that is essential to the velvet in a man. The following are some of the most basic needs and characteristics to understand if you are to live with a woman in peace and happiness.

The first two needs have to do with love. I identify these as christian love and romantic love. It would be easier to explain if our language had a separate word for each, for these are not the same emotion. Both, however, are essential to a woman's happiness and feeling of security with her husband. Let's consider these two needs:

Her Need For Christian Love

Christian love is a concern for the welfare and happiness of another person. So far as the wife is concerned, she must know that her husband will stand by her in all circumstances. Whatever trouble or concerns she has are his also. *She knows he will never desert her whatever her need.* When ill or discouraged, she has a true and loyal friend. This assurance is rooted in her confidence that her husband loves her not only because she is pretty or young or vivacious, but because she is a human being who has needs.

It seems that a man who loves a woman romantically would also love her with a christian love. One would think so, but this is not necessarily true. A man may have tender romantic feelings for her and at the same time be selfish. It may be that what she does for him is more important than what he does for her. Should she fail in any way to meet expectations, his feelings could cool. These are subtle concerns usually more than expressed doubts. But her fear of this is terribly disturbing. She must feel *secure* in her love for her husband and his love for her.

A man may resent any implication that he lacks christian love for his wife. He may defend himself saying he has always provided for her, been faithful and done many things to make her comfortable and happy. He will remember times when he has sacrificed and gone beyond the call of duty. But, in spite of many kindnesses through the years, if she doubts his deepest concern when she is in distress, he appears to be, in her eyes, *a fair weather friend.* A woman must have the assurance that her husband will stand by her in all circumstances (not just when he feels like it) if she is to feel truly loved.

If a man lacks this christian love, his romantic love will strike her as superficial and insincere. She may regard his tenderness as manipulative. It will be difficult to forget her hurt when she has been deserted or neglected.

Her Need For Romantic Love

> Love is to man a thing apart,
> 'Tis woman's whole existence.
> - Lord Byron

Romantic love is a tender soul-stirring feeling a man and woman experience for one another. It is, in fact, the all-consuming emotion that brings them to marriage. After marriage, a man needs only a vague assurance that his wife really loves him. In a woman this need is *intense*. It continues

222

from day to day *for the rest of her life*. Few men realize this need. Neglect brings much unhappiness and frustration to women. The following example is typical of a man's attitude:

The story is told of a man who told his wife on their wedding day, *I want you to know I love you. If I didn't, I wouldn't have married you. I expect to continue to love you, but don't expect me to say any more about it. Remember! I've already said it.* She was speechless and, guided by instinct, said, *Oh, I can't remember something like that. I think you will have to remind me again and again.* For a woman to flourish she must have this assurance just as plants need sunshine and water. Deprive her of this and she wilts on the vine, as in the following example:

A man of my acquaintance who loved his wife dearly suffered the terrible blow of losing her in death. He was left with several small children and in his predicament felt an urgent need to find a second wife. His bride had never been married and suddenly found herself with a family and full household. She entered marriage hopefully and determined to succeed in her new responsibilities.

Her husband loved her to a degree, but never sufficiently to allow her to forget his first wife. He grieved her death openly. His attitude was that his new wife was fortunate to get a ready-made family of adorable children and a husband to provide for her. He felt he was giving her everything she required and deserved. His appreciation was the type he would extend to a housekeeper.

Denying her the love and tenderness every woman needs affected her tragically. I saw a withering effect take place, observed the tender blossom fade on the vine until she was reduced to a common drudge. She lost the vitality she formerly had and became harsh and disagreeable. His lack of love destroyed her finer qualities.

Men are not harmed by the lack of love to the same degree women are. A normal man, if denied love, usually throws himself into his work and finds compensating fulfillment there. Or he may concentrate on achievements outside his work where he obtains admiration or praise which is *his* greater need. He manages to survive and make a fairly adequate life for himself. Not so with a woman. If she is denied love, she will suffer as no man could comprehend. Her whole existence shakes at the foundations.

If men realized this need in women and the pain experienced when she is unloved, it would be difficult to imagine how he could be so cruel as to tell his wife he no longer loves her, or that he is interested in another woman. It seems there would be some compassion for her suffering that would prevent this cruelty. He would be driven to plead to God for insight to sustain him until love could be rekindled.

How to Love Her

1. *Cultivate a Feeling of Love:* It might seem on the surface impossible for a man to do anything to awaken his feelings of love for his wife. He would expect his wife to bring this feeling about by her own femininity and charm. But the miracle is that there *are* things he can do to cultivate his feelings of love.

As a beginning, remember the past. Think of how you felt when you fell in love with her. There was a time, no doubt, when she was the center of all your thoughts. You probably thought that if she could be constantly with you that you would need nothing more. No matter how cloudy the day, it would be sunshine if she were there. If she had faults you could not see them. You wanted to shield her, care for her and protect her.

Think now of the sacrifices she makes for you. Life has not been easy during your years of marriage. All marriages have disappointments. and you have had your share of these. Remember how she supported you when you were discouraged. Remember your plans and your hopes.

If you have children, you have seen her sacrifices in bearing them. Think of the hundreds and thousands of meals she has prepared, think of the errands she has run, the trips to school and music lessons, her comfort to injured children, changing dirty diapers, efforts to fix her face when she was dead

224

tired. Think of the *dates* you've had together. Think of the good times, the foolish mistakes, the things you share in common which no one else knows about. She has been an intimate part of your life for a long time. You share a long-term investment together. Reflect on these things. Be appreciative!

Now suppose you remember and appreciate her, as has just be reviewed, but find it difficult to love her in a *romantic* way because she has lost her feminine charm. She just isn't the woman she used to be. When this is the problem, the following thoughts will be of special value to you:

Remember, it is *the man* who awakens a woman's feminine charm. *He* is the one who makes her blossom and bloom, by the way he conducts himself and the way he treats her. He can make her beautiful, charming and radiant, or he can make her ugly and disagreeable.

To solve this problem, apply the teachings of this book. Be a man. Protect her, provide for her and lead her with firmness. Treat her like a queen and help her have a feeling of self-worth. Apply all of the velvet qualities. In this way you can make her blossom into her full womanhood, regain lost charms so you can love her as you once did. This is the miracle that cultivates your feeling of love for her.

2. *Express Love:* It is not only important that a man *feel* love for his wife, he *must express it*. This love can be expressed in a variety of ways, such as words and tender affection. A man needs not be adept with words as the poets to express the feelings of his heart. A woman thrives on the humblest of speech when it is sincerely given. Tenderness is one of the most appreciated expressions of love for a woman. A touch of the hand, a pat on the shoulder or the head, a tender word or term, or any act of affection moves her emotions. She thrives on these small manifestations of love.

Most men have no idea how important it is to a woman to hear expressions of love. This is like the food she eats which sustains her life. Just because you feel love for her is little assurance she understands the measure of the love you feel. You must spell it out! And this must be part of her daily fare. Because you spoke lovingly and tenderly yesterday will not be sufficient to tide her over today.

3. *Prove Love:* It is deeply embedded in the nature of a woman to count love as sincere only when a man does something to prove it. Perhaps this is why little girls are so attracted to fairy tales in which the hero rescues the princess from a castle wall, or from the clutches of a witch or from a villain who ties her to a railroad track. In each case the hero does something to prove his love. This is illustrated in the story, *The Gift of the Magi,* by O. Henry:

The story concerns a young married couple deeply in love. In near poverty, they have only two possessions of real worth - Della's beautiful long hair and Jim's gold watch that had been his father's and his grandfather's. Della had often looked longingly in a shop window at two tortoise shell combs with jeweled rims - something she knew they could never afford. On Christmas Eve the two young lovers found themselves penniless. Eager to prove their love for each other and without knowledge of one another, they made a noble and willing sacrifice. Della sold her beautiful hair to buy a gold chain for Jim's prized watch. Jim sold his gold watch to buy the two beautiful combs for Della's hair. As the author said:

And here I have lamely related to you the uneventful chronicle of two foolish children in a flat who most unwisely sacrificed for each other the greatest treasures of their house. But in a last word to the wise of these days, let it be said that of all who give gifts these two were the wisest. Of all who give and receive gifts, such as they are the wisest. Everywhere they are wisest.

In the mind of a man, having a distinctly different orientation than she has, he no doubt feels he proves his love by hours of toil in providing the living, his devotion and loyalty, his patience with her weaknesses, and of course his fidelity. This is a tangible evidence of love and duty, but don't think this is sufficient in her eyes. She looks at these as your obligations, just as she has an obligation to serve you meals and keep the house tidy. She looks for something beyond the call of duty to prove love.

In proving love there must be an element of *sacrifice*. It ✓ is voluntary and beyond the call of duty. There must be an extra effort given, something one goes without, some trouble in attaining the object of proven love. It also requires being sensitive to her needs, her desires, deep feelings and even whims.

Without being sensitive to her needs, a man may make a sacrifice but fail to prove his love so far as she is concerned. It is like the little boy who thinks his mother will be excited about having the little toy car he gives her. The sacrifice must be for the exact thing needed. For example, had Jim bought a new dress for Della rather than the combs, he would have been insensitive to her need. Often it is an insignificant item or small favor a woman wants so desperately, but because a man is dense and unaware of these desires, he misses the opportunity. Sensitivity to her needs affects her profoundly, as you may now realize. A personal experience illustrates this point:

We lived in a house with a serving bar between the kitchen and eating area. The eating space was small, and my wife often remarked that it would greatly improve the kitchen if this bar were removed. I had some doubts since it required considerable patch-up of the tile on the cabinet, the floor coverings and the walls. But her desire persisted without much hope. She didn't ask, but I was aware of her wishes.

While she was visiting relatives for a few days, I decided to surprise her by remodeling the kitchen. It was a trying job as most small jobs turn out to be. But when it was finished, it looked great and I wondered why I hadn't thought of it. I bought a round table and some new chairs and had the job completed when she returned.

I shall never forget her joy in my thoughtfulness. She leaned against the doorway in total silence. Then she began weeping. She has reminded me many times since that this was one of the happiest moments of her life.

Sometimes in desperation a woman will ask a special favor merely as a test of a man's love. She may not feel so much a need for the favor as a need to see tangible evidence of his love. Children often do this - just a little checking on their part to see if their parents still love them.

There is something in the male psyche which causes him to resist giving his wife something he thinks she expects. If he also senses that the desire is more to prove love than satisfy a legitimate need, he will probably resent the whole thing and determine to give her nothing. If she hints for a birthday present or to be taken to dinner, he puts the idea aside although he may have previously thought of it. The very thing she wants and needs she is denied because she made the mistake of asking.

Although it runs counter to the masculine nature to give in to such requests, it is wise to give in and do it in good spirit. There is a biblical scripture which asks, *If a son shall ask bread of any of you that is a father will he give him a stone? Or if he ask a fish, will he give him a serpent?* If a woman needs proof of a man's love, should she be denied this proof? *If she asks for bread, should she be given a stone?*

Proving love when asked is certainly not the most significant way to demonstrate one's feelings. But temporarily it will fill a need which is very important. When requests are made, this indicates that a man may have failed to assure her of his love. In the future it is hoped he will seek opportunities to fill this need without being asked.

Romantic love is of great significance. It has always been the theme of impressive music, art, and literature - the very center of the drama of life. To have life center around love is the most sound of reasoning. Is any subject of greater importance to both men and women? Are other efforts a man can render of more worth than love and tenderness in his marriage relationship - the very center of a happy home?

Treat Her Like A Queen

Treat a woman like a queen and she will act like one. It is a fact that if you place a high value on a person and let him know that you regard him highly, he will grow to be that finer person. Especially is this true with women. If they are held in high esteem they take on a regal attitude which makes them queenly.

The story of Johnny Lingo bears out this message. This story concerns a young Polynesian girl who was downgraded by her father to the point that she and everyone else considered her an inferior person. She deteriorated until she no longer combed her hair, and often hid behind the banana trees to hide herself from the mockery of society. So diminished was she in the eyes of everyone that she had no feeling of self-worth.

A young man who lived on another island knew her when she was a little girl. He always remembered her and recognized her true worth. When he grew to manhood, he decided to go back to her island and ask for her hand in marriage. He was evidently aware of her deterioration, but believed in her intrinsic worth and meant to rescue her.

As was the custom in this society when a man asked for a girl in marriage, he bargained for her with *cows*. If a woman was considered ordinary he may have to pay only one cow for her. If she was of great worth and the competition was keen, he may have to pay three or four cows. Women took pride in how many cows they were bargained for, and there was a special value in having their suitors sacrifice for them.

When Johnny came to the home of the girl, he set out to bargain with her father. Her father was prepared to give her away for one cow and feel he had the best of the bargain. But to his astonishment, Johnny offered eight cows. When asked why he did not bargain for the girl, he said he wanted everyone to know, and especially his wife to know, that she was worth this higher value. As he took her by the hand, a change came over her - a realization of her worth. She took on the dignity befitting a person worth *eight cows*. She unfolded like a lily in the spring with the fascinating charm of a real woman.

Unfortunately, men usually fall short in making a woman feel queenly. By criticism or slighting remarks they treat women like inferiors. I was offended to hear a business associate speak of his wife as *the old lady*. Men are quick to criticize *women drivers* and yet expect women to drive and run errands for them. Some men make demands on their wives to the point of causing them to feel like slaves. They ignore them or treat them with indifference. Anything which depreciates them in value diminishes their womanliness.

The evil effects of this downgrading has more far-reaching and destructive effects than most men realize. Many women have been lured into the feminist movement because they feel men have let them down. Most women would not give the feminists a second thought if their men honored them in the many ways women expect and deserve to be honored. I quote from a pleading letter.

Let the men who are contemptuous of the women's liberation activist take a good look at themselves and take a personal inventory of their attitude towards women in general. Perhaps they will develop some insight as to where they have failed as men - failed to show appreciation for true womanhood and all that womanhood represents. Perhaps they will come to realize that women are members of the same human race they themselves belong to.

Prior to the fall of communism, Russian women were not treated as queens. (Hopefully, over time, this will change. But with the desire of many of them to follow American tradition this possibility seems unlikely.) They were regarded as equals with men and required to do the work men do. Now they are crying out for tenderness and chivalry that they might feel like women.

It has been a backward step in the United States. The emergence of the feminist movement has downgraded the woman's position so that she is treated often as one would treat a man. Some women have claimed this is what they want, but many are now rejecting this philosophy. They do not always know what they want, but they do know they are unhappy as things are. A woman becomes what a man esteems her to be - be she queen or slave.

Allow For Her Mistakes

Being human, women make mistakes. They may be late, or fail to have dinner on time, or the food will not taste just right. Sometimes the house is not well kept, especially when there are children. Women may not handle children wisely or may spend money foolishly. They make stupid remarks. The usual male response is to be harsh or critical. She may have pleased her man in a hundred other ways, but let her make one mistake and he expresses harsh disapproval. We want an angel for a wife, but she will make mistakes. Do not give her reason to believe her greatest mistake was to marry you.

Your wife's mistake gives you an excellent opportunity to turn a lemon into lemonade. The husband who has patience to smile and withhold criticism, and especially to say something endearing, does something that is most unexpected. If you not only allow for a mistake, but are forgiving, understanding and sympathetic and even more - help her correct the consequence of her error, she will probably be brought to tears. She will realize her husband is a rare jewel. The following suggestions will help as you allow for her mistakes:

1. Develop Humility: A man who is humble is not quick to criticize the mistakes of others. He realizes he is imperfect and subject to error. His mistakes will not be the same as hers. A woman who is habitually late is exasperating to a man who is punctual. But she will have a compensating virtue he lacks, and it may well be a more important one. A critical person is vulnerable to embarrassment, for he is sure to be caught in the fault he criticizes others for.

2. Look to Her Better Side: Looking at the positive is good therapy. When the spotlight is not concentrated on the fault, it does not seem so important.

When a woman continually makes mistakes which burden others, it becomes her husband's obligation to teach her, if he has the capacity to do it. If she is a poor housekeeper or poor cook, perhaps he can encourage her to get instruction. She needs to know how important it is to you to have a well-organized home and meals which are adequate and on time. She must know that a part of the success in her life is to become adept in these skills, and a serious responsibility attaches to it.

If she is habitually late, help her understand how

inconsiderate it is to keep others waiting. She may not understand that such a habit is a selfish disregard for the time and comfort of others. Teach her as you would a child, if her fault is a childish one. If she spends money foolishly, she can be taught the principles of economy either by yourself or by special instruction. Let her know that it places an extra burden on you when she is careless with money.

If this instruction is given with kindness, free of sarcasm or ridicule, and with an assurance that you do not consider yourself perfect, a woman will usually respond favorably. Otherwise she will resent unexpected criticism, especially when she is tired or overwhelmed with her duties.

In review, we can say that it is never wise to criticize. Express sympathy and be understanding and forgiving. Help her overcome the problems caused by her failure. If you don't do this it will compound the problem. The mistake itself has caused suffering enough. Don't add to it. If she continually makes the same mistake, you must teach her with kindness and patience.

Understand Her Responsibilities in the Home

In understanding the woman's role as the wife, mother and homemaker, there are three important things to understand: 1) Her pressing and demanding responsibility, 2) the tendency for her life to be confining and monotonous, and 3) the importance of her work and *her need to understand its importance.*

In viewing the woman's life, we must remember that not all women have the same demands in the home. Some have no children, others have one or two, and others have four, five, six, or more. Some women will have reared their children and may have less pressing responsibility. But all women who are running a household must have consideration for their duties, which under any circumstance are demanding.

1. Her Demanding Responsibilities as a Mother and Homemaker: In her role as a homemaker a woman faces a life of long hours and demanding responsibility. She must prepare meals regularly and for every day of the year.

She must continually shop for food, considering costs, nutrition, and pleasing the family appetites. If she is a good cook she may spend hours in the kitchen in a single day, hours which are seldom noticed or appreciated. She must continually fight dirt and wear and tear in the household. Carpets, floors and furniture become soiled and worn. Clothing must be washed and rewashed. Clothes, shoes and socks wear out and must be replaced by sewing or shopping. If her husband moves her from place to place, she must adjust her household furnishings to the new environment. There is usually painting to do, new curtains to make, and a period of getting settled to make her new place attractive.

Her role as a mother is demanding. Her children are not like little stuffed animals. They are human beings with a need for love and understanding. Her children need instruction, discipline, attention, and even entertaining. She cares for them when they are sick or injured. She escorts them to music lessons, doctors' appointments and to activities and recreation. Her life is made up of a myriad of tasks, many of them menial. No one of them seems great, but when viewed as a total responsibility, it becomes overwhelming. Her responsibility is different from a man's. Only when her children are sick does she feel urgency. But her demands are continual, often lasting before sunrise and after sunset.

When a young woman marries and has children very soon, she may have a difficult adjustment to this new responsibility. As the burden of family life is suddenly thrust upon her, she may lose the bloom of her youth. The light may go out of her eyes and the laughter fade as she faces the tremendous burdens of the household. She may have a marvelous attitude and feel life is giving her what she has always wanted and hoped for and dreamed about, but she may not feel adequately prepared for her new and overwhelming tasks. There are a number of things a man can do to preserve his wife's bloom both in her young years and throughout her entire life by understanding her responsibility and seeking to minimize her work.

The first thing is make certain you are not the one who

233

is burdening her by expecting too much. Very often it is the man who makes unnecessary demands, requesting special food which takes hours to prepare, demands his pajamas be ironed, his shirts hand-made, or his shoes polished. If his wife is already burdened, it is thoughtless and unkind to add anything to that burden. Often by lessening demands, he can ease the load enough to make her load bearable.

Some men even go so far as to bring office work home for their wives to do, such as typing, bookkeeping, and research work. They apparently have no thought as to the burdens she has already. Many sweet wives willingly obey.

Among the first things a man should do is to get his wife settled as early in married life as possible. Sometimes his career will prevent this, but if he will pursue his career quickly (as when he is still in school) and not waste time on foolishness, she can get settled into *her* career sooner. Some women want the change and excitement of a move, and some adjust very well. But it is nevertheless difficult for her to function in her role and devote herself to husband and family if she is wandering around.

Next, get her settled in a home of her own. A man would do well to listen to his wife on housing, since it will be the center of her world and responsibility. Consider her feelings, giving them priority over your own. Throughout this book I have been emphasizing that a woman has an important career as wife, mother and homemaker. The facility in which she manages this career should meet her needs as completely as possible. Show her the respect she deserves. The only thing a man has a right to insist on is that it be within his means.

Choose a location that is convenient to schools and shopping on a street with a homey atmosphere. Choose a home that is not too large or small for family needs. A man often wants a larger home, the utmost he can afford. This is his desire for status or perhaps a wish to give her the best he can provide. It can turn out to be a disservice if management is beyond her capacity. Don't buy her a castle unless you can supply the servants as well. A woman needs a house she can manage. Once you have an adequate house, work to make it convenient for her. Build shelves where needed and good laundry facilities. Buy essential furniture and play equipment for the children. Prepare her for her life ahead.

As children come and responsibilities increase, help her minimize her work by getting rid of too many possessions. The accumulation of excess baggage by either husband or wife often creates needless problems. I am not talking about *junk*, but such things as furniture and clothes. Most families have too many *things*. People who can simplify their lives by having only what they really need often avoid problems.

If she is disorganized, help her create a smooth-running system where each person has specific duties. Help her list her responsibilities in priorities and encourage her to concentrate on the important things and let minor details go. Help her see where she is wasting time and energy on non-essentials. Sometimes women try too hard to please on non-essentials and then find it difficult to find time for the more urgent matters. This help needs to be given with patience and kindness, assuring her that you are anxious to do everything you can to ease her burdens.

One of the greatest responsibilities a woman has day-in, day-out is the meals. If her work is burdening, encourage her to have simple meals, easy to prepare. Rather than demanding elaborate meals, tell her you will be satisfied with simple nutritious food. When she voluntarily spends hours in the kitchen preparing food to please you, don't make the mistake of over-doing your appreciation as this will encourage her to spend more time in this pursuit. Instead, explain that although you appreciate her efforts, you prefer she spend her time and energy on preserving her health and beauty.

Certainly not the least thing a man can do to ease burdens is to pitch in and help when he is available. There is no way his masculinity is lessened when he fixes the meals, changes the baby, does the laundry, or cleans the house. Under such circumstances, he is really more of a man.

And last, express understanding for her continual responsibility, and appreciation for her efforts. Somehow, whatever we do no matter how difficult, seems easier and

235

worth the effort if it is appreciated.

2. *Her Confining Life:* When a woman is tied down with little children, her life becomes confining and may seem like a narrow existence. She needs a broader view and diversion from the home scene. The trouble is that when a man comes home, his needs are usually different. If his work has been demanding, he may want to shrink inside his four walls and get away from the world. He does not necessarily want to go any place or do anything. This incompatibility requires understanding of both man and wife. There are things you can do to relieve these feelings of confinement.

First, tell her about your life away from home. The broader the picture, the better. Be honest and let her know the good and the bad. Some men give a blown-up picture of life away from home, hoping to win praise and gratitude. Others emphasize the negative, hoping to find sympathy. An honest picture will help her see life as it really is and will be more likely to make her content with her own circumstances.

A man should take his wife out of the confines of her home frequently, especially if she is tied down with children. Even though he does not need or desire the diversion himself, *concern for her* demands that he do it. If circumstances permit, take her to distant places, as it will broaden her whole scope of life. I know a man with a large family who has taken his wife all over the world. This is not something most people can do, but it has done everything for this woman and made her a better mother and wife.

If a man is self-employed or circumstances are otherwise favorable, it will also help if he will occasionally take his wife to work and let her see him in action. Ask her advice about your problems and let her feel a part of your world. Do not think it beneath your dignity to share your world with her. This is customary with men and women who are very close. The counsel a man receives from his wife may well be the most valuable advice he receives.

Provide breaks in her routine by entertainment and diversions. Women love going out to dinner, not so much for the meal as for the opportunity to get dressed up and have a break away from the routine of home life. She usually returns refreshed and anxious to assume her duties again.

A woman can also overcome her narrow feeling by giving benevolent service. If she can increase the circle of her love and concern for people beyond her own family, she will broaden her perspective. As she becomes aware of the problems of others, her own world expands tremendously and she loses the self-centered feeling she might otherwise have. This requires cooperation on the part of her husband - something he may find hard to give, for she is going to have less time for him and some of the things he has grown to expect. Many men are selfish and feel a woman must spend all her time on him. This attitude is defeating, for although he demands her time, he will lose the benefit of her broader experience. Benevolence truly enriches a woman's life and makes her a better person.

3. Her Need to Feel Her Work Is Important: I read of a doctor's wife who developed a feeling that her work in the home was meager and insignificant when compared to that of her husband who was saving life. He took time almost daily to assure her that her work was as important as his. She was shaping human life, which is as important as saving it. She was a builder of society. Her work in the home was appreciated as one of the most essential contributions for the good of humanity that could be given.

Because men have failed to make women feel important and have even depreciated their work, women themselves have felt inferior and many have rejected their life in the home. They have pushed out into the man's world, seeking careers and hoping to find a greater feeling of importance. Men can decrease this problem by helping women see the importance of their work in the home, a valuable contribution to society equal to the work of men. In the overall, *the role of the woman in the home is a more vital one than the role of the man in his working world.* Such an appreciation on the part of a man will give a woman an entirely different perspective of her life and one that will assist her in finding contentment and fulfillment within her feminine role.

√

A woman's most basic rights in marriage are a voice in matters which concern her, consideration for her feelings and desires. and a certain amount of personal freedom.

We have already learned of the woman's subordinate position, and that she has an obligation to yield to her husband's authority. She is in this position although she must bear the consequences with him. She is also dependent upon him for a living, for personal things she needs, and for places she needs to go and for the freedom to do things she wants to do. He holds power over her. To a certain extent, her human rights are in his hands.

A just leader will grant her these rights willingly and without disparagement. He will give her a voice in matters which concern her and will carefully consider her viewpoint, feelings and desires and will respect her need for personal freedom. Not all men are so just and in tune with a woman's needs. Let us illustrate:

A man and wife were building a home. The wife had a plan for the kitchen, but her husband had different ideas. He had it designed his way, giving no consideration to her desires. She said she often thought as she lived in that house, not of the inconveniences she suffered in the kitchen, but of how her human rights were denied.

In another case the husband was transferred to another city and went before the family to select a home. His wife's only request was that it be on a quiet street and near the schools. But he became carried away with his own desires and bought a house which was on a busy street and quite some distance from schools. Such a disrespect for her only two requests was a denial of human rights.

Contrast this with an experience Phyllis McGinley relates in her book *Sixpence in Her Shoe*. They were remodeling their home, and she selected blue tile for a bathroom shower. When the shower was completed, she was disheartened with the color which looked so much brighter on the walls than what she expected from the tiny sample. She called her husband at work and asked him what to do. This understanding man, knowing a woman's feelings and her predicament, said, *Have them tear it down. It's cheaper than a nervous breakdown.*

Such a man as this is a jewel to a woman. He goes beyond the call of duty, but will receive rich dividends in love and appreciation. The interior of a house means a great deal to a woman. It is her world - the center of her career. Her desires need to be met whenever possible, and given enthusiastically. If an over-riding reason prevents this, a loving explanation needs to be made. She must know that she is respected.

Men make other serious mistakes. Some hover around their wife like a shadow, not allowing her the freedom of a world of her own. When a woman's work is done, she is entitled the time and privacy to do things she may want to do. Some husbands expect their wives to be both queens and slaves, centering all their time and attention on them.

Women need time of their own, money of their own, a world of their own in addition to the one they share with their husband. They need to do some of the things they long to do and have some of the things they long to have. They are dependent upon a man for most of these privileges. His justice rules them.

A denial of human rights is one of the major causes of the feminine rebellion. Had men been more considerate of women in their subordinate and dependent position, had they respected their rights and needs, women would not consider themselves in an inferior position and would not be seeking a place in the man's world where they compete with him and neglect their feminine sphere.

The role of the man and the woman is God's plan. Man is the divinely appointed leader of the family, and the woman is his subordinate helpmeet. This plan is the perfect plan whereby a family can function in peace and harmony, but it is all dependent upon the justice of the leader and his respect for human needs and wants. As God is just, so must man be just. As God will give to those who ask and to those who knock, so must a man heed the heartfelt requests of his family members and *turn them not away*. I stress again that it is not necessary to violate one's convictions in granting family requests. As God sometimes withholds things from us which He feels in His wisdom is not for our benefit, so must a loving father withhold from his wife and children those things he deems unwise. But in his justice and mercy, he considers the feelings of both wife and children and lets them know his concern for their desires.

Her Need For Security

All human beings need security, but a woman's feeling of security is not derived from exactly the same source as a man's. This is important for a man to understand. A woman's security comes principally from three sources: 1) From her husband's strength as the dominant leader of the family; 2) From his adequacy as the provider and money manager; and 3) From his ability to protect her or shelter her.

Therefore, anything he can do to more adequately function in his role as the guide, protector and provider will bring his wife the security she needs. Since we have already covered this subject in previous chapters, we need only stress here that it is an essential part of understanding a woman's needs.

It should also be added that security comes from within the woman herself, in her ability to shoulder her own responsibilities and solve her problems within her feminine sphere. But even if she is competent as a woman, she will feel insecure if she is denied a strong man to lean on. Otherwise she is in the unfortunate position where she develops manly traits to relieve her need for the security of masculine care.

Her Need to Express Resentments or Anything Which Troubles Her

Often feelings of anger, hurt, disappointment and frustration well up in a woman's breast in the form of resentments. If these feelings are not expressed, it can cause her to act strange, distant, and sulky. She has likely been trained to be a *nice person* and will resist *flying off the handle*

240

or expressing anger or bitter thoughts which might offend. She may feel no choice but to suppress these unhappy feelings, but the price both man and wife pay is a break in their relationship.

The usual treatment a man offers is to leave her alone and hope she gets over it. He may ignore her completely, getting interested in other things, or may even leave the house. His actions only compound her problem, for his lack of concern demonstrates, in her eyes, a lack of love. *If he loved me,* she may reason, *he would not leave me alone in my suffering.* This makes bad matters worse.

If she is forgiving and feels secure in her husband's love, she may get over her distress alone. But most women feel too shaken by this apparent lack of concern to be truly forgiving. *How can you forgive a man who has a heart of stone?* she may reason. *If he really loved me and cared about me, he would not turn from me while I'm suffering.*

There is a great principle of truth to follow in this case: Whenever you detect that someone is offended with you, whether you are guilty or not, it is your responsibility to go to that person and try to be reconciled. If you can follow the reasoning of this principle, you will see that it is not the offended person's responsibility to take the first step. It would be too difficult and counter to principles of human relationships for the offended one to seek out the guilty party and express disapproval of his actions. With a little thought, we recognize that only when the person who has committed the offense, or supposedly committed it, has taken the first step can good relationships be restored.

Following this principle, when the woman has been offended by her husband, or even thinks she has, it becomes *his* responsibility to go to her and become reconciled. He should first tell her that he detects something is wrong. Then he can invite her to express herself. As she begins talking freely, he can encourage her to continue until she discloses her innermost feelings. If he is guilty, he should admit it and make amends. Then he should go a step further and show sympathy for her feelings and the pain she has suffered. If he is not

241

guilty, or feels he is being misjudged, he should not take a defensive attitude, at least not while she is expressing herself. This can come later when her feelings are quieted.

This is a difficult procedure to follow. Even if a man is in the wrong, he will not like to admit it. No one likes to be in a *bad light*. But when a person will admit a fault, or an error, and take steps to rectify it, he moves into a *good light*. Asking forgiveness brings warmth and understanding into a relationship. Sympathy and concern for another is a mark of good character. Both are velvet traits women appreciate.

If a man is innocent, after his wife has fully expressed herself and the troubled waters are calm, he can point out her errors in a way as non-defensive as possible. Even though it is difficult, he will aid the situation if he will forgive her misjudgment and not cause her humiliation because of it. Here again we are reminded that men and woman are not alike. To a given situation their perspectives will often differ.

If a woman is guilty of harsh judgment or a bitter attitude, sometime later, when there is no crisis, a man may give her instructions about developing a more tolerant and forgiving attitude. Sometimes a woman has never been taught the meaning of humility and will listen to a man's instruction if given in a spirit of love and concern. By growing as a person she will overcome her faults and appreciate her husbands's part in this personal achievement.

Sometimes a woman will have distressing problems on her mind. Whatever the situation, when a woman is troubled, a man can greatly relieve her by telling her he is aware of her distress. Invite her to express herself, showing sympathy and concern.

Her Needs In Sex

In sex a woman's most urgent need is to know for sure that her husband's advances are motivated by genuine love and will be expressed with tenderness and consideration. She wants to know that she is not just a female to satisfy a masculine urge. A common fault with many men is that they use sex as

242

a gratification of the flesh - a degeneration to the animal instinct of self-concern with no feeling for his wife.

His failure to consider her feelings frequently causes her to be unresponsive. She may want to respond, but cannot, for she does not feel cherished. This is not a deliberate action or retaliation, but is involuntary because of the delicate tuning of the female nature.

To assist her to respond more positively a man should provide things to awaken her senses, such as beautiful and romantic music, art, the beauties of nature, quiet waters, moonlight, and tasty food. Tender words are indispensable. It is also important to eliminate the things which reduce her sexual response, such as too much outside responsibility, pressure and deadlines, or worry. She needs to be separated from the nagging problems which occupy her mind throughout the day.

I must emphasize that arousing the senses in a proper way is not the sensual arousal that many so-called authorities advocate. To them it may be purely an arousal of uncontrolled passion or lust which, although it may increase responsiveness, does so at the expense of one's finer nature. (It's interesting that this negative arousal, as with all sin, does not produce a lasting response that edifies, but must be constantly reinforced by more absurd stimuli until one is finally consumed in complete frustration.) If a woman is still slow to respond after using the positive methods described above, one can increase her desire through restraint, depriving her for a period of time.

For this to be effective it must not be done as a punishment, but should be done while supplying an abundance of tenderness and loving concern and applying the other positive suggestions we have discussed. Her barriers will be broken down as she realizes your feelings are for her as a person and not because she is a woman who can satisfy a physical need.

When the sexual needs of man and wife are encouraged in this way, they can expect a long life of sexual satisfaction without the *wearing out* or debilitation which often sets in at middle-age. And this satisfaction needs no further outside stimuli but blossoms from the pure love that only such respect and fidelity can produce.

We come to the end of this very brief study of Understanding Women in which I have explained some of a woman's most basic needs. It has been said that Sigmund Freud, near the end of his lifetime study of human needs, said that he could never discover what women want. I readily admit that we need a great amount of light on this subject. My experience is that some of the most important things a woman wants are the following:

Some Things Women Want

1. To be loved and cherished.
2. Gentle but firm leadership.
3. A voice in matters which concern her.
4. Sympathy when she suffers.
5. Appreciation.
6. A feeling that her domestic work is important work.
7. Personal freedoms: Time to do things. Right to go places.

14

Gentleness, Tenderness, Affection

Gentleness is a softness of manner and disposition. A man who is gentle is quiet and refined. He is tender and kind with people, mild and smooth in conduct. His temper is not easily provoked. There is an absence of harshness, fierceness or violence. He is not severe or tempestuous.

This gentleness comes to some men seemingly by inheritance. To most, however it must be developed, as it is generally lacking. Man's firm, rugged masculine nature does not encourage these gentle qualities. His gentleness must be acquired by subduing the masculine nature as one would tame a wild colt. His hot feelings must be schooled, his harsh temper restrained. He must be trained to mildness in conduct.

Gentleness is to the steel qualities what mercy is to justice. When justice is meted out alone, it is cold, undeviating, and unsympathetic. Although justice is in reality given for the benefit of the individual, without mercy it appears intent on the suffering or even the destruction of the person. As mercy softens justice, gentleness softens the steel in man.

Because gentleness is strong in the feminine nature, many men avoid being gentle, thinking it a mark of femininity and softness. This may be true if one is lacking in steel. Without a strong masculine nature, gentleness would be offensive in the male. But the careful blending of gentleness with firm masculinity produces a fascinating combination in a man which is attractive and admirable.

Women especially need the combination of gentleness and the firmness of steel. They need the support and strength of steel, but they cannot take it unless administered gently. This man of steel must not be too foreign to their own gentle make-up. Children also require gentleness constantly. A gentle voice, kindly manner and soft expression build good relationships with children.

Gentleness is a God-like quality and was strongly evident in the life of Jesus Christ. He gathered children about Him; they sat on His knee and He took time to converse with them. When the apostles sought to dismiss them as a nuisance, Jesus rebuked them saying, *Suffer the little children to come unto me and forbid them not, for such is the kingdom of heaven.* He was gentle with women, and they worshiped at his feet.

He was also gentle with men. Although He knew in advance that Peter would deny Him and Judas betray Him, He did not rise in angry protest. His gentle nature restrained him. When the angry mob gathered to stone the adulteress, He did not grab a sword in her defense, but said, *Let him who is without sin cast the first stone.* He recommended that we love our enemies, do good to them that hate us, and control the hard and fiery nature with gentleness.

With all this gentleness, He was masculine and firm. When confronted by those seeking to entrap or destroy Him, He stood fearless, and His gentle nature was temporarily masked as He demonstrated a strength which struck fear into the hearts of those who heard Him.

King David was an impressive example of strength and gentleness. As a young shepherd boy, he slew both a lion and a bear. With only a sling and a few pebbles from a brook, he killed the feared Goliath. He led armies and governed a kingdom. And yet he had a gentle nature. He loved music and wrote poetry. He spoke of *clean hands and a pure heart, of roses, lambs and green pastures.*

Many men lack this gentleness of spirit, much to the pain of their families. I remember in my youth such a man. He wanted his boys to grow up to be men, not *sissies.* Even as small children he spoke to them like a drill sergeant giving orders. He always had a sharp word of criticism for them. His wife and children lived in constant fear and seemed relieved if he had occasion to be out of town. When I occasionally visited the family with my parents when I was a little boy, I thought as I walked up the steps, *I hope he isn't home*.

One day as we were playing, one of his sons thoughtlessly put his finger in his nose. His father slapped him across the face saying, *Don't you know it's crude to do that?* The little boy was almost too astonished to cry. I've thought since how much more crude it was for him to slap a child in the face - not crude only, but cruel.

As I have followed this family, I have observed a lack of closeness for one another. The boy still remembers the slap across the face and has confessed to me that he never liked his father. And yet this man provided an excellent living. They lived in the most expensive house in town, his wife was always well- dressed, and there was ample of all life's needs. But what reward did he have for all this service if he killed their spirits by his harsh attitude?

The spirit of God cannot dwell in the heart of a man who is harsh. It is a part of the gospel of love to be gentle and kindly. *The fruit of the spirit is love, joy, peace, long-suffering, gentleness, goodness, and faith.* (Gal. 5:22) If the gospel of love teaches a gentle nature, we cannot hope to teach it to our children unless we demonstrate it ourselves. They will not likely listen to our instruction if we fail to win their hearts with a gentle disposition. There are steps we can take to overcome a harsh nature and replace it with gentleness.

1. *Restraint and Self-Control:* Bring the actions and emotions under control. Bridle the tongue as one would bridle a horse and lead it where it should go. School your feelings - restrain and subdue the harsh temperament. In other words, one must train the fiery temperament to become a mild one. There are impressive words to an old church hymn which give such instruction:

> School thy feelings, O my brother;
> Train thy warm impulsive soul;
> Do not its emotions smother,
> But let wisdom's voice control.

School thy feelings, there is power
In the cool, collected mind;
Passion shatters reason's tower,
Makes the clearest vision blind,
Charles W. Penrose

2. Develop a Gentle Character: Man's harsh conduct can be brought under control by restraint, but he will never be gentle in nature until a change takes place in his character. He must have a character which automatically prompts him to deal kindly with people. Gentleness comes as we grow spiritually - as we develop love and forgiveness, learn to concentrate on people's virtues rather than their faults.

3. Develop Humility: The key to humility is in learning to see our own mistakes, weaknesses and vulnerabilities. When this occurs we soften our attitude towards the errors of others.

For example, if a child breaks a lamp or spills paint on the floor the usual reaction is to shout at him, slap him or threaten him. What he has done is undoubtedly less serious or thoughtless than mistakes we make. If we could see a movie re-run of the scene, and then see a scene of ourselves in our own ridiculous and thoughtless behavior, we would blush in embarrassment. This would change the way we discipline our family.

Tenderness and Affection

Tenderness is to be softhearted, expressive of the softer feelings of love, kindness and compassion. One who is tender is susceptible to other positive emotions. He is especially sympathetic to pain or suffering. The Good Samaritan displayed tenderness when he treated the wounds of the injured man, lifted him onto a donkey and took him to the inn. So does a father who comforts the pain or disappointment of his little ones, or shows concern for his wife when she is distressed, or assists an injured bird or animal.

Tenderness and affection are awakened when we have feelings of love or a fond or tender attachment for another person. Some acts of tender affection are a squeeze of the hand, a pat on the shoulder or cheek, a soft, gentle expression, and a tender tone in the voice. The eyes can say more expressly how one feels than his words. When these emotions are seen in a thoroughly masculine man, the effect is penetrating. This is because it doesn't happy very often. The unexpected and very pleasant effect kindles deep emotions. It is such a perfect blend of virtue. A thousand words of eloquent language would not say so much.

Tenderness and affection, like gentleness, are usually associated with femininity. Because of this some men hesitate to appear tender, for fear of appearing effeminate. I say again, this may be so if a man is already a little effeminate. His tenderness may appear offensive. But when a man is strongly masculine and also tender, he can become a hero to his family and society, as was Abraham Lincoln. There is a poem which beautifully describes the need for tenderness:

'Tis the human touch in this world that counts,
The touch of your hand and mine,
Which means far more to the fainting heart,
Than shelter and bread and wine;
For shelter is gone when the night is o'er,
And bread lasts only a day,
But the touch of the hand, and the sound of the voice
Sing on in the soul alway.

Spencer M. Tree

The world is a harsh place, filled mainly with people who are busily occupied with their own pursuits and problems. They are not thinking of others.

I was watching a family of eight preparing to board their van enroute to church. The family dog who had been sleeping by the door step immediately began wagging his tail and jumped to his feet as he heard the family approaching. Excitedly brushing up against each person as they passed he was hopeful of a look or perhaps just a pat. Not a single person paid any attention to him. His eyes reflected his disappointment, but without any malice he returned to his place as they drove away. He would be ready with the same expectation when they returned.

Like the neglected dog, people everywhere need tenderness and affection. They need these more than they need blankets. And it will bring more warmth and peace than material things will ever do.

15

Attentiveness

An attentive person is watchful, observant, and heedful of the comforts and needs of others. He is a sharp contrast to that person who is so concerned with his own feelings and desires that he ignores, neglects or is indifferent towards others, taking them for granted. This is a particularly easy habit for married men to fall into who believe that the legal contract of marriage is sufficient to assure a woman that her husband is devoted to her.

It is indispensable for a woman to know that her husband is aware of her as a person. His thoughtful attention to her comfort is a visible demonstration of his love. It provides a unifying bond between them, for as he shows this thoughtful concern for her, she blossoms as a flower in the sun. He feels an expansion of his better self through remembering her. We shall consider some of the ways a man cam be attentive to a woman.

1. *Small acts of chivalry:* An attentive man will open a car door for a woman, help her with her coat, lift in the groceries. If they are attending a picnic and a small breeze blows up, without a word he will take off his coat and place it around her shoulders. He will see that she has the first hotdog and will check to see that she is comfortable. When they are on a busy street, he offers her his arm or hand. He pulls up her chair at dinner. He is aware of her needs, and his attentions come automatically. All this is a demonstration of the value he places on her. She is on his mind, and he cares about her.

2. *Notice her:* When she enters a room, he is aware of her presence. He looks at her, comments about her being there and talks to her. She is not like a piece of furniture.

She is a woman, and he notices her as one.

If she has done something to look especially nice, he compliments her. He notices her hair, her dress, her beauty, her figure, or anything that is distinctively feminine. (She wants to be appreciated as a woman, as you want to be appreciated as a man.) Nothing escapes his glance. If there is opportunity, he seeks her company and prefers her to other interests.

Noticing a woman helps her to *come alive.* She will have a new excitement in getting up in the morning and making herself beautiful, for there is someone who makes it worthwhile. She has a new incentive - someone to please, someone to look nice for. She will enjoy making a new dress, shopping, or standing before the mirror wondering how to wear her hair. She is like a little girl who anticipates a birthday party full of surprises, wondering just how he will react.

Such an attentive man knows her best features. She may have a beautiful nose, shapely figure, well-formed neck and shoulders, a special color or glint to the eyes, long graceful hands, an engaging smile or beautiful hair. Whatever her best features, her husband is aware of them and comments about them frequently. If she is not physically beautiful, she may have a charming laugh or cute manners.

3. Little attentions, indications of thoughtfulness: He remembers her birthday, anniversary and every other special occasion. Sometimes without special reason he brings her flowers -her favorite kind. It may be only a flower he picked in the yard, but it is of special significance because it is spontaneous. She will probably remember it most. He buys her perfume, a nightgown, a scarf, just to let her know he is thinking of her. She may not need these things, but this only convinces her that it is a gift of thoughtfulness and love. Sometimes he writes her love notes or delivers the message personally. His language may be simple or eloquent, but it indicates he is thinking of her, knows she is alive and is important to him.

4. Remember heartfelt desires: An attentive man has an educated heart. He is observant, knows his wife's favorite

252

flower, color, and favorite perfume. He knows which styles of clothes she likes, the kind of sweaters and jewelry she prefers. He is aware of her special desires. He remembers the time she looked longingly in a shop window at a Spanish shawl. She does not have to hint. He knows her desires.

The movie, *The Unsinkable Molly Brown* illustrated this point. In early marriage Molly had expressed a desire for three items: a red silk dress, cups and saucers that match, and a big brass bed. They had little money at the time but her remarkable husband kept these childlike whims in mind and later, when they became rich, the first things he bought her were a red silk dress, cups and saucers that match, and a big brass bed. Molly was overwhelmed. She had not imagined he would remember, especially after such a long time.

Men are busy with concerns which make forgetting easy. Pressing business matters, family budget, church and civic assignments occupy his mind. It may seem absurd that he should be asked to keep in mind the whims of his wife. But what is more important than her happiness? An attentive husband can bring *radiance* to a woman who knows she is the focus of her husband's attentions.

Few virtues stir a woman's heart like attentiveness. If men only knew its motivating power, they would not neglect this virtue. It is one of a woman's greatest pleasures and the lack of it her greatest pain. I have often thought of how many marriages could be restored if a man would show his wife proper attention - bring her a gift, tell her she is beautiful, remember her birthday. This will put new vitality into a mediocre marriage.

Attentiveness is sadly lacking in most men. When they come home from work they take their wives for granted. There they are just as expected, and in the environment that has become so ordinary. They are part of the scenery, like the furniture, the walls, the draperies. They are background.

The man sinks into the sofa and reads the paper or watches T.V. The woman feels no more significant than the kitchen sink. If she talks to him, he mutters a few words and continues to read the newspaper or goes to the basement or the garage to work on his hobby. His wife begins to think, *He doesn't even know I'm alive.* Is it any wonder women begin to neglect their appearance? A woman simply has to be noticed to have a reason to be attractive to a man.

I have recently read of Russian women and how they long for the return of chivalry. According to authoress Natalya Baranskaya, *A man will rarely open a door for a woman.* She pleads for more male attentiveness for the Russian women. The authoress told of the Russian women's reaction to the British T.V. series, *The Forsythe Saga,* which they viewed. The women were impressed mostly by the courtliness and family fidelity of hero Soames Forsythe (forgetting the social point that he was a plundering capitalist). *How sincere he is. His daughter is fortunate. Everything was for her.* The Russian women could not even dream of chivalry. And the authoress' appeal to Russian men is: *Men, look after the women.*

In another interview with a Mrs. Perevoznikova, the lady was asked what women in Russia want. She replied, *They are looking for those material comforts and conveniences that will liberate them in the home and add that touch of glamour and color to life that is still so lacking.* And what do they want from their men? Mrs. Perevoznikova became thoughtful. *I would like above all, attentiveness. When a woman does not feel she is liked and respected, she does not even want to comb her hair.*

In the movie *My Fair Lady*, Eliza complains of Henry Higgins because she did not want to be *passed over,* or in other words ignored. She could stand to be corrected, remade, revamped, transformed into a different person, but she could not stand to be treated with indifference. And such is the pain in the hearts of thousands of women who are set aside, like the pictures on the wall.

There are some men who are more attentive than others. The Italian men are known to be so, and the women love it. Women who have not seen this masculine attention so lavishly given are especially impressed when they visit Italy.

The Associated Press carried a release from Rome under the title *Women Defend Wolves.* It seems that Italian officials were going to take action against the sidewalk Romeos when the American Women's Club of Rome resisted the action. They said, in part:

An American woman is accustomed to walking the street as if invisible. The fact that Italian men aged seventeen to eighty will, without exception, turn their heads at her passing, is a thing of wonder and joy. It may take a bit of getting used to, but it is an adjustment women are happy to make. The Italian attitude is the important thing. If you are a woman, you are worthy of admiration . . . It's so charmingly un-American.

Italian men also use elaborate language. *Never have I seen anyone more beautiful than you,* or *You make the whole world like sunshine,* they can say it with ease, as though they were speaking about the time of day.

Polynesian men are much the same and have a lavish way of expressing their affection. Perhaps such expressions seem insincere and overstated. I certainly do not recommend insincerity, but there is something about the wholehearted way these men express themselves which could be used as a lesson.

Why Flowers

Many men are at a loss to know why women so appreciate flowers. A short time ago a young man asked me to suggest something he could send his mother for her birthday. *Flowers,* I said, *women always love to receive flowers. But they are so perishable,* said the young man. *That's why they are such a meaningful gift,* I replied. *If a man is willing to spend his money on them, it's a token of love.* He had never thought of it this way.

I uncovered this mystery about flowers from the Polynesians. While in their islands I watched a lady making leis. She explained that it was often necessary for women to stay up all night to make beautiful leis for early morning ships coming to port. *That's a lot of trouble to go to when they only last a day or so,* I said. *That's the beauty of it all,* she replied. *Because they are so perishable, they convey only the true meaning of love.*

This concept of flowers makes them appropriate to show

attentiveness. It is clear demonstration that a man is perceptible to the thoughts of a woman. A gift of great worth is perhaps a greater method of proving real love, since it indicates greater sacrifice. But since these gifts are given only rarely, they are not the type to show attentiveness. Flowers are fragrant, beautiful, inexpensive, and therefore fitting to carry the message, *I'm thinking of you.*

Other Gifts to Show Attentiveness

If a man is careful to observe his wife he will probably have ideas for gifts. He will know her favorite colors, perfume, and those special things she has been wanting. But if he is lost for ideas he can rely upon the following suggestions:

1. Seek the Advice of Women Close to Her: Closest are her mother, sisters, daughters, or close friends. They will likely know her favorite styles, colors, and taste. If not, they have a way of finding out.

2. Rely Upon the Things All Women Love: Women always love things which are feminine, pretty, soft, scented, silky and in any way beautiful. Perfume is always appreciated, but unfortunately the best kinds are the most expensive. Do not buy anything second rate. Sweaters, soft scarves, beautiful purses, jewel boxes, mirrors, vases, pearls, and well made jewelry are good standbys.

3. Things to Avoid: Avoid things which are overly practical, unless she has expressed a specific desire for them. Avoid things which, although she may need them, she may not necessarily want. It is relatively easy to observe what someone needs, but remember the key - does she also *want* it? Gifts should not necessarily serve the purpose of filling needs unless they are also desired. One's needs are likely to be filled anyway, but the special attention that stirs a woman is to receive something she wants very much, but would not likely receive otherwise. Would you believe that I know of a case where a man actually gave his wife a chain saw for her birthday, and told her to cut down some trees for firewood.

Occasionally a gift will be given which does not fit or suit the need as expected. In this case, suggest it be exchanged or returned. This will save your wife the embarrassment of making the suggestion. It is really not appropriate for her to make such a suggestion, although something very near to the gift given might be exactly what she wanted. If in any way you detect that she is not entirely happy with the gift, you can greatly ease the situation by suggesting it be returned. She will appreciate your sensitivity to her feelings.

There are at least two circumstances when gift-giving can be a painful experience. One occurs when she criticizes the gift; the other is when she complains that it is too expensive. In both cases it is cutting to a man and humiliating for the woman. There is only one satisfactory solution in such a case.

The woman, being unaware or insensitive to the value of gift-giving, needs to be taught. If a man will patiently teach her these values, she will be relieved of future mistakes, and the tenseness of the moment will likely be eased as a man takes the opportunity to express himself.

Unfortunately most men do not behave so wisely. Instead they clam up, resolving to *teach her a lesson* by determining never to buy her anything again. This is a sad mistake. A man should not let her ignorance eliminate the pleasure of gift-giving - an act which can bring them closer. Teaching her will not only keep open the opportunity to give, but will ease pain on her part.

I discussed this once with a woman who years before had criticized her husband because he purchased a lovely leather handbag which she felt was an extravagance. It was not until years later that she understood her mistake and the effect it had upon him. Since he alone realized the impact of her mistake, the ill feelings would have been minimized if he had explained the situation. This is admittedly difficult, since she is the one in error. But it is the only practical way to resolve the hurt feelings under such conditions.

1. When She Needs Assistance: In her household duties a woman frequently gets *snowed under* and needs help. At such a time a man demonstrates his awareness of her needs by doing the dishes, changing the baby, fixing the baby's formula, going to the market, or doing whatever is needed. If these things are done, not by routine, but when such special needs are noted, they are acts of genuine attentiveness.

2. When She Is Not Well: This is a time when a woman especially needs attention. An attentive man will look after her physical well-being as a mother does her child. He is the first to notice the tired look in her eyes and suggest that she may be working too hard or needs medical attention. His concern gives her a wonderful feeling of security, an assurance that she can rely on him in times of need.

Often this attentiveness is sadly missing. I have heard women say, *My husband is the last to notice when I'm ill.* They feel alone in the emergency. They have to faint or go to the hospital before such a husband realizes anything is wrong. This lack of concern causes a woman to feel like she could die without being missed.

A well-known newspaper columnist received a complaint from a young husband, married four years, who stated that his wife had lost all incentive to fix herself up or to keep up her domestic duties. Before marriage she was immaculate in grooming, energetic and full of life. Now she let herself go and had become a complainer and seemed always to be tired. He mentioned, as if in passing, that they had four children, all of whom came in four years.

For such a man to be so insensitive as to think a woman can manage four children, all of whom came in four years, and keep up the same energy as previously is beyond understanding. It is obvious such blindness could only make them more severe and cause her to feel like a common drudge.

There are cases when a husband gets so upset when his wife is ill that he becomes silent and distant towards her. He has become so dependent that he is frustrated to think of life running along without her usual assistance. Such a selfish attitude is wounding to her. She may feel like a crutch - her value that of a servant. She senses his lack of concern, lack of sympathy, self-centeredness and even lack of love. Love and concern are inseparable to a woman. Such neglect on her husband's part is, to a woman, unforgivable.

Some men fail to demonstrate concern for fear it will encourage psychological illness. A wife may so enjoy her husband's attention that she creates an imaginary illness to prolong the pleasure. Usually an opposite reaction is more apt to occur. If a woman feels her husband's lack of concern, at the first sign of illness, she may, perhaps unconsciously, encourage the illness for the express purpose of winning his attention, or seeing to what extreme she need go before he is alarmed.

Husband and wife must realize that they are dependent upon one another, *for better or for worse, in sickness and in health*. They need each other in times of joy and health, but even more so in times of suffering and trouble. These are times true love is tested. To let another down at such a time is difficult to redeem. It is a source of emotional pain for the neglected one.

3. At Childbirth: A special time when a woman needs a man's attentiveness is when she is expecting a baby. And yet I have observed men who give this dramatic occasion little attention.

A man once told me, with an attitude of pride, that when his wife was ready to deliver their baby, he drove her to the hospital, dropped her off at the curb, and came back that evening to see his newborn child. He had thought of asking her to take a taxi, but felt restrained from doing that.

Women suffer pain from such neglect, perhaps pain more distressing than the childbirth. Yet some women will not reveal their sensitive feelings. It is too humiliating. They also have pride and self-respect. If one must ask for such attention, it means nothing. Attentiveness must be given voluntarily and willingly.

Every consideration should be given to a woman in

childbirth. Traditionally, women want the presence of their husband. They want to hold his hand, feel his sustenance and comfort. They want to know he is there. Nothing in life is so intimate as the relationship which produces a child. In the culmination of an event which includes both the *joy* and *pain* of childbirth, it is especially comforting to a woman to have her husband present.

This was customary when women had their children at home. This tradition is more commonplace now as hospitals permit the father to enter the delivery room. They are of little assistance to the doctors, are perhaps a hindrance, but are of real value in giving the wife comfort so needed at this critical moment.

Although childbirth is a natural function and seldom ends in a fatality, there is a moment at birth when a woman hovers close to death. Her heart momentarily stops and there is a time of crisis. I think women sense this danger and reach for the person who means the most. It is also a time of intense suffering and great joy, strong reasons why the husband should be there to share them with his wife.

4. *When She Has Problems:* Sometimes a man thinks he is the only one who has problems and expects his wife to do all the giving. He becomes frustrated if she is troubled or not her usual cheerful self. He may even become irritated or resentful because she has a problem. This is a particular time when she needs attention. She may be suffering emotional pain or turmoil or physical pain.

At such times her husband's concern is essential. And yet, men are not so willing to give of themselves in these moments. They are so frustrated at the task of trying to comfort their wife, have so little knowledge of what to do, and perhaps even worried about her, that they leave the room or escape from the house in despair. Such men do not mean harm, but they do not know what to say or do. It is regrettable that they do not realize that desertion at such times greatly intensifies her problems. Her greater need - more than a solution to the problem, is the concern of her husband. If this is denied, her problems are multiplied.

The solution is very simple. When a man senses his wife is troubled, he will help her immensely if he will say tenderly, *I can tell that something is wrong. Please tell me what it is. I want to help.* I challenge any man to keep these words in his wallet, to use them when needed and see the miracle that happens. See the barriers come tumbling down. It is important to listen carefully to her problems and offer sympathy and give all the assistance one can.

But do not take a negative attitude. In other words, don't make her feel ashamed for her suffering. Don't minimize the problem or defend someone who may have caused it. It is sympathy and concern she needs. This is the approach that reduces the problem.

When She Does Not Deserve Your Attention?

Sometimes a man feels his wife does not deserve his attentions. She may be so neglectful of her responsibilities, so unfeminine, and perhaps unappreciative, that she is not deserving of any special considerations.

My answer to this is that God gives me many things I am not deserving of. If I had to be worthy of everything I have, I would have much less than I now enjoy. Further, we are commanded not to judge others. As with so many things, it is difficult to judge. Certainly she is not perfect. In some ways she will fail miserably. But she does have a better side. Concentrate on this.

During a period of a few years, the meals a woman prepares number thousands. She will likely have children and countless tasks incident to that - nursing in illness, feeding, washing, and tending. These may be the *first mile* tasks, but they are certainly worthy of appreciation.

It may be that a man may be responsible for his wife's failures, at least to some degree. But even if convinced that she is undeserving, one might remember that *God maketh the rain to fall on the just and the unjust.* Should we not then give to the undeserving as well as the deserving?

Often a small act of kindness will so impress a woman

261

that she will make a new determination to live a better life. If she feels she is not worthy of the kindness, it will move her even more. The message that it brings of continued concern and thoughtfulness may awaken a new spirit in her.

We are often inclined to *withhold* our fellowship from those we consider undeserving. This is a form of punishment. It is well to remember that God has said, *Vengeance is mine. I will repay.* It is not up to us to make certain that God meets His obligation to render vengeance to the deserving.

When She Appears to Reject Attention

Sometimes a woman will strangely reject a man's attentions and even appear to be irritated because of them. He brings her flowers and she accepts them coolly. He brings a gift and she gives thanks stiffly. Obviously something is wrong.

Perhaps a man should check on himself to see if he has offended her in some way. She may be suffering resentments and consider these attentions a cover-up for bad deeds. Offenses will extend from the most trivial to those of great magnitude in which she may have suffered extremely.

A man who has been unfaithful and presumes that a gift of flowers will compensate for such a great sin has something to learn about repentance. Although God has promised forgiveness to the truly penitent, He has His own criteria to make the divine judgment. Under conditions such as these, a wife's hurt and disillusionment may be so severe that it will take a period of time to recover.

In any event, if her coolness is the result of an offense by her husband, proper acknowledgement, retribution and forgiveness are first required. Only then will she be in the frame of mind to fully accept a token of warm feelings.

When She Asks for Attention

Is a man justified in withholding attentions when a woman asks for them? This is another instance when the nature of man resists that which is expected.

A business associate once confided to me that when he was first married, he and his wife had the habit of walking each evening down to a certain place where a lady sold carnations. Each evening he bought one for her. This went on for quite a long time until it became a tradition.

One day he decided not to buy her one. She was terribly disappointed and wondered what was wrong. She asked him to buy her one. This so irritated him that he determined never to buy her flowers again. He said that in the fifteen years that had elapsed since that event, he had never bought her flowers.

I thought, *Oh foolish man. You deny yourself the joy of giving and diminish your wife as a woman.* He could have explained that it is better not to ask, since the flower would only convey meaning if it were *his* idea. To withhold this evidence of love was to me almost inhuman. I knew this lady and wondered why she was so harsh and impatient. After hearing her husband's story, I wondered if it could have begun with the flower incident.

Actually the solution is quite simple. If a woman makes the mistake of asking, inform her that it detracts from your joy in giving. But do not make the mistake of denying her the very things she needs to keep her spirits alive.

Attentiveness With Children

We generally think of attentiveness as being given to the wife only. Children also require it. It is important for a father to greet them when he comes home, acknowledge their presence when they enter a room, and give them the courtesy of listening when they speak. They need a pat on the head, a touch of the hand or a squeeze, to convey the feeling of concern and warmth. If a father will sit by their bedside and show them special attention, he can draw them to him and make them susceptible to his teachings.

Little children frequently have difficulty in getting their father's attention. He may be reading, watching T.V., or talking to someone. These pre-occupations are frustrating to children who have no way of communicating with their father, other than to create a disturbance. They must compete with these demands if they want attention. It is therefore imperative that the father take the initiative to give them attention without their having to demand it. They, too, must know that they are considered important, and are not just *fixtures* around the house.

Little girls need special attentiveness. Their father will train them by assisting them with coats, opening the car door for them, seating them at dinner. In short, he treats them as the ladies they will some day become. In this way they are trained to accept such attentions when they become adults. It would be wise to educate their brothers to treat them the same way.

Children are apt to become spoiled if given too many material things which only clutter their lives and lessen their appreciation for these things. But little thoughtful attentions will add security and happiness to their lives and are vitally more important than material things. In review, consider the following means one can employ to demonstrate his attentiveness:

How To Be Attentive

1. *Extend small acts of chivalry:* Open doors, assist her with her coat, give your arm or hand when walking.
2. *Notice her:* Look at her, notice things about her such as her hair, her figure, her clothes, her better features.
3. *Remember little attentions:* Let her know you are thinking of her. Bring her flowers, perfume, remember her birthday, or something she has been wanting. Write her a love note or tell her personally.
4. *Remember her special desires.*
5. *Help in times of emergency.*
6. *Notice when she is not well.*
7. *Offer attentiveness when she bears a child.*
8. *Offer help when she has problems or is suffering.*

It is masculinity to which femininity responds. The masculine art of attentiveness brings a moving response in women. It melts their hearts and makes them womanly. It makes a finer person of her. The need for this male act of chivalry is deep and almost haunting. Evidence of this is expressed in a song, on the opposite page:

Little Things Mean a Lot

Blow me a kiss from across the room,
Say I look nice, when I'm not.
Touch my hair as you pass my chair,
Little things mean a lot.

Give me your arm as we cross the street,
Call me at six on the dot.
A line a day when you're far away,
Little things mean a lot.

You don't have to buy me diamonds and pearls,
Champagne, sables or such,
I never cared much for diamonds and pearls,
For honestly, honey, they just cost money.

Give me your hand when I've lost the way,
Give me your shoulder to cry on.
Whether the day is bright or gray,
Give me your heart to rely on.

Give me the warmth of a secret smile,
To show me you haven't forgot.
For now and forever, for always and ever.
Little things mean a lot.

16

Youthfulness

An attractive characteristic of the man of velvet is a spirit of youthfulness. This spirit is exemplified by a zest for living, an inquisitive and inquiring mind, a love for adventure, and a daring to try something new. It is a spirit of optimism with a sense of humor and an ability to see the challenges of life as opportunities to test one's ingenuity.

Youth is a time for dreams, plans, and enthusiasm. When one of my sons was sixteen years old, I took him with me on a business trip to Australia. His youthful eagerness for life was inspiring. He had a map he referred to constantly. His eyes were scanning every landmark he could identify on the map. Flying high over the Pacific he spotted island groups and atolls which he would identify. Even at night he could scarcely sleep because of his curiosity. At every stop, he made the most of the opportunity to investigate everything new.

Our destination was a cattle station in the outback of the Northern Territory. There he found endless interest in the plant life and the animals and insects. He was like a sponge soaking up everything in sight. I contrast this with the bored attitude of some of the passengers on the plane who drew the curtains and read a detective story with the same interest as if they were at home in an easy chair.

Unfortunately men are constantly subjected to the idea that age is overtaking them. Throughout our lives we are continually conditioned to age in a negative way by forever being aware that we are so many years old. This information is required on an endless number of forms. We associate ourselves with our contemporaries we have known in school, at work, or in the service. The passing of years goes on relentlessly, and we are reminded of it as we celebrate birthdays, observe the New Year, and see the inevitable changes that take place in ourselves.

It is true that we have all lived so many years, and this is a matter of record and exactness and cannot be altered. We are so many years old and nothing can change that. But it is well to remember that this age in *years* is not necessarily all important. One's physiological age is more important, since it has to do with the aging process. We realize, of course, that the body does not age uniformly. The brain cells, for example, are much slower to deteriorate than the muscle structure. One should find his mind expanding beyond the time when he has reached the zenith of his physical capacity.

This physiological aging or deterioration can be slowed down remarkably through diet, exercise, positive thinking, and constructive work. It is not uncommon to see men aged sixty or seventy who are physically younger than men of forty. These older men have a more promising life expectancy and may have thirty or more years of productive life ahead.

It is pathetic to see the negative thinking that invades the minds of so many, telling them they are so old and must limit themselves to playing shuffleboard or checkers. Gray hair does not necessarily limit one's activity in any of the important adventures of life. The thought that one is getting old should be discouraged, for it generally brings with it the concept of being weakened, exhausted, worn out, and depleted of vigor. All of these negative ideas militate against one's attitude and performance. And we must remember the truth - age is not so much a matter of years as it is a matter of attitude, and there is something we can do about that.

There are a few unique men who retain their spirit of youth into old age. They are eager about life and noticeably unaware of their advancing years. One such man is the famed anthropologist Dr. Leakey. The National Geographic magazine carried a feature on this interesting man. He was photographed in Africa on his hands and knees, a shock of white hair hanging down on his forehead, studying specimens he had uncovered in his diggings. One could tell from the intent look on his face that he was enthusiastic about his work and was certainly not aware that he was well advanced in years.

I studied the picture carefully. It intrigued me. I felt respect for this man who had such an obvious zest for living. It reminded me of the writing of Thoreau, who said, *I do not want to find when I come to die that I have not lived.* Dr. Leakey had not only lived, he was still living!

I also thought, as I continued to look at this picture, of other men I have known who had lost their spirit of youth at an early age. Some became disillusioned and bored. One such man was a famous movie actor who committed suicide, leaving the note, *I am bored with life.* Other men complain that life has dealt harshly with them. They withdraw from the battleground of life to nurse their wounds in self-pity.

My father-in-law was an example of a man with the spirit of youth. I am still amazed when I think of him at seventy-three, and after he had retired from the active practice of dentistry, began life anew by opening a dental practice in a frontier town in Alaska. This was a small town entirely new to him, but he threw his heart into his work and soon had a successful practice. While there he also enjoyed hunting and even slept in the rain in a pup tent.

Another man with zest was an architect who designed his finest creation when he was ninety years old - a magnificent building which stands like a monument on the top of a hill. During his lunch hour I observed him poring over his plans as though life had just begun. He enjoyed the mental challenge of his work and even worked out difficult mathematical equations daily just for mental exercise.

To one with a youthful disposition, life is good. He can get excited about a new idea or the prospects of seeing a new place, meeting people he has not seen before or doing something which has not been done before. To such a man the endless prospects before him in a world so large and varied stagger his mind. He thinks of all the books he would like to read, not books of diversion only, but books that excite the mind because they broaden his comprehension on the many frontiers of new learning as well as the learning of the past.

He wants to be familiar with the customs and problems of people who are far removed from him. He would like to understand them and see into their hearts. He is interested in the earth - the infinite variations in typography, climate, landscape, and peoples. It may not be his opportunity to travel widely, but the opportunities available do not make this a necessity. One can saturate his mind from many other sources.

John Goddard, the famous explorer, is a man of daring who has a zest for living. When only fifteen years old he outlined one hundred and twenty seven goals he wished to achieve during his lifetime. He had achieved one hundred of them by his mid-forties, and was pushing ahead on the remaining. He has sailed the full length of the Congo and Nile Rivers in Africa, and has also explored the Amazon River and climbed Mt. Kilimanjaro and several other peaks.

While visiting with him, I inquired about his plans. He enthusiastically said that the following month he was going to visit the Galapagos Islands and the month after that was going to do further exploring on the Congo River. There was no sign of lessening of enthusiasm for his adventures. In fact, the past seemed to strengthen his spirit of youth.

One who is youthful has a mind open to new ideas. A. P. Gianini, founder of the Bank of America, possessed this quality. Although he was an immigrant and had no experience in banking, he had ideas which he felt would be an improvement to the conventional methods in use. Established bankers who sat in their oak-paneled offices behind marble columns, familiar with all the *sound* practices of their profession, ridiculed his ideas. They wondered at the audacity of one who would suppose he could introduce ideas that were at variance with their time-tested methods. Yet this young man entered their sanctuary and succeeded beyond anything they had known. Here is a direct confrontation between a young man with imagination and faith and those who are set in their ways and closed to new ideas.

A special gift of youth is to ignore the limits of time and age. Youths, of course, ignore it because they have so much time ahead, but some men retain this quality in a most remarkable way into old age.

Several years ago I made an exploratory trip to Brazil to search for business opportunities. Sometime after returning, I received a call from a man I had never met who sought my services in assisting him in a similar undertaking. I was impressed with his enthusiasm. He had done considerable studying and planning and felt that the potential in some of the large, underdeveloped countries offered excellent *long range* opportunities, as he put it. Later a mutual friend inquired about our conversation. After explaining I had only talked to him by phone, he said, *You should meet him. He is eighty-nine years old.* I never would have guessed. He didn't mention his age, and I'm sure he felt no barrier because of it. This man was planning for the future as if he were forty years younger.

On another occasion a man age ninety-five called on me to see if he could accompany me to Australia. He was more agile than most men of sixty. As we talked, he became so animated that he was literally sitting on the edge of his seat. Although he had traveled extensively, the idea of going somewhere he had never been intrigued him immensely. To him the world was an interesting and challenging place.

I am always amazed with old people who disregard their age. They seem so youthful. One such man was a neighbor who lived next door to me, age eighty-nine. This man was left a widower after sixty-five years of marriage. He lived alone although several of his thirteen children wanted him to live with them. But he liked the independence of living alone. He worked in his garden, pruned his trees, drove a tractor in the fields part time, and even canned fruit he had grown.

After several years living alone, he considered the option of marrying again. He went to a physician for an examination to see *what his chances were* for an extended life. After the examination the doctor said, *It looks to me like you have another ten years or more.* With this encouragement he decided to remarry, and took a bride age eighty-three.

Shortly after his marriage, he decided to climb into the upper branches of a fruit tree to prune it. I was working in my yard and heard his wife say, *Joe, you come down out of that tree*

270

immediately or I'll call the fire department. I'll never forget his answer. He said, *They will laugh you to shame if you tell them to come and get a ninety-two-year-old man out of a tree.*

I have observed many such men who defy the press of years. Another was a production manager in a television studio, age eighty. He was so thoroughly wound up in his work and enthusiastic about what he was doing, almost schoolboy fashion, that I could hardly get his attention to ask him a few questions. His youthful attitude of enthusiasm had greatly preserved his physical appearance and manner. He gave the impression of being a much younger man.

I have, of course, met other men who have lacked this spirit of youth. One was a friend age forty-two. He had a fine medical practice, a wonderful family, and the esteem of the community. One day I asked him how he was getting along. *Terrible*, was his reply, *I won't live to see fifty.*

Maybe this discouraged friend was just having a bad day, but it is poison to the mind and body to allow such horrible thoughts to dominate. More than that, such an attitude is offensive to God who has provided us with life and the exciting opportunities it offers.

Sometimes we slow down because we do not feel good. Someone has said that most of the world's work is done by people who do not feel good. This is probably true to a great extent. Muscles may be sore and perhaps there is a headache. For most of these simple maladies the best treatment is an involvement in some challenging work in which one can raise some enthusiasm. One wonders if many of the common complaints are not due to boredom or perhaps a fear of life.

Those who accept the challenge of a difficult situation and look to the opportunities such difficulties provide, stir the admiration and interest of most everyone.

A shut-down of a large industry put hundreds of men out of work in a certain community. Some of these men had been working all their adult lives in this one place and knew nothing outside this familiar community. The article describing these conditions referred to the plight of a particular man who had lost his job and who was now at home while his wife brought

271

in the pay check. He was doing the domestic duties and would have the dinner prepared when she returned from work. It was noted that he was suffering emotional blows - adjustments to his ego in not being the one to provide the living.

There are numerous cases where perhaps a man would have to adjust to this, at least temporarily. It turned out in this instance, however, that he had been offered a job in another city, but declined it because he hated to move from the town he was familiar with and leave the friends, the only people he had known all his life.

Here is a man lacking courage and daring. He had a job in another city. The only daring required of him was to adapt to a new environment. Making new friends can be a stimulating and gratifying experience. He voluntarily relinquished his position as the provider for his family to stay in the shell he was used to and avoid the mental exertion of the change. Such an attitude does nothing to raise the level of esteem he has for himself, nor does it encourage the esteem of his family for him.

This brings up the matter of risk. A willingness to take risks is a youthful characteristic. In a very real sense the progress of the world is attributable to those with the daring to do that which has not been done before. Certainly there was a time when no one had flown, and to dream of such a thing would bring only ridicule. Every invention, every piece of literature or art requires an investment in time and money and is therefore a risk. Politicians risk their time and resources in seeking office. Launching a new business requires risk. Doing anything which has hope of gain carries a counter-balance of risk.

A careful line must be drawn between that which has substance and is worthy of risk and that which is foolish and over-speculative. Too frequently the hesitancy encountered by the older-thinking person is a lack of courage, an unwillingness to make an extra exertion. Excessive caution is more likely due to fear than prudence. Perhaps it is a realization that past failures have resulted from a lack of effort or planning, and a new venture would require more dedication than one is willing

272

to give. So it is easy to become an armchair philosopher and content oneself with dreaming rather than doing.

Fear of taking action frequently has its roots in the doubt one feels as to the worthiness of his own ideas. Being open to the new ideas of others is important, but being open to flashing thoughts of inspiration one occasionally receives himself is also important. It is possible you might get a sudden insight into something no one else has thought of. People become so accustomed to a stereotyped procedure or pattern of thought that it is never questioned. To change would be heresy. So it is often difficult to accept a new idea especially when we recognize that people hate to be different.

When such negative thoughts enter the mind of one who is striving to gain a youthful attitude, he pushes them aside and deliberately replaces them with some logical positive thoughts. He remembers that the wise are not afraid to appear foolish. He remembers that exploring new paths will invigorate the mind and keep him young despite the passing of years.

Sense of Humor

A man of youthfulness has a light-hearted sense of humor. This removes much of the drabness from his daily work which is bound to become routine and monotonous at times. Being able to see the humor in commonplace situations makes the carrying of one's load so much easier.

It has been observed that a characteristic of healthy and long-lived persons is a sense of humor. It is as though their optimistic attitude were supplying a physical nourishment to their bodies - a sort of vitamin supplement. These people realize that to take themselves too seriously is a deadly mistake. Life is going on anyway, and somehow things always work out regardless of how gloomy the picture looks at some low point.

Humor will often bring the picture into sharper focus. Abraham Lincoln was gifted in this respect, and through this means cut down gigantic problems to a size he could manage. Bitterness and rancor are impossible when one's sense of humor is functioning. It brings a smile to the face, and everyone succumbs to this touch of human warmth.

Bruce Barton tells this story about Lincoln: *Around his table in Washington sat the members of his Cabinet, silenced by their overwhelming sense of responsibility. It was one of the most momentous meetings in our history. To their amazement, instead of addressing himself directly to the business in hand, Lincoln picked up a volume and began to read aloud a delightful chapter of nonsense from Artemus Ward.*

Frequent chuckles interrupted the reading, but they came only from the President. The Secretaries were too shocked for expression! Humor at such an hour - it was well nigh sacrilegious! Heedless of their protesting looks, Lincoln finished the chapter, closed the book and scanned their gloomy faces with a sigh.

"Gentlemen, why don't you laugh?" he exclaimed. "With the fearful strain that is upon me night and day, if I did not laugh I should die; and you need this medicine as much as I."

* * *

These characteristics of youthfulness are not an exhaustive list but will suffice to indicate the nature of a youthful person. It is always to be remembered that youthfulness is a state of mind and not a matter of years. When a man has this quality, he adds a breadth to his personality which is a rare distinction. It is an indication of maturity and is in sharp contrast to the childish men who long for *the good old days* and revert back to the pranks of their youth.

Sometimes men are afraid to learn and adopt these qualities of youthfulness for fear of *losing their dignity*. It is only the unsure who would harbor such a feeling. Or perhaps one has let life beat him down to the point that the spark is dead. This, of course, is one of the terrible tragedies which we see all too often.

But it is fortunately true that man is not bound by having to accept things as they are. The human being is far more adaptable than most persons realize. Even long-established patterns are alterable.

17

Humility

Humility is freedom from pride or arrogance. One who is humble may have many virtues and achievements, but he realizes his weaknesses, mistakes, and limitations. He does not rise in pride over his wife, his children or other men. His achievements do not blind him to the fact that he has much more to learn and do. He also recognizes and appreciates the achievements of others, including the contributions of those whose efforts are commonplace but essential to the public welfare. He sees in them strengths *he* does not have. Despite his own achievements he does not glory in them, but views the good works of others and seeks to learn from them.

Humility is not, however, a groveling or self-effacing attitude, in which one deliberately depreciates himself beyond justification. *It is a correct estimation of ourselves as God sees us.* Humility is not pretended modesty in which we control bragging for the purpose of impressing others. There must be a quality within which causes one to truly feel his own limitations and weaknesses.

The Savior set a perfect example of humility. Although He was the chosen Son of God, having no sin, and was able to overcome all things, yet He lived among the common people and dined with sinners. Although His disciples worshiped Him, He did not rise above them in an attitude of superiority. He demonstrated His humility when He bowed before them and washed their feet. By this act He impressed upon them in a dramatic way the requirement that men remain humble. How can anyone elevate himself above others when he remembers this action of the Savior?

Humility is one of the most desirable traits of the human

personality. No man is truly great without it. It shows a respect for all life and a greatness of spirit. A humble man recognizes himself and others as participants in a divine plan which glorifies the human potential and recognizes that from the most inauspicious beginnings may arise greatness. Humility adds velvet to a man which tempers the hard steel and balances his self-confidence. Without humility, self-confidence tends towards arrogance.

Arrogance or Pride

Humility can best be understood by reviewing its opposite - arrogance or pride. Arrogance is an ungrounded feeling of superiority and an inability to see one's own weaknesses or limitations. This fault can be commonly viewed in the following areas of life:

1. *Worldly goods:* The possession of wealth causes many to be lifted up in pride. Wealth is easily flaunted and is unfortunately considered a yardstick of success by far too many people. Since the seeds of pride are in everyone and grow so easily, the temptation to use wealth in this way is almost irresistible.

For those who obtain wealth through sacrifice, risk, and years of labor, it is not difficult to view themselves as superior to persons who have not exerted themselves as they have. It is satisfying to display their possessions for the feeling of self-importance they derive. This pride, which is contemptible in the eyes of God, causes men to glory in the corruptible things of the earth - the things of no lasting value - things which not only do not ennoble, but blind men to the things of real value.

Wealthy people themselves are not entirely to blame for this unwarranted emphasis given to their possessions. There is great homage given them because of their money. Others scrape and bow and foster these feelings of superiority. To eliminate this evil from among us, it is essential that we neither elevate ourselves nor anyone else because of worldly goods. Wealth in itself is not an indication of superiority or worthiness.

2. *Knowledge:* Persons who obtain a higher education sometimes feel superior because of attaining a position many are unable to achieve. Such a person may find it difficult to accept a new idea from a man with less education. The truly educated man has an open mind, but unfortunately there are many whose education has not extended that far.

The key to retaining humility is a realization that knowledge is not reserved for the highly educated alone. God sometimes puts it into the minds of the most unsophisticated by way of inspiration. There is the further thought that although a man may know a great deal about some subjects, there is an infinitely broader field of learning about which he knows little or nothing.

3. *Skill, ability or talents:* A man who can perform a skill with great ease as a result of natural talent may feel superior to a man who must strive diligently to acquire the same skill. For example, a man attending a trade school or professional college may notice that he stands out because of his native ability and adaptation. Under these circumstances he is likely to feel superior.

Other men acquire skill and competence, not through talent alone, but because of years of experience and hard work. Such a man may look upon men new to his field as inferiors. And yet some remarkable men are able to retain their humility along with great experience. They are eager to find ways of improvement, even from younger men, and are anxious to assist others to achieve what they themselves already have. They have no fear that their station will be less if they help someone else achieve the position they now occupy.

I know a medical doctor who achieved special skills and had earned several degrees and citations beyond his M.D. degree. Yet this man was a man of unique humility. When a young doctor joined his staff as an associate, he sought out the young doctor's advice, asked him for the *latest knowledge in medical school,* and was respectful of the young man's ideas.

4. *Accomplishments, achievements, honors, position and status:* It seems to be human nature for people to stratify

themselves into social classes with preferential treatment accorded to some. There are many things which can put a man *at the top*. By definition, being *at the top* means you are in a position for special benefits. Since there is an inborn desire for status, when it comes, it may *go to his head*. It is easy for a person to think the applause and attention accorded him is because of *who he is*. (Public officials, for example, are sometimes disillusioned to learn when they leave office that the acclaim was not for them but for the office.) Being in the limelight is an opportunity for growth in learning to be humble, despite public efforts to make one feel otherwise.

When a man has earned his acclaim through effort and dedication, he cannot help feeling satisfaction in his accomplishment. This is a justifiable feeling, but in no way should cause him to feel superior as a person.

One only has to look at certain famous musicians and artists of the past to realize that, although they had talent and often great dedication to a goal, they were human and therefore as full of weaknesses as other men. In almost every case they did not stand out as superior men, only as superior artists. They had every reason, then, to be humble.

But again, it is often the clamoring crowd that causes the famous to feel superior. They seek their autographs, follow them in the streets, and are awed by every word they utter. If we would give credit only where due, these persons of fame and reputation would have a less distorted view of themselves.

5. *Good works or righteousness:* Being lifted up in pride for what we consider our righteous endeavors was the great weakness of the Pharisees, the Sadducees and the scribes in biblical days.

They took pride in their long fasts, prayers in the streets, observance of the Sabbath and the rituals laid down by their forefathers. They made outward demonstrations of piety as a means of impressing others. They reserved for themselves special seats in the temple and avoided the contact with the publicans and sinners whom they felt were inferior to themselves. This group of pretended saints received the strongest castigation the Savior uttered. He condemned them, not for their faithfulness, but for their lack of humility.

There seems to be a predisposition among people towards self-righteousness, a feeling of being better than others, more honest, more fair, generous or dependable or in other ways better than someone else. For this reason we criticize, depreciate or even condemn another person. We do not allow for his mistakes. Rather, we judge. This negative attitude has its roots in lack of humility. If we could see ourselves as God sees us, we would realize our weakness. This would not only restrain us from attacking others, we would shrink in embarrassment.

You can count on it, whenever you find a faultfinding person, quick to criticize, you have also found a person lacking humility. He may feel he is humble, he may reason that he is, but he is not. Somewhere inside he views himself as superior. His judgment of himself and others is not made with the same yardstick.

Because our faults are different, it is easy to criticize. One person may be more generous than another, another more punctual. Differences always invite comparisons, which are not justifiable, if for no other reason than *we don't know the facts*. Humans have not the ability to judge. God has never listed the virtues in order of importance, nor has he given us the insight to make a fair judgment under all circumstances. We therefore lack the ability to make a valid judgment.

How God Dislikes Pride

Where pride arises from a feeling of wealth, knowledge, special ability, self-righteousness, or any source whatever, it is a trait which God condemns with strong emotion. We read in Proverbs 6: 16-19:

> These six things doth the Lord hate: yea seven
> are an abomination unto him: A proud look, a
> lying tongue, and hands that shed innocent blood,
> An heart that deviseth wicked imaginations, feet

that be swift in running to mischief; A false witness
that speaketh lies, and he that soweth discord
among brethren.

It is significant that pride is described as an abomination and one of seven things God hates, being listed in company with lying, wicked imaginations and murder.

The Marks of Pride

Pride is demonstrated in a variety of ways. Typical is an air of arrogance. The person of conceit and vanity shuns people whom he feels are not his equal and is harsh and critical in his judgment. For such a one to teach others is impossible, since his attitude will never allow confidence to exist. Who can take instruction from one who is harsh and whose very attitude suggests superiority?

The proud, arrogant person is not open to new ideas and will shun and resent an opposing viewpoint, for he is unwilling to submit himself to the changes such learning will demand. Suggestions and opinions of others will probably be taken as an offense so that free and easy communication is broken. Characteristic of this arrogant type is an unwillingness or inability to allow for the mistakes of others, thus producing an unforgiving attitude.

The greatest problems comes to the person with pride. From him springs the malicious seeds which make a close relationship with others difficult. His personality is dwarfed by his overbearing ego. With such a hindrance or flaw in his make-up, a man is headed for marital and family problems. He will not deal fairly with his wife; he cannot instruct his children effectively. He is not the example he should be.

We hear much about the generation gap. One wonders if the seat of the gap is not a lack of humility on the part of parents. If one is harsh in judgment, slow to listen, and critical, he has established an environment which makes adequate communication impossible. He has defeated himself in accomplishing the most important thing he has to do in training his family. Of course relationships with others will be similarly affected.

Arrogance Stops Progress

The problem with an arrogant person is that he is not open-minded. His mind is set. He thinks he knows it all. He has all the answers. When a new idea comes along he resists it. In this condition he is very satisfied and comfortable, and changes are upsetting to him. This attitude stops his progress.

When the growth process stops, it is like giving a hormone to a child at six years of age that would prevent his growth and give him a permanent stature at that point. Unless the nature of arrogance is understood for what it really is, a person will suffer continued irreparable damage throughout his life. It could easily be the most disabling influence he has. The cure to this dilemma is a humble attitude.

Humility and a Winning Personality

An arrogant person repels people while a humble person draws others to him. People shun anyone who makes them appear deficient or inadequate, as one shuns anything in the physical environment which makes him uncomfortable. There is a softness -a velvet - about the person who is modest, who, in spite of accomplishments, talents, or money, puts himself on a plane with everyone else - considers others worth as much as he is and seeks their ideas as supplements to his own. The truly great people throughout history have exemplified this quality and have won people to them.

How Humility Can Cure Criticism

A critical attitude is largely the result of a lack of humility. It follows, then, that the development of this attribute will be a deterrent to criticism. As we acknowledge our weaknesses and mistakes, we will find it impossible to criticize others. There is satisfaction in fault-finding, since it is an ego-builder.

This is particularly true if the fault in question is not one he has himself. This is less of a strain to the conscience.

Or if a fault can be seen in someone of importance, there is a temptation to depreciate that person in an effort to elevate oneself or to *justify another fault in oneself*.

One may even feel that his criticism is a justifiable means to establish better habits in another person. If the motive is actually to point out a better way, it should be realized that this is the poorest way to teach. Responding to criticism in a positive way is most unusual, since the natural reaction is a withdrawal from such a person. As we come to see a person's total worth, his weaknesses and his strengths, and as we learn to overlook the weaknesses and acknowledge our own we develop humility. Biblical teachings point out that it is best to remove the beam from one's own eye before attempting to remove the mote from a brother's.

How Humility Can Make a Better Father

As important as anything in the parent-child relationship is a realization on the part of the parent that he is dealing with another individual with as much importance and worth as himself. In theory no one would deny this, but its practice is a far different matter.

How many times, for instance, have you seen a child waiting for service in a store while an adult who came in later is served first? Or how many times have you seen the questions of a child ignored as though they had never been asked? Acquiescence to the principle is much easier than its practice.

Because of their youth, children will naturally make mistakes which an adult would not make. The parent probably made the same mistakes in his youth, and more than likely even later on, but now he is harsh and critical to see this mistake made by another, especially his own child.

The lessons the parent has learned over the years he expects will also have been learned by his offspring, as if by osmosis. But more than this, the parent has not overcome all his mistakes even at his more mature age. He is going to feel very foolish, for example, when he gets a ticket for traffic violation when he knows there was no excuse for his getting it since he knew the law and had probably received citations before. In dealing with his child, a father who is humble enough to acknowledge that he has faults himself is in a far better position to teach. The child will recognize errors on the part of his parents and will resent being criticized or punished for his errors when his parents avoid censure by virtue of their being adults.

A parent will not *lose face* by admission of an error to his child and, if necessary, by asking forgiveness of him. Quite to the contrary, the child will feel that he is dealing with someone who is fair, and his esteem for the parent will increase. This comes through even with a very young child who is unable to analyze the situation in any logical way, but will only be going by his feelings. When it is necessary to administer discipline, if it is given for the benefit of the child without anger or disgust, even though the punishment might be rather severe, the child will submit to it without resentment. A man who possesses humility will not be unfair in his discipline, but will be sympathetic, knowing that all people make errors. His purpose is to help his child overcome the pitfalls and errors which confront him.

Humility and Leadership

A leader, of all people, must be a person of humility. He realizes that, although he is the leader, he does not have all the knowledge and ideas necessary to fulfill his assignment just because of the assignment. Others have valuable contributions to make. He will respond to the suggestions of others by saying, *That sounds like a good idea*, or perhaps, *I would like some time to think about it. I appreciate the thought you have given to this.*

When Andrew Carnegie was asked the secret to his success in business, he responded by saying, *I surround myself with people who know more about business than I do.* Certainly he recognized that if his business was going to expand and succeed to the extent he wanted it to, he was going to have to get more ideas and help than he could possibly come up with as a single individual.

Again we go back to the idea of defining humility as the ability to see oneself for what he is - no exaggeration or depreciation of value, but an honest recognition of real value. To admit that someone else may have a better idea is no threat to one's confidence, since he knows that under certain circumstances he will also be the one to see the problem more clearly than anyone else. But every individual has limitations. As Abraham Lincoln once said, *We are all ignorant, only on different subjects.*

Good outside ideas will come to a man whose respect for others is such as to establish confidence in them that they are free to express themselves. We know so well that sometimes we come up with an idea which, even before the words are out, we realize has a flaw in it. A person with an idea which he felt truly had merit would hesitate to express it if he thought it was likely to be received with criticism. Certainly anyone who is expected to be a follower, whether adult or child, in a home situation or a business situation or whatever situation, would have a similar response. Good leaders are amenable to the suggestions of others not necessarily to adopt them, but to listen open-mindedly so a reasonable evaluation can be made.

Humility and Marriage

Some of the rebelliousness of women is traceable to the injustices they have received from men who lack the humility to acknowledge that women are just as important and intelligent as *they* are. Some men are critical of their wives, critical of their housekeeping, their mistakes, burned food, the way they drive a car, shopping errors, or mistakes in the way they handle the children. This criticism may not be confined to her personally, but may be uttered in public to her great humiliation and embarrassment. Or it may be less personal and be just a *dig* at women generally, suggesting that in some way they are less efficient, less alert, or less intelligent.

Men often feel they are superior to women, that the work they do is vastly more important than the menial tasks in the home which they feel could be done by anyone with a minimum of skill and ability. As the work of the woman is depreciated, so is her value. She will come to feel that the domestic endeavors are not important or challenging enough to warrant her time, for she realizes she has skill and intelligence to offer the world which is commensurate with that offered by men.

Since they are the leaders, some men dominate women, ruling with high-handedness. Their arbitrary rulings and demands produce injustices which are offensive and unbearable. Certainly such behavior makes a marriage difficult since the woman is made to feel subservient and inferior. As a man grows in humility, realizing his position as leader is only an assignment of responsibility and does not vest him with any qualities of superiority, he will accept suggestions and ideas with an unbiased mind.

Since men are the breadwinners and must receive special education for this responsibility, it is frequently the case that their formal education is superior to that of their wives. But for men to suppose that their position is superior by virtue of increased education is a fallacy which is easily exploded.

While they may have a more specialized training in one direction or even generally, their innate ability is no greater, on the average, than the woman's. She may be deprived from extending herself only by dedication to goals that are even more worthwhile. The knowledge of any person is tremendously small when compared to the vast store of knowledge available. Should it be that the learning of the wife is less than that of her husband, this does not indicate a lack of brains or ability. Does an attorney feel inferior to an architect because he knows little or nothing of this latter profession?

It is not uncommon to find men who, after they have obtained acclaim or worldly success, desert their wives. The wife who has assisted him to achieve an education or sacrificed to help him get ahead in business is sometimes put on the shelf while he goes out to make a life with a younger woman, or a different woman. His ego would be shattered in many cases if he realized that this younger woman has motives of her own.

The *heart* that a woman puts into the home and marriage is certainly of at least as much value as anything supplied by her husband. A man will gain humility as he sees things in the correct perspective. With this humility he will contribute much more to his marriage.

Humility and a Man's Success

A lack of humility is a strong deterrent to achieving success either in one's business life or home life. As noted, this lack indicates a basic character flaw, pointing up a failure to understand and appreciate the contributions of others or their inherent worth. It is barrier to growth.

One who is humble will recognize his weaknesses and will work to overcome them. His appreciation of others makes working with them easier; he can influence better, and the channel for helpful suggestions will be strengthened. The very nature of our existence demands that we get along with people. Our development of this attribute is a big step in the right direction.

In gaining humility it is necessary to rid ourselves of any feeling of self-righteousness or superiority. Not many people feel guilty of these two weaknesses. But in refusing to listen to suggestions or by a self-determination to pursue their own course, they reveal an underlying attitude arrogance. Although it is not profitable to dwell at length on our weaknesses to the point of allowing self-respect to wane, it is imperative to be aware of our limitations so that improvements can be made.

18

Refinement

Refinement is defined as a state in which the dross, coarse or vulgar elements have been removed and the pure remains. This is an excellent word for our purpose, being so descriptive and capable of illustration. We think of gold which usually occurs in nature in combination with impure matter from which it must be separated. To accomplish this, the raw ore is placed in a furnace where it is brought to the melting point, and through the application of fluxes a separation occurs, leaving the gold free of the contaminants with which it was originally associated. I will apply this analogy to the two refinements that make up a polished gentleman:

Inner Refinement

A refined gentleman is not born. He is hammered and forged in the fiery furnaces of life. Through years of meeting the challenges and adversities of life, he is polished and refined, like *fine brass*. This transformation is brought about by his courage in facing difficulties, the lessons he learns by the choices he makes, and the sacrifices he endures for the benefit of others. Moment by moment, year by year, these experiences mold him into, not only a man of character, but a refined man of velvet.

We tend to resist such experiences because we associate them with pain - the pain of frustration, adjustments and disappointments. When success seemed inevitable and we were already planning the benefits we felt certain would be ours, we had to face bitter disappointments. Now we must go through the pain of altered plans and adjustments, and perhaps the humiliating pain of defeat.

When we seek the easy, comfortable life, devoid of difficulty, and when we limit ourselves to *easy to reach* goals, we deprive ourselves of the opportunity to grow into refined individuals. On the other hand, when we set *high and noble* goals for ourselves, and maintain the stamina to reach them, the process inevitably brings the inner refinement we seek.

Outer Refinement

Outer refinement consists of good breeding, good manners, courtesy, consideration, thoughtfulness, propriety, polished language and good taste. These qualities are sometimes inborn, but if not, can be acquired by being *trained* in all of the graces that make up a refined gentleman.

By his nature man is course and rough. The elements of life tend towards vulgarity, self-interest and lack of consideration for others. In addition, there are unceasing, unrelenting pressures to tarnish the polish one tries to grace himself with. The human tendency is to relax and *do what comes naturally*. This takes off the sheen.

In the name of freedom some people have concluded they have an inalienable right to say anything they please or dress and act in any fashion they choose. Because effort is required to overcome the dross, it is thought to be undesirable. These are some of the influences and attitudes we must overcome to become refined.

In some ways men are like animals that are valued for their breeding and training. This would be true at a horse or dog show where prize specimens are exhibited. We see to what an excellent state many of these animals are brought. Thoroughbreds may be relied on to behave in a certain way on order. They have a majestic bearing and confidence which makes them seem almost human. The well-trained quarter horse will be valued at many thousands of dollars, whereas the wild Australian *brumby* may be worth no more than his hide.

Refinement will open many doors for a man and impel

him to success. Even a poorly educated man who is a refined gentleman, may outshine the man with the titles and degrees. Such men have been invited to walk with kings and dine with dignitaries. Refinement is also a supreme quality in building good relationships with all people. For a woman, it is an essential part of the velvet that makes up the ideal man.

The unrefined man has the latent ability to be processed as ore, or trained as the thoroughbred horse, to command a higher value.

Manners

That anyone would have poor manners is most unfortunate, since many times the impression given is far more negative than is justified. There seems to be some corollary between good morals and good manners, but apparent good manners are by no means a guarantee of good morals. I say *apparent* since one of *genuine* refinement would *have* good morals. But occasionally we see a man of fine character who lacks ordinary table manners or general manners.

I knew a young man who had cultivated many of the social graces and gave the appearance of excellent refinement. His appearance and dress were proper and his language cultured. But his table manners were atrocious. For the period he was seated at the table he seemed to be in another world where only his gratification mattered. Not only did he eat fast and noisily, but he lowered his head to the plate for quick and effective consumption which he devoured in quantities to the point of embarrassment.

These moments at the table seemed so foreign to his nature as to be a *Jekyll and Hyde* syndrome. Selfishness moved to the front to the exclusion of the finer qualities in his character. The poor impression given was out of proportion to the seriousness of the offense, but that is the way it is with something that is so obvious.

Far more offensive is the use of crude, vulgar, and profane language. The language one uses gives himself away in the manner of placing a price tag on him. By listening to someone speak, particularly on an issue where strong feelings exist, it is possible to make a fairly accurate estimate of his character. You will know in advance what his feelings are on many other issues.

For example, one cannot profane the name of God and yet be a reverent person. The two are completely incompatible. Lack of reverence is a serious character deficiency, indicating not only a disrespect for God, but also for His creation.

Crude language is not only an evidence of deficiency in the language, it indicates a selfish disregard for the sensitiveness of others. For anyone who reverences the name of Deity, profane language cuts like a knife.

While sitting at a noon luncheon with a men's service club, one of the men profaned during the conversation. Noticing a minister at the table, he apologized to him. Why didn't he apologize to the rest of us? Deity is certainly reverenced by people other than clergymen. Had women been there he would have apologized to them also, I presume, but for some reason he failed to realize that profane language is offensive to anyone who loves God. This was probably due to the misplaced idea that masculine men are immune to vile language, or will at least overlook it.

Sitting in the presence of such an unrefined person is uncomfortable and embarrassing, for at any moment one is subjected to having to correct him on his speech, which will prove embarrassing to both parties. Very likely he is speaking out of habit with no realization of the offense he is creating. Such a person will be shunned by anyone whose sensibilities are offended by such usage.

Such a man places an unnecessary limitation on his acceptability, giving himself a handicap, as it were. Getting along in our relationships is difficult enough without handicapping ourselves.

One finds among the advocates of *free speech* an invariable pattern of crudeness and irreverence. While it is difficult to prove, one may presume that such advocates lack basic moral values in sex as commanded by God. Their language gives them away. Lacking restraint, they want their vileness made acceptable to all

The use of the language falls into all degrees of acceptability. The morbid utterances of the blatantly uncultured represent the more extreme cases, but there are many more thoughtless and unrefined terms used by a greater number of people which brand them immediately. The fineness of one's clothing is no gauge to go by nor is the position held. The need for an improvement in speaking cuts across all levels and strata.

The battle to clean up the language is made the more difficult by lower journalistic standards using *the language of the street*. It is hoped this trend will be reversed. It is inconceivable that public dignity will continue to tolerate this.

Crude Behavior

Closely allied with crude expressions is crude behavior. The thought and expression precedes the act, so it is difficult to have the one without the other. Occasionally we see a man whom we describe as *fresh*, i.e., he is overly friendly or overbearing. He may touch or pinch or in a variety of ways impose himself on others. Few people appreciate such intimacy, and most people highly resent it. This is another case where a man places himself under an unnecessary handicap. His type of humor or friendliness is an offense to most everyone, and he is immediately marked as one to avoid.

The "Dirty Joke"

The *dirty joke*, like spoiled food, is always out of place. There is no conceivable way it can be made appropriate. To cloak the dirty joke with humor to make it acceptable is like putting whipped cream on moldy pie. No matter how enticing the whipped cream, the rotten pie below is revolting.

Indecent thoughts go into the mind. Some of them last a life time. This is pollution in one of its more virulent forms. Dirty stories are not innocuous indiscretions, although most are repeated without intend to offend.

But they do offend. And not the least to be offended is God. The subject mostly deals with sex and the sanctity of the human body. These matters Deity guards very zealously.

The Ideal Man as presented in this book would never resort to telling a dirty joke. The trust placed in him as the guide, protector and provider demands that he be above such behavior. What would one think if a president of the United States should begin his inaugural address with a dirty joke? His office is no more to be respected than is yours as the leader of your family.

Women are told in the scriptures to reverence their husbands. How can a woman do this if her husband is dirty minded? Most women want to be led, they want an example, and unless contaminated by an unwholesome experience would like to reverence him. We can see that if a man is the measure of the Ideal Man as we describe him, he would be worthy of reverence.

Diplomacy and Tact

This is an art which the refined man will cultivate, for it is like frosting on the cake. It has its roots in sympathetic understanding for others, consideration for feelings, and a desire to make life as easy as possible. It is delicate in nature and very much the velvet we are striving to cultivate.

Occasionally we see an individual who prides himself on his bluntness. This is the type who comes forth with a comment completely raw and unprepared for serving. He is like a cook, who, rather than place a salad neatly ordered and arranged on a side dish, tosses you a handful of greens with a gob of dressing on it, expecting you to catch it and place it on your plate yourself. The same ingredients may be served in each case, but the manner of service is as far apart as the poles.

A salad nicely arranged shows respect for the one who eats it, whereas throwing it at him may be supplying a need, but shows gross disrespect. The tactless person is a crude person with demonstrated selfishness. This is the common thread running through all traits which are unrefined.

Lack of tact may be traceable to a desire to injure another, or a desire to see an unusual reaction under a strained circumstance. Illustrative of this is the anxious person who cannot wait to spread sad or bad news - the death of a friend, for example.

Tact demands a consideration of the time and place where correction or bad news is given. Correction is bad news to many people, i.e., they do not want to receive it at any time, although they may need it desperately. The only excuse for instructing people or disclosing some bit of information is to help them. Doing it in such a manner as to indicate your concern for their feelings is most important.

One of the responsibilities of a leader is to instruct, and a man will find himself in this position frequently. He may be instructing his wife and children almost daily. They expect this instruction, but it must be served with love and consideration for tender feelings. Some men learn to receive blunt instruction, but the feelings of women and children are more sensitive. They are not the privates being given orders by the sergeant. The ego of a small child can be as great as that of an adult.

Refined Appearance

Refinement is rooted in self-respect. The story is told of a British diplomat who was assigned as a provincial governor to a small island in the West Indies. Very few people resided on the island, and his contact with the refinements he knew in Europe was almost nonexistent. In spite of this, and although he ate his dinner alone, he always dressed properly and had a formal table setting. This he did out of respect for himself and the culture he knew. One is not well-mannered, refined and polished because other people will be impressed so much as he is because he believes in such a way of life for the inherent value in it.

This point is illustrated by a man who entered an elevator. Seeing himself in the company of a woman, he removed his hat. She, being an advocate of the feminist philosophy, said sarcastically, *I suppose you did that because I am a lady?* His response was, *I don't know whether you are a lady or not. I did it because I am a gentlemen.*

One's appearance may be thought to consist of two parts - himself as a person, and the clothing and accessories he uses in dress.

Beginning with himself, the refined person is going to see that cleanliness is an inseparable part of who he is - that his hair, teeth, nails, complexion, and posture are the best possible. This concern is rooted in self-respect. He values who he is, not in an arrogant or over-bearing manner, but because of his awareness that he has a destiny and is a person of worth.

From this point, he then dresses himself appropriately. He does not slouch around nor wear gaudy and ridiculous clothing which makes him a public spectacle. On the other hand, refined appearance has nothing to do with the amount of money spent, since it is possible to spend considerable and still come out looking ridiculous and offensive.

What a piece of work is man! How noble in reason! How infinite in faculty! In form and moving how express and admirable; In action, how like an angel! In appearance how like a god! The beauty of the world! the paragon of animals. — Shakespeare

For a man to see himself as Shakespeare sees him is to place a value of far greater significance than is ordinarily recognized. A beautiful diamond or ruby is not displayed in a showcase with nails, but is placed in a setting with a velvet background, ruffled border, controlled lighting, and uncluttered so its beauty can be appreciated without distraction. Could we say that a man is less valuable than a precious stone? Why, then, would he slouch around or present himself as though he had no self-respect for the being he is?

Refinement in dress suggests that the appearance be modest and restrained. For a man, his dress should be masculine and reasonably conservative. The line between masculine and feminine is being so closely drawn, mainly by women, that one wonders which is which.

A Hollywood men's shop featured a fashion show where a young man modeled a full-length coat, trimmed in fur. Beneath it he was wearing a femininely tailored suit of light pink. On stage he pointed one foot and raised his chin slightly in turning around for full exposure of the clothing. His manner was so feminine as to be revolting. For men, the fashions of the world are not conducive to the masculine appearance in many instances. Some argue the point strongly, but for a man, a refined appearance is a masculine one.

Consideration for Others

In countless ways one has the opportunity to show his concern and respect for other people. Again, it is the overcoming of selfishness which is the key.

In conversation the ideal man will extend to others the courtesies he would expect for himself. It is commonplace for some fathers to fail to show a child the courtesy of looking up from the paper when a question is asked. The child may be asking for advice or seeking a favor. In his subordinate position he can hardly demand attention and remain the disciplined youngster you have hopefully taught him to be.

The *cold water* treatment is deflating and hard to take. Enthusiasm is becoming more rare all the time, and to kill it out when it appears is akin to setting a fire in our diminishing forests. Enthusiasm adds zest and excitement to life, and when one is burning with it, a refined man will respect it.

This is not suggesting that all enthusiasm is justified or that encouragement should be given to something you cannot support. But out of consideration, redirect the enthusiasm if you can't support the idea. Do it in a way that is positive.

It is a little like waking someone from a sound sleep, if you must. Rather than shout in a loud voice, jerk off the covers, and physically pull him out of bed, it would be much more appreciated to gently and pleasantly awaken him with music or by opening the shades and allowing the gentle sunlight to fall on his face. This may not always be practical, but it is illustrative of the idea.

The spectrum of good manners and breeding is so broad as to be a study in itself, and our reference to it is only in a superficial way. But it is vitally important to realize that the development of the velvet side of one's nature requires some study in the social graces as well as the more mundane matters of earning a living.

Some childish habits persist into adulthood and become serious blocks in later life. Such include nerve or cheekiness wherein one asks for or expects special consideration and will do so at the expense or inconvenience of others.

Such cases go to such extremes as to be humorous. There is the case of some friends traveling from another city who, when they found the family they intended to visit not at home, (they had not called in advance) went into the house and settled themselves for the night - this after they invaded the refrigerator.

In the close relationship of the home, the privacy of individuals must be respected to insure an atmosphere of love and confidence. Not only does this embrace the obvious restraint to knock before opening, but precludes asking inappropriate or nervy questions. *How much money do you make?* or *How much did you pay for this?* are embarrassing questions to some people and are not the business of anyone else. This morbid curiosity is a childish trait and will be a bothersome handicap unless brought under control.

Material-Mindedness - Physical Excess

While emphasis must be placed on man's duty to provide for his family, and while it is admitted that he does not measure up as a man if he deliberately fails in this responsibility, yet an excessive concern for worldly goods, dependence upon them or over evaluation of them shows a coarseness in character. It is like the food we eat which we must have to survive, but which one eats in a proper way rather than to lie on his belly at a trough.

Or for that matter, he would not have to eat with poor manners. The gourmet-type individual who is so concerned over the appeasement of an appetite as to be constantly seeking new and exotic ways of satisfying it, is not too much above the level of a glutton.

Material-mindedness leads to ostentatiousness since the material-minded person not only finds satisfaction in his self-indulgence, but loves to parade it before others. Such preoccupation with worldly things is a distortion of values leading into many other problems.

It is a most interesting study to consider the very close tie between the things material and spiritual. They are not unrelated and cannot be actually separated, as a matter of fact. Yet gross distortion results when the proper balance is not maintained.

In frustration, some ascetics have chosen to renounce materialism entirely and have withdrawn into themselves for a life of meditation. They renounce materialism, yet they are an inevitable part of it in ways they probably would not admit. Some extremists will not kill a fly or pluck a plant which would destroy life, yet they find themselves under the necessity of eating. Somehow they rationalize that they are absolved of guilt if someone else does the deed.

The material things of this earth were placed here by God for the use and benefit of man - for him to get his hands into, exploit in the proper sense, enjoy and increase and in every way benefit from their use. But such wealth is not to become an end in itself. It is an aid to spirituality in freeing men, elevating them, expanding their horizons and refining their natures.

One sees that refinement, as viewed in this discussion, is far broader than a set of manners that may be learned from a book of etiquette. While etiquette is a fundamental part of it, a vital and important part - it is conceivable that an acceptable amount of the social graces may be applied as a veneer to cover a basically unrefined and calloused character.

It is doubtful the facade would escape detection over a prolonged period, but it might prove deceiving in the short range. Like a steel beam which must be tempered to withstand the stresses placed upon it, so must the character be tempered with refinement which is an actual part of him, functioning whether he be by himself or in affluent and distinguished company.

Conclusion

To achieve the steel and velvet is no simple task. Its accomplishment promises rewards thought by many to be completely unattainable. Whereas the cynic has come to doubt that life holds any more than fleeting glimpses of genuine happiness and fulfillment, he who achieves a reasonable measure of steel and velvet knows that rewards promised are as genuine as any can be.

We learn once again that life exacts a toll for rewards. There is no shortcut to success or happiness. The violation of eternal principles invariably brings frustration and disappointment. But we learn that when we determine to comply with eternal truth, success is the predictable result.

A false philosophy teaches that happiness comes through pursuing the *easy life*. Work has been demeaned, and people are urged to avoid its demands. Doing the easy thing is taught as the desirable way.

As it turns out, everyone has problems and life is never easy. It was not designed by our Creator that it should be. But the source of our problems is worthy of some consideration, as they tend to fall into one of these categories:

1. Problems that arise because of one's own weakness, foolishness or slothfulness. These problems result in unnecessary hardship as they are the natural consequence of our deliberate actions. Such tend to beat us down and place upon our backs burdens and handicaps which discourage us and deprive us of our greater potential.

2. Problems that arise during the course of living from "acts of God" or the trials which naturally befall man in being in a world that is designed as a testing ground. These trials provide opportunity to gain increased strength by meeting them courageously. These come as a result of the principle that men gain strength as they overcome obstacles. Deity has made our environment one where there is opposition.

3. Problems that arise by setting high goals: A man can provide his own opposition, his own testing ground, by setting worthy and difficult goals for himself. As he engages in a worthy cause and assumes responsibilities which are great, he finds opposition, problems, tests and trials sufficient to prove his worth and refine his character. And the most important point is this: The problems will be of such a nature as to result in greater happiness rather than in sorrow and defeat.

Determining to be a man of steel and velvet is such a worthy goal. While there will be times of disappointment, pain and weariness in achieving this noble objective, all this promises the reward of a full and satisfying life. We determine our own reward as suggested in the following lines:

MY WAGES

I bargained with Life for a penny
And Life would pay no more,
However I begged at evening
When I counted my scanty store;
For Life is a just employer,
He gives you what you ask,
But once you have set the wages,
Why, you must bear the task.
I worked for a menial's hire,
Only to learn, dismayed,
That any wage I had asked of Life,
Life would have paid.
                    Jessie B. Rittenhouse,

From *The Door of Dreams*, Houghton Mifflin Co.

About the Author

Aubrey Andelin received his D.D.S. degree from the University of Southern California and has practiced dentistry in California and Idaho. His business activities include commercial and agricultural developments in the United States, Australia, Japan and Brazil. He is the founder of a successful publishing business. Dr. Andelin is co-founder of *Family Living International* where he has had broad experience in the field of human relations. He and his wife, Helen, are the parents of eight children, and they have fifty six grandchildren. Mrs. Andelin is the author of *Fascinating Womanhood, The Secrets of Winning Men,* and *All About Raising Children.*